YOURS TRULY, DELLA COLEMAN

CASE TWO: THE SPIRITS

Written and Illustrated by:
AMELIA R. RIKSTAD

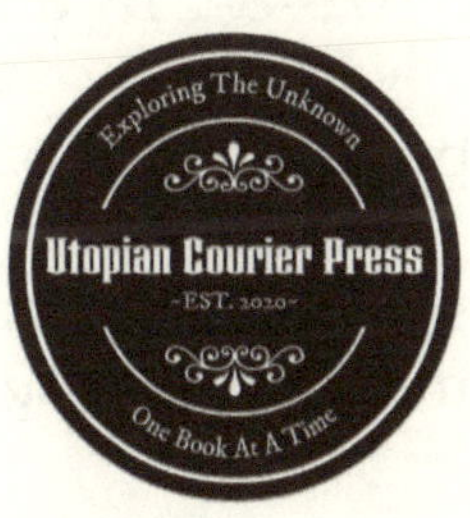

First paperback edition: October 31st, 2023

Book design by Amelia R. Rikstad
Cover art by Amelia R. Rikstad

Edited by Danielle Rikstad and Amelia Rikstad

ISBN: 979-8-218-30752-3

Published by: Utopian Courier Press™

For more information, email:
theutopiancourier2020@gmail.com

PRAISE FOR
YOURS TRULY, DELLA COLEMAN:

"Yours Truly, Della Coleman swept me away to a magical world that breathes life into the magic of friendship. From Amelia's sensitive dexterity for creating distinctive and vibrant characters, to her (some might call it uncanny) knack for building drama and intrigue, and her adept handling of cryptids so realistic they leap off the page, Case Two: The Spirits is sure to keep me turning pages late into the night."
-Laura L. Fox, Author of Initiate

"5/5 for suspense, a mystery I didn't figure out for once, and for the strong character building that was clear the writer wrote from the heart. It felt real."
-Amanda Insco, Book Witch Press

BOOKS BY AMELIA R. RIKSTAD

Yours Truly, Della Coleman
Case One: The Grunch
Case Two: The Spirits

COMING SOON

The Extraordinary Tale of the Man in the
Paisley Suit

Saga of the Winter Witch

For Danielle and Erica.

To the lightworkers, cycle breakers, and
inner-child healers.

CONTENTS

PROLOGUE

The man in the paisley suit was at his wit's end.

The floorboards were rattling again. Blacklight, almost plum in hue, seeped out from beneath the cracks. Protective sigils sparkled to life with each thump.

Those old sigils had been painted on the walls in *Undark* long ago.

Like the ever-present problem below, painting such symbols in that Godforsaken radium paint had been a mistake.

Even the magical community got fooled occasionally. Especially by humans.

Mavericks sighed heavily, standing as he adjusted his tie. With his head held high, he crossed to one of the old jukeboxes dotting his office. With a few quick button presses, the jukebox whirred to life and began to play one of his favorite songs from the seventies. Mixing with the melody was a mechanical clicking. With a spring in his step, Mavericks danced toward the clicking sound. One of his bookshelves was descending, disappearing into the floor. Left in its place was a long hall illuminated by the same purple-black light beneath the floorboards.

As Mavericks' song played, he swayed down the winding staircase, the rhythm consuming him. On the last step, he spun, bowing with a flourish of his hands.

"Am I meant to clap?" a disembodied voice asked.

Mavericks slowly stood to his full height. "That'd be the kind thing to do."

Before him sat a living corpse. His pallid gray skin was pulled tight over his bones, making him appear skeletal. Black veins writhed beneath his skin like sickly leeches. Greasy black hair hung over his purple-black eyes like a veil.

When Mavericks first met this young man, he admired him. He'd been ever so wise, ever so caring. In fact, this corpse had been one of the brightest souls Mavericks had ever met.

Now, all he had inside was darkness.

The young man's eyes drifted away from the pile of bones in his hands, those empty voids sweeping over Mavericks. His sunken features displayed a perfect picture of disgust. "What do you want, old man?"

"For one, I'd appreciate it if you'd stop making such a ruckus. This is still a place of work. And work I must," Mavericks sighed, eyes on the bones. Rat bones, from the looks of it. There must be a hole in the wall. He'd have to send someone in to patch it.

Someone nobody would miss if the corpse decided to kill them.

The young man laughed. The sound was as dark as the shadowy tendrils vibrating around him. With a creaking of his bones, he stood, the purple-black light moving around him as if afraid. He paced back and forth before Mavericks like a lion stalking his prey.

There were few things Mavericks was afraid of.

Unfortunately, this young man was one of them.

"Percival, Percival, Percival," He cackled, his voice almost demonic. "'Holier-than-thou' doesn't look good on you," he said.
He paused his pacing, smiling crookedly as he turned to look at Mavericks with a tilted head. The light pulsed, collecting around him as his face slowly changed into a picture-perfect copy of Mavericks himself. It was like looking into a mirror, without the voids where his eyes should be.

"If you're going to play God, you may as well see me made in your image. Maybe then—" The light flashed a reddish shade of purple. "—you'll see the flaws in your grand design."

Mavericks' eye twitched. "Did you get that off the internet?"

The young man's smile dropped as his face melted and morphed back into his own. "Don't," he said, his voice strained as his head twitched. "Don't mock me."

Mavericks whistled over his shoulder.

The sound of heavy, clunking footsteps came from the hall.

Shivering and whimpering, taking its own sweet time, was the old alligator-skin chair Mavericks loved so dearly. It lingered at the base of the stairs like a scared puppy, causing the young man to smile.

"Believe me, chair, his bark is worse than his bite," Mavericks said with a scoff.

The chair hesitated but eventually came to stand behind Mavericks, who sat, making a show of getting comfortable. He loved getting on the corpse-man's nerves. While Mavericks had his creature comforts, all the young man had was a musty cot and the remnants of a shredded straitjacket.

The young man glared at him through his eyebrows, presumably wishing he could kill the legendary Percival James Mavericks right then and there. But Mavericks knew his future, and he wasn't to die at the hands of someone whose only character trait was black magic.

"What do you want?" he spat, his purple-black light collecting at his back like a snake ready to strike.

Mavericks had been putting this off for weeks now. What had transpired leading up to this moment had been messy. People had died, feelings were hurt, and enemies had been made. These things had to happen. Mavericks, of course, knew this. He knew more than people gave him credit.

Improbable people were surrounding him. There always had been. And he'd vowed long ago to protect them. That's what he was and always would be—a protector. But in recent years, Mavericks had found that to protect those he loved, he'd have to play puppet master, even if it meant hurting them.

Mavericks was not proud of this conclusion. A better man would have found a better solution.

Percival James Mavericks had spent the *better* part of his *better* life trying to be a *better* man.

Apparently, that just wasn't in the cards for him.

With a heavy heart, he turned his attention back to the young man before him, reaching into his pocket. He procured a paper airplane. Sighing, he tossed it through the invisible barrier between them. The corpse in the cage caught it, his fist clenching it so tight it no longer resembled a plane by any stretch of the imagination.

"What is this?" he asked sourly.

Mavericks shrugged. "An early Christmas gift."

The young man's eyes narrowed. Curiosity got the better of him. Mavericks watched in morbid amusement as he unfolded the paper, his purple-black eyes scanning the page.

"What is this?" The corpse-man repeated. This time, his voice was filled with anger.

Mavericks couldn't help but smile. "A case for my favorite writer."

"You cannot send her back there, Percival," the young man spat. "It won't end well." The shadow-like light writhed around its master. "You can't send her back," he repeated. "You can't. You can't. You can't!" he screamed, thrusting his hands forward.

The once invisible barrier surrounding him sparkled green, blue, purple, and pink. Mavericks felt the pull of energy at the edge of his consciousness. Among how he died, he also knew how this young man would escape.

Shivers raced down his spine.

"Why?" Mavericks asked. The black light surrounding his most dangerous secret began to transform, the edges glistening gold. "Afraid she'll start remembering things?"

The young man's eyes were wild, the void inside them swirling like a whirlpool. "You sweep everything beneath the carpet until it serves you, Percival." He was pacing again, repeatedly running his hands through his hair, a crazed look in his eyes. "You're going to get her killed. She's not ready. I can feel it."

"That is not your decision to make," Mavericks said. "I believe she is. I say if we don't start exposing her to the truth now, we won't ever be able to. Her mind is broken, Quincy. Maybe this will heal it. Being back there, realizing that there was so much going on right under her nose—"

"Shut! Up!" Quincy Coleman spat. "You don't understand! You don't know how it was before you tried to fix it all!" His black light condensed into spikes around him. "She was my best friend, Percival! And you screwed it all up!"

"Quincy—"

He spun, throwing spikes of shadow at the barrier as he screamed. "If you genuinely wanted to protect her, you'd let me see her! Seeing me would make her remember!"

"Seeing you in this state would send her spiraling," Mavericks sighed, annoyed by Quincy's outburst.

"You never cared for us!" Quincy snapped. "You're just like the rest of them."

Mavericks had had enough emotional torment for the evening.

"LET ME SEE HER!" Quincy screamed with all his

might.

Like lightning through a storm cloud, the golden light burst through Quincy's darkness, embedding itself in the young man's veins. Mavericks alone was not powerful enough to purge the black magic from him, but he could subdue him.

For now.

The screams that followed him as he walked back up the stairs burned his eyes with tears.

There were few things Mavericks feared and even fewer things he loved.

But the Coleman kids?

Their names were on both of those lists.

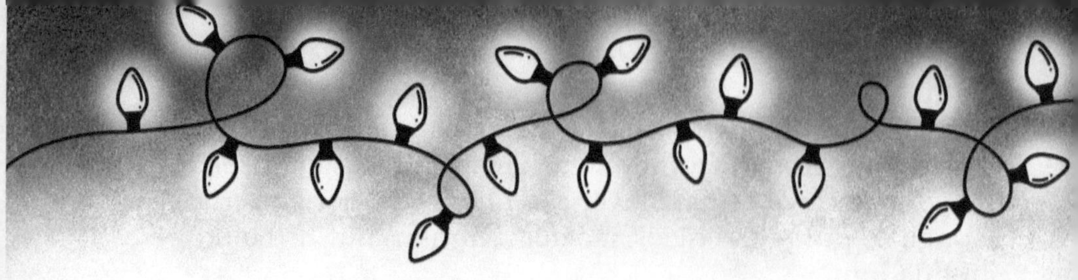

CHAPTER ONE

A Story to Be Told

Who are you?

Who are you, *really*?

How do you know who you are?

Does our family define us? Is the daughter of a mob boss destined to be his successor? Is the son of a baker meant to follow in his mother's footsteps?

What about the color of our skin? Is our person solely determined by color? A race?

A species? Werewolf or vampire? Human or witch?

Boy or girl? Other?

See, I don't see the world like that. All I've ever seen are souls, what lies beneath skin or fur.

Where others can only pick apart and shame, I've always tried to uplift. Sure, I've been known to practice tough love, and I can often come across as harsh, but that's just who I am.

Or at least that's what I've been told.

Some may say truth is my destiny.

But I don't believe in destiny.

Destiny tells me that no matter what I do, I cannot change what has already been set out for me. No matter how many times I erase a set of words, the indents will always be left on the paper.

Destiny says that who I am is already written. In thick, black ink, no doubt.

Like a vampire, destiny can only bother you if you invite it in through the front door. Otherwise, it will move on to its next victim.

And I will never be the victim.

Never.

So, I'll ask again.

Who are you?

Who are you, *really*?

How do you know who you are?

Did someone tell you? Or did you come to this conclusion yourself? Did you let fate and destiny whisper in your ear while you slept? Or did you take matters into your own hands? Did the people around you push you in the wrong direction until you lost all sense of self? Or are you completely and utterly self-made? Did the world wrap its cold hands around you, forcing you to believe you were never truly you? Or have you been lying to yourself for years on end?

Who are you?

~ ~ ~

"Wow. That was beautiful, Della. Truly. Ei especially like the part about—Well, all of it, really. Rivetin'. Now, would ya like yer oatmeal with blueberries or bananas?" Max asked through tight lips once Della had finished her speech.

Della's eyes twitched. "I just gave you a whole piece on identity—one that would trigger an existential crisis in most—and that's all you have to say?"

"Yes, well, last week's topic was Nephilim, so Ei've come to expect a lot of nonsense from ya," Max winked, leaning back against the grimy countertop in the communal kitchen at The Courier.

"You are no help whatsoever," Della snapped.

Max pretended to tip his hat to her. "Ma'am."

"Blueberries," Della said, crossing her arms over her chest.

Max nodded, walking over to the fridge to rifle through unclaimed lunches for a container of blueberries. Many things had begun to change in Moss Hollow, Louisiana since October had passed, but the only one Della cared about was her friendship with Maximilian McGregor-Mavericks. Della had never really had a friend before, at least not like this.

"So," Max began, rolling up the sleeves of his tattered blue sweater. "Where is our little adventurer off tuh tuhday?" he asked as he grabbed a carton of milk and sniffed it, wrinkling his nose.

Della kicked her feet onto the scuffed-up table she sat at, folding her hands behind her head. The Courier was quiet this morning. From the communal kitchen, they could barely make out the faint din of their coworkers starting up printers and computers a few rooms away. These sounds brought mystery and foreboding into the small kitchen. On days like this, The Courier reminded Della of an abandoned office building haunted by disgruntled workers.

"I have to review a few photos for my article with Norman. Then I'm going to run down to that little general store, pick up a box of cake mix, and make myself a cake because I'm worth it," Della yawned, watching the dust and cobwebs blow like the bows of a willow as the heater kicked on.

She hadn't realized how cold Moss Hollow would be this time of year. Part of her thought it would be blistering and humid all year. Still, even though it was cold out here, it wouldn't snow. Della didn't know whether to be happy or sad about that. Snow gave her mixed feelings.

"Please don' burn down yer apartment," Max sighed heavily, pouring a packet of instant oatmeal into a bowl and popping it into the old microwave beside him.

"What of you, Maximilian?" Della asked with a smirk. He hated it when people called him that.

However, he didn't seem to mind when Della did.

"Dad has me decoratin' the foyer, and Ei have tuh fix the Wi-Fi upstairs," he explained, gesturing around loosely. "Love how being tech guy makes me the only person who can plug in a string of lights and place them round a Christmas tree without gettin' electrocuted," he said sourly.

Della choked down a laugh. "Lenora can't do the decorating?"

Max shriveled his nose, looking over his shoulder at her, his eyes as wide as dinner plates. "Yer not serious, are ya? Last time Lenora decorated this place, we blew three fuses in an hour, the whole place smelled like cinnamon on steroids, and all the wreaths spontaneously combusted," He thought for a minute. "Okay, maybe that last part was my fault, but Ei was stressed, and Ei still have an alibi."

"Ominous," Della laughed.

Max chuckled to himself. "Ya celebrate Christmas too, right? Have ya decorated?"

"Ugh, not yet," Della said with a roll of her eyes.

Max gave her a funny look. "Ah, don' tell me yer a bah-humbug-er," he frowned.

Della shrugged, looking away. "Christmas has never really been my favorite holiday."

Max raised an eyebrow as the microwave beeped. He fixed her oatmeal, his eyes not leaving her. Not even for a split second. "Ei thought ya were intuh the whole 'Jesus is the reason' thing," he said, tapping her feet for her to move.

Della begrudgingly removed her feet from the table, sitting as stiff and straight as possible. "It's complicated," she said, side-eyeing him.

Max elegantly placed her oatmeal in front of her. He'd arranged the blueberries into a smiley face. Whenever her friends cooked for her—which was quite often since everyone seemed to think she didn't know how to feed herself—they always made a smiley face on her food. Maybe they thought if she ate happiness, she would become what she ate.

Della couldn't help but grin.

Max dusted off the seat opposite her, then sat down, scrutinizing her. "How so?"

"It's the same as the destiny thing I was talking about—too many rules. Too many—" She sighed heavily, pulling her bowl of oatmeal to her. "I believe in God. Always have, always will. I pray every night, knowing the Lord will judge me when I die. But for me, that's where it ends. Once I crack open a Bible, it's like everything I believe in is wrong. That *I'm* wrong."

"Not sure Ei follow," Max admitted, stealing a blueberry.

"Up until recently, believing in magic was just a coping mechanism. It was the only thing that kept me going back home. But when I pick up a Bible or go to a Church, I'm expected to renounce everything I believe in. To be this perfect person. I can't do that. I don't believe it's one or the other. Magic had to come from somewhere, right? Who's to say God didn't create it," Della explained glumly. "Who's to say that people like us are evil?"

"Ei like the way ya think, love," Max said, flashing her his cat eyes for a minute. Max was a familiar, a witch born with the ability to transform into an animal at will. "In this perfect world ya seem tuh yearn for, where would Ei be?"

"That's just it. Everyone would have an actual choice. No one would force an opinion down another's throat," Della smiled sadly. "You could be science and magic. No one would make you choose."

Max patted her shoulder, stealing another blueberry. "Well, Ei'm gonna be late." Della knew he wasn't leaving because he didn't want to talk anymore, but she couldn't help but feel that way.

"Time is a fickle concept created by man to add further control to his comrades," Della said through a mouthful of oatmeal, dangerously pointing her spoon at him.

"Now that's a conspiracy theory Ei can agree with," he laughed, bowed deeply, then left her alone in the communal kitchen.

When she was sure he was out of earshot, she sighed heavily, sinking into her seat. Like every other one since Halloween, the day had gone by like a blur. Della could barely remember what she had done throughout it as she sat alone in the bellows of *The Utopian Courier.*

Even this part of Moss Hollow had changed, though not as violently as the rest of the town. And the worst part was you wouldn't notice if you didn't care. You would miss it all if you didn't have Della's keen eyes. But if you took a moment to stop and look around, you'd see it.

You could see it in how the fridge was devoid of advertisements and silly drawings. You could even see it in how the lightbulbs were slowly burning out, echoing the darkness filling the rest of the town.

Other changes were even less noticeable, like how the townsfolk carried themselves. Though they hid it well, it was clear to Della that their sparks were dimming. Maybe she was just paranoid, but she couldn't shake the feeling those sparks would die out completely one day soon. Not that she blamed any of them. Her own spark was flickering.

But what would happen if the entire town lost faith in each other? What was brewing in the bottomless cauldron that was Moss Hollow? Everyone seemed to know something was coming. Something they were trying so hard to ignore, to put behind them.

She tried not to think of it, distracting herself with trivial things like everyone else.

Given how strange November had been, distractions were easy to come by.

Many in Moss Hollow regarded Della, Max, and their other partner in crime, Porter Garroway, as heroes. After all, they had saved a bunch of kids, rid the town of evil, and cleared the name of the town's most notorious criminal. Once word had spread of their deeds, the townsfolk took any chance to thank them. The general store had given Della a giant coupon book for her deeds. One of the victims— Clara Dixon—sent her flowers once a week.

Not to mention that a few of her colleagues at *The Utopian Courier* seemed to admire her and Max for solving the town's greatest mystery. Even Mavericks had made sure their names would be remembered for decades.

With all this praise, you'd assume Della was over the moon. This was what she'd always wanted, after all. It must feel great to be recognized for solving a mystery instead of being ridiculed for meddling in things she shouldn't.

However, that just wasn't the case.

There was an air of jealousy to all the praise.

Just a sliver of fear whenever Della mentioned Porter to Clara.

And, of course, half of those coupons she'd received were expired by now.

The truth of what happened that fateful day had

spread through the magical community like the plague. At first, everyone had thought Eric Steiniger—the man who had kidnapped abused children, murdered their abusive parents, summoned monsters, and even brainwashed Porter—had just been some deranged lunatic. But those who knew the truth quickly realized there was more to his villainy than they had thought. Soon, most of the witches, vampires, werewolves, and others not only saw Della as a hero, but they feared her. Rumors spread about how she'd managed to stop Eric, and Della didn't know how to stop wagging tongues from spreading lies. She had even heard that the magical folk outside of Moss Hollow now knew of her and her friends. She was something of a legend now. But not everyone loved legends the way she did.

They all knew what Della had done.

Knew she had killed Eric.

Knew she was one of them.

But they didn't know *what* she was.

She could be more powerful than all of them combined. She could be a savior sent to them from beyond. Or she could be their destruction.

Throughout November, the events of October weighed down her shoulders. So far, December wasn't treating her any better. Della saw herself as a villain, still felt off in a way she couldn't explain. And if she sat and laid it all out, something didn't add up. There were too many loose ends for her liking. All those unanswered questions would eat at her until the day she died.

Yet despite that nagging dread, she weathered on, refusing to let any of it sideline her.

Even with Eric Steiniger's picture plastered on the nightly news as a constant reminder, she pushed through.

Even though Theodore Heiser—one of the only people who knew what was happening in the shadows—was dead.

Even though much of what Theodore had said didn't seem to add up.

That was another thing nagging at her.

He'd known about. . . *something.*

Something bigger than just Eric.

Mavericks and Nicoletta did, too. They'd known of her and her powers for a long, long time. But how? She'd never had a vision before Moss Hollow. Never been able to cast a spell. All she'd ever had was her innate lust for knowledge of the unknown.

Multiple times had she asked the two of them what they'd meant that fateful October thirty-first.

Each time, her question had been met with the same response: They'd known of her magic the second she set foot in Moss Hollow.

But Mavericks had said things that made her think he'd known about her since she was a child. Didn't he outright say that? She'd tried rationalizing it all. Maybe she'd misheard him. Perhaps he'd read through her whole blog. After all, she'd nearly had it for ten years. That had to be the case.

Otherwise, the people she trusted most were lying to her.

Della shivered as she sat in the communal kitchen, pulling her blush-pink corduroy jacket around her tiny shoulders.

Max was the only person who knew how she was feeling, but she hated burdening him with all this. She didn't dare talk to Porter about any of it. She didn't want to drag him down any further than he already was.

At the thought of him, her heart skipped a beat. But not because it was full of childish love. Her problems may be weighing heavy on her soul, hidden from the light, but his were now out in the open twenty-four-seven.

Skeeter Jacobson had been promoted from deputy to chief at Moss Hollow Police Department. Despite the rest of the brigade's distrust, he'd let Porter keep his job in the morgue. When he wasn't digging graves or embalming bodies at *Garroway Cemetery and Mortuary*, he allowed himself to be ridiculed by MHPD. Not once did he stand up for himself. But Jacobson would punish anyone who spoke against him with the fury of a self-righteous schoolteacher.

Della's heart ached for Porter. None of this was on him. It wasn't his fault he hadn't seen through Eric's carefully crafted guise.

Della kept thinking that if she had just talked to Eric sooner. . .

She shook the thought away. It wasn't good to dwell on what could have been. Mistakes are mistakes; you learn from them so you don't repeat them.

Max kept telling her that, and she hoped she would believe it one day.

Speaking of the puddy cat, it seemed Max was the only one who had spent the month of November with a genuine smile on his face. He soaked in every drop of praise like a sponge. Nothing bothered him like Della and Porter.

Della suddenly realized how bitter jealousy tasted on her tongue.

But nothing was as sour as the kitchen door banging open, revealing P.J. Mavericks, her boss and the namesake of the cover-up company that hid *The Utopian Courier*. Barefoot, hair combed in a perfect swoop, his half-moon spectacles hanging loosely from his nose. Eccentric as always. His arms were full of books, his face set in a scowl. At least *he* was still normal. If you could call anything Mavericks did normal.

"Everything okay?" Della asked, her eyebrows furrowed over her mahogany eyes.

Mavericks looked up from his stack of books, his expression unchanging. "Ah! Just the girl I was looking for!"

"She's gonna say no!" Came Max's thick Irish accent as he came bounding back into the kitchen.

"To what?" Della asked skeptically, dread filling her instantly. The communal kitchen now felt suspiciously like a tomb.

Mavericks rolled his eyes, setting his stack of books on the table before her, reaching into his filigree suit jacket, and pulling out a manilla envelope covered in what looked to be coffee stains. He shoved it into Della's hands, smiling tightly. Inside was an entire newspaper and a tiny note. Scanning the newspaper, she was about to ask why they were acting so weird when she read a familiar name at the top of an article. Her heart skipped a beat as she flipped to the newspaper's front page, the color draining from her face when she read another familiar set of words.

"Abso-freaking-lutely not," Della snapped, eyes wide, heart pounding. She stood abruptly, rolling the newspaper into a tight spiral, ready to throw it as hard as she could at Mavericks' smug face.

"You'll be going home for the holidays anyway!" Mavericks argued, putting his hands up in defense when he realized she was aiming at him.

"No, I'm not! I'm staying in Moss Hollow," Della snapped. "I'm not going back!"

"But it's a case!" Mavericks persisted.

Della's nostrils flared with anger. "Just because some weird things are happening around my hometown doesn't mean there's an issue. It's not a dead body. Not a missing person. Not ghoulish happenings. Not our department!" She accentuated that last statement by squeezing her fist tighter around the newspaper.

Max inhaled sharply, side-stepping around Mavericks to stand somewhat between them, a gentle hand on Della's shoulder.

Mavericks rolled his gray eyes. "You didn't read the full article. Nor the note."

"Just drop it; she's not gonna go," Max said sternly, giving Mavericks the death stare.

Mavericks stared Della down, the look on his face telling her that he wouldn't give up.

She hated it when he did that.

Della loosened her grip on the newspaper before sinking back into her chair and flattening it out. Mavericks gave Della a knowing look as she begrudgingly read the full article.

And the note.

The newspaper detailed several accounts of petty theft, some missing pets, and a handful of other rather mundane and ridiculous happenings back in her hometown. Nothing exciting. And the note was nothing more than a plea to get Della to investigate. When she was done reading, she stuffed the letter and the newspaper back into the envelope and shoved it into Mavericks' expectant hands.

"No," she said, scowling deeply.

"'No' as in 'No way, I'm so excited?'" Mavericks asked.

"Dad," Max said sternly, looking apologetically at Della.

"Whoever wrote to you seemed genuinely frightened! It could be something!" Mavericks proposed, looking giddy.

"The man who wrote me? Ashton John? He's a druggie and an idiot. Nothing he says is worth anything. This is a cruel joke or the result of his drug-induced delirium," Della snapped, angrily pulling her bowl of oatmeal towards her. "Not to mention that going through my mail is a crime. I could decide I want to press charges."

Mavericks waved that thought away. "It was sent to The Courier, so technically, it is still my mail," he laughed, clearing his throat before continuing. "He could be on to something! Why not just go and check it all out?"

"Dad," Max said again. This time, his voice was filled with the irritation of a parent trying to dissuade their child from doing something mildly life-threatening. Funny how they were always in role reversal.

"Abso-*friggin*-lutely not!" Della hissed again, yanking a book off the stack he'd placed before her, chucking it at Mavericks with all her might.

Mavericks ducked out of the line of fire lazily, but Della's aim had been off. Instead of going anywhere near him, the book hit Max square in the shoulder. He yelped, glared at Della, and then motioned as if to strangle his father.

"I know your feelings about your hometown, but I think—" Mavericks began.

"See, I don't think you do," Della snapped, pointing at him accusingly. He flinched, staring at her finger like he was staring down the barrel of a pistol. "If you knew, you wouldn't be sending me back."

"Told ya!" Max said, rubbing his arm angrily. "It's

not worth it. We have others we could send if yer so freakin'
paranoid about it."

Della nodded. "I'm not going back, especially not
right now. You could ask me to go to the Caribbean to find
giant crabs or—or send me off to find the Mongolian Death
Worm, and I would jump on the case and be out of here
yesterday, but not for this," Della snapped, tripping over
her words, her blood boiling. "Not this," she repeated sourly.

"It's almost Christmas, Delphee. Don't you want
to go back? See your family? Just once?" Mavericks proposed half-heartedly. The way he said it sent an odd shiver
through her.

Was he trying to get rid of her?

Della paled at the thought. "No," she said for the
thousandth time.

Mavericks squinted at her, trying to fake a judgmental look, his cold gray eyes full of an intensity she couldn't
quite pin. She couldn't tell if he was angry with her, disappointed, or using those emotions as a mask to hide something else.

"I don't have to explain myself to you," she said flatly,
returning to her glorious oatmeal. All she wanted to do was
eat in peace.

"Della," Mavericks said sternly, his tone like a booming thundercloud. "I am your boss. You can't refuse a direct
order from me."

"Watch me," Della dared, her voice quiet. "You're not
a drill sergeant. I'm not a soldier."

He sighed heavily. "I have a feeling about this. There
is something out there; I just know it! It's like—" He paused,
eyeing Max carefully. "It's like something has changed in
the air recently, and I know this is connected. There is
something in Sycamore Heights, something that shouldn't
be. Whatever this Ashton John saw, he had the nerve to
contact you for a reason."

Della bit her lower lip, running a hand through her
brown and green hair. Ashton was just as much of a black
sheep as she was, but she was pretty sure he hated her
guts just like the rest of the town. Maybe something *was*
wrong. That thought made her shake with fury. After all
these years of trying to help, Sycamore Heights only realized it needed her after she had left.

"Not only that," Mavericks said, his voice heavy. "But
I think you all need a distraction. And maybe with everything going on right now, Sycamore Heights would be. . .
safer. Take the boys. Fix whatever this is."

"This boy wants tuh stay home," Max butt in, his

face reddening, a look of desperation in his eyes.

Della shot him a mournful look. "Can't you ask Alexis or Bart to go and figure it out?" she pleaded, rounding on Mavericks, ignoring the word 'safer.'

Mavericks inhaled sharply. "Maximilian, please go wait in Della's office," he said, straightening.

Max tried to protest, but when Mavericks turned to give him that fatherly look of his, he stomped off without a word. Mavericks waited until they could no longer hear his footsteps to start speaking again.

"I cannot ask this of anyone else. You know I can't. Everyone here is needed where they are—" he began.

Della scoffed. "And I'm not?"

Mavericks raised a disapproving eyebrow. "Your cases are nowhere near what I assign to others. No one can do what you do. And I'm not talking about the way you write," Mavericks said, crossing his hands behind his back. He was closing himself off from her, disconnecting from the situation emotionally. Something *was* wrong. *Really* wrong. He was hiding something. He wanted them gone—all of them.

"Why?" was all Della asked.

Mavericks fought himself for a minute before finally sighing. "Because."

"What are you? Five?" Della laughed.

"Delphee Coleman, you are about two seconds away from being put on probation." The look in his gray eyes was fiery.

Della straightened.

"We're very good at keeping things from the human population, but with the events of October, we are under watch. I know I've discussed my theory that Eric Steiniger didn't act on his own volition once before, but I worry whoever worked with him may reveal themselves soon," he paused. "And I don't want the three of you here when that happens."

"Meaning?" Della asked, crossing her arms. She scrutinized him, trying to find the truth beneath his ever-present façade.

Mavericks let his hands drop from behind his back. Hesitantly, he placed his hands on her shoulders. He suddenly looked much older. Like the years were finally catching up to him: all four hundred and some.

"Meaning, whoever it is could still be in town. Meaning they could have sympathizers. Meaning there could be people who want Eric's spellbook. Any number of things," he began, his voice full of sadness and exhaustion. "We are playing a dangerous game, Delphee. One that I'm afraid that if we lose, we lose *everything*."

A memory like a bee sting flooded her mind. "A chess game?" Della asked, the words getting caught in her throat.

Mavericks shut his eyes, the dark circles under his eyes darkening by the minute. "Chess would be easier than this," he whispered.

Della froze, thinking back to the blood-chilling vision she had seen after she had killed Eric. She knew it was a glimpse into the future. She had just hoped it was the very distant future. She couldn't believe what she was hearing.

"Why can't I help?" she asked quietly. "From here?"

When Mavericks opened his eyes, she knew not to ask any more questions.

"Because you, Della, are like me," he said softly. "And people like us will never be safe. Not even here. And it's people like us who take the blame when those who have truly done wrong are nowhere to be found. We are a rare breed of truth seekers. It is a burden we share, my dear."

Della just stared at him, feeling lost.

"I just don't want any of you getting hurt. So what if I'm wrong about Sycamore Heights? At least you'll be far away from here. Far away and safe," Mavericks said pleadingly.

She nodded glumly. "I understand," she admitted, feeling like she was caught in a war she didn't want to fight.

That she *shouldn't* fight.

"Good," he smiled weakly. "Like I said before, I will be here for you no matter what. I picked you for a reason. I believe in you, Della. I believe in your potential and that you can do a lot of good in this world. Which is why I need to send you all away. You are no good to this world if you're caught in the crosshairs of something you don't understand." He paused. "Or lost to us for other reasons," he said knowingly, gesturing to her head.

Della swore thickly, struggling internally. This sounded like a goodbye for some reason. This speech raised many questions, but one look at his face told her he wouldn't answer any of them. Not now, anyway. Her heart ached for him to tell her everything, but her mind told her she couldn't shoulder it yet. She had to figure this out for herself like she always did. Put the pieces together like a puzzle. But not now. Now, she had to watch how things played out. Maybe he knew that. Maybe that was his point.

So, she did the one thing she hated. She complied.

"You owe me, old man. I mean, *owe* me," she hissed.

Mavericks' eye twitched at 'old man.' "Anything you wish."

She stood, her appetite disappearing. Just as she was about to say something snide, Mavericks hugged her, squeezing her tightly. Again, this felt like a goodbye. Mavericks hated touching people. Sometimes, he would forgo contact with even Max. But he had hugged Della. And that made her nervous.

He pulled away, reaching up to push a strand of her hair behind her ear. He was looking at her with such immense sadness. Yet deep in those storm-gray eyes of his, she saw admiration and love. Fatherly love.

As he stared at her, his usual playful aura returned. "Promise me one thing," he smirked, trying to hide the tremble of laughter in his voice. "That even if I piss you off—even if I make you go find Mongolian Deathworms and giant crabs—that you will *never* call me 'old man' ever again."

She laughed, nodding solemnly. "I promise."

He pulled away, sweeping her out the door. As she turned down the hall, she heard him whisper, "Old man, my ass."

His laughter, quips, and joyful spirit were the only things that made any of this okay, but in her heart of hearts, she knew it wasn't.

None of this was okay.

Not one word of it.

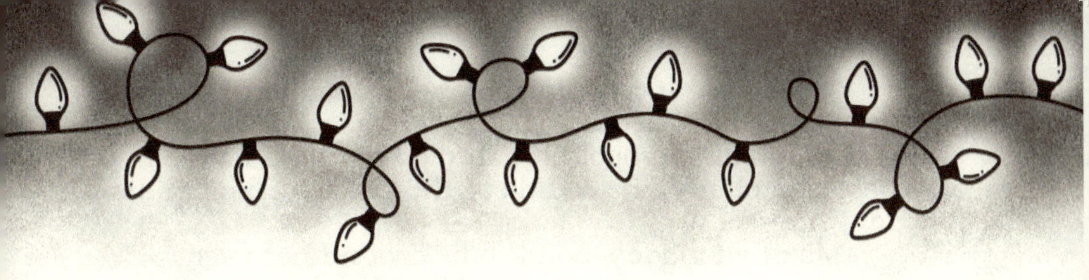

CHAPTER TWO

Over My Dead Body

For once in her life, Della didn't know how to feel. On surface levels, she missed her family—well, she missed her mom and siblings—but that didn't mean she wanted to go home.

But her parents hadn't invited her home once. In fact, she hadn't gotten a call from them since the beginning of October. In all honesty, she was relieved about that. If they were going to avoid the subject of why her migraine medication had been a placebo or the fact that their daughter had a seizure, so be it. Della didn't feel like talking about it either. This time, her curiosity shied away.

She'd think of them, how they lied to her and seemingly suppressed a part of her, and all she'd feel was bitter betrayal. And Della was so very tired of being bitter and angry all the time. Yet no matter how hard she tried to let it all go, the world wouldn't let her.

She sighed heavily as she opened the door to her office, her fragile mood darkening like someone was snuffing out candles inside her mind.

She wasn't mad at Mavericks anymore. She trusted him, even if she wondered why he kept things from her. From the sound of things, he had little control over what was happening in town. That scared her. If Mavericks couldn't stop whatever was happening, she definitely couldn't.

No, she wasn't mad at him. She was just furious with herself for thinking she could escape Sycamore Heights. She wanted to kick herself for thinking she could leave so easily and leave it all behind. When Della left her hometown in Washington, she never intended to return.

And that wasn't just because of her powers and the secrets behind them.

"So?" Max asked, startling her out of her thoughts. He was lazily sprawled across the couch in her office, flipping through an old book. He studied her for a moment. "What's the plan?" She could see the gears turning in his head.

Max had made a point to be around her twenty-four-seven. He was with her at The Courier. He was the one to walk her home or to the bus stop. He was there whenever Nicoletta tried to teach her spells. And on days when the world felt like it was crashing down around her, he was the only one who could calm Della down. Hearing his voice snapped her back to reality. It was like a breath of fresh air when he was around, though Della couldn't understand why.

She shrugged. "Guess we have to go," she said gloomily, crossing her arms over her chest. Her heart thumped away anxiously.

A storm was brewing inside her chest, but it wouldn't fully form. She often felt the same whenever Nicoletta tried and failed to teach her a spell, as if she couldn't quite access her true self.

"Ei told him not tuh make ya go," Max whispered angrily, chewing on the sleeve of his sweater, tossing his book aside.

"Ashton did sound pretty freaked out about whatever is going on, but those articles are vague," Della said quietly. She hated that she was even considering if his claims were legitimate.

"That could be any number of things," Max grumbled.

She nodded. "But he wants us out of town, Max," she blurted out before she could stop herself.

Max nodded. "Which is why Ei really hate this."

He glanced at her, his face darkening. He looked her up and down, his eyes tracing the edge of her bright purple spider-web printed skirt, her corduroy jacket, and the thick purple headband covering her ears from the cold. Obviously, he saw something he didn't like since he shriveled his nose and looked away. A pang of disappointment filled her.

"What all did he say?" he asked finally.

"What I have suspected. That the town is in shambles. He's scared; I know that much. I just don't know why," she sighed, dragging her feet over to him. "I don't understand why everyone is freaking out," she added quietly.

"So. . . just another day in Moss Hollow, then?" Max laughed grimly.

Della nodded.

"Fine. We'll go. At least ya won' be goin' alone?" was

all he managed in return.

"It's not about that. My mom hasn't spoken to me in weeks, and I know if I show up unannounced, my dad will have a full-on temper tantrum," Della sighed, laying her head on his shoulder. "This sucks."

Max reached for her hand—the bruised one that the Grunch had broken a month and a half ago—carefully interlocking his fingers with hers, studying the cloud-like bruise patterns that traveled up her arm. She winced. She'd gotten the cast off a week ago. Max had finally convinced her to let him perform a healing spell. Della hadn't wanted to cause him any pain by over-exerting himself with a spell like that. She was thankful; the pain had been immeasurable. However, she'd felt guilty seeing him struggle to mend her broken bones.

Max sighed heavily, laying his head on top of hers.

"It's our job tuh help people, whether we like it or not," he said, though it didn't sound like he believed his own words. "And look at it this way, maybe we can finally figure out where yer powers came from? A mystery inside a mystery? Sounds right up yer alley."

"Funny how everyone keeps saying that," Della scoffed. She wished he wouldn't have said that. "Last time I checked, I signed up to be a researcher and a writer. Not some—some—some savior of souls," she snapped half-heartedly.

"Then why are ya still here?" Max asked, his tone soft but his words like bullets to the chest.

Della inhaled sharply, scowling at everything and nothing at all.

"Because deep down, ya want tuh help people more than ya want tuh make the front page. Ya just hide under all the false pride, anger, and daddy issues." She felt him smile against her head.

"I hate it when you're right," she grumbled.

"No, ya don'," he laughed. "Ya find it comfortin' that Ei understand."

Della rolled her eyes.

'Daddy issues' wasn't even close to the word Della would use to describe her relationship with her father. And 'anger' wasn't a worthy word when referencing the town of Sycamore Heights. It was more than just how her family treated her. The whole town had harbored a vendetta against her since birth, though Della had never figured out why.

It was something she rarely admitted to herself. Her loathing for the town that had made her. Her hatred for her childhood.

Leaving Sycamore Heights had been the best thing she could have ever done.

And now everyone wanted her to go back.

Sure, maybe there was a story. Maybe Mavericks was right in thinking it wasn't safe for them in Moss Hollow. But wasn't it her job to protect everyone here? Shouldn't she stay and fight whatever was coming?

"You'd tell me if you knew something I didn't, right?" Della blurted out.

Max jolted back, looking quite hurt. "Of course!" he said almost angrily. "Why would ya think otherwise?"

Della shrugged, kicking her feet up onto the coffee table. "It feels like everyone is keeping a secret nowadays. Would be nice to know who I can count on."

Max nudged her, smiling sympathetically. "Trust me when Ei say, Ei wouldn' lie tuh ya. Unless, of course, ya were possessed or somethin', but that's a whole other can of worms," he said with a wink. When Della didn't respond, he sighed heavily, reaching up to tap his finger under her chin, telling her to keep it up despite everything. "Listen. Christmas is a week from now. Maybe the whole 'tis the season' bull-crap will distract everyone, and we can wrap this whole thing up while the rest of the town is digging into their figgy pudding," he said, trying to sound reassuring.

"You make it sound so easy," Della whispered.

~ ~ ~

After her chat with Max, Della headed toward Garroway Mortuary, looking for Porter, hoping he'd be her last line of defense. Hoping he would sympathize with her and convince everyone to let her stay home. She'd ducked into the tiny room where she often found Porter singing to himself while working on a corpse. But this time, she found a casket, the lid barely cracked open, a pair of muddy steel-toed boots on the floor beneath it.

Della lightly knocked on the coffin. She guessed he was asleep inside, headphones in, either listening to an audiobook or angry pop music. She knocked harder, tapping her foot impatiently. She could hear his blissful snoring seeping out of the crack when she leaned closer. Somedays, he was more of a vampire than any of the Ambrose's. She rolled her eyes, finally deciding to wrench the casket open. The hinges screeched, the latch dusting her teal combat boots in rust dust.

She smirked.

He wore a devilish smile as he slept.

"Really?" Della asked loudly, trying her best not to

laugh. She wanted to be irritated with him, but she had to admit, this was hilarious. Still, her patience was wearing thin. When he didn't move or answer, she decided to flick the side of his nose with her long fingernail.

Porter snorted awake, blinking away the cold light from the lightbulbs hanging over Della's head. He smiled groggily, propping his head up behind his arm. Della held the lid of the casket open, amused.

"You know, they make these for two," Porter said lazily. "They are quite comfy. And you look like you could use a nap, *meu amor*." He'd been calling her that a lot lately. He said his dad used to use that phrase whenever he deemed it necessary.

Whenever they had downtime, he'd been talking about his dad nonstop. About his memories of him, about what little Portuguese he knew. About how he wanted to learn more. About how he missed him. Della frowned. The look on his face whenever he said his dad's name caused her immense pain.

"I called you like ten times! Why didn't you answer?" she teased.

Porter frowned, reaching up to tap the inner lining of his nap casket. "Here at *Garroway Cemetery and Mortuary*, we have only the finest coffins, caskets, urns, mausoleums, and other fine containments for your deceased loved one. You and your dearly departed can R.I.P. knowing their body will be in the utmost comfort for eternity. For those worried about resurrection, this baby right here is soundproof when fully closed. No one will hear your loved one screaming for help, and *they* won't be bothered by that pesky north wind. Or—for the bloodsuckers in town—it can block out the calls of an angry lover." When he finished his little speech, he smiled his best salesman smile.

"It scares me that you have that so well-rehearsed," Della said dryly. Then she realized that her word choice had made him smile even wider. Specifically, the 'hearse' part of 'rehearsed.' "No pun intended," she said disgustedly.

Porter's eyes sparkled with delight as he sat up in his casket. His charm was a defense mechanism at best, but it was welcome. That handsome, melancholy, yet sadistic grin gave Della an ounce of comfort.

"We need to talk," Della sighed, propping her elbows up on the edge of the casket, resting her pointy chin in the cup of her hands.

Porter paled. "Nothing good comes after those words. Especially from your species."

"Relax, lover-boy," she yawned.

Porter chuckled to himself, swinging his legs out of

the casket. He studied her for a moment before scowling. "You okay?" he asked, eyeing her awkwardly.

"Mavericks put us on an assignment," Della explained, her tone dark.

"Oh. What happened?" He tried to play it off as genuine curiosity, but Della knew he had hoped they would never have to hunt for monsters again.

He was content working on dead bodies but hated finding or creating them. That fear of his had only magnified as of late.

He had never explicitly said he didn't want to talk about it, but he would flinch or change the subject if she or Max mentioned anything about their unique line of work. And Porter *never* brought up what happened in October. Della was half convinced he had blocked out the memories altogether. Under a different set of circumstances, she would have forced him to talk, but one look at him told her he was beginning to buckle under the pressure. So, instead, she let him be, leaving him to wallow. He'd snap out of it eventually; it would just take time.

She cleared her throat, looking everywhere but at his magnificent green eyes. "Some guy saw something," she shrugged.

Porter furrowed his eyebrows. "I haven't heard anything new over the police radio upstairs. When did it happen?"

"You wouldn't have heard anything unless that radio was tuned into Sycamore Heights' police radio," Della said, briefly explaining the dilemma, hoping against all hope he would tell her to leave this problem up to someone else to solve. That he would say he'd been waiting to surprise her and Max with that trip to the Caribbean he'd always wanted. That he would sweep them all away in the middle of the night, and they wouldn't have to return if they didn't want to.

But Porter didn't seem to understand her hesitation.

She would be surprised if he did, to be honest. She rarely spoke of her hometown, but when she did, she left out certain details. The picture she had painted for him of Sycamore Heights was nothing but ordinary. Who was she to grumble about her family members with what he had dealt with? It wasn't fair to call what she had experienced trauma when she was around him.

"This could be fun!" he announced after a while. His eyes were now full of child-like excitement. She frowned, turning away from him. He scoffed. "I mean—er—can't he stick it on someone else? I mean, what's his deal?" he corrected.

"He said no," Della said simply.

Porter sniffed a few times. Usually, he did this when he was trying his best not to get excited about all the different books he'd read that week. "What did Max say? Maybe he can plead your case?" How sweet he was to try and be polite when he looked like he had won the lottery.

"Max tried to stop him before he even said anything. When Mavericks makes up his mind, there's no stopping him." She puffed out her lower lip, knowing damn well it made her look like an unappreciative five-year-old. She should be lucky that this 'internship' Mavericks had her on was paying her bills. Instead, she was complaining about being sent off to do the one thing she wanted to do with her life: investigate the unknown.

"Hey. Look at it this way. I finally get to meet your parents. That's a big step, right?" Porter couldn't contain his smile anymore. So that's what this was all about?

Della couldn't help but glare at him. "A step toward what?" she snapped. She instantly regretted it, but it was the truth.

Porter recoiled, looking betrayed.

That was another thing they hadn't talked about. Whatever there was between them, it was unspoken, leaving Della extremely confused. For a girl who knew how to read a person like a book, she could barely figure him out. One minute, he kissed her, told her he loved her and called her adorable little pet names; the next, the space between them was full of tension—and not the romantic kind.

"You need to work on your motivational speeches," she said before he could ask any awkward questions.

"Significant bother, dearly detested, loathe of my life, you truly need to smile more," he said, ruffling her hair. He tried to play it all off, but there was darkness in his eyes.

She swatted him away. "Careful what you wish for. If I start smiling, it'll be because I've done something unspeakable to Mavericks' *beautiful* little face," she said through gritted teeth, clenching her hand into a menacing fist in front of his face.

Porter chuckled, stretching as he hopped out of the casket. "How long do you think we will be in the mountains?" he asked.

"Max is hoping not more than a week."

Porter stiffened. "So Max is making our vacation plans now?"

Della gave him an odd look. "What?"

"Nothing, never mind." He looked away, then sighed. "I just. . . I just thought you would come to me first," Porter admitted.

"I already told you he knew Mavericks' plans before I did. Why does it matter anyway?" Della said, confused by his sudden change in mood.

"It doesn't," he said quickly. "I just thought—never mind." He cleared his throat, scratching the back of his neck. "Should I pack heavily? Will it be cold?"

"It's Washington. What do you think?"

"Right. . ."

They were quiet for a while. The whole house was. It was so quiet they could hear the old mortuary moving with the heavy winds outside.

"Sorry," she said quietly.

He immediately changed the subject. "So, what are you thinking? What's the case?"

"This guy, Ashton, sent me a newspaper from early November. Some weird things are happening in town. For some reason, he thinks this is a 'me' problem. I don't know what to think. He's not a very trustworthy source," Della said. She was sure she had already said this, but hey, why not repeat herself for the millionth time today?

"It's worth checking it out anyway, right?"

Della sighed, tapping her foot angrily. "I don't want to go, Porter."

"I know. But at least Max and I are coming with?" Porter proposed with a smile.

"Max isn't thrilled either. He hates the cold more than you do."

Porter stiffened again, his expression turning frigid. "Yeah, well, he has a layer of fur he can jump into at any time, doesn't he?" he grumbled. "This could be good for us. Mavericks needs new stories to keep his readers engaged, and we need something to keep busy." His cheeks reddened as he looked at her.

"Will Jacobson let you take some time off?"

He opened his mouth to say something but stopped himself. His eyelids flickered with frustration. "I'll figure it out."

"Mavericks wants us heading out tomorrow," Della sighed. "From here, it's about a two-day drive."

"Wow. He isn't messing around, is he?"

Della shook her head. "It only gets worse from here."

A shiver ran down her spine. For once, she hoped all these conspiracy theories inside her and Mavericks' heads were just that: theories.

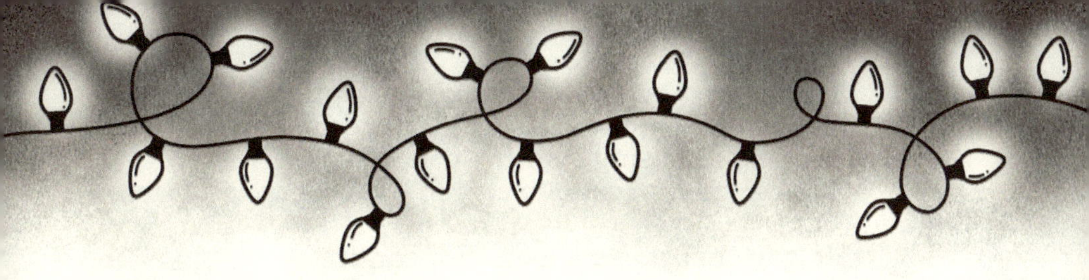

CHAPTER THREE

Road Trippin'

Della couldn't sleep that night as she sat on her bed folding her cold-weather clothes as she stuffed them into a suitcase. Porter had talked with Jacobson, who happily let him take a few weeks off. He and Max were somehow already packed. Mavericks had allotted them gas money. Everything was ready to go. But Della wasn't. As she packed, she went over her options. She could always run for it, hide somewhere Mavericks wouldn't find her. She had heard Ireland was lovely this time of year. No one would ever find her there.

Angrily, she zipped her suitcase shut, looking around her bedroom warily. This was the first place to feel like home, and she hated leaving it, even if it was only for a week.

Wasn't Della supposed to be the brave one? The one people could count on? Why was she acting like this? Brave people didn't feel this way. Brave people sucked it up and made hard choices. They did the things they didn't want to do. They didn't cower in their bedroom like this.

"Fine," she said to the universe, falling back onto her bed and directing her words to the ceiling. "You want me to go back home? I'll go back home."

Sycamore Heights wouldn't know what hit it when Della came back into town, and when she left, she was determined to leave the place in ruins.

~ ~ ~

With a scowl, Della came waltzing down the stairs at full speed the next morning, a suitcase trailing behind her, a book bag slung over the shoulder that didn't kill her to move. As soon as Richie Ambrose saw her from behind his desk, he appeared before her, looking skeptical.

"Be careful," he said as she walked by, nodding to her, a dark look passing over his ashen face.

She raised an eyebrow at him. "Is that worry, Richmond?"

He gave her a stern look. "I mean it."

"So, you know something, then?" Della asked lazily.

"I didn't say that," Richie said quickly, somehow paling despite his already pallid vampire skin.

"It's *how* you said it," Della smirked, leaning against the reception desk. She studied him—all veiny skin, tousled hair, blood-red lips, scrutinizing blue eyes that held centuries of worry. "Richie?" she asked warily.

He nodded at her, donning his usual bored expression.

"You've known Mavericks for a long time, right?" Della began. He nodded again, raising an eyebrow. "In your opinion, do you think he has been acting. . . *weird?*"

Richie tapped his fingers on the reception desk. "Define weird. I mean, it is Mavericks we are talking about," he said, looking over his shoulder nervously as if he expected the man, the myth, the legend to appear behind him.

"You know what I mean," Della said impatiently, watching Porter's hearse pull up to the glass double doors a few feet away.

"No clue." Richie shrugged, but his tone told her he had an entire cupboard full of clues.

She was about ready to tell him everything Mavericks had said, but something inside her made her stop. She didn't know Richie. For all she knew, he could be one of the people in town who sympathized with Eric Steiniger. Or worse.

So, instead, she smiled lazily. "If anything happens while I'm away, you have my number," Della said, removing herself from the reception desk.

"I'm not supposed to use that unless it's an emergency." Richie yawned.

Della stopped, her shoulders sagging. "Richmond Ambrose. If something happens, no matter how small, call me."

"Sure thing," was his lazy little answer.

Della gave him a curt nod and then headed for the door. Porter honked at her when he saw her. Not a rude 'hurry up' honk, but a honk that sounded like an out-of-tune song she couldn't quite pin. She smiled at him, waving at Max, who was half asleep in the back, looking like he regretted every decision that had led him to this point in life.

"All ready?" Porter asked as he jumped out of the

hearse and ran to help her with her luggage. He was beaming, absolutely giddy, his cheeks flushed pink, his eyes
glittering like gemstones.

She nodded. "Hopefully."

Porter shoved her suitcases into the back with the
rest of their baggage—it was quite roomie back there thanks
to it being a hearse and all—then herded Della into the
front seat. He was humming that same off-tune song as he
skipped around to the driver's seat.

"You're chipper this morning," Della noted, a sly
smile on her face.

He winked at her.

Della sighed contently, reaching into her book bag
for something she'd packed for Max. She dug around
past notebooks, pens, scrunchies, broken eyeliners, loose
change, and other odds and ends until she found the tiny
baggie of sweets she'd picked up. She tossed them back to
him. When he saw what they were—an assortment of cara-
mels, chocolates, and buttered popcorn jellybeans—his eyes
lit up.

"You're welcome," she said proudly, then handed him
another plastic container filled with raspberry and poppy
seed scones.

He hesitated before grabbing those. "Who baked
those?" he asked skeptically.

"Eloise," Della said snidely. "If you don't want them—
"

"No! No! Ei want them!" he screeched, wrenching the
container from her hands.

"Where's mine?" Porter pouted, pulling out of the
parking lot and heading towards the main road.

Della held up a baggie full of black licorice, sour candies, and mint gumdrops. She smiled slyly at him. She hated black licorice, but he loved it. "We can share my scones.
Eloise didn't make many. But you can have all those to
yourself," she added, pointing to the licorice.

"Sweet!" Porter exclaimed, riffling through his candy
bag for a handful of black licorice.

"That's disgustin'," Max breathed as they watched
him shovel in one after another.

"They're Scotty dogs, just like you!" Porter laughed,
holding one up for him to see.

"Ei've never been so offended in my whole life," Max
hissed, flashing his cat eyes at him.

Della grinned at them, then turned to look out the
window. Early morning fog separated them from the world.
This was nice. This is what she craved. Good company,
good memories, good food. Maybe she'd get more of these

little moments this week. Maybe Max was right. Hopefully, everyone would be too distracted with Christmas to care about them.

"Can Ei put on a podcast?" Max asked, leaning forward, resting his elbows on the center console, and shaking his phone in Porter's face.

"No," Della and Porter said in unison, surprising each other.

"What? Why?" Max asked, looking hurt.

"Because all your podcasts are about finances, the law of attraction, and the latest science news. I don't want to spend thirty-some hours listening to that," Porter said defensively.

Della nodded solemnly. "Maybe later?"

"Yeah, when I'm asleep. Oh! Wait! I'm the only one here qualified to drive! Never mind! Oh no, I'm so sorry. So sad," Porter said dryly.

"Well, Ei'm not gonna listen tuh any of yer stupid audio dramas then," Max said matter-of-factly.

Porter made a *tsking* sound. "Nope, I've already made plans to show Della one of my favorites."

Max turned to her, a pleading look in his eyes. "It will be a cheesy South American soap opera. Please, for the love of God, don' succumb me tuh this torture."

"Brazilian," Porter corrected. "And it's only cheesy because of the American voice actors. The original is pure perfection."

"Right, and how does that work? Dubbin' an audio drama? That's the stupidest bull—"

Della laughed, watching them argue over what to listen to. It took them thirty minutes to realize she'd put on the radio and that she was singing along to *The Beatles*. It seemed that was a happy compromise for the time being.

They drove for hours, listening to music as they all caught up. It had been ages since the three of them had been alone like this. There was no stress, no tension, nothing bad between them. They talked about everyday things. About life. About memories of Christmas from when they were young. Porter talked about the book he was reading and how it had almost made him want to write his own book. Max spent a full hour arguing with Della about space travel. Della gave hints as to what she'd gotten them for Christmas. They talked about anything and everything. Della felt almost ordinary. Like she didn't have to be something she wasn't.

"Ei think Ei'm gonna grow my hair out," Max announced at one point, looking at himself in the rearview mirror, a curious expression on his face.

He'd been styling it as of late. No more messy afro. Instead, he'd opted for tight ringlets that made him look more youthful. It suited him, Della thought.

"How come?" Porter asked, turning down the radio as a song none of them liked filled their ears.

"Well, usually Lenora cuts it, but Ei'm kinda tired of it. Like, Ei've always had an afro. Ei kinda want dreadlocks," Max said, looking at Della, who nodded her approval.

"It'd be cool to have rune beads in it like a Viking," Della smiled. She felt her cheeks redden. She glanced at Porter, noticing he was gripping the steering wheel tightly, a far-off look in his eyes. "What do you think, Venus?"

Porter glanced at her, then at Max. There was something dark in his eyes, something she didn't like. "Oh, uh, I don't know. I'm not sure it would suit you."

Max glared at him. "Well, good thing Ei'm the one with fashion sense and not *you*," he leaned over to Della, pretending to whisper in her ear. "Ei mean, look at this kid. Hoodie, leather jacket, and—Oh my—Ya pierced yer ears!" Max exclaimed, yanking Porter towards him, examining a small silver cross stud on his ear lobe and a thick black ring on his helix, connected by two thin chains.

Porter went maroon. "Both sides. Thinking about getting my nose done, too."

"Ew," Max said, shriveling up his nose.

"Dreadlocks and piercings are hot," Della said. "Equally," she laughed.

Both looked embarrassed.

"Dreadlocks are better, though," Max said after a while.

"If you mean they don't cause you pain, then yes, they are better," Porter said, holding his head high.

Della rolled her eyes, reaching over to change the radio station. "Why'd you get them pierced then?"

Porter shrugged. "I've sworn off alcohol, figured I needed a new hobby."

Max and Della exchanged a look. Getting piercings wasn't exactly a hobby. Neither was drinking.

"I thought you cooked when stressed," Della said carefully. "And what about reading?"

He shrugged again. "I need one destructive habit, or else I'll go insane."

"What ya need is therapy," Max scoffed. "How's meetin' with Ellie?"

Porter fingered the cross hanging from his ear. "It's been going good."

Della thought for a minute. "Could you imagine the

three of us showing up to like family counseling?"

"Ei'd be like, 'Oop, mom and dad are fighting again!'" Max laughed.

Porter broke out into a huge smile. "You mean Mavericks and Della?" he snorted.

Della giggled. "Yeesh. I'm not that old."

"Of course not, yer the baby," Max smiled.

Their little road trip continued like this for hours. Full of laughs, snarky remarks, and genuine happiness. They stopped at hole-in-the-wall grocery stores and gas stations, eating copious amounts of junk food. It was pure bliss for a couple of young adults who usually couldn't relax, even if it meant they won the lottery.

Twenty hours into the drive, Porter grew weary, and Della forced him to pull into a dimly lit park so they could all sleep. After that, it had just been the two of them trying to keep their voices down. Max had already been passed out in the back for a few hours.

The stars twinkled above, giving Della the feeling they belonged solely to them. The moonlight illuminated Porter's face as he turned to Della, a tired smile on his face.

"So, what can I expect when I meet your family?" he asked groggily, snuggling into his seat and pulling his hood up to keep him warm.

Della turned to him, wrapping a fluffy blanket around herself. She shrugged. "It could go a couple of ways, honestly. I know my mom will love you, though," she smiled.

"And your dad?" Porter asked nervously, again tugging gently on his earring.

"Not sure," Della said quietly.

Porter thought for a minute, studying her face like a long-lost painting by one of the greats. "Are you close with your dad?" he asked finally.

"Nope," she said softly, looking at her hands.

Porter nodded to himself. "I'm sorry."

"Thanks."

He looked her over, a sad look on his face. "I hope you have a good time while we're there. I want to see you smile like this all the time."

She blushed, glancing at Max to ensure he was still asleep and not just faking it so he could eavesdrop. Nope, he was snoring now, sprawled out in the backseat, one hand on the floor, the other straight up in the air resting against the seat. He looked extremely uncomfortable. Della snickered.

"Me too," she said finally.

Porter yawned, shutting his eyes softly. "Night, love."

"Night," Della sighed.

Porter fell asleep almost immediately, but Della lay wide awake, overseeing her friends. No one had ever done this for her before. No one ever offered to take her places. No one invited her to do things. No one wanted to be in her company. They were more than just friends; they were her family.

A selfish, twisted thought entered her mind.

She couldn't wait to see her family's faces when they saw her—saw *them*. She hoped they looked disappointed in themselves. Maybe they would realize they let her slip away.

Her mind traveled to her older brother, Quincy. She was following in his footsteps. He'd left them, too. No remorse. Without a word. At least she had the decency and opportunity to leave for a job. At least she was coming home. Even if she didn't want to. Quincy never called them, never sent letters, never emailed—nothing. But Della tried. Even when her heart told her to cut ties completely, she tried. Plus, there was the matter of her younger siblings, whom she loved with all her heart. She didn't want to leave them the way Quincy had left her. That didn't seem right.

Her mind told her she should care for her siblings and put aside her transgressions against her parents and Sycamore Heights. But her heart told her to leave and never return, that she didn't deserve this responsibility.

Things could go either way. She could be welcomed with open arms and sorrow and remorse, or she'd walk in, and they'd see the same rebellious teenager who died her hair neon green to spite her dad. Whatever happened, she silently vowed she'd make up her mind on whether to return or not.

Deep down, she already knew what conclusion she'd come to.

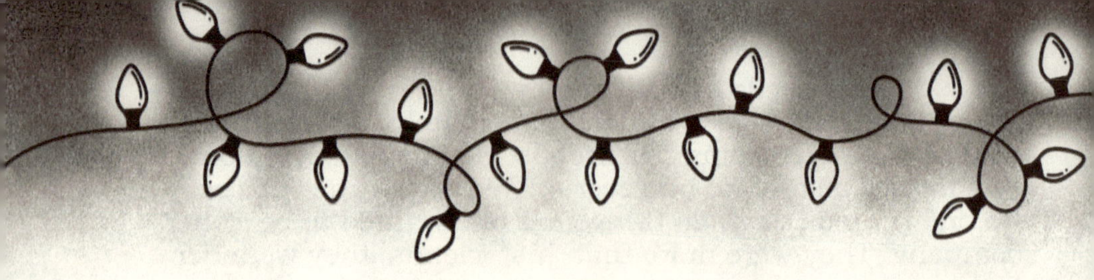

CHAPTER FOUR

'Welcome' Home

After around thirty-five hours of being stuck in Porter's rusty old hearse, they were finally driving through the snowy cul de sacs of Sycamore Heights.

"It's that yellow one on the left. The one with the kid shoveling snow," Della said, trying to keep her leg from bouncing up and down, gesturing loosely as Porter parked the hearse on the curb.

Her heart somersaulted. Her childhood home stood before them: a prison cell and a sanctuary all in one.

She really should have called first. If they turned around now, they might find a cheap motel nearby. Even sleeping another week in the hearse would be better than knocking on that front door.

The boys pressed their faces against their respective windows, peering out at the pristine, egg-yolk-yellow abode before them. Tiny smiles pulled at their lips. Whatever they were expecting, this was not it. Max's smile widened as the boy who was shoveling snow waved at them.

"Aw, shit," Della breathed, panicking, slouching in her seat to not be seen immediately. She needed a few more minutes to gain her bearings and decide what to say.

That was no ordinary winter slave hired to do the drudgery her father refused to bore himself with.

Porter glanced at her as she popped the collar of her jacket to hide her face. "What? Who is he?"

"Just a guy I know," she breathed, craning her neck to see the boy had set the shovel on his shoulders.

"Is there a problem?" Porter asked, immediately full of concern. "Should I go around the block again? Will he come hit my car with his shovel or something?"

She bit her lower lip, shook her head, and took a deep breath. She froze out of fear for a good minute before grabbing her book bag and ripping open her door. It was too late to turn back now. He would knock on the window out of suspicion if they didn't get out soon. And that would be humiliating. Della forced her lips into a smile, though her eyes were as dead as the trees that lined the sidewalks of this cul de sac. Begrudgingly, she gestured for Porter to get out, shooting Max a look in the rearview mirror.

"Woah, who died?" *His* familiar voice rang. High-pitched and whiny, yet still raspy enough to be perceived as manly. Sort of.

Della edged around the hood of the hearse, watching the snow shoveler's preoccupied eyes scan Porter and the shivering figure that was Max.

"Thankfully, no one—" Porter began to joke.

The snow shoveler's eyes finally locked onto Della's. They widened as his fingers loosened their grip on the shovel atop his shoulders, sending it clattering to the cleared pavement below. His face erupted into a gigantic smile as he ran to Della, flinging himself onto her with the might of a golden retriever puppy.

Della's eyes twitched with irritation as he squeezed his arms around her. "Hello, Sebastian. Nice to see you, too," she said in a motherly tone as she wiggled her hand free to pat him on the back. "You're hurting me," she said, his bony elbows digging into her sides.

Sebastian pulled away, beaming, ignoring her.

Some would say that Sebastian Breckenridge was Della's first and only friend. Until recently, Della would have called him nothing more than an acquaintance. The whole 'friendship' thing hadn't been Della's speed. Nevertheless, a small—miniscule, in fact—part of her was happy to see him.

"I thought you weren't coming!" he exclaimed, running his hands through his dirty blond hair.

"Heh, me either!" Della chortled, giving him an awkward snap and point. Max gave her a confused look, shaking his head as if to say, 'Please don', love. Yer embarrassin' yerself.' She reddened, clearing her throat. "Uh, Seb, this is Max and Porter. Boys, this is Sebastian."

Sebastian turned, crisscrossing his arms, offering his hands for the others to shake.

"Pleasure," Max smiled, loosely shaking his hand. His eyes were on the patches littering Sebastian's camo bomber jacket. All of which were either science puns or something from some lesser-known show about space travel and aliens. Right up Max's alley.

"Nice to meet you," Porter said kindly, shaking Sebastian's hand firmly. His eyes were set on Sebastian's face, analyzing every part of him.

"Same to you both!" he exclaimed. He stared at them momentarily, then whipped around to face Della. "They aren't staying, are they?" He must've thought he was whispering. Subtlety wasn't exactly Sebastian's strong suit.

"They are." Della nodded, daring a step towards the front door. Thinking of opening it made her want to throw up that cheap convenience store hotdog she had for breakfast. She really should have convinced Porter to stop at a coffee shop instead.

Sebastian turned green. "That's. . . oh boy. Uh—best get you all inside. Please tell Jasper I had no idea you were coming. I—I really need the money."

Della rolled her eyes to hide her fear. Porter wore an odd look, but the excitement was getting to him. Max shrugged, exchanging a worried glance with Della behind his back. Sebastian grimaced, stepping past them all. They kicked the snow from their shoes as he swung open the front door. He knocked on the door frame several times, poking his head inside. The fresh pine wreath on the door burned the inside of Della's nose, the bells hanging from it stinging her eardrums as they rang.

"Mrs. Coleman, you have guests!" Sebastian called into the bellows of the prison that paraded around as a lovely suburban home.

A rattling sound came from the direction of the kitchen. "Let them in!" A voice sang afterward. Della had gotten her innate clumsiness from her mother.

Sebastian inhaled sharply, pushing the door open and stepping aside to let them in. Porter was the last in, offering to hold the door for Sebastian, but he was already pulling it closed, trying to disappear outside without them noticing.

"You aren't coming?" Porter asked skeptically.

Sebastian stared Della dead in the eyes, then shook his head. "I have no intent on being at the station when that train crashes," he said, eyes the size of dinner plates, his finger pointed between Della's eyes.

Porter began to ask what he meant, but the door slammed shut, cutting him off. He turned slowly to Della, his thumb pointed over his shoulder, eyebrows furrowed.

"What was that all about?" he asked.

Della's face cycled through hysterical expressions. She choked out a laugh. "He's just antsy," she lied. "Honestly, I—"

A blood-curdling, ear-piercing, heart-wrenching scream filled the room. Max choked on thin air, Porter's hand went to his hip holster, and Della froze.

"DELPHEE!" Kimi Kitchi-Coleman screamed at the top of her lungs. Suddenly, two hands wrapped around Della's waist from behind, pulling her into another tight hug.

Instantly, the air squeezed out of Della's lungs. "Hey, Mom," she choked out, trying and failing to escape her mother's bear hug.

Kimi spun her around to see her face. "I didn't think you were coming! And you brought *friends*!" Her mother always emphasized that word, forcing it into Della's brain, letting her know that it was good to have people who crave your undivided attention twenty-four-seven.

"Indeed, I have," Della smiled.

Kimi paused for a moment. She had probably expected Della to say something like: 'No, they're just co-workers!' or 'Nope, they're off-duty cops; I just got arrested. Mind paying my bail?' But she was over the moon when she realized Della was serious in saying they were friends.

Her honey-gold cheeks glowed brightly, illuminated by the Christmas lights coiled around the staircase to her left. She tucked a strand of ebony hair behind her ear, pulling the boys into a hug. Kimi loved people. She loved company, loved long chats with strangers—she was an extrovert in every way. However, Della couldn't remember the last time she had been this excited to meet someone new.

"I'm Kimi, Delphee's momma," Kimi said proudly, letting the boys go. Max rubbed his ribs, and Porter smiled, looking winded. "You are?" she asked happily.

"Yes, I'd like to know that too," a sour voice added.

Della involuntarily coiled in on herself, slowly looking over her shoulder to see Jasper Coleman standing at the top of the stairs, his arms crossed over his chest, eyes locked onto Max and Porter. Jasper, with his permanent pout, always resembled spoiled milk. But since it was 'tis the season' and all that, Della thought he looked more like curdled eggnog.

Porter straightened to his full height, looking more like a soldier than a gravedigger. "Porter Garroway, sir," he said, his face red. "Friend of your daughters."

Jasper scowled. "You're a little too old to know Cassie," he said dryly.

Porter chuckled, taking it as a joke, though Della could tell he had no idea who Cassie was. Della, on the other hand, knew otherwise.

"I'm Maximilian McGregor-Mav—"

"Why are you here?" Jasper interrupted, looking at Max like he had just screamed profanity in his face. His eyes floated back to Della, his scowl deepening.

"Work," Della replied, trying her best not to sound

too cold.

"Why are *they* here?" Jasper corrected, pointing to Max and Porter.

"What's Christmas without the people you love?" Della asked haughtily, adjusting the strap of her book bag, instantly regretting that sassy comment.

Jasper's eyes narrowed threateningly.

Della recoiled further, feeling like a scared animal caught in the headlights of a semi-truck. Something deep inside her told her to run, to get out while she still could. Slowly, she backed up until she was safely wedged between Max and Porter. Using them as human shields was another option, but that would have played into the cowardice she was trying to fight.

Jasper Coleman was the one thing on Earth Della was terrified of.

She looked around, trying to find something else to discuss and change the subject. A plate of half-eaten cookies and crumpled pieces of paper lay on the coffee table. Her eye twitched again. "Bible study?" she asked, rocking back and forth on her heels.

Jasper shriveled up his nose at Porter and Max. "Luckily enough, everyone just left." He was about to say something else when his gaze fell upon the bruises left over from her broken arm. Even though she was on the mend, the damage wasn't completely erased.

Jasper's face filled with a questioning expression.

Kimi cleared her throat. "Della, what happened to your arm?" she asked, roughly grabbing her arm and rolling up her sleeve.

"Oh, I, uh, tripped—"

"She got in an accident," Max cut in.

"I fell on her," Porter said over him.

Della turned to stare at them in disgust, particularly at Porter. "Yes," she said with a discreet 'what-the-literal-Hell' kind of look. "I came down the stairs at my apartment and ran into Porter, who fell on me and broke my arm," she explained. "I guess you could say that was me getting in an accident."

"Yup," the boys said in unison.

They were horrible liars. Had she taught them nothing?

Jasper raised an eyebrow, but at this point, he probably knew he wouldn't get anywhere with another question.

"You poor thing. . . And look at you! So pale!" Kimi said, frowning deeply, pinching Della's cheek. "You aren't staying cooped up in an office twenty-four-seven, are you? I thought for sure being in Louisiana would give you some sort of tan! You look so sickly!"

Della flushed. "Mother, dear, you're embarrassing me."

Jasper rolled his eyes. "I hope you aren't staying long. We have things to do. December—"

"Is the busiest time of the year. I know," Della said, biting her tongue the best she could. "We were actually hoping to stay here for a week?"

"Absolu—" Jasper began, raising a finger to object.

"Absolutely! What a perfect idea!" Kimi said, glaring at her husband. "Cassie took over your room, but I'm sure she will gladly share. Porter, Max, you can bunk with Leonel or stay in the living room."

"What about Quin's room?" Della dared, though she knew better.

Jasper glared at her.

Kimi paused, then shook her head. "It—It's a mess. They'd be more comfortable elsewhere." Jasper gave his wife a questioning look. Kimi waved him away, pulling Della into another hug. "I'm so happy you're home," she whispered tearfully.

Della glanced at her father, forcing a smile. "Me too," she whispered back.

Even after everything, that might've been the biggest lie of Delphee Chrysanthemum Coleman's life.

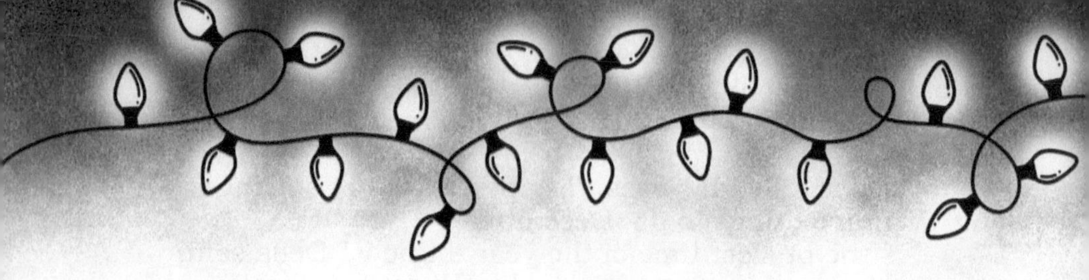

CHAPTER FIVE

Revelations

In some cases, when you leave someplace you think you know, returning to it shows you just how wrong you were. Your heart is so full of joy that you realize not everything was as horrid as you made it out to be. Unfortunately, this wasn't the case for Della. Home was exactly how she remembered it. Maybe even worse. The beautiful blue skies and crisp mountain air covered the smell of carbon monoxide. 'Put Jesus First' signs hid the fact that most of the teenagers in town hadn't left room for Jesus since the womb. Even the welcome signs were a lie. The fences were covered in layers upon layers of stark white paint, but inside, the wood was rotten to the core. The houses barely differed in color, mirroring the mindset of those living in them. Della's family was no different.

It was a miracle she'd grown to be the person she was.

Della smiled mischievously as she led Max and Porter up the creaking staircase, luggage in tow. The walls around them were covered in picture frames. Most were full of pictures of Cassandra and Leonel, only a few of Della. Never Quincy, whom her parents pretended didn't exist.

"Bathroom on the left, next door down is Leonel's. I'm on the right with Cassandra," Della explained, crossing the hall to knock on Leonel's door.

"Password!" Came Leonel's tiny voice.

"Open up, or I'm leaving, Squirt One," Della called back.

There was a crashing sound and a yelp from across the hall before both bedroom doors were wrenched open.

"DELLA!" The twins screamed, tripping over themselves to get to their big sister. Leonel launched himself onto Della's back, squeezing her tightly. Cassandra hugged her quickly, then pulled away, looking lovingly into Della's eyes.

"Mom said you weren't coming home!" Cassandra exclaimed as Della struggled to pry Leonel from her back.

"I changed my mind," Della smiled, ruffling Cassandra's striking black hair. The twins were far too innocent to be let in on the strife Della caused her parents. They were utterly oblivious to everything that went on around them. Truth be told, they had probably believed she was too busy for Christmas.

"We missed you! I didn't have anyone to help scare off the trick-or-treaters on Halloween!" Leonel said, puffing out his lower lip.

Della knelt and hugged them both, her grip lingering a little longer than she cared to admit. She had missed them so much. The twins were a spitting image of Kimi: dark hair, golden skin, and brown eyes. Della had always been jealous of their appearance. Della matched her father all except for his eyes. And though the twins mirrored Kimi's personality, Della didn't share either of her parents' qualities.

Della smiled up at Max and Porter, who wore the dumbest grins she had ever seen.

"This is Porter and Max. Boys, this is Leonel and Cassandra," Della explained. Cassandra rolled her eyes. "Right, sorry. Cassie, not Cassandra."

Leonel saluted the boys. "Pleasure to meetcha!"

Cassie gripped Della's hand, waving shyly.

"Leo, mind if they bunk with you? I swear they don't bite."

Leonel's eyes widened. "Really? Yeah!" he said excitedly. Della could see the wheels turning in his mind, though she had no idea why. An impish grin spread across his lips. Oh, the trouble he could get into.

"Can you bunk with me?" Cassie asked.

"Wouldn't have it any other way," Della smiled.

"I can help you with your bags," Leonel said, offering a hand toward Porter.

"Oh, thanks!" Porter said, taken by surprise, handing over a lighter suitcase. "Lemme get the door for ya." He reached around to help Leonel, both disappearing inside the bedroom. "Wow! Is that a lava lamp?" Della heard Porter ask as the door closed.

Max rolled his amber eyes.

Cassie watched him carefully, her eyes tracing him with the utmost curiosity.

"Go on," Della said, nudging her.

Cassie blushed. "I think your pants are cool," she

said quietly.

Max looked down at his olive and orange pinstriped pants, smiling ear to ear. "Thanks, love. Ei like yer. . ." He looked to Della, who mouthed a word with a wink. ". . . socks," he added. Della nodded approvingly.

Cassie's eyes sparkled at the sound of his accent.

"He's Irish," Della said.

Cassie gasped, leaning forward. "Have you ever seen a leprechaun? Della says they don't really hang out at the end of rainbows, but I think she's lying."

Max thought. "No, Ei've never seen a leprechaun, but Ei hear they're angry little buggers. As for the rainbows, well. . . Let's just say Della needs tuh use a wee more imagination."

"Called it," Cassie breathed.

Max smiled kindly.

There was a crash from inside Leonel's room.

Max tensed. "I swear, if he broke another lava lamp, Ei'll—" He paused, looking down at Cassie.

"You can swear," Cassie said exasperatedly, brushing her hair from her eyes. "Della does all the time."

"Hey!" Della blurted out, feigning a hurt expression.

Max opened and closed his mouth several times, caught between a smile and a look of bafflement. "Well, Miss Cassie, Ei'll see ya later." And with that, accompanied by another crash, he departed to Leonel's room.

Cassie giggled, pulling Della toward what used to be her bedroom.

"You've missed so much! So, you know that kid who lives across the street? Well, she—" Cassie launched into a long-winded discussion about all the crazy third-grade drama Della had missed out on.

Indeed, some things never change.

~ ~ ~

"Dad! Dad!" Leonel shouted, racing past Della while pulling Cassie down the stairs. "Porter works at a mortuary, and Max is a scientist! He said my science fair project should've won first place!"

"Ei said that for a third grader, Leonel knew a lot about pyrotechnics," Max corrected, smiling to himself.

"Leo tends to bend the truth," Della explained, leading the boys downstairs. Come to think of it, Leo probably learned that from her.

"He is very inquisitive," Porter said. "And hyper," he added, terror filling his eyes. Watching someone who didn't have siblings be stuck with little kids was always amusing. Della wondered how long the boys would last sharing a room with Leonel. She guessed two days at the most.

"You should have opted for the living room," Della laughed.

Leonel and Cassie had planted themselves at the kitchen table, talking Jasper's ear off while he set out plates and cutlery.

"Need any help, Mr. Coleman?" Porter asked.

Jasper looked up, staring at him for a moment before reluctantly nodding. He handed over napkins, pointing to where they went.

Della leaned against the kitchen counter on high alert, not knowing what to expect tonight. Jasper Coleman had a unique way of embarrassing his children. Most parents would lovingly poke fun at their children and their friends. Jasper, on the other hand, tended to make a scene.

"So, Max," Kimi began, chopping up a cucumber. Great. She was making her signature salad, which somehow tasted like it came from a garbage disposal. "How do you know Della?"

Jasper whipped his head around to listen.

Max reddened. "Ei work with her."

"Leonel said you were a scientist," Jasper said suspiciously.

"Aye, as a hobby. Ei am the tech guy at the newspaper we work for," Max explained, nervously pulling the collar of his shirt away from his neck, eyeing Della. "My dad runs the place."

Jasper's face lit up in mild surprise.

Sighing and clearing her throat, Kimi continued. "And you, Porter?"

Porter fumbled with the napkins, nearly knocking over Leonel's glass of water. Max snorted. Della smirked. Who knew napkins could be such a pain to handle?

"I—uh—Well, among other things—reasons—among other reasons, Miss Coleman found evidence at the cemetery I work and live at," he explained, his face rotating through all the colors of Christmas. "Not raccoon hair, I might add."

The three of them chuckled grimly.

Jasper, on the other hand, was far from amused. "Evidence? Evidence for what?"

"The article," they said darkly.

"Ooh! What kind of article?" Kimi asked, putting her hair up into a ponytail.

Della completely checked out, her thoughts overflowing like a bubbling cauldron. Max and Porter exchanged a look, searching every corner of the kitchen for the right words.

"Small crime. Nothing important," Della lied, her voice small. It was strange. She could almost feel the far-off look in her eyes.

"Petty theft," Porter tried to explain, giving her a questioning look, silently asking if she was okay. The answer was no. He cleared his throat. "I found some fur out by one of the mausoleums. It turns out it had come off the perp's jacket." He tried to laugh, but it sounded more like a choking horse.

Jasper narrowed his eyes in Della's direction. She stiffened, pinning herself to the counter, head bowed, waiting for him to say something she didn't want to hear.

"So, you caught the bad guy?" Cassie asked.

Max and Porter nodded. Della just stared at her father, anticipating a reprimand.

"You guys are like superheroes!" Leonel exclaimed.

"I wouldn't say that," Della said quietly, finally tearing her eyes from Jasper, choosing to stare at her feet instead.

"Ei would," Max said solemnly, nudging her.

Porter was silent as he finished setting the table. Della glanced at him, the look on his face a mixture of pain and resentment. She wished she knew what was going on in his head. If the option arose, she would trade her visions for mind reading in a heartbeat.

Jasper took one look at them all and plopped himself down onto one of the fancy chairs that lined the kitchen table, crossing his legs in a way that made him look like a mob boss. "So, what makes a paper from Louisiana send an intern, an I.T. guy, and some boy who works with the dead to good ol' Washington state?" he asked. Della suddenly realized where she had gotten her 'interrogation mode' from.

The three of them stood lost in thought. If Jasper knew why they were here, he would be spasming on the floor from a heart attack in less than half a second. Or call the nearest psych ward to come pick them all up.

"We have assets a couple of towns over. We're following up on something," Della explained slowly. "And I'm not just an intern," she added under her breath. Not that he would care. Journalism, to him, wasn't the kind of job you should be proud of.

"Anything we can help with?" Kimi asked.

Porter smiled, shaking his head. "Letting us stay here is more than enough, Mrs. Coleman."

"She was talking to Delphee," Jasper interjected before Kimi could reply.

"It's *Della*, not Delphee," Cassie corrected innocently, though she was ignored.

Porter looked extremely hurt, but he said nothing.

"He can speak if he wants to," Della hissed.

Jasper scowled, shooting Della a warning look. Porter looked between them, a look of realization washing over his face. He rocked back and forth on his feet momentarily before taking a seat. Della glared at Jasper in disbelief. Porter was staring at the kitchen table in such an odd way. Della thought for sure his face would stay like that forever. Max discreetly reached for Della's hand, interlocking his pinky with hers. He squeezed tightly, then went to sit next to Porter. Della didn't move, eyes back on her father.

"My house, my rules," Jasper said, grabbing the salad bowl from his wife. He came to stand close to her, whispering in her ear. "You should know better. Bringing people like *them* here," he spat.

"What exactly do you mean by that?" Della snapped back.

"You know what I meant."

Della leaned in close, nodding to cover her face with her hair, dropping her voice so only he could hear.

"I don't care if this is the white house. They are my friends, and you will treat them as such," she hissed, her blood boiling.

Jasper rolled his eyes. "Della, you don't have any friends. And I doubt you ever will with how you treat the people around you." He looked down at her, smiling toothily.

Della bit her lip hard, biting back tears. He turned away from her, satisfied.

"What? No witty comeback?" Jasper whispered over his shoulder.

Della inhaled sharply. There was a bomb in her chest that was dangerously close to igniting. She tried to push it down and ignore it, which unfortunately only sent fire closer to the fuse. That feeling terrified her. She knew what was happening. This was the same feeling she'd had when she'd used her powers to kill Eric Steiniger. All that anger, fear, pain, and sadness culminated inside her, and she feared what would happen if she gave in to it again. She felt like she was on the verge of losing control of something ancient, dark, and far too powerful to control.

"No snarky remark?" Jasper asked again. "Has Louisiana made you soft?"

Della turned away from him, looking to her mom for help, but she didn't say anything. Again, she wanted to flee. But her hands were tied. If she did that, the consequences would be worse than what she would endure if she stayed.

Porter cleared his throat, cutting through the silence. "Food looks great, Mrs. Coleman," he said awkwardly.

"Yeah," Della whispered, her voice coming out choked. "Super great."

CHAPTER SIX

In The Minds of The Ignorant

Dinner had been a quick affair. Leonel and Cassie bombarded their sister and her unusual guests with endless questions as Della tried not to have a breakdown. Jasper hadn't stopped glowering once, and Della couldn't bring herself to smile through the tension. She'd sat next to Porter, who held her hand under the table the whole time. Max spent the entire evening watching her from the corner of his eye. Neither of them said a word the whole night. Della kept as quiet as possible, too afraid she'd melt into a puddle of tears.

Morning came, but the night hadn't washed away the tension. Keen to avoid another stressful meal, the three slipped down to the living room before anyone else woke up. Christmas lights illuminated their faces as they sat huddled on the sofa.

Porter was lost in thought.

Max seemed pissed.

Della was a mix of the two. Her entire body tingled with expectance, waiting for the other shoe to drop, waiting for the yelling to start, the arguments, the lectures. She shivered beside Porter on the couch, pulling her knees up to her chest, feeling morose.

"So, what all do you know about this guy?" Porter finally asked through a mouthful of pumpkin-flavored toaster pastry, startling Della. He sat perched on the back of the sofa, scanning one page of the newspaper that had brought them here.

"Ashton John," Della explained. "Town screw-up. Type of guy that won't be missed if he ends up dead in a ditch. However, in some ways, he is perceptive. If there is anything weird going on in town, I bet he would know about it. Just. . . Just not. . . not our kind of weird, if you catch my drift."

"Yikes," Max said as he picked the frosting off his *Poptart* and handed it over to Porter, who smiled in delight.

"I busted him about two years back for dealing steroids to the seniors before one of the big football games. I'd love to talk to him in person," Della said, gesturing to the front door. "Maybe even one of his ex-clients. I bet they would love to rat him out for something."

"What makes you say that?" Porter asked.

"Up here, if you cooperate, you get a slap on the hand and college tuition in exchange for a felony. I guess it keeps things interesting. Cops told Ashton to tell them who he had been selling to, and he wouldn't go to jail. And don't get me started on all the stereotypical rich kids 'round here," Della grumbled, feeling a headache coming on. She hadn't been able to sleep much on the road, and last night was no different. She was already exhausted and achy.

"Ugh. Nothin' like bitter rich kids tuh put a sour taste in yer mouth," Max yawned.

". . . but you. . . You are a bitter rich kid. . ," Porter said carefully.

"Ya know what Ei meant."

"I—I really don't," Porter sighed. He thought for a moment, then shook his head. "Bets out!" he announced, tossing the newspaper aside and reaching for his wallet. Max sighed heavily, he and Della following suit. "I think we are dealing with the ramblings of a drugged-up mind. I doubt there is anything magical in this town. Or it's werewolves. Thirty bucks. Forty if anyone brings up *Twilight*. It is Washington, after all," Porter said, slapping money onto the coffee table before them.

"Werewolves?" Della asked. He shrugged innocently.

"Hundred even. Witch. Doper. Curse of some sort," Max said lazily, sliding a crisp Benjamin next to Porter's thirty bucks.

Porter winced. "Might have to pay that off in intervals. What say ye, Coleman?"

Della sat back, thinking. Porter had started this little game to distract his companions—or maybe himself—from any blunders or mishaps they had. Anytime Della began working on an article, Porter found a way to bet on it. Max tended to bet the most. Maybe out of spite, knowing Porter would have a debt to pay if he won.

"All right," She began. She played this game for his benefit, knowing he only did it to try and raise their moods. "Seventy. If it's magical, I'm betting on a poltergeist. Or absolutely nothing is happening here, and Mavericks sent us here for no reason." She paused before putting her money on the table. "If that's the case, you'd better start biding on how quickly it will take me to snap and kill him."

Porter grimaced, collecting the money and placing it safely inside one of the zip-up pockets that lined his jacket. "That's two hundred and pending."

Max smiled cheekily. "Make it double."

"Yeesh," Della smiled.

"All right, four hundred and pending. I—"

"I'll throw in one of my signed CDs," Della added quickly.

Porter rolled his eyes. "No one wants that."

Max's hand shot up into the air. "Ei, personally—don' know about the rest of ya invisible contributors—" He looked around the room. "Ei want that."

Porter scowled, sighing.

"She has the greats, mate!" Max exclaimed.

"Fine. Four hundred dollars and pending, plus a signed copy of one the worst band's worst albums," Porter said, smiling smugly.

Della gasped, indicating being stabbed in the heart. "And you call yourself a music lover," she said dramatically.

"No, I call myself Porter Garroway," he said sarcastically.

Della rolled her eyes playfully.

"You three are up early," Kimi's voice rang behind them. Della turned to see her coming down the stairs, dressed in clean white overalls, her hair braided and pulled into a bun on top of her head. Kimi was the only person Della truly thought was beautiful.

"Getting all the facts straight before we head out," Della said.

"Where are you guys headed?" Kimi asked, leaning over the back of the couch to look at them all. She smiled at the boys, giving them sympathetic looks.

"Into town. Are the O'Malley twins still working at *Ole Joe's*?" Della asked lazily.

Kimi frowned. "You haven't even been back a day, Della. Don't start anything."

"She's done more in less. You should be proud," Porter smiled. Della shook her head at him disapprovingly.

"Precisely. Stay out of trouble. All of you," Kimi pleaded.

"I just have a few questions for those idiots, then I'm off. Trust me; I'm not here to start anything," Della said quietly, standing.

Kimi sighed heavily. "Be back by lunch. I'm off to the historical society. Jasper is taking the twins to Church for the day."

Della gave a thumbs-up as she beelined for the front entryway. With more aggression than necessary, she slipped on her neon green sneakers.

"You work at the historical society, Mrs. Coleman?" Porter asked, trying to clear the air. Della could feel his eyes on her as she bent down to tie her laces.

"I do! My family has been here for a long time. My people have graciously donated many things to the society. I'm a representative," Kimi explained. Her voice was enthusiastic, but Della imagined her face was blank.

A moment of silence before Porter asked the question Della knew had been burning a hole in his head. "What do you mean by 'my people?'"

Kimi scoffed. "I am part of the Mukwa Tribe. My father is the current Chief," she said, an odd tone to her voice. She didn't sound proud to say that.

"Oh, cool! I never knew Della was Native," Porter said.

"Indigenous," Kimi snapped.

Kimi cleared her throat and apologized, but Della looked over her shoulder, fury in her eyes. Della didn't have a preference like her mother, but she was still livid.

"What am I supposed to do? Wear moccasins and do a rain dance for you?" Della grumbled at them. "Am I supposed to wear a headdress twenty-four-seven?" No one dared answer that. She rolled her eyes, turning back to her shoes.

"What it's like? Being part of a tribe like that?" Porter asked, his voice a little strained.

Della paused as she tied her laces, staring at where the hardwood flooring and the carpet met. The division between the floors mirrored her mother's separation from her heritage. Kimi was well versed in all things Mukwa, but discussing anything related to the subject outside of the historical society was unheard of. Almost everything Della knew about that percentage of her being had come from her grandfather or the internet. It was such a taboo subject; the twins didn't realize they were Indigenous until a few years ago.

"It's definitely an interesting experience being Mukwa," Kimi said, her voice an ounce harsh. "A lot of challenges you wouldn't expect. We're small. Not recognized federally. We've had to work very hard for what we have," she explained sourly.

"Oh," Porter squeaked. He hadn't been expecting an answer like that.

"We should get going; we have a lot of ground to cover," Della lied, standing and nodding at the door.

Porter shook himself from his thoughts, reaching over to shake Kimi's hand. "Right. Thanks again for having us, Mrs. Coleman," he smiled, joining Della reluctantly.

"You are very welcome." Kimi smiled tightly, a crease forming above her eyebrows.

Quickly, the boys gathered their coats, and the three of them headed out. Crisp air stung Della's lungs. A light breeze blew snow into the sky, creating a tiny glittering tornado. The Universe must know she needed something to calm her down.

However, it didn't work in time. As soon as he was sure no one else would see, Porter gave Della a very judgmental look.

"You could at least *pretend* you want to be here. I mean, at least she cares. She's just trying to look out for you," he said as he opened the passenger door for her.

Della opened her mouth to say something when Max cut her off.

"Hey, if roles were reversed, she wouldn't be telling ya off for snappin' at Jed. Leave her be," he said matter-of-factly.

"Max," Della scolded, panic rising in her throat like bile. She couldn't believe it herself, but she would rather have Porter dig at her than tell him how messed up her childhood was. The rational side of her knew that was a red flag.

A red flag she would ignore for the time being.

"That is a completely different situation!" Porter barked. "Jed has nothing to do with this!"

"Knock it off, both of you," Della snapped, shoving Porter away so she could get in the car. Shortly after she shut the door, Max's door slammed shut.

The only words spoken the entire drive were Della's directions.

~ ~ ~

Ole Joe's was a small coffee shop and bookshop. Although other businesses would argue, this café was one of the biggest money makers in Sycamore Heights. Filled with sweet, flaky pastries, home-brewed beans, and plush seating, it made for the perfect hang-out. Dates, study sessions, and meetings were always happening here. Once upon a time, Della wanted to spend the rest of her life slaving away behind a coffee machine. Her favorite view would be these brick walls covered in chalkboard paint and plastic ivy.

Maybe if she hadn't had to grow up so quickly, she would be here now, not galivanting around with beings who weren't supposed to exist. But then again, she, too, had powers. Meaning she wasn't supposed to exist either.

How lovely.

Kicking snow out of the way, Della walked up to the door, gruffly opening it. Someone had oiled the hinges—usually, they squeaked as incessantly as a mouse whenever the door opened. As soon as her feet crossed the threshold, every head attached to every freezing body turned. They looked to stare in disdain, their beady eyes unblinking as she led the boys to the front counter.

"Oh. . . My. . . *Lord*. . ." a voice came from the counter. "Not *you*. Anyone but *you*."

A boy with flaming red hair stood behind the counter, his hand stuck in a water glass, looking utterly disgusted. Cyrus O'Malley. Half of the pair that had made middle school Hell for Della and Sebastian. To say the young super-sleuth had been happy to bust him for buying steroids from Ashton was a massive understatement.

"O'Malley." Della nodded curtly.

He rolled his eyes, staring past Della at the boys, his eyes lingering on Max. "We're at full capacity," he grumbled, wrenching his fist from the glass.

"Luckily, we aren't staying long. I have a few questions for you. About Ashton John," Della smiled tightly.

"Last time I checked, you aren't a cop," Cyrus smiled back. The audacity. But that statement struck her as odd. Was he waiting to be questioned by the police?

"But," Della began, pulling a notebook and pen out of the army-green book bag slung over her shoulder. "I am a journalist, which means I have privileges. Oh, and not to forget you are too scared of me to throw me out."

Max snorted a laugh.

"I'm not scared of you," Cyrus said, reddening as he slammed the glass he'd been cleaning onto the counter.

"I got a letter from him in the mail. What's been up with old Ash lately?" Della began, clicking her pen several times, locking eyes with him.

"I haven't seen him since he went missing, and if he sent you a letter, then you need to tell the authorities. You know. The people who are *supposed* to investigate disappearances and the like," Cyrus said, wrinkling his nose.

Della furrowed her eyebrows. "What do you mean?"

"Wait, that's not why you're here?" Cyrus asked, looking suddenly concerned.

Della shook her head. "No, I'm here to talk to Ashton about the contents of his letter. I didn't know he was missing."

There may have been a case here after all.

She hated that thought.

Cyrus struggled with himself for a minute before leaning forward. "No one has seen him since Church a few weeks back."

Della studied him, then nodded. "What have you been up to recently?"

"I've been here," he snapped. "Thanks to you, I can't get a job anywhere else." True. *Ole Joe's* was known for both its drinks and how often it let street urchins join the bean brewing ranks.

"Had you been in contact with Ashton before he disappeared?" Della asked, eyeing Porter, who was inspecting the glass case of quiches before him.

"After you busted him, he cleaned up his act. Yeah, I talk to him, but only because we're in the same help group," Cyrus explained, grabbing another glass and holding it to the light before scrubbing it with a wet cloth. "Four-fifty a slice," he said, glancing at Porter.

"Did Ashton have any enemies?" Max asked, scanning the drink menu.

"Other than the one standing next to you, not really. A lot of the people in town he dealt to moved away." The way Cyrus looked at her boys made Della want to choke him. Or worse. Probably worse. "For one reason or another," Cyrus added, looking Della up and down. "I'm surprised he even wrote to you. What did he say?"

"Confidential, O'Malley. Can I get the name of that support group?" Della asked through gritted teeth, looking away.

Mistakenly, she glanced over her shoulder. No one had moved since she had walked in. Everyone was still staring. Whispering. Judging.

Cyrus rolled his massive green eyes. Compared to Porter's, his eyes were a pale, ugly chartreuse. "Unaddicted, Unafraid. We meet every Sunday after Church. Because of you, it's mandatory. I suggest you come alone," he added, trying to nod discreetly in the boy's direction.

Della scowled at him, fingering a container of toothpicks, debating whether to flick it over and cause him the inconvenience of picking it all up. "Where's Lorelei?" she asked.

Cyrus shrugged. "With a boy, at home, or passed out with a bottle somewhere she shouldn't be. Take your pick. Trust me. She had nothing to do with him either."

Della nodded, turning to leave.

Cyrus made a sound akin to a strangled cat.

"Hey, Coleman?" he called. Della turned back, giving him an exasperated yet questioning look. "I know we aren't supposed to encourage your—" He made a show of air quotes as he rolled his eyes again. "—'fanatics,' but I don't think Ash is passed out somewhere in the woods like the cops are trying to say."

Della doubled back, crossing her arms over her chest. "What makes you think that?" Her heart felt like it would beat out of her chest while she waited for his response.

He cleared his throat, lowering his already husky voice. "Things have been weird lately. I mean, nothing happens here. Sure, druggies, cheaters, petty theft, your usual corrupt people—but people don't just disappear. Things don't go missing and turn up the next day. You don't see shadows out of the corner of your eye. Not like this." His voice was barely audible by the end.

Cyrus was tall, muscular, and as strong as a twenty-something who wasn't born with magical powers could be. Some would say he was devilishly handsome, but Della left off the 'handsome' part. He was a class-A bully and used to be captain of several sports teams. The only thing that had ever scared him was Della. At least, that's what she had thought. But now, there was something more terrifying than a cranky teenage girl who was Hell-bent on clearing her town of jerks like him.

"Just catch the bad guy like you always do, okay?" he finished, a strained terror in his voice. "But don't tell anyone I helped you. And, uh, talk to your mom? I'm pretty sure Ash's been hanging around the Sycamore House lately."

A nervous chill flooded Della's spine. She would have rather had him say never come back to *Ole Joe's*.

"I will," she said.

This time, she would do it the right way: no loopholes and no room for error.

"See you Sunday," Cyrus nodded, dismissing them.

Della turned, watching the collective herd of sheeple turn their heads as she left the café. She could still feel their eyes on her as she followed Porter back to the hearse.

"Well, he was kind of an ass," Porter said as he unlocked the hearse. He looked disappointed he wasn't walking out of there with a slice of quiche.

"It's something in the water, I swear." Della nodded.

Max was silent, chewing on his sweater, watching the door of the café out of the corner of his eye. He looked like an animal in a cage.

"Take everything they do with a grain of salt, okay?" Della said, smiling apologetically.

Max shrugged away her solace. "So, where now? Ei'm

assumin' he meant the historical society?"

Della was about to suggest finding some of the other ex-addicts when Porter cut her off.

"You think Kimi would be okay with us visiting?" he asked excitedly.

The answer was supposed to be a no. But what came out was a broken, "Worth a shot, I guess. . ."

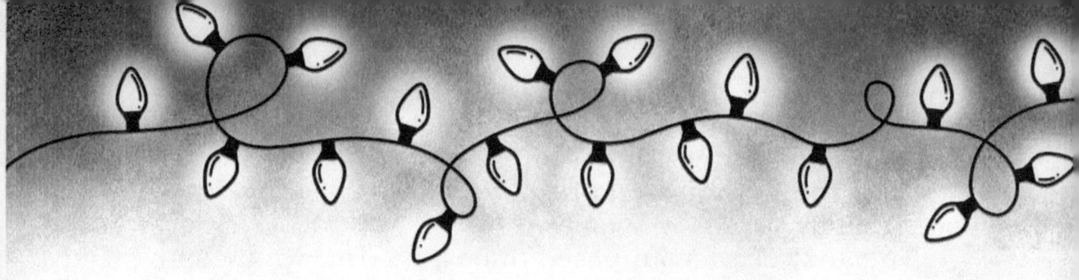# CHAPTER SEVEN

"Don't touch anything. Everything here is worth twice our combined worth. Financially and culturally," Della warned, paving the path to the historical society.

If the first place you saw when visiting Della's corner of the world was the historical society, you'd realize how hoity-toity this town was. The Sycamore House was the most prominent building in town. Painted the color of cheap wine, featuring two stories, four wings stretching out in every direction, complete with a vast front garden, every inch perfectly manicured. It looked more like a palace than an old homestead.

The inside of the house was just as grand. Massive chandeliers hung from vaulted ceilings, floor-to-ceiling windows made the outside world look like a *Van Gogh* painting, dusty velvet carpet—it was pretty much Ambrose Apartments if they had a bigger budget.

"Instead of a cemetery smack dab in the middle of town, Sycamore Heights' crown jewel is the Sycamore House. Just like everything else, it's named after the family who founded the town and the trees they planted. Everything is the original structure other than the pipes and wiring," Della explained, bitterness in her voice as she swept her hand through the air.

The tiny cracks in the walls and worn-down carpet told her the magnificent exterior was still just for show. If she were in charge, she'd have spent every waking minute making this place as glorious as it once was.

"Ya know quite a bit about this place, don' ya?" Max asked, stopping to observe a case of patinaed belt buckles beside an old military uniform.

"I do. This town is rich in stories." *Stories I've tried to exploit*, Della thought, grimacing. She cleared her throat, nodding at the uniform next to the fireplace. Her arms crossed behind her back, her head held high. She must have looked like a tour guide to them. "This is Willard Sycamore, eldest son of the guy next to Max—Earnest Sycamore."

"They look like mean old fellas, don't they?" Porter asked, grabbing a pamphlet from a nearby holder and flipping through it.

"A few years after the Civil War, Earnest packed up his family and moved them here. Earnest was keen to move to disputed territory to escape the remnants of war. He had traveled many parts of the world but decided this was as good a place as any to settle. Although the Sycamores moved here in the late eighteen-sixties, Washington wasn't founded until eighteen-eighty-nine. At first, all his family wanted was a house, but soon, this place grew into the town we know today," Della said. "This was the drawing room. Most of the furniture has decayed over the years. However, a few antique shops and carpenters in town have found or made reproductions."

"Wow," the boys breathed.

'Boys' was the perfect word to describe them. They looked as excited as Leonel had been last night, completely entranced by the things around them. Della wished she shared their excitement.

"You two want to see my favorite exhibit?" she sighed.

"Yes, please!" They said in unison, equally excited.

Della chuckled despite herself, leading them upstairs. A couple of doors down, she turned into a dimly lit room.

"Most things in this old house have to do with the Sycamore family, but I couldn't care less about them. This is what I care about. Everything here belongs to the Mukwa people. Scraps of clothing, wood carvings, arrowheads—and him," Della bragged, pointing to a brightly lit glass box in the center of the room. "That is one of my ancestors."

Inside the glass, perfectly preserved, was a jawbone. It was a morbid sight to most, but for the longest time, Della thought it to be the only exciting thing this town had to offer.

"So, why didn't you tell us about your heritage?" Porter asked as he surveyed the room. "I had no idea until I saw your mom."

That was a phrase Della had heard her whole life. And every time she heard it, it hurt. She had the misfortune of looking like her father's side of the family, making her the butt of jokes from both sides. Just another reason she felt like an outcast.

"Okay, one, that's kind of rude, and two, it never came up in conversation," Della said sassily, hands on her hips. "I never guessed you were Portuguese until you said something. No one would know Max was Irish if he kept his mouth shut."

"Love ya too," Max said from the corner as he stood looking over a few rough carvings lined up in a lighted case.

Porter stared at Della for a while before nodding to himself, changing the subject. "You'd think the Mukwa wouldn't want this here," he breathed.

To him, it was probably just another bone, just like the ones he had to lay to rest. To Della, this was sacred. Everything here was just as important as a Church to her.

She rolled her eyes, trying to ignore the fact he wouldn't look at her anymore. "Most of what we now call Washington was inhabited by Indigenous Americans. When the Sycamore family arrived, they had to befriend the local tribe or suffer the consequences. For several years, they lived in peace with each other. So much so that the Sycamores had a young Indigenous man living with them. Their kindness toward him was something you don't hear much about. This was his room. Not much was known about him. One of the granddaughters briefly wrote about him in her journal. In exchange for education, he helped out around the homestead," Della explained, pointing out a window. "There used to be fruit trees as far as the eye could see. This side of the mountain was farmland. Cattle, sheep, wheat, orchards—everything. They chose this part of the mountain because of the basin-like shape. Like how, in Moss Hollow, the cemetery was built on a plane with hills so there could be burials *and* mausoleums. The basin made it easy to cultivate up here. Plus, there's a river that runs through the forest. Made by the snow melting off the peaks."

"I wonder what it was like back then. . ," Porter said wistfully.

Della heard Max whisper the same word she was about to utter. It would have been a joke from her, but it was heart-wrenching coming from Max's lips.

"Torture," he whispered, glancing at him.

As they walked through the room, looking over every artifact, soaking in the mass amounts of history like rays of sunlight, voices and footsteps floated in from the hallway.

". . . that about covers it, Mrs. Coleman. Again, I thank you for your consideration."

Della didn't recognize that voice. She thought she knew everyone in Sycamore Heights.

"Of course." That was Kimi. "I just hope she listens. I'm surprised she's willing to meet up. She's stubborn."

A heavy sigh and a light clacking of heels were followed by the appearance of a woman in a pale pink pencil skirt and sparkling white stilettos. She stopped in front of the door to the Mukwa exhibit, tapping her foot on the floor impatiently. She swept her curly golden hair behind her, hand on her hip.

"Mom?" Della asked, leaning against the door frame. Max and Porter were right behind her, just as concerned and confused as she was.

The woman—her tight blonde ringlets bouncing in a way Della could only describe as irritating—turned to her, eyeing her suspiciously.

"Elvi, this is my daughter, *Delphee*—" Kimi stressed her name oddly, the woman's eyes widening. "—and her friends, Max and Porter," she explained. The simple act of gesturing towards them seemed to take the life out of her.

"Elvi Sinclair. Nice to meet you. Your mother has told me an awful lot about you," the woman began, her words quick and cold. "Your mother and I were just discussing the foreclosure."

Della offered a hand to shake, which Elvi practically refused. "F—Foreclosure? Is there something I should know about?" Della asked.

"Poppy got in over her head. Again," Kimi sighed heavily, giving Elvi a look of disapproval. "We're in a tough spot. We have two options: let the bank have it or sell the historical society to Ms. Sinclair. She's graciously allowed me to continue working here on the weekends." It seems she thought adding that would lessen the blow.

"You *what*?" Della breathed, eyes wide.

Kimi opened her mouth, but Elvi held up a hand, cutting her off in a way she must've thought to be professional.

"There is nothing to worry about," Elvi explained sharply. "In fact, your mother will be paid more for her time here." She spoke like she surpassed Kimi in everything but, most importantly, age. Yet underneath the fancy outfit and the mile-long fake lashes, Della suspected she'd look barely older than Porter.

"You can't just—" Della began.

Kimi gave her a warning look. "This doesn't concern you, Della, don't meddle."

She stared down at her mother, mouth open in complete disbelief. There were only a few families in town struggling with money. Most of the town wore its wealth like some ribbon won at the county fair. Proudly, yet unjustly so. And the owner of the historical society, Poppy? She was practically small-town royalty.

Slowly, she turned back to Elvi, observing her like she was suddenly the villain. No ring or mark of one on her finger, no brand on her heels, no fancy jewelry. Her hair may be in perfect coils, and she may dress like she had all the money in the world, but Della suspected otherwise. The real kicker was the smell. Her perfume was horribly familiar to Della's nose. It was the cheap body mist most of the local girls had worn in high school, a cheap mixture of cherry blossoms and sweet peas that came in an ugly silver bottle.

Della straightened, removing herself from the door, crossing her ankles, then her hands. "May I get one of your business cards?" she asked as politely as she could, but she couldn't make her face display any amount of pleasantry.

Elvi eyed her suspiciously but nodded, producing a thin, glossy card.

"Sinclair Credit Union," Della read, scrutinizing the card. It was simple in design and felt cheap between her fingers. How was selling to Elvi—who, apparently, worked for the bank—any better than foreclosing?

"We took over for the old bank. Some things need changing, don't they?" Elvi sighed happily.

She glanced around the historical society, looking as though she knew exactly what she would change in a place like this. Her eyes trailed to Della, then behind her. Della followed her eyesight directly to Porter, who both cowered and blushed under her gaze. Della shot him a look. Max glowered at Elvi, arms crossed defensively.

"Indeed, some things do," Della chose to reply, turning back to her. "I guess I'm just a little confused about why you'd want to buy the place to begin with."

Elvi adjusted her jacket, not meeting her eyes. "I have a vested interest in old artifacts and muddled history."

No one would lay a finger on this place as long as she was in town. Even if it had been sold, Della would ensure the history and culture stayed here. Places like this were few and far between. She would *never* let anyone like Elvi ruin it.

"Well, I'll be off. Think about what I said, will you?" Elvi said, casting a glare in Della's direction. Kimi nodded as Elvi turned to leave, waving over her shoulder as she waltzed down the hall.

When she was out of sight, and the click-clack of her heels faded, Della rounded on her mother. She wanted to yell at her, but one look at her called back what she'd said earlier:

Don't start anything.

It took her quite the effort, but Della inhaled deeply, pushing down her anger in search of concern.

"Are you okay?" she asked, reaching for her mother's weathered hands.

Kimi flinched away but nodded. "Everything is under control."

"Yeah, but by who?" Della asked softly.

Out of the corner of her eye, she saw Max and Porter share a confused look.

Kimi glanced at them, then back at Della. "You really should have called before you came back, Delphee," she whispered as if speaking louder would take too much energy.

The thing was, Della couldn't decide whether Kimi meant that she didn't want her daughter to see the town falling apart or that Kimi hadn't wanted her around simply because there was nothing Della could do. At least not without an arrest, a search warrant, or a lawsuit. All of which seemed insignificant to what Della had gone through lately.

Della was fuming on the inside. The tiny librarian she imagined organized all her thoughts was running rampant, kicking over shelves, pulling her hair out, and swearing at the top of her lungs. How un-ladylike. But maybe that's what this town needed. One outcast. One bad apple. One delinquent.

One spot of colored ink on a perfectly white canvas could show an artist their next masterpiece.

"Why didn't you tell me? I could have helped—I would have *wanted* to help. If money was the problem, I could have taken something out of my savings. You know how much this place means to me, Mom. How could you let this happen?" she asked, trying to keep her voice calm.

Jasper being the Pastor's pet didn't exactly pay the bills. And since the Mukwa tribe wasn't recognized federally, they didn't get any benefits. Though her family lived relatively comfortably, that didn't mean they never had to stretch a dollar.

Kimi's hand fell from her face, her eyes full of rage, but she kept whatever she thought to herself. Maybe for Della's sake, not wanting to embarrass her in front of her friends, perhaps because she knew once she started listing off any issues she may have, she wouldn't be able to stop.

"I didn't want to burden you with that. And how could I ask that of you? I know how long it took you to save up. I knew your plans. I didn't want to take that from you," Kimi sighed, giving a half-hearted shrug. "You wanted to forget about Sycamore Heights, and I was willing to let you."

Translation: *You didn't have to—nor need to—come home anytime soon.*

Della felt like a sinking ship trapped in a maelstrom. "You should have told me. I would have found a way to help."

"And would one of those 'ways' consist of—" Kimi began, raising her voice, pointing an accusing finger at Della, her eyes wide, lips parted, revealing what Della imagined as razor-sharp teeth. And Kimi used those teeth, chewing into her daughter like a rabid animal. "You know what, I'm tired of sidestepping it. Whenever you think you are 'helping,' you screw everything up for yourself and others. Please, please, *please*—for once, just this once—just let me handle this. Let someone else fix things."

Della stiffened. She glanced at Max, who looked furious, and Porter, who wouldn't meet her eyes. When she looked back at Kimi, she'd gone pale.

"I'm sorry I—" She took a deep breath, then shook her head angrily. "I can't deal with this right now."

"You mean you can't deal with me," Della corrected, tears stinging her eyes.

Della usually argued with Jasper. Not Kimi.

Kimi rolled her eyes. "I have to file some paperwork. Let me know if you need anything," were her parting words.

Della watched her mother walk back down the hall, thoroughly gutted. Max put a comforting hand on her shoulder, but she shrugged him away. Her mind was spinning. The *world* was spinning. Standing there, surrounded by dusty display cases and mannequins dressed as soldiers, she felt trapped, like another exhibit. Someone had put her heart on a pedestal and shattered it.

Suddenly, she remembered why they had come here to begin with. To ask about Ashton. She swallowed her tears, turning away, feeling like the world was about to crash down around her.

"Are ya okay?" Max asked quietly.

Della looked him dead in the eyes, taking in the concern on his face and the confusion on Porter's.

"No," she whispered.

In no ordinary world would Kimi have said that—especially in front of Max and Porter. Something was wrong in Sycamore Heights, and she hated to admit it. Because if there wasn't anything wrong here—if no supernatural force had screwed up the fragile ecosystem—then the apocalypse was upon them. Monsters, ghosts, witches, or aliens? Della could deal with that. But not the apocalypse.

It took the boys a moment to realize that Della hadn't responded with her usual 'I'm fine' or 'It's nothing' and, for once, had told them the truth.

"How do we fix it?" Max asked, nodding at Porter like he was supposed to say something, too. All he did was stare at Della; his eyebrows furrowed deeply over his peridot eyes.

"I don't know," she admitted, fiddling with the zipper on her jacket. "I really don't know."

All she wanted to do was run. Porter reached for her, but she swatted him away, backing down the hallway. It was like all the walls were closing in around her. She needed out, to be as far away from here as possible.

"I need some air," she said, then left.

Neither of them followed.

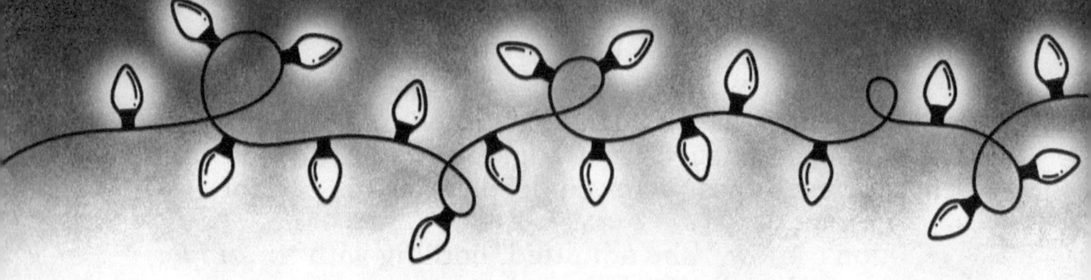

CHAPTER EIGHT

Barricade

"Ei think Ei'm gonna start a fight," Max said eventually, then turned down the hall toward where Kimi had gone.

Panicked, Porter grabbed him by the collar of his jacket, shaking his head disapprovingly. "Please don't."

"Ya can' just let Kimi talk tuh her like that. That was rude and uncalled for," Max snapped as Porter spun him around. His eyes flashed, slit like a cat for a split second.

Slowly, Porter put a hand on Max's shoulder. "It's not our place," he said with a shrug.

"Maybe it isn' mine, but it sure as Hell is yers!" Max whisper-yelled.

"I'm not going to start a fight with my girlfriend's mom, Max. I'm trying to make a good impression."

"Oh, so that's what ya are? Boyfriend and girlfriend? Could have fooled me," Max snapped, shaking free of Porter's grip.

"Low blow," Porter grumbled back.

Max crossed his arms, ever defiant. Porter, hands on his hips, stared down at him, fuming.

"Ya can just speak yer mind," he said under his breath, barely loud enough for Porter to hear.

"Max."

"*Porter.*"

He looked up at him, giving him puppy-dog eyes. Porter recoiled, his nose wrinkled up. That look had gotten them both into a lot of trouble when they were younger. Flashbacks to Max's thirteenth birthday came flooding back. That had been the first and only time Mavericks had yelled at them.

Porter should have put his foot down right then and there, but as usual, he followed Max. He blinked, and there they were, standing in a cluttered office. Porter mirrored Max's defensive stance. Guess they were playing bodyguard this fine December morning.

"Oh, now don't you two start," Kimi breathed. "I'm not wrong, and you know it."

Max had a murderous look in his eyes. Porter instinctively grabbed hold of his shoulder again. He couldn't help but feel like he was holding back a rabid dog from killing a rabbit.

"Ya shouldn' have said that," Max said hotly.

Kimi took in the sight of them. Admiration flickered across her face, but she hid it behind fear immediately. "She responds well to tough love."

"She just stormed out into the cold," Porter sighed.

"Wouldn't be the first time, and I doubt it will be the last," Kimi shrugged, then grabbed a pile of papers off the chintzy desk before her. Muttering to herself, she angrily tapped them into a neat stack. "Best to let her cool down," she said with an exasperated sigh as she filed those papers away in her desk.

Porter doubted that highly. He hadn't seen Della this angry in quite some time. Not since *it* happened. In fact, the only emotion he had seen from her was a sad sort of numbness. Yet Sycamore Heights had awakened every negative feeling buried this last month.

Kimi looked up at him and Max, then sunk further into her chair. "I'm sorry you had to see that," she whispered, adjusting the straps on her overalls nervously.

Max gave Porter a funny look. He shrugged, tightening his grip on Max's shoulder when he tried to take a step toward Kimi.

Porter found that when it came to Della, they both could be. . . *dangerous*. . . if necessary. Max was always on Della's side, no matter what. She could do no wrong in his eyes. And though part of Porter felt the same, he knew Della needed a serious reality check. Sure, he was disappointed in Kimi, but she wasn't exactly wrong. Everyone makes mistakes, but Della was the queen of them.

"She never used to—Never mind," Kimi said defeatedly.

Porter and Max exchanged another look. Della didn't talk much about Sycamore Heights. As far as Porter knew, Della was a stereotypical rebellious teen with a problematic relationship with her parents. That's where the story ended. She hated this place, but Porter couldn't fully understand why. This place was perfect. It was the kind of town he would want to raise his kids in. Quaint, well-manicured, full of picket fences and houses that weren't falling apart.

Perfect. Sure, Jasper seemed strict and a little rude, but he couldn't be that bad, could he? Surely, Cyrus O'Malley was the worst of the people here.

If he was to be honest, he felt Della was being rather ungrateful. Sycamore Heights was everything Moss Hollow wasn't.

Yet—from what little Max had relayed—Della saw this place as a Hell hole.

That thought suddenly made him want to chase after her. He could admit that he was jealous of Della's other relationships, but what bothered him the most was that he was completely out of the loop. He always had to hear her damage from Max, and even then, he wasn't getting the whole story.

His brain told him he should've raced after her the minute she walked away. But his heart told him he shouldn't have to. She shouldn't have run in the first place. However, he would push her farther away if he didn't go after her.

He sighed heavily, swearing under his breath. "Mrs. Coleman?"

Kimi's heavy eyelids fluttered with irritation.

"Do you know where she would be going?"

Kimi nodded. "I might have an idea." She shuffled through the papers on her desk, finding a pamphlet and handing it over to Porter, tapping the map on the back.

"Thanks," Porter smiled. "Come on, Max."

If there was one thing Max couldn't do, it was hide his emotions. His gaze was colder than the icicles hanging outside. "This seems like a 'Porella' moment. Ei'll stay here. That is, if ya don' mind, Mrs. Coleman." He fluttered his long lashes, smiling tightly.

"Max," Porter said sternly.

Max turned to him and gave him a stubborn smile. "Ei won' kill anyone," he said under his breath.

Porter raised an eyebrow.

"Trust me!" Max whispered.

"You know I don't," Porter replied, waving him away.

They both looked at Kimi expectantly.

She rolled her eyes. "We will head home, and I will make lunch. Sound good?" She waited for Max to nod before continuing. "Tell Della I'm sorry, will you?"

"Sure thing," was all Porter could manage.

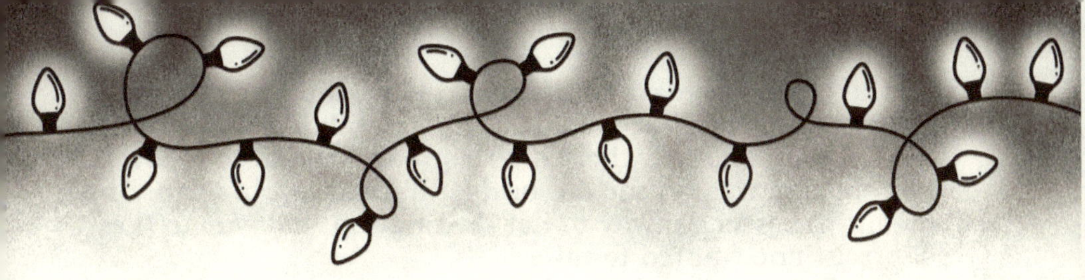

CHAPTER NINE

It's Up To You

Della walked silently through the lightly falling snow, happy to be ignored by anyone who passed by. A few people did glance her way, though all they did was shoot her a dirty look. No one stopped her. No one said anything. She smirked to herself. She couldn't tell if they feared her or if they thought her rebellious nature would rub off on them if they got too close. Whatever it was, she was thankful to be left alone in the cold.

To the boys, cold, blustery, snowy days like this were like taking an ice bath naked in Alaska, but not for the residents of Sycamore Heights. Even though she shivered, the freezing air was nothing but a cool breeze to Della as she stomped along the sidewalk, her sneakers now wet from the snow. Her toes may feel like ice cubes, but that familiar feeling reminded her of simpler days.

But simpler days were long gone for her, and she knew that. No amount of reminiscing would change that.

She walked down the icy pavement, following the footsteps of many before her, wondering why the place she hated and was glad to leave needed her more than ever. And why, oh why, did part of her want to help? She'd be more than happy to see this town burn to ash before her eyes. There'd even been a time when she might have started said fire.

But that wasn't her, not really. No matter how angry she was, she could never do anything to the people here. Eventually, all their transgressions would catch up to them even if she wasn't around to see it.

Still, a tiny voice inside her head wanted her to speed it all up.

A honk startled her from her thoughts.

She turned to see Porter driving beside her, almost

on the curb. She gave him a bored look, then turned her eyes to the horizon. She didn't feel like talking to anyone.

Soon enough, there'd be no road for him to follow her on. She was on the old bridge that led out of town. That meant she was halfway to her destination, halfway to the shortcut she wanted to take.

Porter rolled down the window, slowing the hearse to stay next to her as she tried to walk briskly away from him.

"Go away," Della said in a sing-song tone.

"Didn't your mom ever tell you not to talk to strangers?" Porter said, putting on a gravelly accent that made him sound like an old seadog.

Della made sure his eyes were on her before she flipped him off.

"Ouch," Porter laughed from the driver's seat. It wasn't a real laugh. It was a pleasantry. The laugh you give a child when you can't understand them, but you don't want to risk hurting their feelings.

Della scowled, crossing her arms defensively. So, she was just a child now? Always the juvenile delinquent.

"Jump in, I'll take you wherever you want, *meu amor*," Porter called, turning his eyes back to the road.

"I'm sure you would, but I'm fine out here, thank you *very* much," Della said, holding her head high.

"Delphee Chrysanthemum Coleman, if you don't get your butt in this car right now, I will drag you in here myself," Porter said sternly, waving to a passing truck, his face reddening. He probably looked like he was harassing poor Della. Technically, he was. Not that anyone would care.

She stopped abruptly, reveling in how he kept driving for about two minutes before lurching to a stop and pulling back, scowling deeply.

"Don't do that," he hissed, leaning over to unlock the passenger door for her.

"I like watching you squirm," she said matter-of-factly.

"Della."

"Porter."

"Del-LA!" he roared. "Car! Now!"

"Like I said, I'll take my chances with pneumonia." She winked, then kept walking.

He followed.

"I just want to talk," he sighed.

"Obviously. But I don't. I want to walk until I feel like I'm normal again. And if I don't feel normal by the time I reach the edge of town, I will keep walking until I do," she said nonchalantly.

Silence.

She glanced at him to find he looked bored. "I could jump off this bridge into the freezing water below just to get away from you. You know that, right? I'm that reckless," she said, stepping dangerously close to the railing, letting her hand hover over it.

"And you know I'm stupid enough to jump in after you. Spare us both becoming popsicles by getting in the car?" He smiled a toothy grin, raising an eyebrow, daring her.

She weighed her options, staring down the bridge and the stretch of road that followed. Cold mid-afternoon air or warm car? Alone with her thoughts or suffocated by Porter's? Honestly, jumping off this bridge didn't look so bad after all. Then again, it would be easier to drive where she was headed. Her shortcut may not take as long, but the trek would be much more perilous than a lecture from Porter. Plus, the cold was making her bones ache.

"Fine," she sighed, begrudgingly sliding into the hearse. The pros only slightly outweighed the cons.

"That's my girl."

"Shut up."

It was so irritating when he did that. Couldn't he tell that she wanted to fume? Not once had she asked him to coddle her. She wanted to simmer in anger right now. Why couldn't he save his little act for later?

"Where's Max?" she asked dryly, turning to find the back seat empty. Without him here, she regretted her decision.

"He's with your mom," Porter said shortly.

Della nodded, buckling herself in and turning up the heat. "You made him stay behind?" She hadn't meant to say that aloud. She cleared her throat, settling into her seat. "Are you mad at me?" she asked softly.

"I'm not mad at you. Disappointed, maybe," he said, gripping the steering wheel tightly. "I just want to see you happy. You know that. I thought that coming here, you'd change." She could tell that last part hadn't come out right.

"Well, Prince Charming, you'll be waiting quite a while for that."

"What?" he asked. "I thought I was Robin H—"

"The script changed," she said quietly, pulling her knees to her chest and leaning against the cold window.

Porter inhaled sharply, shaking his head angrily. Della imagined steam blowing out of his ears.

"If you have something to say, why don't you just say it?" she mumbled, not daring to look at him. If her mom was going to lecture her, she might as well allow the other overbearing figure in her life to do the same.

"You wouldn't listen to a word I have to say, so how about you just tell me where you want me to take you." His voice was far too steady, almost robotic.

"Just stay to the right, and we'll get there eventually. The trees will get thicker. I'll tell you when to turn," Della whispered.

It's not that she didn't want to tell him why she was so upset. Most days, he was the only person she ever wanted to confide in. Porter was the only person she *should* talk to, after all. But every time she tried to form the words, they got stuck in her throat. She kept telling herself that it was because he had his own problems, but she knew deep down it was for a much darker reason. She felt guilty for being so upset with her parents.

For running out.

For making her problems into a mountain she couldn't climb.

Or maybe that's just how everyone said she should feel. Perhaps it was Porter who should feel guilty for making it seem like she could never honestly say what was on her mind.

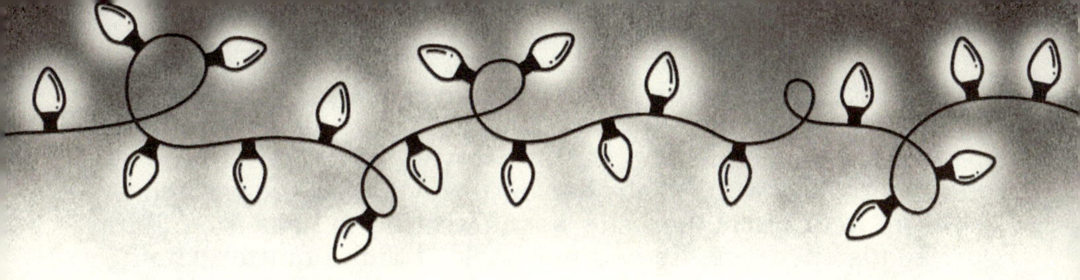

CHAPTER TEN

A Thousand or So Questions

Max had opted to wait in the historical society's entry while Kimi finished arranging bones, dusting old books, or whatever you do when you run a place full of ancient relics no one seems to care much about. Maybe that's why Della liked it here. All the forgotten things were on full display inside these walls. They'd finally found a place to shine.

His Pluto fit in perfectly.

Just like she did in Moss Hollow.

"Sorry I took so long. I had to lock up everything," Kimi said breathlessly, snapping Max from his thoughts.

He shrugged, pretending to be interested in a pistol almost as old as Mavericks. Give or take a few hundred years. He smiled to himself. His father would love a place like this. Max imagined that if The Courier wasn't so low on funds, Mavericks would have donated more than enough money to keep this place afloat. The second Della would've told him, he would have offered as much as he could.

"I know you think I'm the bad guy, but—"

"Ei'm sorry," Max said, turning to Kimi, who stood wringing her hands a few feet away.

"You'll understand when you have kids of your own. You won't want to see them sabotage themselves like Della does," she sighed.

"No, darlin', Ei meant Ei'm sorry that ya feel the need tuh explain yer side of the story tuh someone half yer age. As well as someone who doesn' care in the slightest," Max said through a tight smile.

"All I mean is—"

"Listen, Ei think yer a nice lady, but Ei'm Della's friend first," Max said, putting up a hand to stop her from rambling on. Kimi gave him a confused look. "Yer not gonna change my mind on her. Everyone else seems tuh have given up on her, but not me. So ya can save all yer 'motherly' talk for someone who can be swayed."

Max would fight her battles whether she wanted him to or not. When she wasn't around to hear the talking heads spew lies, he had her back. It didn't matter who it was or what they said. Whether they were in Moss Hollow or Sycamore Heights.

No matter the consequence, he'd protect her.

Always.

Kimi rolled her eyes as she walked away. He took that as his cue to follow. She tried again to explain her side, but Max shut her down. Talking bad about someone behind their back was a surefire way to lose his respect. Especially when that person just so happened to be one of his favorites.

When they finally returned to the Coleman household, all Kimi asked was if he had any allergies. The answer was a curt shake of the head.

Max couldn't help but imagine invisible landmines floating in the air. The tension between himself and Kimi was enough to kill a lesser man.

Mavericks really should have come with them. Max didn't know how to smooth things over like everyone else. All he knew was the truth and how to use it—a poor habit for a reformed kleptomaniac to have. Mavericks, on the other hand, would have crafted some sort of lie by now. Something about how family always makes things work. How blood is thicker than water. If he were here, Della wouldn't have run off, and Kimi would be laughing at how weird he was. Maybe even Jasper would be a little kinder.

Max would never admit it out loud, but he missed his crazy father. Never since he had come into the protection of Percival James Mavericks had he been this far from him. Max had always been the kind of person to rely on others to fix things that were out of his control. That was part of the reason he hadn't argued with Mavericks when he told Nicoletta she couldn't teach him magic anymore. It was why he liked science so much. He could control that. He couldn't control magic. Magic always ended up controlling him instead.

Magic fed on emotion. And though he hid it well, Max was ruled by feelings. Logic was a mask he never took off. Beneath his calculating calm, his mind was full of ringing alarms.

He knew Della felt the same, which was why he was so worried right now. He knew the signs. He knew she was buckling even before she confided in him all her deep and dirty darkness. He had seen it in himself and seen it in Porter. She was angry, depressed, and beating herself up for something she shouldn't. He was terrified to think of what would happen if—

Kimi dropped a plate and a butterknife. She swore heavily, angrily grabbing a napkin and placing a crudely made sandwich on it. She stomped out of the kitchen and practically threw Max's sandwich at him.

"Thank—"

"It's not like I want Poppy to sell the place," Kimi suddenly said.

"Okay, so we're gonna go there," Max sighed, rearranging his sandwich as Kimi sat across from him.

"I love that place. Despite all the negativity. I just don't want her involved. She doesn't need to be. I just want her to stay a kid for as long as possible, y'know?" Kimi asked, taking Max's sandwich and angrily biting off the corner.

Max stared at her for a minute, then sat back like he was some parental therapist. "But she's eighteen. Ya have tuh realize that she stopped being a kid a long time ago."

"Not by my choice. Not by hers."

"What's done is done. If ya live in the past, yer gonna risk her future, love. Ei may not have kids, but Ei have one Hella protective father. But he doesn' coddle me. He knows Ei can handle myself. But that's because he gave me the resources tuh do so," Max explained.

Kimi took another bite of what Max thought was supposed to be his sandwich, nodding to herself. "I just don't want her to get hurt. She's going to end up way in over her head."

"How so?"

Kimi shrugged. "Things took a turn for the worse shortly after Della left. Della's aunt, our beloved mayor, Poppy Hawthorne, broke ground to expand the town. She underestimated the cost—even though we all told her she was making a huge mistake—now she's in debt up to her chin. That old house takes a lot to keep the lights on. Things are constantly breaking, sparking—everything. Not to mention all the other problems in town. . ."

"What other problems?" Max was suddenly glad he stayed back. At first, he wished he would have boarded the 'Porella' ship, even though it was sailing choppy waters.

"Promise not to tell the super sleuth?" Kimi asked, her mouth sticky with peanut butter.

Max shrugged, lazily drawing an 'X' over his heart.

"A kid that worked at the historical society disappeared. And before that, he kept reporting weird things happening in the woods behind the trailer park," Kimi shook her head.

Max's excitement dropped, causing him to roll his eyes. He had been suspecting something far more interesting, something he didn't know already. A cheating wife found dead. The principal of that school Della always complained about losing her job. A bunch of circus performers ransacking the town.

Something.

Anything.

Everything.

Just not another long-winded rant about Ashton.

"It's usually so quiet here. Almost storybook-like. People don't just disappear," Kimi sighed.

Max looked around the house, nodding distractedly. It was such a contrast from Della's apartment back in Moss Hollow. There, socks littered the floor, books were piled on every flat surface, mismatched furniture was welcomed, and herbs and witch bottles hung from the ceiling. Here, not a cushion was out of place. Even the Christmas decorations were squeaky clean. Yes, this place was storybook-clean. It was almost like Mrs. Coleman had an unseen set of hands to do her dirty work.

A thought struck Max like a bowling ball to the head.

What if an invisible force was helping around the house? Say, some telekinetic powers like her daughter? Max watched Kimi carefully for a minute, wondering how far he'd go to get the answers he'd come for.

Max heard everything—observed everything. Very few things got past him. He'd heard Mavericks and Nicoletta talking about Della when they thought no one was around. He knew Nicoletta wondered if she'd been wrong pronouncing Della a Seer. He knew Mavericks was keeping something from all of them. Something that had to do with her. And he intended to find out what. Something told him that all the answers they needed were held here. What he didn't know was how deeply they were buried.

He cleared his throat, shifting uncomfortably in his seat. He knew Della would not have wanted him fishing for information, but someone had to look out for her. Della would hate him, but he'd have to carry this burden for her if she refused to investigate her past while they were here.

He began, a pang of guilt flooding him as the words came out. "Yeah, Ei mean, Ei'm sure not much happens around here. Ei would have thought the biggest story would've been what happened tuh Della. It was pretty scary when she was in the hospital, huh? Rumors probably spread like wildfire in this place," he said casually, watching Kimi's face. He didn't know the tells of the human race, but maybe he could catch her in a lie just like Della could.

Kimi choked on her peanut butter and jelly sandwich. "You know about that?" she asked, her eyes wide.

He nodded. "Della tells me everythin'," he said, narrowing his eyes at her.

"Was it really a seizure?" Kimi asked shakily. Her eyes held flares. He could hear her heart beating rapidly, thanks to the abilities his familiar side lent him.

Max furrowed his eyebrows. "What makes ya think it wasn'?"

"Nothing!" Kimi said quickly. "It just came as a shock. One minute, she was calling asking about her migraine medication. The next I got called by some doctor in Moss Hollow. At first, I thought it was a prank call."

"When did ya realize it wasn'?" Max asked darkly.

She didn't answer.

"Is that why ya never got back tuh her? Ya thought it was all a prank? That yer daughter hadn' had a seizure?" Max laughed darkly. Della definitely didn't get her intellect from her mother.

Kimi sighed heavily. "How'd it happen?"

"Porter found her. . . passed out. Don' know much more than that. She was in the hospital for a few days in October," Max chose to say.

Finding out about your daughter's seizure from an outside source was one thing. Finding out from an external source that your daughter had a boyfriend who liked to stay the night was another, even if those nights comprised only board games and rom-coms.

Max tried to ignore the sudden burst of jealousy in his heart when he thought of Della and Porter together.

Kimi stared at Max, the color draining from her skin.

"Do ya have a history of seizures in yer family, Kimi?" Max asked.

Kimi set down her sandwich, her face going eerily blank. "On my mom's side," she whispered.

"What triggered them?"

"Why do you want to know?" she asked defensively.

"Ei'm just concerned about Della. Ei want tuh make sure she's gonna be okay, and if her family has a history of bad seizures, maybe if we look at what her ancestors did tuh stop or help them, she can apply that now," Max explained. It wasn't a total lie. However, he was more concerned about whether anyone in the Coleman or Kitchi family had magical powers.

"I'm sorry, I don't remember. I assumed her migraine medicine would have helped," Kimi said. He noted the flinch of her shoulders, the widening eyes. She hadn't meant to let that slip.

"What makes ya say that?"

No answer.

Max wanted to call her out on her lies right then and there. He knew what was in those placebos. Knew Jasper and Kimi had been poisoning their daughter with oleander, lemon verbena, and betony. But he knew that was a card he couldn't play just yet, so he kept it tucked in his deck, deciding to go a different route.

"Can Ei talk tuh yer mom?" Max asked carefully.

Kimi shook her head. "Unless you can talk with the dead," she laughed, then grimaced. "If you can, I'd understand why Della keeps you around. I bet she's been getting into all sorts of trouble with people like that in Louisiana."

Max ignored her attempt at trying to change the subject. "How'd she die?" He knew exactly what had happened to Della's grandmother. But maybe hearing it all from Kimi would put together some of the puzzle pieces he'd been mulling over for the past month.

Kimi thought for a second, the flares in her eyes turning to the burning tip of a recently fired gun. She scooted her chair closer to him, wringing her hands under the table.

"We never really figured that out," she said, her tone filled with caution. "Maybe heart attack, maybe a seizure, maybe something else." Her eyes were full of expectance. She wanted him to prove her wrong.

"Interestin'," Max whispered.

So, Della's grandmother had a history of seizures and died under mysterious circumstances. There was the lead he'd been needing.

"Would there be any possibility of lookin' intuh yer mother's medical records?"

Kimi sighed heavily. "Some things are better left in the past, Max."

"Not this. Not if Della's health could be on the line," Max argued.

Kimi nodded, chewing her lower lip. "I—I'll see what I can find. Just don't be disappointed if there isn't anything of substance for you to stick your nose in."

"Is there a reason there wouldn' be?"

Kimi laughed darkly. "Knowing my mom? I'd have to sell my soul for the answers you seem desperate to have." She stood, nodding towards the front door. "I have to go pick up the twins soon. I'll stop by the clinic to see if I can access my mom's files. Will you be okay here by yourself?"

Max nodded, filled with a sense of triumph. "Ei'll be

fine."

She smiled sadly at him, not saying another word.

His skin tingled with the possibility he was close to figuring out Della's abilities. He knew deep down that something was wrong with her. He just couldn't figure out what. Her powers had only manifested once she stopped taking the placebos. Everything in them had been used in old wife's tales to prevent nightmares, and all of Della's visions seemed pretty nightmarish. Either this was done in a good-faith effort to help her, or Della's parents were more in tune with the magical world than they wanted to admit. But the thing was, ever since the Eric Steiniger incident, her powers had been absent as if she'd locked them away.

Max knew Porter and Nicoletta would be more than happy to let her keep her abilities locked up. Especially if they harmed her any more than they already had. But Max knew how magic worked. Magic was put on this Earth to create balance. The powers magical beings had were given to them for a reason, no matter how they chose to use them.

From what he'd seen, Della's powers may have been bestowed upon her to do something great. Which was something Mavericks seemed to believe as well.

And in his experience, when Mavericks kept secrets, it was best to uncover them before they destroyed everything you love.

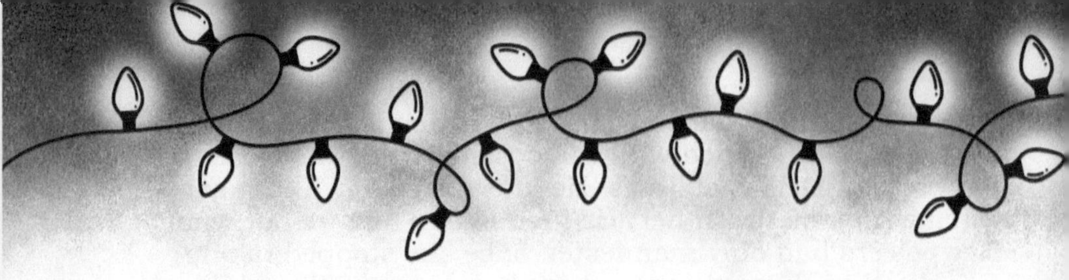

CHAPTER ELEVEN

Geeking Out

Max had rarely been left alone back in Moss Hollow. Someone or something was always looking after him on account of Mavericks being overprotective. Sitting by himself in this suffocatingly immaculate house made his skin crawl. Unlike his friends, Max had never liked being left alone. That might be his greatest fear. Empty rooms made his heart race. Silence made him antsy. He flinched every time the heater kicked on while he sat in Leonel's room, scrolling away on his phone.

He was back to wishing he'd boarded the 'Porella' ship.

He sighed heavily, tossing his phone aside and shutting his eyes. Though he was a nervous wreck, sitting for a minute was nice. The bat and the rat had been working nonstop since October, throwing themselves into anything that needed their attention. It was probably for the best if Max was being honest. The less time they spent dwelling on all the bad, the quicker they could move on. Nevertheless, Max—the laid-back, shape-shifting cat he was—just wanted to rest.

Was it too much to ask to get an hour of sleep? Twenty minutes, maybe?

A knock on the front door below him made him jump.

Apparently, it *was* too much to ask for.

He swore. His accent was the thickest when he did that. It was a subconscious thing he'd picked up from TV. Mavericks had the strangest taste in television. All those old Irish shows he'd watched as a kid were unsuitable for a child.

Then again, neither was living in a haunted mansion or tagging along when he went monster hunting.

Dragging his feet and rubbing his eyes, Max begrudgingly went downstairs. Another knock on the door graced his ears before he finally ripped it open.

Sebastian stood in the doorway, red from the cold, adorned in a puffer jacket two sizes too big.

"Hey! Is Mrs. Coleman home?" he asked.

"Just missed her," Max yawned. "Everyone else is out, too."

Sebastian frowned. "Oh. Mind opening the garage?"

Max nodded, shutting the door in Sebastian's face.

Upon entering the garage, the chill that took hold of his bones furthered his irritation. Back in Louisiana, he would have been able to get away with only one of the three layers he needed here. Eager to get back inside, he slammed a button to his left, watching the snow blow in as the garage door opened.

"I didn't wake you, did I?" Sebastian asked, immediately rummaging through the garage.

Max groaned, shaking his head. So much for going back inside. He wouldn't let Sebastian make a mess and then take the blame for his blunders.

"What are ya lookin' for?" he asked, hugging himself against the cold as he peered over Sebastian's shoulder.

"Della used to have a microscope, but science really isn't her thing. Anything out here is free real estate. I was going to borrow hers since mine broke," Sebastian explained, absent-mindedly digging through a box of old photo albums. "Oh, Kimi was looking for these," he said, taking the box into his hands.

"How does one break a microscope?" Max asked, disgusted.

"It's old, one of the ones the school got rid of when they upgraded. The bulb burnt—er—blew up last night. Melted the plastic and broke the lenses," Sebastian frowned.

"Ei have a portable one Ei brought. Ei can set it up in the kitchen."

"Really? Thanks!" Sebastian exclaimed, his eyes lighting up.

"Sure. What are ya needin' it for?" Max asked, holding the door back inside open for him as Sebastian struggled with the box of photographs.

"Found something. Not sure if it's real or not," Sebastian said.

"Why do Ei get the feelin' ya aren' goin' tuh tell me what yer up tuh?" Max smiled.

Sebastian chuckled. "Can you keep a secret?"

Max blinked slowly. If he only knew. "Ei can try," he

said flatly.

"There's a dig site out in the woods near the reservation. Weird things keep happening out there, so, being the sane person I am, I went to check it out. They had piles of bones up there, discarding them like garbage. I snatched one. It's full of bite marks, but I couldn't figure out what kind of animal made them," he explained excitedly, his eyes so full of wonder that he looked bug-eyed.

Max suddenly realized why Della had kept this idiot around for as long as she had. Which also made him realize why she'd kept himself around. Every super spy needed a trusty nerd.

He smirked, quickly running upstairs to grab his tiny portable microscope.

"What kind of weird things?" he asked when he returned, taking his microscope out of its protective case. This was the first Mavericks had ever gotten him—a reward for not stealing it himself.

He handed it off to Sebastian, who began setting it up. Satisfied with his work, he procured a dirty *Ziploc* bag with a bone inside from his pocket.

"The workers say they keep hearing this weird voice in the distance. Lots of growling, too. They paused construction after Ashton—this guy—"

Max waved him away. "Old news, keep goin'."

"Right, well, they stopped because the police are worried a bear might have got Ash. They think that maybe the construction noise has been waking them up too early, and now they're angry," Sebastian finished.

The house fell silent as Sebastian broke off a piece of the bones and set to work. Max sat beside him, watching him turn the dials, trying to figure out what exactly Sebastian was doing. He hated watching other people do all his favorite scientific things. It was so boring. He bit his lower lip in frustration, letting Sebastian fiddle with the microscope for another minute before clearing his throat loudly. Sebastian almost jumped out of his seat.

"Right, sorry. What did ya find?" Max asked, snatching the microscope—*his* microscope—away so he could look at the piece of broken humerus bone Sebastian had grabbed. Judging by how easily it fell apart on the slide, it was older than the two of them combined. And then some.

Max grimaced, realizing the construction site might be an old burial ground. Della could be right in wondering if they were dealing with ghosts.

"What do you make of the teeth marks?" Sebastian asked, scratching the back of his neck as he slid the rest of the bone to him.

Max gently picked up the ancient bone, careful not to break off another piece. Digging into his pocket, he found the miniature magnifying glass he always had. Two teeth marks were left on it, but they had been smoothed down over time, so much so that Max wasn't sure if they were teeth marks at all.

"This is all ya got?" he asked, looking up at Sebastian judgmentally. Half of what they thought to be a humerus bone wasn't much to go off.

"Della always had better luck with the whole research thing," he admitted. He scratched the side of his nose nervously, looking embarrassed. "I was always the guy in the black van with all the cameras and surveillance."

Max nodded, sitting back, still holding the bone. They could always try and find a lab willing to carbon date it, but who knew how long that would take. Or how much it would cost. A spell would be their best bet, but he doubted Della would allow such a thing.

"Hey, uh, Max?" Sebastian asked. Max looked up from staring at his microscope with a questioning look. "Does she ever talk about me? Er—us? As in her family and me?"

Max stared open-mouthed, not knowing how to respond. Della had only mentioned his pock-marked face a total of two times.

"Eh, it's okay," Sebastian sighed. "I wouldn't have expected anything less. I knew that once she left, that'd be that. I wouldn't say she's selfish or anything. It's just—"

"Della is not a selfish person," Max responded somewhat angrily.

If one more person attacked her character today, he would attack them. Physically. Claws a' blazing.

Sebastian laughed darkly.

Max rolled his eyes, shooting him a disapproving look.

Why did this town hate her so much? He couldn't think of one thing she had done to warrant this treatment. Was Sycamore Heights just that prejudiced?

"Do any of ya realize just how much she's done for ya?" Max asked before he could stop himself.

Sebastian gave him a questioning look. Max angrily shook his head, looking away. Sebastian just continued to stare at him. After a while, he readjusted himself in his chair.

"I don't want to offend you, but can I ask you something?" He gave Max a skeptical look as he spoke.

Max sighed a long, heavy, exasperated sigh. "It's called vitiligo. It's a skin condition that caused certain patches of my skin tuh lose pigment. No, it's not contagious. No, Ei'm not going tuh die," he said, pointing to his face, staring Sebastian dead in the eyes.

"That's. . . that's not what I was going to ask. . ." Sebastian said.

Max furrowed his bushy eyebrows.

"It's just—" Sebastian leaned forward. "Why are you friends with her?"

Max squinted. "Because she's Delphee-friggin-Chrysanthemum-friggin-Coleman. Ei've never met anyone else who sees the world like she does."

"Yeah, 'cause she's paranoid."

And there it was, the thing that sent him over the edge.

"She's not paranoid," Max started, settling in to lecture Sebastian the way Mavericks always did. "The way she looks at the world is with the eye of an adventurer. Cautious enough to calculate every move but brave enough to take necessary risks. She—She sees the world like she can fix it. Like she alone has all the broken pieces in front of her," he finished.

"Yeah, I get that, I just. . ." Sebastian sat back in his chair, sighing heavily. "For the longest time, I have been the only one who would give her the time of day. Most people don't see her the way we do. They see her as a project."

Max studied him. An angry vein popped forth from Sebastian's forehead, his fingers clenching the armrest of his seat.

"People are blind," Max shrugged.

Sebastian nodded, chewing on his lower lip. "I'm glad she found you—and Porter. I was terrified when she left. I thought I would find her on my front doorstep crying her eyes out. Or worse," he shivered.

Max nodded, knowing exactly what he meant. He had often thought about the 'worse' that could happen to all of them. Knowing perfectly well he would be the only one left standing if something terrible happened. Such a thought made his skin crawl.

"I'm guessing y'all are here because of Ashton, then?" Sebastian asked, clearing his throat.

"Yeah, that paper we work for sent us here."

"You guys talk with some of the ex-druggies he dealt to yet?"

Max nodded.

Sebastian thought for a minute. "What are you guys going to do next?"

"Not quite sure. Della ran out of the historical society. Her and Kimi got intuh it."

"I doubt what you saw was bad. If there wasn't screaming, crying, or something broken, it was just another day at the Coleman house," he chuckled darkly.

Max's eyebrows furrowed. "Ei figured as much."

"Does Porter know? I mean, about what Jasper is like? About what she had to deal with? I can tell you don't like it here, but he seems to think this place is Heaven."

"She won' talk about it with him. Ei've told him a little here and there, but it's not my place," Max sighed. For someone who was a wizard with words, Della was horrible at communication.

Sebastian smiled sadly, standing and brushing himself off. "I should go start shoveling snow before anyone gets home. Thanks for letting me use your microscope."

"No problem," Max smiled as he began to walk away. "Hey!" he called a little too loudly.

Sebastian stopped, turning to give him a questioning look.

"For what it's worth, she was lucky tuh have a friend like ya. Even if she couldn' admit it."

Sebastian only shrugged before walking away. Max wondered if Della knew how much he cared about her. If she knew how much any of them cared. It seemed she was used to being thrown out like an unwanted Christmas present, not cherished like the gift she was. Sure, she was stubborn, snarky, and sarcastic, but she was kind and caring, and all she wanted was to do good. She tried her best to be the hero.

If people couldn't see that, then it was on them, not her.

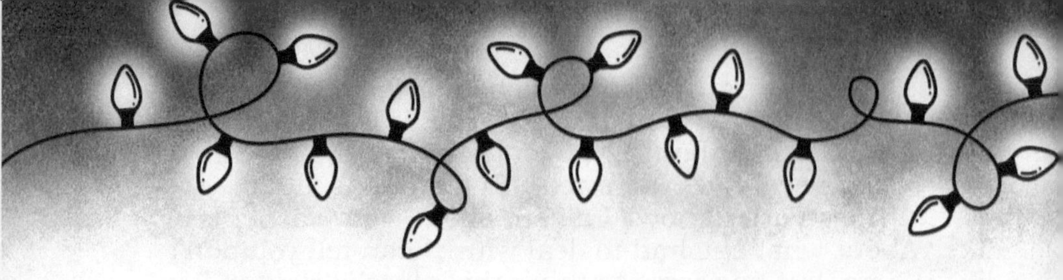

CHAPTER TWELVE

Lost In Translation

Della had directed Porter to the one place in Sycamore Heights that had welcomed her: The Mukwa Reservation. Coincidentally, that place had been forbidden until a few years back.

The only memories she had of this place before age fifteen were few and far between. Just fragments of Christmases past, family reunions, maybe a birthday or two. Just pleasantries. When she was old enough to realize certain people in her life were keeping her from where she felt she belonged, she snuck out at any given opportunity to get here. They had always told her it was a bad idea to come.

She didn't want to admit it, but she suspected she knew why.

Though she was still rather furious with Porter, she was glad he got to see the reservation. Della didn't know what was going through his mind, but his face darkened when they pulled up to the giant, moldy archway.

"They aren't going to come out with bow and arrows to shoot you," Della smirked, pointing to a parking spot. Then she paused. "Don't—Don't make jokes about that," she said sheepishly.

"Noted," Porter whispered. She gave him a questioning look, which he ignored.

Deciding it best to drop all animosity, she left the confines of the hearse.

As soon as you set foot on the reservation, you could sense how dramatically the atmosphere had changed. The air was crisper, the sun a little brighter, and above all, you felt safe. Truly safe. Della led Porter past houses and people, happily waving to her distant family. You could tell she had changed too. It was written all over her face that she felt she fit in here. Porter finally let himself smile as he watched her. This must be the kind of happiness he wished to see from her.

Della took to a raised wooden path, taking in the sights as she wove her way through the reservation. The trees grew thickest on this side of the mountain, encircling the Mukwa Reservation like a protective barrier. Every branch and totem pole was blanketed in snow, the sun making everything glisten like this place was made of diamonds. Eventually, they came to a large log building that looked like a modernized plank house. The Mukwa tried to hold onto as many traditions as possible while still being able to function in the ever-changing world.

"This is like the town hall. Back in the day, a place like this would have communal areas and enough space for several families to live," Della explained, gesturing loosely. "Now there's a kitchen, a dining room, and some game rooms."

The building wasn't pristine, but Della preferred the ramshackle buildings and log cabins with sagging roofs to the rest of the town. The Mukwa Reservation felt more human to her.

She also loved this place because the regular townsfolk stayed away. They weren't exactly welcome. If the outside town could be prejudiced towards the Mukwa's, they had every right to keep the townsfolk out.

"Little bear!" A familiar voice said, a laugh to his tone, just as she was about to lead Porter inside.

Della whipped her head around to see her uncle—the only one that mattered to her—standing a few feet away. Kohen Kitchi, Kimi's younger brother. Or, as she and Quincy had always called him, 'big bear.'

She ran to him, tackling him to the ground in a hug that fit their nicknames. He growled at her playfully, then swung her around into the snow, pinning her to the ground, laughing, his braided hair tickling her face. He smiled brightly, then caught sight of her hand. He scowled.

He tilted it to the side, sitting heavily in the snow. He signed to her questioningly as footsteps echoed behind them.

"I'm fine, really," Della said, unable to stop smiling.

Kohen gave her a knowing look. "Since when has one of your escapades ended in injury, little bear?"

She shrugged, throwing a handful of snow into his face, standing, and brushing herself off. He stood, too, hooking his arm around her shoulders. He took in Porter as someone else wrapped their arm around Della. She turned to see her grandfather, Mingan Kitchi, staring down at her like the king she thought of him as. He tapped his long cane on the path several times in greeting.

"Hi, Grandpa," Della smiled, accompanying her words with ASL.

Mingan smiled, his face wrinkling. His hair was grayer than the last time Della had seen him, but his eyes were as full of life as they had been when he was Porter's age. Those magnificent brown eyes scanned over Porter, a cheeky smile on his face. He nodded to Kohen, who rolled his eyes.

Mingan pointed to Porter, making a motion with his hands like he was grabbing the bill of a baseball cap, touched his fingers together like an 'X' twice, then drew a question mark in the air.

Della reddened, though not because of embarrassment. He was asking if Porter was her boyfriend. "This is Porter," she explained, signing every word. But secretly, she told them both no. Kohen giggled like a schoolgirl.

Porter waved awkwardly.

Della continued translating as they spoke. "This is Mingan, my grandpa. He is the Mukwa Chief. And this is Kohen, my uncle."

"Unfortunately," Kohen laughed, then kissed the top of her head.

Mingan smiled proudly, puffing out his chest.

"Nice to meet you both," Porter said, offering a hand to shake.

Mingan got to him before Kohen could make a move. Instead of shaking Porter's hand, Mingan pulled him into a tight hug. When he finally let go, he put two fingers to his face, making two circles in the air. Della laughed, nodding in agreement. Kohen rolled his eyes.

"What's he saying?" Porter asked, watching them all intently.

"He says you are handsome," Della said teasingly. Mingan always tried to sell the men around him to his feisty granddaughter like he was selling her a used car. Just as he'd done with the women to Quincy.

Porter blushed. "Thank you, sir."

Kohen smirked, turning to Della. "Well, I'll see around, little bear. Glad you're home."

Della felt all the elated air drain out of her. "Where are you going?"

"I have a life, y'know," Kohen laughed. "But I'll be hanging around. Catch ya on the flip side." He winked at her, bowed to Porter, then skipped away.

Mingan waved after him, but after a moment, he began moving his hands through the air. "It's nice to meet you. What brings you two here?" Della translated.

"In town for the holidays and work. Thought we'd stop by," she explained.

Mingan squinted at her, blew steam out his nose, and tapped his cane on the wooden path several times. Not all of his communication was sign language. He had little ticks Della had nicknamed Mingan-isms. And this meant he wanted the truth. Two taps for 'welcome' and four for 'cut the crap.'

Della's smile faltered. "I just needed out of the house," she admitted. Mingan nodded to himself and then pulled her into a hug.

How's your mother? He signed. His eyes held a sadness Della knew all too well.

As far as Della knew, Kimi hadn't been to the reservation since last year. Even longer before that.

Fine, I guess. She doesn't talk to me much, Della signed back.

"Care to share?" Porter asked, watching Mingan with the utmost curiosity.

"Private conversation," Della said a little too sharply. Porter frowned, taking a step back.

Mingan looked between them, eyeing Della carefully. Whatever was on his mind, he kept it to himself, which was probably for the best. Mingan seemed to be the only one who knew when to keep his thoughts to himself. Just like Max, he loved weaponizing his bluntness.

He snapped his fingers to get Della's attention so she could continue translating. He was smiling excitedly now, giddily signing.

"'Tell him the story,' he says. He loves bragging," she sighed. "He was in the army. Ranked pretty high, I might add. He fought in the Vietnam War. He lost hearing in his right ear due to shooter's ear. A couple of years later, he lost the left, too. What was it? Fifty-some years ago?" Mingan angrily shook his head. "Right, sixty. You don't have to swear," Della scolded. Mingan laughed. "He prefers sign, but you know he's angry with you when he uses his voice."

Porter was listening intently. "That's so cool—er—not cool, but interesting—like in—" Porter looked to Della for help, but she only shrugged. "Thank you for your service, sir."

Mingan nodded. He pointed to himself, then put two fists in the air, dragging them through the air twice.

"He's cold. Well, maybe you shouldn't walk around in the middle of December wearing nothing but a cheap pair of sweatpants and a t-shirt," Della scoffed, putting her hands on her hips once she finished signing.

Mingan rolled his eyes, pointing to Porter, asking

Della to tell him something.

"She's bossy, isn't she?" Della asked dryly.

Porter squinted at Della. "She is, but usually for a good reason." Mingan nodded his agreement.

This time, Della blushed for real.

"We skipped lunch. What's at the hall?" she asked, keen to change the subject.

Mingan shrugged, asking them to follow him up into the meeting hall. Della was about to grab Porter's hand to pull him along but couldn't bring herself to interlock her finger with his. Though she tried to convince herself otherwise, it wasn't because she was still mad at him.

Sure, she had kissed Porter. Sure, she was attracted to him. Sure, he always acted like he cared about her. . . But what if it was all a rouse? What if she was just his distraction? What if that's what she was using him as? How was she ever supposed to know what they were if she couldn't bring herself to ask?

Porter must've felt the same since all he did was clear his throat and nod toward the hall. They walked in awkward silence for a few paces before he began fiddling with one of his earrings. Della could see his shoulder blades tense up, telling her just how upset he was.

"He thinks you're cool," Della said to try and lighten the mood.

"Hmm? Mingan?" he asked. "That's—That's nice. He seems nice, I mean. Reminds me of you," he said distractedly, giving her a weak smile as he ran a hand through his thick black hair. "That's cool how you can translate so quickly."

"Mom taught me. I could sign before I could speak. Grandpa and I like to make fun of people behind their backs," Della said proudly, a mischievous grin pulling at her lips.

"You weren't making fun of me, were you?" Porter frowned. He framed it like a joke, but she could tell he was dead serious.

Della shook her head. He would know if she were to make fun of him. "He asked who you were. I don't bring people up here often, so he was suspicious," she chose to say.

Porter paled. "What did you say?"

"I said you were my friend." Not a total lie. It seemed she was having to use a lot of half-truths lately.

She would much rather see him frown than try to fake a smile. He was so bad at hiding his emotions. Della imagined a mind reader would have a hay day in his brain.

"Nothing else?" he blurted out.

"Was I supposed to say something else?" Della asked, feeling all the color drain from her skin and her heart somersault.

"No, no, I just—Never mind." His fake smile turned sour.

"What?"

"Nothing," he snapped, moving away from her.

"Porter," Della pleaded, grabbing him by the elbow and twisting him around to face her. His eyes were flickering between green and gold.

"I just thought that after everything, we—"

CLAP!

Porter wrenched himself away, a look of fright passing over his face as Della, startled, whipped her head around to see Mingan angrily signing at the two of them from the entrance of the meeting hall. Porter shoved his hands in his pockets, looking embarrassed, his head hung low as he turned to Mingan.

"We'll talk later," he whispered. "What's he saying now?"

"Get your asses in here before I die of pneumonia," Della translated, pursing her lips, an irritated eyebrow raised.

"You heard the man," Porter said, gesturing for her to lead the way. He wouldn't meet her eyes.

She complied, though not without wondering how much of a lecture or how heated an argument they would have later. Trying not to think about it too much, she let the warmth of the meeting hall engulf her. The smell of cinnamon and pine hit them hard as they walked along. There had been many a day when Della had snuck out of school only to wind up sitting in front of the massive fireplace in the entrance, her nose stuffed in a book while one of the tribe members—usually Kohen—serenaded her with their musical instrument or chatter from the day. If it wasn't that, she was curled up on one of the old armchairs, talking with Mingan about anything and everything.

Or she was admiring the giant bear carving that Porter was staring at now. Taking this as an opportunity to change the subject, she decided to give him another one of her tour-guide-esque speeches.

"Mukwa means bear," Della explained, pointing to the statue. Every detail was perfectly carved into honey-colored wood, the eyes made of a dark green gemstone. "The tribe was formed when the Great Spirit Bear spoke to a member of the Algonquin tribe. He'd been wanting to leave his people and start a new life, and the Spirit Bear said it would protect him if he chose to leave. We don't kill bears around here, but we do kill the deer. Sometimes, we leave parts of the meat out for the bears as a sign of goodwill."

"Interesting," was all Porter said.

That was something Della had learned all on her own. Mingan hadn't told her. Kohen hadn't fabricated a story. She'd read and researched and listened in hopes of showing her worth and that she knew something about her family and culture. That ephemeral factoid was beyond important to her.

And Porter had just shrugged it away.

At that moment, she decided she would rather get a lecture from him now, out in the open where he was vastly outnumbered, rather than wait for the confines of the hearse.

"Porter," Della sighed, gripping him by the sleeve and pulling him towards an empty corner.

"What? What now?" he asked shortly. Again, his eyes flashed gold. He was beyond angry and was desperately trying to hide it.

Della stared at him, taking in his features. The way his nose was a little bit crooked. The way the skin around his left eye was permanently tinted gray from Jed's fists.

"What?" he asked again, searching her face as well.

She looked away, hugging herself. "I'm sorry if I hurt your feelings or something, but—"

Porter scoffed, pulling away from her. "It's more than hurt feelings, Della."

"That's my line," she said brokenly, refusing to look at him.

"It seems to be *our* line now, doesn't it? I don't know what you want from me, Della. I'm trying my damnedest to figure you out, and every time I think we are back on good terms. . ." His voice trailed off as someone walked by. When they were gone, he didn't feel the need to finish.

"We weren't ever on bad terms," Della said, utterly confused.

"It certainly feels like we are!" he whisper-yelled.

She finally looked up at him, his eyes finally settling on that gorgeous glowing gold, a fury in them she couldn't quite understand. She squinted at him for a minute, then swallowed hard, looking everywhere but at him when she spoke.

"Am I just a distraction for you?" she asked, the words tasting bitter on her lips.

That knocked the wind from his sails. "What the Hell are you talking about?"

"What are we, Porter?" Della asked, placing a hand over his heart. "You and me."

He stared at her like she was stupid, making her want to slap him. She wished she had a milkshake to dump on his head like she had that time at *Bayou Gil's Crab Emporium*.

"Where is this all coming from?" he asked lifelessly.

"I don't know," Della admitted.

"Delphee, I love you. You know that. Why would I kiss you if I didn't?"

The words began spilling out of her like a crack in a pipe. "It's been weeks since you offered to take me on a date. You don't come and hang out at my place anymore. You don't—we don't—you—" Her throat tightened as she tried to keep from sobbing through her exposition. Panicked, she looked around for Mingan, noticing that the world seemed to sway and that her depth perception had disappeared. "If we are a couple, we don't act like one," she finished, then shut her eyes, feeling dizzy.

"Okay, yes, I have asked you out. I'm not hanging out with you because I'm exhausted by the time I'm done digging graves or fixing up bodies, I just want to go upstairs and crash. And how am I supposed to know you feel like this if you never talk to me about it?" Porter snapped.

"I'm trying to give you space and time to heal!" Della hissed, daring to open her eyes. She could have sworn for a minute that he was glowing a deep, muddy brown.

"I don't need space, Della; I need *you*," he said, his voice breaking.

Della sighed shakily, swaying on her feet for a moment. With a start, she realized this was what a panic attack felt like. Which only made things worse. Porter must've realized something was wrong, for he tried to reach out to steady her, but she ducked out of his grip.

"I don't know how to be there for you," she said, putting a hand on the wall to avoid falling over.

"Yes, you do. You've helped me out of a rut before, and I need you to—"

"Porter, I'm not going to be your therapist, and I'm not going to be your girlfriend just because you think I can fix you. My mom made it pretty clear that I ruin everything I touch. I don't want to ruin you, too." Her voice was barely audible over the thumping of her heart. Again, she swore he was glowing. She had to turn away from him; she couldn't stand to look at his face.

"I'm not—You aren't going to—"

A cane tap.

Della was shaking. She wrapped her arms around herself, cocooning herself from the rest of the world. She ignored Mingan, shutting her eyes, trying to calm down.

"Della?" Porter asked, an edge to his voice.

She swallowed her emotions, shoving the hurt into the darkest corners of her mind. She inhaled sharply, set her face in a smile, and then turned to Mingan as if nothing was wrong. Porter rolled his eyes, stepping back, looking disgusted at how easily she could shut it all off. If only he knew she did it so Mingan didn't try to kill him. If he knew Porter had upset her, her grandpa would be livid. The entire tribe would be livid.

Yes? Della signed, trying to remember to keep her face full of wonder and light.

Are you okay? Mingan asked, glancing at Porter. Della just nodded, causing Mingan to sigh. *There is chili in the kitchen. Will you be staying? Or is something wrong?*

"Do you want chili?" Della asked Porter, who shook his head angrily and stuffed his hands in his pockets.

We have places to be, but thank you. I love you. Della said, panic making her heart somersault as she realized she would have to sit in the hearse with him and then return to her angry mother. She should have taken that shortcut. Shouldn't have gotten in the car with him.

Mingan scowled but nodded. *I love you, too. Tell him to drive safely. Visit me again soon.*

I will. I promise. Della smiled.

Though on the inside, she was screaming and crying and having a full-on mental breakdown.

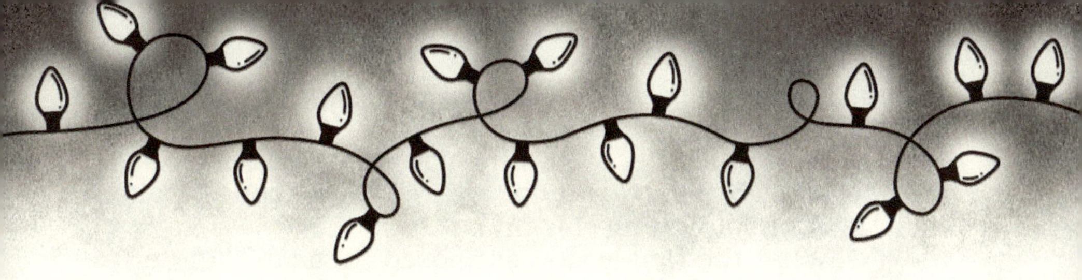

CHAPTER THIRTEEN

Quarrels

Porter and Della left quickly after that, as usual, not saying a word to each other. Though the silence wasn't exactly refreshing, she was thankful. She didn't want to fight with him while on the road. Knowing him, he might accidentally swerve off and send them into a ditch.

Della had always loved long drives. It gave her time to listen to music and daydream. Even silent drives were welcome. You could listen to the wind or rain or watch the passing scenery peacefully.

Now, however, the silence was too much to handle. The absence of sound allowed her darkest thoughts to roam free.

They had finally reached the Coleman household, and Della stood, frustrated, fumbling with her keys, trying to remember which one went to the front door. All the keys on her keyring looked the same, minus the one to her office, which was covered in peeling sunflower-yellow paint.

"You have prophetic visions, but you can't remember which key goes to the house you have lived in your entire life?" Porter sneered.

Della stomped her foot on the ground, brushing hair from her eyes. Her mind was full of buzzing thoughts she wished would go away. It made it hard to think of anything else.

"I can barely remember what was on the toast I had for breakfast, let alone this," she snarled, shoving a key into the lock. Miraculously, it fit.

"We had *Poptarts* for breakfast," Porter corrected.

"No, we didn't," Della replied.

"Yes, we did," Porter scoffed.

"No, we didn't. I made toast."

"You grabbed three Poptarts out of the pantry and

slapped them on the coffee table, Della," Porter said, a mildly concerned look on his face.

Della rolled her eyes, unlocking the front door. "Whatever. Obviously, you don't care much about breakfast, let alone anything else."

"What the Hell is that supposed to mean?" Porter snapped, yet he held the door open for her as she waltzed in.

She ignored him, sweeping into the house to find Max and Sebastian sitting at the kitchen table, their voices hushed. Besides them, the house appeared empty. Max stopped mid-wave, reading her like a book. He looked to Porter, his expression darkening. Della gave him a discrete look, which he returned with a scowl at Porter.

"Oh, big surprise," Porter mumbled. He said something else as he kicked off his shoes, but Della didn't hear it.

No one stopped him as he stomped upstairs.

The lights flickered. Della shivered. No one else seemed to notice the sudden drop in temperature and the impending doom that Della felt.

"You guys okay?" Sebastian asked.

Della sighed, eyes on Max as she sauntered over to them. She sat on the table's edge, then leaned back, lying across her mother's carefully positioned tablecloth and runner, staring at the light fixture above her.

"I'll take that as a no," Sebastian said, then patted her shoulder affectionately. "Max told me what you guys are up to."

She turned her head toward Max, who gave her a bored look as if to say, 'Ei didn' tell him everythin'.' Della gave him a grateful look.

"And?" Silence as Della turned her head back to stare at the ceiling.

"We can talk about it later," Sebastian said finally.

"I'd prefer talking about it now."

"And I'd prefer you plant your feet on the ground," said Jasper as he descended the stairs.

"My feet aren't on the table," Della said matter-of-factly.

"They are on the chair," Jasper said sourly.

"So?" Della spat back.

"Attitude," Jasper snapped back.

Della mocked him silently. After a while, she scoffed. "Lay off it, Jasper."

Sebastian flicked her arm in warning.

Begrudgingly, she sat up, staring her *lovely* father dead in the eyes. "I'm tired of playing nice."

"Well, if that was your nice, I'd hate to see what your mean looks like," Jasper said smugly.

"Well then, I guess you hate looking in the mirror, don't you? Where's mom?" she asked, afraid Kimi would come down and start yelling at her.

Jasper narrowed his eyes at her, glanced at the boys sitting on either side of her, then shook his head angrily. That look on his face was the kind every kid had nightmares about. You knew you were in trouble when your father was scowling that deeply. You might as well start digging your way to Hell before he could throw you there himself.

Sebastian stood slowly, glancing at Max. "I'm. . ." he began. "Well, it's going to snow tonight, so see you guys later," he said, then quickly made for the door.

When the door closed behind him, Jasper glared at her so deeply she was sure his face would be permanently set in that position. Then again, Jasper was always scowling. She doubted anyone would notice if his face did get stuck like that.

"Mom ordered pizza," he said dismissively, grabbed a water bottle from the fridge, then walked back upstairs.

Della didn't say anything as he walked away. She wanted to cry then. To burst into tears and hide under the table.

Max gave her a knowing look. "Are we burnin' all yer bridges tuhday, love?" he asked.

"Burning implies that I accidentally dropped a match or a torch," Della said with the air of a writer from the eighteen hundreds. "Darling, I had dynamite and a fuse."

Max smirked. He studied her for a moment. "Ya look exhausted."

She shrugged. "It's been an exhausting day."

He nodded his agreement, clearing his throat as he shifted uneasily in his seat. Della looked him up and down, freezing with dread.

"Oh no," she breathed.

"Now listen—"

"What did you do, Maximilian?" she groaned.

He tented his fingers, crossing his legs dramatically. "Ei may or may not have asked yer mom if yer family had a history of seizures on either side," he said in a squeaky voice.

Della stared him down, unsure whether she should be angry or excited. "Why?" she choked out.

He blinked at her. "Well—Ei figured ya'd need someone lookin' out for ya while we're here, so Ei took it upon myself."

"Th—Thank you," Della said softly. "What did she say?"

Not wanting anyone to stick their nose in her business was a contradictory trait for an intrepid reporter to have. If it were anyone else snooping around in things that should stay buried, she'd be furious. But this was Max. She knew deep down he only had her best interests at heart.

"She mentioned yer grandma had seizures, Ei talked her intuh goin' tuh find some of her medical files tuh look through, and we chatted about how Ei'm disappointed in her parentin' skills," he smiled proudly. "Yer not the only one burnin' bridges tuhday."

Della smirked. "Dually noted."

"Ei also talked tuh Sebastian. He's somethin' else, ain' he?" Max grimaced, an ounce of fear crossing his face. "He's an eejit."

"He means well," Della laughed.

It was obvious he wasn't convinced. "Anyway, he mentioned a construction site out in the woods. Said something weird is goin' on up there. They shut it all down after Ashton went missin'. People think a bear got him."

"They think the sound woke the bears up?" Della asked. Max nodded, and she rolled her eyes. "It's a possibility, but I doubt it. Bears don't just go after people. You have to be in their territory, threatening them or trying to take away their food. If anything, they'd flee deeper into the forest."

"My thoughts exactly. Which is why this might be our kind of case." He was smiling smugly, but he didn't sound too thrilled.

"We should check that place out tomorrow," Della said, lost in thought.

Weird things were happening all over town, but what kind of weird? Sure, missing things, missing pets, and a disappearance were all strange, but what had everyone so freaked out that Cyrus O'Malley and Ashton would tell Della, of all people, to figure this out? What kind of weird things were happening at that construction site? Was machinery going haywire, or was something else happening? Something darker?

"Okay, hear me out," Max began after a while, looking uncomfortable with her silence. "We tackle that tomorrow and spend tonight following a different lead."

"What kind of lead?" Della asked with a sigh, not feeling up to much of anything. Back home in Moss Hollow, she would spend tonight curled up on the couch watching all the weird late-night shows on the *History* and *Discovery* channels.

He shrugged, his eyes lighting up with a dark sort of delight. "Yer mum gave me an idea. She joked about talking tuh ghosts, and at first, Ei thought tuh summon the ghost of yer grandmother, but. . ." He waited for her to finish his thought.

Della snorted with laughter. "Maximilian Cormac McGregor-Mavericks. Are you asking me to summon a spirit with you? At the historical society?"

"Hmm, now that's a proposition," Max said, a twinkle in his eyes. "Would it be yer first time?"

"Shut up," Della laughed, trying her best not to smile.

For the first time today, she'd said that word playfully. With endearment. Sarcasm. For the first time, she hadn't meant it. She could listen to Max talk for hours and never get bored.

They locked eyes as Della finally smiled. He returned her smile with an arched brow and dazzling eyes. Della now knew what danger was and why so many put that word and 'men' together. She should have walked away from him and turned towards the kitchen or the living room, but instead, she leaned in closer. After today, she just wanted all her problems to melt away. And Max always had a way of doing that.

"Think you can do it?" she asked, daring him.

"For *you*, Della?" he asked. "Of course. For ya, Ei'd do anythin'."

And deep down, she knew that was true.

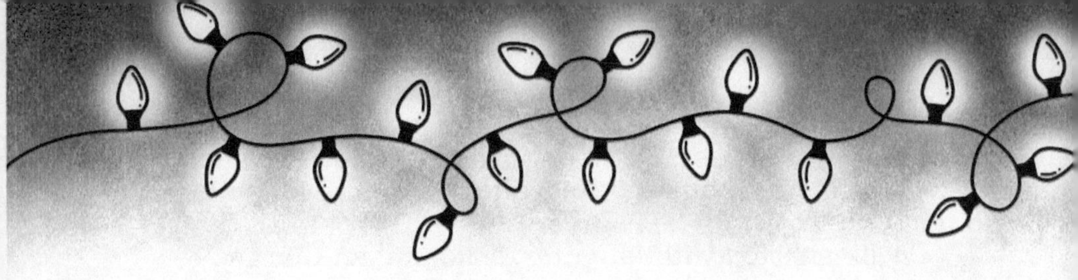

CHAPTER FOURTEEN

Séance 101

No one came down when the pizza showed, so the two of them claimed it for themselves as they gathered all they would need for a quiet night of summoning potentially evil spirits. When they were all packed, Della stole Porter's keys from his jacket, which was haphazardly hung up by the front door, and they quietly slipped outside. Della—so anxious she kept accidentally hitting the brakes—drove them to the historical society.

It was late. No one would be around at this time, but if anyone caught them, they'd surely spend the night in one of the teeny holding cells at the local police department. Della *did not* want to spend any amount of time there.

"Think you can get us in through the back?" Della asked, parking a few streets down.

Max held up his wallet, letting it fall open. It wasn't a wallet at all. It was a miniature lock-picking set.

"I kind of meant magic, but hey, that works, too!" Della smirked, thinking about how he said he was a re-formed kleptomaniac, yet he still carried a lock pick set.

Max winked at her. "Ei don' always think of magic. Never grew up relyin' on it." Then his face went blank. "Okay, maybe that's not entirely true. Ei had my moments."

Della shook her head playfully as they exited the hearse. She grabbed her book bag, all the ghost-hunting equipment stuffed inside rattling away. Max grabbed his own bag—a beat-up leather satchel with test tubes sticking out the sides and burn marks on the straps—and rifled through it for a flashlight shaped like a beaker. Della laughed to herself.

Max looked up at her innocently as he switched on his flashlight. "What?"

Della gave him a knowing look. "Oh, nothing."

He raised his eyebrow but shrugged.

They crossed silently in the dark to the back of the historical society, and Della watched as Max picked the lock to the back door with finesse. Something she couldn't do—though it pained her to admit—was pick locks. Well, she could, just not well. And if Della couldn't do something perfectly, she might as well not do it.

Within seconds, they were inside.

"Where do we start?" Max asked, observing their surroundings cautiously as Della quietly shut the door behind them. She knew he could see better in the dark than she could. He would've told her if anything was off. Still, it was ominous being here so late. Alone. With him.

"Uh. . . Upstairs! With the bone. There's a key in my mom's office. We can use the bone as a conduit!" Della said excitedly.

"So ya think we're dealing with a pissed-off Indigenous American spirit?" Max asked skeptically. "That's a little cliché. Even for us."

"Worth a try. I mean, it's either one of mine or one of the Sycamore's. And there's a perfectly good bone right above us. It'd be a shame not to use it." Della knew he wouldn't say no, at least not to something like this.

"Fine. Get the keys. Ei'll set up shop," Max said, taking Della's book bag from her.

They creaked up the steps, hyper-aware of the sound of their footsteps on decades-old steps, aware of how their shadows moved, the flashlight, and most importantly, their hands brushing against each other. Parting on the landing, Della rushed to her mother's office and kyped the keys off the wall next to the light switch. She made sure not to drop them as she bolted back to Max. There was no shame in admitting she was afraid of the dark. After all, she was one of the few who knew what was hidden in the shadows.

Max had already set up one of his devices when she returned to the room with the bone. It was similar to a *REM-pod*, a spirit communication device that would light up if a ghost was nearby. However, this particular ghost communication tool was made by Max himself. He liked to tinker in his free time and had whipped up a few of these flat, circular gadgets for The Courier. Everyone lovingly referred to the device as the MAX-pod.

Other than that gizmo, he'd taken out the container of salt Della always kept on her. The jar stood open before him as he sat, messing with the setting on his EMF meter. Della crossed to the display case that held the bone and unlocked it.

"Gloves, please," she called down to Max. He rifled

through his bag, then threw a pair of neon green gloves at her.

She wondered if he'd always kept neon green gloves or if he'd had the normal blue or black ones until he'd met her. Why did she care if he'd changed the color of his gloves to match her? That was stupid. Childish even. It had to be a coincidence.

"Thank you," she said, her movements suddenly awkward as she pulled on the gloves and carefully removed the jawbone from its enclosure.

She sat down next to Max and placed the bone near the MAX-pod, startled for a second that it went off, forgetting that not only could ghosts affect it, but ordinary people could too. The sensors were hypersensitive to movement.

"Ya wanna do the flashlight thing? Turn on one for yes, two for no?" Max asked.

Della nodded. She switched off his flashlight and took out another from her bag, placing both on the floor. The darkness was consuming, but in a way, it was thrilling. This is what she had always wanted. Ghost hunting with someone who understood. Someone who—though skeptical—would humor her theories.

"Magic as a last resort, okay?" he asked. "None of yer little *Discovery Channel* people use magic. There's no sense in depleting sources that are already dry."

"Agreed," Della said, scooching as close to him as possible. "Speaking of: For a guy who says he's strictly into science, you always carry an awful lot of herbs and candles on your person," she said accusingly. Those candles weren't hers, nor was the jar of spices she'd seen him take out of his satchel before the flashlight went off.

"Maybe. . ." he began, turning towards her. She couldn't see his face, but she knew he was giving her a wistful smile. "Maybe that's how Ei had tuh be. Maybe Ei thought Ei couldn' have things both ways."

"Until. . . ?" Della prompted.

She felt him shrug beside her.

Until you, she had hoped for him to say.

She paled. She shouldn't be thinking that. Why was she thinking that? Something was seriously wrong with her tonight.

She cleared her throat and gestured toward the MAX-pod and flashlights since she knew he could see it. "You first or me?"

"Well, Ei'm a gentleman, so, ladies first?" he asked. She could hear a slight twinge of fear in his thick Irish accent.

She nudged him comfortingly, then focused her

metaphysical attention on the spirits that could be surrounding them.

"Hello," she said kindly, trying to welcome any
non-corporeal listeners. "My name is Della, this is Max.
We'd love to speak with you tonight."

"Oh, yer good," Max whispered teasingly.

"Is anyone listening?" Della asked, then waited for a
response.

Nothing.

"If ya—" Max began, but the MAX-pod went off, and
the lights on top flashed, turning blue. The EMF detector he
held also began to beep, the screen lighting up in an array
of colors before settling on green. "Green's good," Max said,
though his words came out quick and tight. Both of them
were terrified, and it showed.

"Good evening," Della said.

"And now ya sound like a vampire," Max snickered.

Della flicked him. "Good evening," She said louder.
The MAX-pod flickered. "We have a few questions for you. If
you could, two flashlights for no, one for yes."

"Next, ya'll be askin' them about their current insurance plan," Max whispered.

Della shushed him, then gestured for him to ask a
question. He hesitated, then shifted uncomfortably next to
her.

"Are we speakin' tuh several spirits?" he asked. The
MAX-pod lit up and beeped. So did one flashlight. "Well,
hello, everyone!"

"If it isn't any trouble, may we speak with just one of
you?" Della asked.

Silence.

One flashlight.

Yes.

"How are we kinder tuh ghosts than we are tuh each
other?" Max asked thoughtfully, staring at the lit-up flashlight in awe, the low light casting his features in an ominous glow.

Della shrugged, moving on to her next question. "Do
you know an Ashton John? He might have worked here."

Another yes.

"Do you know what happened to him?"

Two flashlights. No.

"Did he know of you?" Della said carefully.

Suddenly, the MAX-pod went nuts. All the lights
were blinking on and off, the flashlights on the floor were
flickering, and the EMF detector Max held flashed every
color on the spectrum.

"What—What does that mean?" Della asked, shivering.

"Uh, well, it shouldn' do that, for one," Max said quietly, fiddling with the nobs and buttons with shaking hands.

Della felt her blood run cold. She couldn't pin what it was, but something in the air felt almost. . . evil.

"Was he good to you?" Della asked, her voice quivering.

The MAX-pod switched off, the EMF detector landed on red, and both flashlights stayed on.

Della felt Max go frigid next to her.

"Did you want him gone?" Della asked.

One. Yes.

Della swallowed hard. "Are—Do—Did you have anything to do with his disappearance?" she asked carefully.

The light didn't change.

Max found Della's hand in the dark and gripped it tight.

"That doesn'—Are we still talkin' tuh the same person?" he asked slowly.

Two flashlights. No.

Della shivered. The longer they sat there, the worse she felt, like someone was breathing down her neck. It was so strange. She could feel malicious intent resonating off the walls.

She opened her mouth to ask another question but was cut off.

Cold hands clamped around her shoulders.

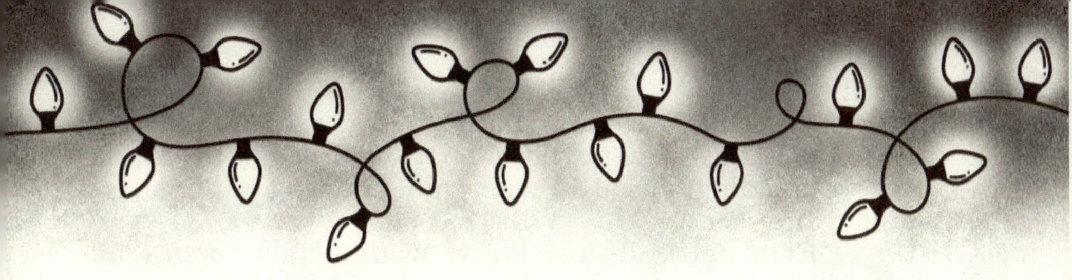

CHAPTER FIFTEEN

Spectrophobia

She screeched, jumping up, ripping her hand from Max's, tripping over the flashlights and MAX-pod, knocking over the unlit candles. She smacked at thin air, eyes shut, hopping up and down in a crazed frenzy.

"GET IT OFF! GET IT OFF! GET IT OFF!" she screamed at the top of her lungs as she paddled and swatted at the air like a drowning dog.

"PORTER!" Max screamed over her.

It took her a minute to realize the word—*name*—he had yelled.

Porter.

She opened her eyes to see him doubled over, laughing so hard he was crying.

Della stomped her foot on the ground, fuming. "YOU LITTLE SH—"

"You scream like a girl!" he choked out as Max side-stepped him to turn on the lights.

"I AM A GIRL!" Della roared, then snatched her flashlight off the floor and hit him with it.

He winced, holding up a finger in defense. He was going to object to that, but his face was blank. "Yeah, no, I got nothing to say to that."

"What are ya doin' here?" Max snapped, shaking violently. His fingers had turned into claws, his ears were now pointed and covered in black and white fur, and his eyes were slit and glowing. Not to mention, he was clinging to the light switch like it was the fountain of youth.

"I—" Porter took one look at him and burst out laughing again.

Max willed his appearance back to normal, exchanging angry looks with Della. When Porter finally finished laughing, he was smiling like the idiot he was, looking between them.

"You guys are summoning ghosts, and you didn't invite me? That's like purposely not inviting half the family to a will reading: illegal," Porter said, snorting out one last laugh.

"Ei would really love it if ya wouldn' talk about readin' wills durin' a situation like this. Thanks," Max snapped, but a smile flickered across his lips. He turned to Della. "Yer scared of ghosts."

Della straightened, holding her head high. "Am not."

"Are too," the boys said in unison.

"D-2," Della said haughtily.

Porter lost it laughing again.

That is until all the lights around them suddenly went off, and a cool breeze entered the room.

"Okay now, that, that isn't funny," he said, his voice quivering as he looked at Max.

They heard Max flip the light switch on and off several times, each flip of the switch more desperate than the last. Nothing. "Ei—Ei didn'. . ."

He didn't have to finish that sentence. He and Della immediately grabbed Porter's arms, looking around the room, squinting into the darkness.

"Wow, guys. Real mature. What am I supposed to do against a friggin ghost?!" Porter hissed, but he crossed his arms tightly, placing a hand over each of their hands to comfort them. Or maybe he was just concerned that two ghosts had grabbed him, not his friends.

"I don't know! You deal with the dead! Maybe you can reason with the *un*dead!" Della said shakily. She could feel eyes on her from every angle.

"Could—Could that upset them? Me working with the dead? Max says he can smell it on me," Porter said quietly. Collectively, they backed away from the discarded ghost-hunting equipment.

"You smell him?" Della asked in disgust, looking in Max's direction.

"NOT REALLY THE ISSUE HERE, DELLA!" he shot back, punctuating every word with a slightly higher tone.

"I'M SORRY, OKAY! I'M SCARED! SUE ME!" she yelled back.

"EARDRUMS!" Porter screamed over them.

"WHAT?" They screamed back.

Della jumped as they backed against a wall, thinking for a split second that someone was behind her.

"STOP BLOWING OUT MY EARDRUMS!" Porter screeched.

"STOP YELLIN'!" Max replied.

"YOU FIRST!" Porter snapped, then shushed himself.

They all stood in tense silence, Max and Della pinned to the wall graciously using Porter as a shield. They listened, waiting for something—anything—to happen. But nothing did. They were alone in the empty historical society.

Alone except for a malevolent ghost that could have killed Ashton.

"Did—Did you hurt Ashton?" Della asked the room.

The flashlight in Della's hand went off. Yes.

Max yanked it from her fingers and then threw it at the floor, shaking. His eyes were glowing again. So were Porter's. The MAX-pod was beeping rapidly, emitting a shrill, almost angry sound. The EMF detector on the floor was cycling through the rainbow again.

"Ei feel sick," Max whimpered, resting his forehead on Porter's shoulder.

Porter nodded, gripping Della's hand tightly.

They stood there for what felt like hours, waiting for an attack, but nothing ever came. All they heard was the sound of each other's quickened breath, the crescendo of their hearts, and Max's tiny whimpers.

"Maybe the power went out?" Max offered, his voice barely audible.

"I'm going to ask a question," Della said.

"Don't you dare!" Porter snapped.

"Are we alone?" Della spoke over him.

"Della!" The boys screeched.

No response from beyond the grave.

"If that would have said no, Ei would have—" Max began.

As soon as those words left his lips, the lights flicked back on, the brightness blinding them.

Footsteps.

The clicking of heels.

"Oh G—It's a ghost with heels. Those are the worst kind!" Porter whispered, his voice high and tight as he clamped his hands over his eyes.

Max gave him a funny look. "Under what logic—"

"What the Hell are you three—"

They all screamed. Della clung to Porter, and Max tried to edge his way between her and the wall.

"—doing here. . . What is—"

They screamed louder.

"Are you done?" A haughty voice echoed, accompanied by a final click-clack of heels.

Della, shaking from fright, peered over Porter's trembling elbow. In an instant, dread changed to annoyance when she saw Elvi Sinclair judging them from the doorway.

Della watched as her eyes slid over them—Porter specifical-ly—then down at the array of magical objects, devices, and herbs littering the floor. Something changed on her face for a split second, but it was gone before Della could deduce what it meant.

"Oh. It's *you*," Della snapped.

Elvi raised an eyebrow.

"Who?" Porter and Max asked shakily, their eyes still shut tightly.

Della managed to shimmy out from between Max and Porter, placing herself in front of the boys protectively. "Miss Sinclair."

"Miss Coleman," she said in turn, looking bored. "To what do I owe the pleasure? And why—" She gestured to the floor. "—is my floor covered in spices?"

"We're trying to sage the house of your bad energy," Della said flatly, then nodded to Max, who quickly began shoving things into Della's book bag and sweeping up spilled containers of herbs into an empty jar. "And it's not your floor," she added under her breath.

"Charming," Elvi snorted, wrinkling her nose.

"Thank you," Porter said pointedly.

"Get out," Elvi snapped, pointing to the door. "Now."

Della raised her hand in objection, but Porter grasped her firmly by the shoulder and shoved her forward, dragging Max along with him, who protested that he wasn't done cleaning up. One look at Elvi, and he promptly shut up. Elvi saw them all downstairs and to the front door, wav-ing them away with a sarcastic smile and an evil glint in her eyes.

Porter collapsed into the snow when she slammed the door behind them.

"That was the stupidest thing we've ever done," he said, though he smiled and began to make a snow angel, sticking his tongue out to catch a few snowflakes.

Max kicked snow on top of him, smiling mischie-vously.

Della laughed, hugging herself against the cold. "I don't think that would even reach the top *twenty* of the stu-pidest things I have ever done."

Max laughed and nodded in agreement. "That was kinda fun. Breakin' and enterin'. Screamin' like children."

Porter sat up, shaking snow from his hair. "We should do stuff like that more often."

Della rolled her eyes. "We should get home before Miss Pencil Skirt decides to—" She paused, eyeing Max. He'd gone pale, a far-off look in his eyes. "You okay?"

His response was his knees buckling. Della panicked, grasping for his hands. Porter jumped up and caught before he fell backward.

"Holy shit, Max!" Porter screeched, struggling to keep him upright.

Della squeezed his hand, gently lifting his chin. His eyelids flickered for a second as he stared at her. There was something about his stare. Something off. Della couldn't quite pin it.

"Ei feel sick," Max said again, letting Porter place his arm around his shoulders. He leaned heavily against him, holding his head in his hands. "Ei'd like tuh go home now, please."

Della and Porter exchanged a worried look but nodded quietly. They led him across the street and to the hearse—Porter had walked all the way here—and they drove back home.

Max crashed on the couch as soon as they walked in.

Della's heart did a somersault when he did, her mind immediately going someplace it shouldn't. From the look on Porter's face, he thought the same thing. Quietly, they both leaned over the edge of the couch, watching his chest rise and fall. Both sighed in relief, delighted to know he was at least still breathing.

"I thought I was the problem child," Della whispered, pulling Porter toward the stairs in case they woke him.

"Not always," Porter said darkly. Worry lines spread across his chiseled features as his eyes drifted down. Years of memories seemed to catch up to him. Clearing his throat, he glanced down at Della, softening his expression. "It's nothing. He'll be fine," he smiled weakly.

Della inhaled sharply, stuffing her hands in her pocket.

They stood like that for a while, as if afraid departing upstairs would harm Max somehow. Della watched Porter's eyes, thinking about one of their first meetings and how eyes alone could tell you so many things.

"I'm sorry about earlier," he whispered, refusing to look at her. "I love you, Della. I really do. You're not a distraction. I'm not with you because I think you can fix me. I'm with you because you deserve someone who loves you with all their being," he said solemnly, then leaned down to kiss her.

Della turned her head. "I don't want you to kiss me," she said quickly, thinking of Max lying asleep a few feet away.

She regretted it as soon as she said it. It had just come out. She didn't even know *why* she'd said it. It just happened. She felt her cheeks redden as she looked back to

Porter, his questioning expression riddled with sadness.

"I mean, I want you to kiss me, just not right now," she added before he could ask a question she didn't want to answer. "I'm just tired, y'know. I want to go to bed."

"O—Okay. I'm cool with that. Of course, I'm cool with that. I don't want you to do anything with anyone you don't want to do," he said, his words coming out in short bursts as he scratched the back of his neck.

"Okay," Della said, nodding.

"Cool. Cool," Porter sighed, stepping back and clearing his throat. "We are cool, right?"

"Yup."

"Nice."

"Yeah."

Della rocked back and forth on the balls of her feet for a minute, then made for the top of the stairs at the same time Porter did. They bumped into each other rather painfully.

"You first, *meu amor*," Porter said, bowing.

Della nodded at him, then quickly made her way to Cassandra's room and shut the door.

Sheer embarrassment would end up killing her far before any supernatural entity did.

The floorboards outside her door creaked. The door moved ever so slightly. Della expected Porter to open the door and convince her to kiss him. Not in a way that'd be deemed wrong. Just by saying something sweet and charming he'd probably read in a book. She'd expected him to make her ache for him. Maybe that's what she wanted.

As she heard him turn away from the door, she realized something.

She was always expecting something from him.

And the only expectations he'd delivered were the ones she didn't want.

All the color drained from her face as a thought entered her mind. One that she'd been trying to fend off for quite some time. Ever since that night in the hospital when she talked with *him*. With *Max*. The thought came as a burst of color in her mind.

She shook her head violently to clear her thoughts. No. She loved Porter, and Porter loved her. She couldn't— *wouldn't*—think things like that. It was wrong. It was practically cheating on him. And Della refused to be a cheat. Nothing in this world could make her become one. That was one sin she would never have on her resume.

Theft? Sure.

Breaking and entering? Sure.

Murder? Yup.

But cheating? Especially on Porter? Never. Della couldn't live with herself if she broke his heart. He deserved someone to love him unconditionally.

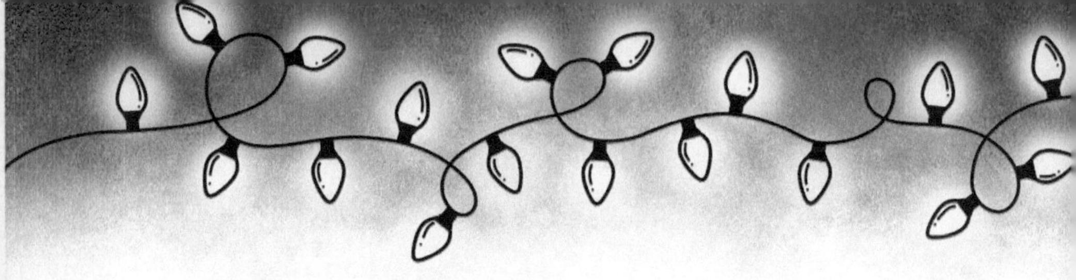

CHAPTER SIXTEEN

Insight

Porter had laid awake that night, his mind spinning with thousands of sickening possibilities. He wasn't a fan of heartbreak. In all the books he'd read, Porter always found the ones that contained tragedies weren't the ones he wanted to read. He craved fairytales. Where the guy always got the girl, and the bad guys always lost. But those were just stories. Figments of someone's imagination. He realized that now. Not everyone was lucky enough to get a fairytale ending.

He just hoped that Della and himself could find a way to work things out. Maybe they wouldn't end up like a fairytale, but they still could find some sort of happiness. Their love didn't have to be perfect. Perhaps he wouldn't lose her if he found a way to explain, to tell her he was willing to work things out.

He knew he shouldn't be jealous of Della and Max. Nor should he feel hurt that they went off without him. That outcome was inevitable, wasn't it? After all, it was his fault for fighting with her. Still, there was a pang of hurt in his chest.

When he'd arrived, he'd seen them holding hands in the dark, the flashlight illuminating their intertwined fingers. Such a sight had made him physically sick.

He knew Della wouldn't do anything to break his heart.

At least not on purpose.

Still, he had to find a way to win her back. Even if she didn't realize it, he knew. He knew her heart wasn't entirely his, even though he'd given his away the minute they'd met. Her heart was in purgatory, floating between him and something else. Blaming it all on Max was easier than wondering what could be more important than true love.

He rolled over in his sleeping bag at that thought, his blood boiling.

His heart ached.

No, his entire *life* seemed to ache.

Part of him had always been jealous of Max. But this? This was different. Della was supposed to be his. He was supposed to be the one she'd confide in. Not Max.

Maybe if he'd read all those books about tragedy and heartbreak, he would have been more prepared. He had a friend in Maine who loved reading tragedies. She was always trying to get him to read her dark and twisted books, pointing out they were already accustomed to tragedy. Reading such stories should feel validating. Instead, those stories reminded him of how screwed up his life had been.

Tired of lying in a sleeping bag that was barely big enough for him, he stood pacing the hallway, wondering if he should knock on Della's door and confide in her all the thoughts clouding his mind. He paced for hours, watching the early morning light crawl up the stairs from the living room. As he walked the halls, a different idea filled his mind.

Maybe he was supposed to cheer her up? He needed to do some grand gesture. Prove to her that he cared, that he wanted to help. Maybe he had to prove it to Max, too.

Porter couldn't remember the last time he'd been in the snow. Last night, making snow angels as he laughed with them had brought him back to the days before his dad died.

Before Jed.

Before he and Max had their falling out.

Maybe all they needed was a chance to act like kids again. He laughed to himself at how childish his idea sounded. A snowball fight, complete with hot cocoa and laughter, was just what the doctor ordered.

~ ~ ~

If someone asked Porter about his dream job, they would know how big his passion for cooking was. Mixing spices in just the right way, the sound of sizzling vegetables in a perfectly oiled pan, the way the smell of ground beef changes as it's cooked—every aspect of it, he loved.

Breakfast was one of his favorite things to cook, and he was awfully good at it, too. For years, he had had to get up and make himself breakfast before school or suffer a growling stomach until lunch. He had found the perfect recipe for scrambled eggs—four eggs, two diced tomatoes, cheese, heavy whipping cream, and cayenne pepper.

One day, he'd experimented with making French toast with coffee cake and found baking even easier.

He was a master in the kitchen. There'd been a time when his mind was full of fantasies of attending culinary school. Of owning a café or a bakery.

He smiled to himself as he waltzed around the kitchen, performing a delicate dance with the frying pan he held precariously in one hand. A plate of cut fruit was on the counter, toast was in the toaster, eggs were hard-boiling on the stovetop, bacon was sizzling in his pan, and a fresh smoothie was blending away behind him.

This was a better use of his time than pacing back and forth down the hallway. Thank the Lord above that the Coleman's fridge was full of fresh ingredients.

Max was still softly snoring on the couch. It seemed not even a jet plane could wake him. Porter would stop occasionally, ensuring he was still breathing when he wasn't snoring. Every time the house went quiet, his heart skipped a beat.

Porter fingered the hot toast as it popped up from the toaster. The smell of warm butter filled the kitchen as he arranged the slices on a decorative plate. Popping a leftover strawberry into his mouth, his eyes lit up with pure, unbridled joy.

He worked quietly until he glanced at the couch where Max had been lying to see him groggily glaring at him. The sight of him staring back nearly scared Porter out of his skin.

"Morning!" Porter smiled.

"Yer loud," Max grumbled, rubbing the sleep from his eyes.

"Sorry," Porter grimaced, then swept his hand through the air to show everything he'd cooked up.

"Are ya stress cooking?" Max yawned.

"I—No! No, of course not! No!" Porter laughed tensely.

Max rolled his eyes and then headed upstairs. "Ei'll be down in a few," he said, his voice full of exhaustion.

"Okay!" Porter said in a sing-song tone, trying to hide his embarrassment.

He one-hundred percent was stress cooking. The cookies in the oven that he would present to everyone later were proof of that. He tried telling himself that he just wanted to decorate cookies with friends, but baking was just another way to keep his mind busy.

Della might be right. Maybe he needed a distraction from the chaos in their lives.

All those dreams of culinary school came flooding

back like royal icing on one of the sugar cookies he was eyeing. Maybe he could apply for some online classes when this was all over. He could even take a course or two at a community college.

He smiled sadly, knowing that would never happen.

There was a reason he stuck around.

Money wasn't an issue like Porter made it out to be. He had rainy-day savings he could dip into if he wanted to pay for school. He could've left anytime he wanted. He could've gone to college or taken a one-way trip to Portugal or the Caribbean like he'd always wanted. But he had stayed for his mom and grandfather. For Max. And now for Della.

In his eyes, he had to protect everyone he cared about.

This weighed heavily on him most days.

He feared they'd end up in a coffin at *Garroway Cemetery and Mortuary* if he weren't around to care for Max and Della.

And if that were to happen, it would crush him.

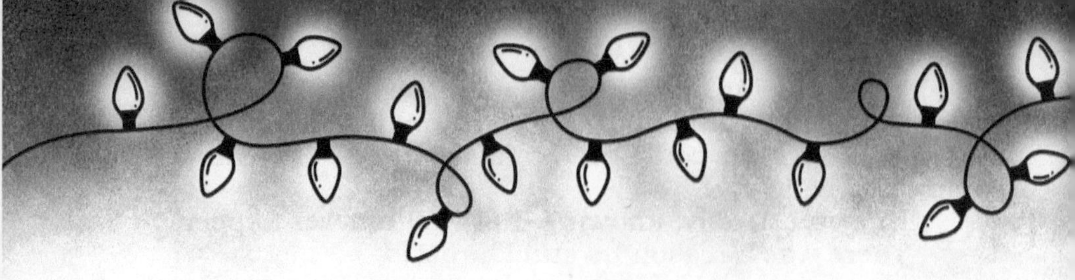

CHAPTER SEVENTEEN

Mars Alongside Pluto

Della woke to the sound of someone rummaging around in her room, a squeaking door, and a blinding light. Muffled footsteps filled her ears, the floorboards creaking beneath whoever dared to wake her. A tiny soft swear. The familiar sound of someone walking into the corner of a dresser. An audible roll of the eyes.

Max.

She shivered beneath the covers. Slowly, Della rolled away from the window to face him. His coiled hair was messy, dark circles forming beneath his eyes, his shirt cock-eyed. She tried smiling at him, but her lips didn't seem to work. She couldn't describe how she knew, but she could tell he was in pain. Something had happened to him last night, and that terrified her.

"Ei didn' mean tuh wake ya," he sighed, plopping down on the bed beside her. He lay beside her, facing her, looking like he could fall asleep at any moment.

"It's fine. What time is it?" Della said quietly, tracing the lines of his face. He looked like he hadn't slept for days.

"Far too early if ya ask me," he sighed, his eyes flickering shut.

Della nodded, letting her eyes close as well. She would never in a million years admit it, but trivial things like falling asleep next to someone or staying up past the witching hour to talk filled her heart with pure bliss. Max shared the same sentiment, for he was always ready to listen to her even after the clock struck midnight. Most of the time, it was over the phone while they both worked on their respective hobbies, but sometimes, he would sneak into the lobby of Ambrose Apartments for a bowl of cereal paired with an existential crisis.

"How did ya sleep?" he asked groggily, rolling over

onto his back.

"Fine, I guess. What about you? You look like shit," Della whispered, opening one of her eyes to watch him. Maybe it was the lack of light, but he looked almost sickly. His espresso-colored skin was alarmingly pale. Sweat glistened on his forehead. "You okay?" she asked nervously.

There was a momentary pause before he answered. "Ei don' do well with ghosts," he choked out. "And there were a lot of ghosts last night. Familiars work on a different frequency, tuh put it scientifically. Ghosts do, too. Their frequency cancels mine out. It got tuh be too much. Just feelin' a little drained," he said it so simply as if it was common knowledge, as if it were okay.

Della sat up to stare at him, horrified. "Max! Why didn't you say anything?"

His eyelids flickered open, the amber of his eyes like a jar of honey lit by the sun. He smiled weakly. "Like Ei was gonna let ya go summon an evil spirit on yer lonesome. Friends don' let friends summon alone, Della," he studied her face for a second, regret filling his eyes. "Ei'm fine, really."

Della didn't believe him for one second. "You are hereby banned from all ghostly interaction," she said sternly.

He rolled his eyes, then snuggled into a pillow. "Ya sound like my dad," he whispered.

"Well, then your dad is smarter than he acts," Della said with a little *humph*.

That made him smile.

"Thank you," she said after a while. "Thanks for not letting me summon something alone."

He gave a half-shrug, the dark circles under his eyes making him look skeletal. "What about *you*? How are ya doin'?"

She laid back down next to him, staring up at the ceiling. "What do you mean?"

"Ei mean, what's goin' on inside that big brain of yers?" Max corrected.

Della went quiet. She let herself forget they had a job to do for a split second. That the only reason they'd summoned anything was to solve another mystery. She swallowed hard, suddenly feeling just as drained as he looked.

"I don't know," she said wholeheartedly. "Porter seemed to scare off the ghosts, and you can't be around them—don't even fight me on that—so I don't know where to go from here."

"Being lost is my thing," Max smiled.

Della stifled a laugh. "Okay, Mars."

"Pluto," he said, saluting her weakly. He coughed a couple of times, his face twitching in pain.

"You don't look very good," Della frowned.

He opened one exhausted eye. "Meanin'?"

"If being lost is your thing, then being self-sacrificial is mine. I mean it, Max; I don't want you getting hurt. You look like death," Della said sternly.

"Right, 'cause ya've listened tuh us every time we've told ya the same," he scoffed.

"I'll take a day to rest if you do."

"Can we stay here all day, then?" Max asked. Every time he spoke, he seemed like he was slipping away. Maybe he was lightyears away in his mind. Della wished she knew.

She studied him again, taking in the patches of vitiligo on his face, the dark circles, his unruly hair, and the way his lips were set in a frown—watching him how he usually watched her. Like she was afraid he'd suddenly shatter into a thousand pieces.

"Porter said I wasn't the only one with magical issues," she said carefully.

"Consider yerself problem child number two," Max sighed. "Lemme sleep, all right? Just for ten more minutes?"

Della nodded, closing her eyes, feeling tense. She could wear herself thin all she wanted. If she got hurt or died or something happened to *her*, it wouldn't matter. If something happened to Max or Porter? She would probably go insane or worse. If she couldn't save them, she wouldn't be able to live with herself. If she was the cause of their destruction? She didn't want to imagine what she'd do.

"Max?" she asked quietly.

"Hmm?" he sighed.

"Promise me that you'll take today to rest. I mean it," her voice broke.

His eyes shot open. He lifted his head to look at her, his eyebrows furrowed deeply over his eyes. "Ya gonna talk tuh Porter about why yer fightin'?" he asked. Not the reaction she was hoping for.

"What? No, this has—"

"Then there's yer answer," he sighed, plopping his head back down.

"Max," Della said, frustrated.

Max snorted, scooching closer to her. "All right, fine. But Porter is worried about ya. Ya should at least talk tuh him. Eventually."

"And say what?"

"The truth couldn' hurt."

"The truth always hurts because that means there

was a lie that led up to it," Della said.

"No arguin' with that logic," Max chuckled.

Della glanced at him, feeling guilty about what she would say next. "We got in a fight yesterday. That's why I was upset when we got home."

"Ei figured as much." He thought for a moment, then laughed to himself. "He's downstairs makin' breakfast as we speak. Eggs, bacon, smoothie—the works. Ei even saw cookies in the oven."

"Wow, he must be really stressed out," Della winced. Coincidentally, the last time he cooked like this was when she'd passed out from a vision.

"At least it'll taste good. Glad he is the stress chef and not *you*. Ei still cannot believe ya ruined popcorn. Popcorn, Della. How do ya screw that up?" Max laughed, sitting up and stretching.

"That was one time!" she laughed, grabbing a pillow to smack him with.

"Ouch! Ouch! Ei've been wounded!" he laughed, placing a hand on his forehead. "Woe is me! Ei shall die by nightfall!"

"Don't worry, puddy cat. I wouldn't let that happen," Della smiled.

He opened his mouth to say something, his face reddening as he traced her with his eyes. He smiled mischievously.

"What?" Della laughed, flicking him playfully.

"Nothin'. Ya hungry? Ei bet he's almost done cookin' by now," Max said over his shoulder, still smiling.

Her heart sank.

No, no, no, that smile wasn't genuine. That smile was the kind you use when trying to hide all the darkness the world isn't supposed to see. A smile that meant he was lying about how he felt.

"Max?" Della asked, propping herself up on her elbows.

"Yeah?"

"Is there anything you want to talk about?"

"Me? No, love, Ei'm fine. Really. Ei swear tuh ya." He nodded almost to reassure himself of his statement. He must have noticed the worry in her face, for he stood and ruffled his hair. "Just need tuh get up and get goin'. Ei'll meet ya downstairs, all right? Get dressed?"

She nodded, watching him walk away.

A rustling to her left caught her attention. The closet on the opposite side of the room opened, revealing Cassie's face.

"Well. Wasn't that awkward?" Her tiny spitfire of a

sister sneered, shaking her head disapprovingly. "I think you need to reassess who you want to, y'know—" She made an exaggerated kissy face.

"Cassandra Lillian Coleman!" Della laughed, tossing a pillow at her. "You little creep!"

Cassie slapped the pillow away, giving Della a judgmental look. It seemed she wanted to say something but thought better of it.

"I'm borrowing your one skirt with the skulls on it. See you at breakfast." With that, she skipped out of the bedroom, leaving Della a little happier.

Or maybe it was Max who had lifted her spirits. . .

CHAPTER EIGHTEEN

Avalanche

Breakfast was filled with tired smiles and groggy conversation. Everyone was content to fall back asleep at the table until Porter mentioned his plan for the day. Cassie and Leonel were excited to play in the snow, but Max and Della were reluctant, wondering what they were getting into. Porter had planned a full-on snowball war. Not a fight. A *war*. Della was worried Max wouldn't be up to it, but he put on a brave face and quietly insisted she do the same. Porter was trying to apologize, so she might as well accept it.

Now they stood in the cold, awkwardly working up the nerve to nail each other with frozen sky tears.

"This is stupid," Max grumbled, hugging himself against the cold. Obviously, he'd changed his mind. He and Porter were bundled up so much that they looked like the snowman Leonel and Cassandra were trying to build in the distance.

Porter was beaming, kneeling in the snow a few feet away, balling fresh powder into his hands. He stood, revealing the worst snowball ever made, aiming it at Max's chest.

"Stop," Max said sourly, shoving his hands in his pockets.

Della laughed a little.

Yesterday's fight had been a bump in the road. This meant a lot to Porter. He just wanted them all to have a good time. So why not revel in Max's annoyance? What was the harm in playing along?

"Come on, Max, it'll be fun!" Sebastian said, smiling widely. He had appeared out of thin air once he finished shoveling snow, happy to join in on Porter's plan.

Porter reached back to throw the snowball.

"I will kill—" The snowball hit Max square in the shoulder. "—ya," he finished. He shut his eyes, then launched to the ground, scooping up snow. A devilish smile lit up his face.

Sebastian and Della stood back for a minute, watching them throw snowballs that shattered in midair.

They glanced at each other with knowing looks. "Amateurs," they said in snobbish tones.

Porter dodged a snowball, his face glowing from the frigid air. "Fine, show us how it's done then."

Della knelt, using her gloved hands to shape a perfect snowball. She arched back like a baseball pitcher, then threw that snowball with all her might at Porter. She struck him in the chest so hard he stumbled back, taking a moment to catch the wind that had been knocked from his lungs.

Max burst out laughing, almost in tears. While he was preoccupied, Sebastian quietly gathered a rather large handful of snow. He crept up on Max, then in one fluid motion, grabbed Max by the hood of his puffy jacket and shoved the snow down his shirt. Max yelped like a banshee, twisting around on the spot before falling to the ground.

"*EEJIT!*" he screamed at the top of his lungs.

It was Sebastian's turn to laugh. "Hey, you were the one who wasn't paying attention!"

Without warning, Porter hit him in the face with a snowball.

Della gasped. Getting hit in the face with a snowball wasn't fun. Especially when an arm like Porter's had thrown that snowball.

A moment of tense silence.

Sebastian bent over, tapping the snow out of his ear. "See, *now* it's a war," he thundered, clearing his throat. "FOR—" He paused. "FOR HOUSE BRECKENRIDGE!" he shouted.

Max screamed a battle cry, allowing Sebastian to help him up off the ground. Della imagined that if her life were a movie, what happened next would be accompanied by epic battle music. Max and Sebastian rounded on Porter, throwing snowball after snowball as fast as they could at him. Light seemed to pour down from the Heavens, guiding their projectiles towards their target. None of the snowballs missed. Not even one. Every snowflake was perfectly aimed.

Seeing as she was meant to be on Porter's side, Della realized she had to take defensive actions. She ran from the battlefield and into the garage, grabbing a long piece of PVC pipe with an oxygen tank attached to the end. She didn't know how it worked exactly, but Jasper and Leonel had made this snowball cannon last Christmas. It was bulky and loud, but the firepower was more than worth the effort of carrying and loading. She ran back to the battlefield, finding Porter cowering against the onset slew of snowballs, unable to move. She darted to the ground, made some quick snowballs, and shoved them into the cannon. Flicking the 'on' switch, Della heard the tiny motor on the cannon buzz to life. Rapid fire snowballs hit Sebastian in the back, sending him face-first into a mound of snow.

Max gasped, turning to Della. Unwavering vengeance was written all over his tired face. As Sebastian tried to remove himself from the snow, Max bent down to make a snowball, and Della tried to reload the cannon.

Just loud enough for her to hear, Max spoke a spell. "*Se' frysis.*"

A rock-solid snowball hit Della in the shoulder. She felt the pain ripple down her arm to her fingertips, feeling like she had stumbled into a concrete wall. She stopped making snowballs, clutching her arm. She swore, her fingers burning with pain. He'd hit the bruised one.

"Wait—Max! DELLA WATCH OUT!" Porter screamed as Della stood.

Just as Della looked up, Max threw a snowball at her face. It sparkled blue with the magic Max had cast, screaming imminent doom.

Della's hands shot up to protect her face. An odd feeling of familiarity filled her chest. Her mind went wild with panicked thoughts, wishing the snowball would magically transform into something other than a mystical cannonball. Maybe something a little softer. She stood waiting for impact, her mind racing, but the pain she expected to feel in her face and hands never came.

"Holy *shit*. . ." she heard Sebastian breathe.

Slowly, Della removed her hands from her face. Max was staring at her, his mouth hanging open, Sebastian looked terrified, and Porter—well, Porter was either really impressed or about to have a panic attack. It was hard to tell sometimes.

"What?" Della asked, looking at her gloved hands.

Sebastian lifted a shaking finger to point at her feet.

She looked down to see bright purple flower petals floating to the ground like a spatter of alien blood on the snow.

Sebastian jumped to his feet. "You—The—Snow—MAGIC!" he screamed, pointing at her.

Della took a step back, feeling slightly faint. "I—Seb, I can explain," she said, her voice shaking.

"How the Hell did you—"

"*RENNIM STETTE!*" Max shouted, cutting Sebastian off. A poof of black mist hit Sebastian in the back of the head. A blank, dazed expression floated over his face. "*Vi-mebes!*" Max screeched. Sebastian collapsed in a heap to the ground.

"MAX!" Porter and Della screamed, racing to Sebastian's side.

"Ei'm sorry! Ei panicked!" Max trembled. He was staring at the flower petals, his eyes wide. "How did ya do that?" he asked breathlessly.

Della ignored him, for she had no friggin idea. She'd turned a snowball the size of her hand into a pile of petals. Even by their standards, that wasn't normal.

"Seb?" she asked, patting his acne-covered face. "Seb, wake up. Sebastian Orion Breckenridge, you wake up right now!" Della pleaded, practically slapping him. Nothing.

"Is he breathin'?" Max asked.

"Luckily for you!" Porter hissed. "What the Hell did you do to him?!"

Max thought for a minute. "Sleeping spell—" He swayed and then collapsed to his knees. "Ei think Ei erased his memory," he panted, holding his head in his hands.

"Think?!" Porter hissed.

"Ei'm sorry!" Max screamed back, throwing his hands up in the air. The dark circles under his eyes were pitch black now, his eyes glowing brightly. His eyelids flickered. He was barely holding onto consciousness.

Della gasped. "Your nose."

He gave her a questioning look, then reached up to wipe his nose, leaving behind a thick, dark blood trail. He gagged, wiping his hands on his pants. "Ei'm gonna be sick," he whispered, then lurched sideways into the snow.

Della screamed, leaving Sebastian and Porter behind to run to his side. She took his head into her hands, watching in horror as his eyes rolled back into his head. "Hey, hey, look at me! Max!"

He cried out in pain, gripping her arm tightly. "It'll—pass! It'll pass!" he choked out, arching up in the snow, blood pouring from his nose.

Della looked to Porter. He shook his head angrily, still trying to shake Sebastian awake.

Max took in a sharp breath, his body going limp as he let go of Della. He was panting heavily, staring at the sky with glassy eyes, and muttering incoherently. Della was sure she heard a few swear words.

Wincing, he sat up. "*Fińń boken,*" he coughed, holding out his hands. Della's heart stopped as a familiar tome appeared in his hands.

"Why—How do you have that?" she asked shakily.

Max flashed her a warning look, ignoring the question. He flipped through the pages of the same spellbook Eric Steiniger had used to conjure the Grunches. The book Eric had used to kill Theodore and kidnap children. The book that Della wished never to see again.

Max stopped flipping through the pages, pointing to something. "*Uakopp*," he said breathlessly, pointing a finger at Sebastian, then slumped against Della, breathing heavily. She held him tight, his cheek hot against her shoulder as if he had a fever.

Sebastian's eyelids flickered. He grumbled something under his breath. "What happened. . . ?" he asked, struggling to sit up.

Max hid the spellbook behind his back. Della saw his lips move out of the corner of her eye, and the book disappeared.

"Della got you in the head with that snowball cannon," Porter lied. "You went down."

Sebastian rubbed his forehead, nodding, trying to convince himself of something.

Porter stood, dragging him to his feet. "Come on, let's get you inside," he said, giving the evil eye to Max, looking at the twins who were only a few feet away. "Leo! Cassie! How about some hot cocoa?" Thankfully, they hadn't been paying attention to them. Or if they had, they didn't seem to care.

Max tried to stand and follow them all inside but couldn't, barely strong enough to keep upright. He stared at Della, his tired eyes full of regret. "Mavericks said—Ei—"

"Why," Della began, trying to keep her voice calm. "Why do you have that damn book?" she demanded, unable to hide the fear in her heart.

Max opened and closed his mouth several times. "It's just a book," he said weakly.

"It's not just a book!" Della whispered angrily, grabbing him by the shoulders, trying to shake some sense into him. "You know what Nicoletta and the other witches said about it! Look what it did to Eric! Look what it did to Jimmy and Theodore! They were terrified of that thing, Max! Mavericks wanted it locked up! We have no idea what's inside it! Spells in that book summon demons. Who knows what else?"

"Not all the spells are bad. Some of them are healing spells. The book isn't evil; the people who have used it are," he said simply, back to leaning against her for support, using his sleeve to dab away the dark blood pouring from his nose. "Not me, though," he added quickly.

"Max!" Della hissed, unable to believe what she was hearing. "Look at you! I haven't seen you like this in forever."

She had sat in on many of his and Nicoletta's training sessions, and one thing always stood out to her. Nicoletta said that magic corrupts people who aren't careful with it. Della had a sneaking suspicion that Max could fall into that category if he didn't heed the warnings of those who knew better than them.

"Ei'll be careful!" Max tried to assure her, his voice small.

Della took in a shaking breath. "I can't lose you," she blurted out. He gave her a funny look at that. "I just can't."

"Yer not—Della," he said, smiling softly. "Yer not gonna lose me," He thought momentarily, avoiding her eyes. "Mavericks said Ei could use it. That Ei could study it. It's not just a spellbook."

"What do you mean?"

"It's an entire encyclopedia of magic, Della. Everythin' from stories about the Loch Ness Monster tuh the Faye Folk. Everthin'. There's stuff on familiars in there, stuff on Ahools, stuff on. . . stuff that sounds like it could be *you*, now that Ei think of it," he whispered that last part. "Ei don' think this book was somethin' Eric took from Theo and Jim. This is different."

"Great," Della breathed. "That's just great." She knew that everything would tie in eventually, but she had sincerely hoped it would've taken longer to come up.

"Ei promise Ei'll be careful with it, but Ei think we'd be fools tuh let it leave our sight," he finally pushed himself away from her, pinching the bridge of his nose. "Somethin' bigger is at play here, Ei can feel it." He angrily waved his hand through the air, his face set in frustration. "Dad has been actin' off for weeks. He knows it, too."

Della sighed heavily, wishing she could convince him otherwise. When Max set his mind to something, there was no stopping. And deep down, she knew that book was important. That one of these days, they would need a spell from it.

"Fine. Just—Just don't bring this up to Porter; you know he gets nervous when we talk about this stuff," she snapped.

"Let the ostrich bury his head in the sand? Fine by me," Max snapped.

Della rolled her eyes, begrudgingly heaving herself off the ground, offering him a hand up. He ignored her, struggling to get to his feet, brushing the snow off his pants. Della couldn't help but give him a judgmental look. There was reckless, and then there was stupid. Max so happened to be acting like the latter.

"We should go inside. It's cold," Max grumbled, nodding towards the house.

White-hot pain rippled through Della's brain.

Max turned back, opening his mouth to say something, but Della didn't hear him.

She was too busy staring at the red mark erupting from his throat. It took her a minute to realize what was happening, but when she did, she choked out a whimper, lunging at him, clamping her hands around his throat. Somehow his throat had been slit. Was this a consequence of his powers?

Max tried to push her away. "What the Hell are ya doin'?" he screeched as Della frantically tried to stop his blood from pouring onto the snow beneath them.

She tried to speak, to scream, to call for help, but she couldn't. She was frozen in fear, watching his blood spill through her fingers. His blood was so dark, it was almost black. Della looked up at Max, her fear turning to all-consuming terror. His dark skin had gone gray, all his veins stark black, his amber eyes completely white.

A demonic voice entered her mind. *That's what will happen to them*, it said.

That's what Mavericks thinks is going to happen. That everyone he loves—everyone she loves—is going to die. And she was sitting here, having a snowball fight like a child. She shut her eyes as tightly as possible, pushing that voice away.

Her stomach churned as it dawned on her. This was just another hallucination.

"Della!" Max shouted, shoving her away, gripping her by the wrists. He shook her gently. "What's wrong?"

She dared to open one of her eyes to find he was fine. No black veins.

No gash on his throat.

No empty white eyes.

Sure, he still looked weak from the spells he had cast, but now the only thing odd about him was the look of worry clouding his handsome features. "What's wrong?" he repeated.

Della finally found her voice as she looked down at her hands—no trace of blood. "I—I—Nothing," she lied, shaking away the foreboding feeling that was building inside her chest.

Max raised his eyebrows. "Y—Ya just grabbed me by the throat looking like ya'd seen a. . . ghost." His eyes widened. "Vision?" he asked, his voice dark.

Della stared at him for a minute. Should she tell him what she had seen? That she had just hallucinated him bleeding out, looking like death reincarnated? She knew that if she saw something, it was bound to come true. This wasn't the first time she had hallucinated something, but could she tell him?

She swallowed hard, pulling away. "It's nothing, I—I—Sorry."

Max looked like he was going to have a stroke. "If that's nothin', then Ei have more than a few concerns."

She couldn't do anything but look away, glancing at the petals in the snow a few feet away. Again, she thought they looked like mystical blood spatter. She cleared her throat, still refusing to look at him, afraid her brain would make her see him lying on the ground dead.

He sighed heavily. He wanted to say something, but whatever was on his mind, he must've thought it unimportant. "Ya sure?"

All she did was nod. Della stared at her hands. Seconds ago, she had thought they were covered in his blood. If that had been real—if she'd lost him—

She could barely stop herself from letting out a broken sob.

"You just looked like you were going to pass out like last night," Della shrugged, her voice broken.

Her hands shook, her body tense, waiting for something to happen.

He gave her a questioning look, looking her up and down, scrutinizing her, but eventually, he nodded.

Then he did something surprising.

He pulled her into a hug.

"Ei'm not goin' anywhere—Ei promise. Ei'm okay now," he whispered against her temple.

A small cry escaped Della's throat as she wrapped her arms around him, burying her face in the crook of his neck. He placed his chin on top of her head, squeezing her tightly.

They stayed like that for a while. Della wondered if he was listening to her heartbeat like she was listening to his. Did he need the same reassurance? Did he need to know that both of them were still alive? That Death hadn't caught up to them just yet?

Slowly, Della peeled away from him, wiping away one of her tears with her thumb, searching his eyes. His eyebrows were furrowed over his striking amber eyes, which were even more enchanting in the morning light.

"Let's go in and take that rest day ya talked about," he said softly, disconnecting from her and turning away.

She yanked his hand back, startling him.

Her foot was tapping the ground nervously as he

turned back to her, a questioning tilt to his head. No part of her wanted to let go of his hand.

Something had been weighing very heavily on her the last couple of days. Maybe it was time to bring it up.

"You died, Max. I saw you die," she said quietly.

Max inhaled deeply, running his free hand through his hair, avoiding her eyes. "Ei know."

"No, you don't," Della said desperately. "Eric killed you, and I had to watch. I don't care if you have extra lives. I don't care if Necromancers exist. I don't care if Fate is in our favor. I don't want to see you die again. Even if I know you'll return to me—I mean *us*—in minutes!"

His eyes trailed up to meet hers. "Yer not gonna lose me, Delphee."

"You can't be sure of that!"

Something clicked for him at that moment. "Yer right. But whatever happens—good or bad—we are all gonna get through this."

Della finally dropped his hand, hugging herself tightly. She shook her head in disbelief.

"Della," Max said with a sigh. "Love, please look at me."

She shook her head.

He lifted her chin with a shaking finger. His eyes were full of fire. "Ei am never gonna let anythin' happen tuh ya. Never. And if my well bein' is the thing that keeps ya happy, then ya have no need tuh worry."

Della just stared at him, sickened by the intensity on his face.

Nicoletta said she was a Seer. Seers were supposed to see the future, yet all she'd seen thus far were lousy riddles and broken truths. But what she'd seen today could only be interpreted one way: Max would die. Sooner or later. And while everyone died eventually, she knew this would be different. She felt it so deeply, as if that truth had been planted inside her since birth. The same way she knew some of her other visions hadn't passed but would one day. The only issue was that she had no idea whether she could stop them.

Max grabbed her hand, pulling her toward the house. "We are gonna go inside, get warmed up, and take a well-deserved day of rest, all right?"

She nodded glumly, gripping his hand tightly as he pulled her along.

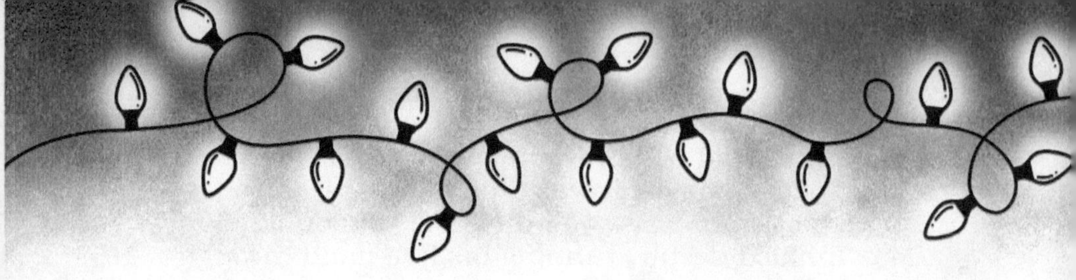

CHAPTER NINETEEN

It was a quiet afternoon in the Coleman household. Porter had his nose in a book, and Sebastian was sprawled out on the couch watching the cheesy Christmas movie Kimi had put on. Jasper was in an old recliner, reading his Bible. Della was typing away on her computer at the kitchen table next to Max, who was half asleep, quietly watching her work. Occasionally, he'd whisper something that she'd shake her head vigorously at, shushing him. He'd sigh heavily, but it seemed he ultimately agreed with her every time.

Porter tried his best to ignore them, trying to focus on the vampire novel Sebastian had found in the garage. The pages were marked with green highlighter, and extensive notes were written in the margins. Della sure had a lot to say, even about the most mundane passages.

Jasper also seemed to be having a hard time focusing on his reading. He glanced over at Porter, giving him a questioning look before turning the yellowed pages of his Bible. Porter wondered what he was thinking. He almost wanted to ask.

"Aww, look at this one! Leo and Cassie look so little!" Kimi exclaimed, handing a photo over to Jasper. She'd been sitting on the floor looking through all the old photo albums Sebastian and Max had brought in.

Jasper leaned forward to grab it, smiling kindly. "When was that? Wow, four years ago," he whispered, looking at the back.

Porter smiled to himself, looking over his shoulder to see Max scribbling away in a notebook. He seemed rather tense. Porter wished he knew what had the two of them so engrossed in their work.

Jasper handed the picture back to Kimi, returning to

his Bible. Porter followed suit, taking one last look at Della, who was running her hands through her hair repeatedly, shaking her head again. He sighed. Whatever they were so upset over obviously wasn't important enough to include him. Part of him was relieved by that, though a bigger part was hurt.

Twice now, they'd excluded him. If that's the game they wanted to play, so be it. He'd ignore them just as they were ignoring him.

If he tried hard enough, he could lose himself in a book and not find his way out for hours.

Plus, this was one of his favorites. He had read it a thousand times before but found something new every time. The main character was a cop, and with the help of her missing daughter's vampire boyfriend, they solved murders while trying to solve her daughter's disappearance. Due to the notes in the margins, Della seemed to think that the vampire boyfriend was an idiot. Porter thought he was charming. He'd have to bring this up to her. He knew she'd love to have a good debate over this sort of thing.

Kimi gasped, cutting into one of Porter's favorite parts in the entire *Vanish and Despair* series. The part where Officer Jupiter finally found out that Sigmund—the vampire boyfriend—was, in fact, a vampire. He looked up, slightly irritated he would have to reread the whole thing. Kimi was holding up a picture, frantically searching through the rest of the photo album.

"Did you find that picture Kohen and I took on Valentine's the year we got married?" Jasper laughed.

"No, I found one of Della and my mom," Kimi said, handing the picture over, her hands shaking.

At first, Jasper's lips pulled into a thin, sad smile. He looked over the picture, holding it close to his face, his smile widening. But then, he paled, his smile disappearing in an instant. He rubbed his eyes, then looked closer at the picture, seeming to see something he wished he hadn't.

Porter glanced over at the kitchen table to see Della had turned, a look of mild curiosity spreading across her features. "What kind of picture with grandma?" she asked.

Max swiveled in his chair, yawning. "And why do ya sound so alarmed?"

Jasper cleared his throat, handing the picture back to Kimi. He fumbled over his words, nothing but strangled noises coming out.

"It's just damaged. Looks like we have a leak in the garage. You know how much he hates housework," Kimi said as smoothly as she could.

Della hesitated, looking back and forth between her

parents. "Can I see it, though?" she asked slowly.

Kimi straightened, clearing her throat. "You seem busy. I'll put it to the side for later, okay?"

Della's eyes narrowed. Something was floating in her gaze that Porter couldn't quite pin. The only way he could describe it was some sort of primordial rage. The kind an old, scorned god would have if they knew how few people believed in them nowadays.

"I'm not that busy," Della said flatly.

"Honestly, Della, it's not worth it. It's so damaged you can barely make it out," Jasper sighed, closing his Bible. "I'll talk to some guys at the Church about fixing the roof while I help set things up for service tomorrow. Speaking of, I'm going to be late."

He stood and stretched, making a face at Kimi. She swallowed hard, avoiding Porter's gaze.

"If it's so messed up, how do you know it was me and grandma?" Della asked, that ancient rage turning to fire in her eyes.

Max looked alarmed, slapping his hand down on the table to catch a pen from falling. Was the table shaking, or was that just Porter's imagination?

Jasper's shoulders sagged. "You really don't know when to give up, do you?" he asked as he turned to her, hands on his hips, scrutinizing her.

Della stared him down, eyes twitching ever so slightly. She looked like a pot ready to boil over.

Now, of course, Porter knew his girlfriend had a very fragile temper, but this was something else. He'd never seen her like this before. It scared him. Even the way that there was something so obviously protective to the way she stayed seated, to the way she chose her words as carefully as she could.

"Fine. I just wanted to look at the stupid photo. Didn't realize that was such a crime," she mumbled, turning back to Max as a glass of water spilled, startling him. He scrambled to clean everything up before it reached her laptop or notebooks, all the while whispering rather aggressively.

"I seriously have no idea where we went wrong to raise a woman who thinks it is okay to disrespect her parents like that," Jasper snapped. "Well, actually, I do know where we went wrong. Can name the date."

Della went stiff.

Jasper smiled crookedly. "Got nothing to say to that, do you?"

Della glared at him over her shoulder. "Didn't you say you had to leave?"

Jasper shrugged. "Well, now I'm debating staying to continue this lively conversation. But unfortunately, you are correct. Try not to bother your mother too much, okay? I heard about your little stunt at the historical society."

"Jasper," Kimi said, eyes wide.

Della rolled her eyes, returning to her pile of notebooks and her laptop. And to Max, who was holding dripping wet paper towels as far away from everything as he could.

Jasper left with a sinister smile on his face.

When the front door clicked shut, and they heard Jasper's car pull out of the driveway, Della turned to Kimi.

"Thanks for that," she hissed.

Kimi sighed heavily. "He's my husband, Della. I tell him everything."

"Yeah, well, you never used to," Della whispered, standing.

"And yet I never got any thanks then," Kimi breathed.

Della gave her a lazy look. "Whatever," She collected her things, rolling her eyes at Max as he asked if she would help clean up her mess. "I've got things to do."

"Della," Porter and Max pleaded.

She glared at them, shoving her laptop into her book bag. "What now?"

"Don' go," Max sighed, nodding at Porter behind her back as if to say he had to fix this.

Della ignored him, stomping towards the front door.

"What do you want me to do?" Porter whispered.

"Talk tuh her!" Max snapped.

"You do it! I don't want to lose my head!" Porter snapped, crossing the room, ignoring Kimi and Sebastian, who were watching them intently.

"Yeah, well, Ei already had to clean up spilled water. Ei'm lucky she didn' break the glass," Max hissed.

"I was worried you were going to say that," Porter sighed.

"I need your keys!" Della called from the entryway.

Porter pinched the bridge of his nose, sulking into the entryway, tossing her the keys to the hearse. "You okay?" he asked, leaning on the wall, fiddling with a loose thread on a jacket hanging next to him.

Della was sitting on the floor, struggling to pull on a pair of snow boots. "Oh yeah, just fine. My favorite thing in the whole wide world is hearing how my dad wishes I was never born."

"He didn't say that," Porter sighed, kneeling to tie her shoelaces after she gave up. Her hands shook violently, so she couldn't even form a simple loop.

"Yeah, well, he implied it," Della whispered, rolling her eyes.

Porter sat beside her, pulling his knees to his chest, studying her. "You two don't get along, huh?"

"Very perceptive, Garroway."

"Hey, don't be like that, okay? Don't take it out on me. I'm just trying to help," he said softly yet sternly. He leaned forward and planted a kiss on her forehead, lingering for a second.

"I'm not trying to. I'm sorry," she whispered.

"All is forgiven," Porter smiled, nudging her legs gently. "What had you and Max so upset?"

Della stared blankly at his eyes, his lips pulling into a frown. "It's not important," she said as she turned away.

Porter shook his head, feeling like she'd betrayed him somehow.

He knew they would've filled him in if he hadn't gone after them last night. He trusted her enough to believe that. So why wasn't she doing such now? He desperately hoped the only reason was her being too upset to talk.

He cleared his throat, not wanting to add to her emotional turmoil. "Where are you running to today?"

"I just want out of this stupid place. I'm at my wit's end with everything. I'm tired and cold and just want to go home." Her face reddened. It didn't seem like she meant to say that out loud.

"You are home," Porter laughed.

Della's face was empty as she stared off into space. "Porter, this was never my home," she said sullenly.

With that, she stood, roughly pulling her jacket from its hanger.

Porter stood as well, unease sliding over him like rainfall. "Seriously, are you okay?"

She nodded. "Yup. I'll see you later, okay?"

He gave a weak thumbs up as she opened the door and left. He stayed in the entry for a while before finally gathering enough courage to face Max, Kimi, and Sebastian.

"Well?" Max asked.

Porter shrugged. "She's in a mood."

Max grumbled, putting his forehead on the table and sighing so deeply that Porter thought his lungs would deflate.

"Are *you* okay?" he asked.

Max groaned something that vaguely sounded like yes, but Porter wasn't exactly sure it was a word at all.

"Okay then. . ." Porter blinked a few times, returning to his place on the couch and picking up his book again.

Kimi looked up from squinting at a photograph. She cleared her throat, putting it aside, locking eyes with Porter as he tried to get comfortable.

"Crisis averted?" she asked.

He shrugged. "I did what I could. You should talk to her when she gets home, though I don't think she's too happy with either of you right now."

"Story of our life," Kimi sighed.

He gave her a disappointed look but left it at that. He didn't want to be the cause of any more problems.

Kimi thought for a moment, then stood and handed him an album.

"Just in case she made you believe otherwise, this is proof we love her. Both of us," she said dryly, then returned to her place on the floor.

The entire book was filled with colorful family pictures. There was a picture of a young Della with flowers in her hair at a fair, one where she was sitting on a bench with Mingan, one with her holding a debate trophy, an irritated look on her face. Porter smiled. There were so many of her but not many of the twins. He wondered what Della would think if she knew that. Maybe she did. Maybe she didn't care.

"You know, I think you should be showing *her* this, not me," Porter said after a while.

Kimi laughed darkly. "Doubt she'd give me the time of day,"

"Jasper should have just let her see the pic with her grandma," Sebastian yawned. "You know how happy that would have made her."

Kimi went frigid.

Della and Max were starting to rub off on him. The only thing he could imagine justifiable for not showing her that picture was something she wasn't meant to see had been captured.

"Can I see it? Maybe she'll believe it's just a boring old memory if it comes from me," Porter laughed, holding out his hand expectantly.

Sebastian eyed him skeptically as Kimi inhaled sharply, nodding reluctantly. She grabbed the picture, held it firmly between two fingers, showed him for half a second, then put it away. The movement had been so fast that Porter wasn't even sure the picture was damaged or who was in it. Porter wanted to believe that Kimi was just irritated none of them took her word as the truth, but she'd obviously done all this to hide something deliberately.

"Enlightenin'," Max said from the table. Porter raised an eyebrow at him, which was returned with a blank stare.

"I honestly don't know what you kids want from us," Kimi sighed, cleaning up the mess of photos scattered across the floor.

Sebastian slid off the couch to help, ignoring Kimi when she repeatedly said she could do it herself. Porter glanced at Max, who had a knowing look on his face.

Something was up. And Porter had a pretty good idea what the problem was.

But this was a problem he couldn't fix alone, and now was not the time to bring it up to Max. So, instead, he opened his book and settled onto the couch for a long day of reading and contemplation.

Oh, how he loved books. At least he knew the problems in them would eventually be solved.

Unlike his life, which seemed to have a million plot holes everywhere he looked.

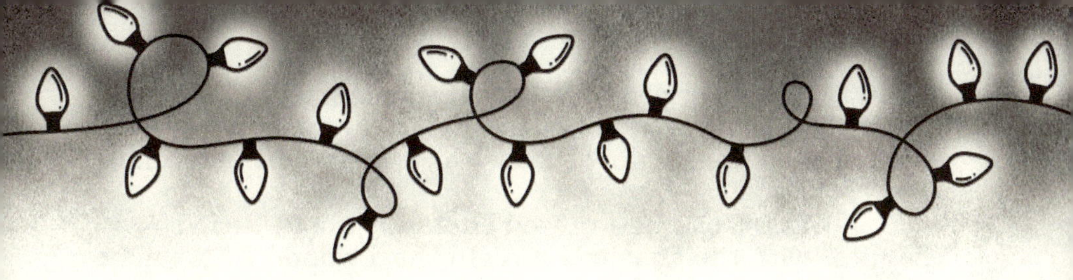

CHAPTER TWENTY

A Theory of His Own

It took every ounce of Max's paper-thin patience to keep himself from chewing out Porter and Kimi. He'd made up his mind that he did not care for Kimi in the slightest. And Jasper? That horrible man made him want to grab one of Kimi's fancy non-stick frying pans and smack him as hard as possible.

He sighed heavily, returning to the notebook Della had lent him. In it, he'd scribbled away a list of all the possible creatures, entities, or beings Della could be. A separate list noted what abilities she did or could have. He'd been compiling and comparing notes like this for a solid month. So far, he'd barely narrowed things down.

He'd considered bringing her in on this little project to distract her from her mounting problems, but now he was glad he'd kept it to himself. She didn't need him filling her head with self-doubt, for he was sure she was not a witch or a simple Seer. Seers don't shake tables out of anger. And most witches don't have unaided future sight.

He'd consulted the spellbook everyone seemed terrified of, but it'd only raised more questions.

Mystical encyclopedias were like that.

Everything from how it felt in his hands to how unknown words translated for him was strange. When he held it, it pulsed like it had a living heartbeat. He could feel the magic resonating off it. It was spelled—or rather hexed—in some way, for better or worse. Della was right to be worried about what he may find between its pages, but it wasn't like he would try every spell in the book. All he wanted was to make sure they knew what it was. If Mavericks and the Weeping Crow witches feared it, there had to be something more to it.

Max wasn't entirely sure Mavericks didn't already

know who it belonged to or why it was created.

But those were all questions for another time. Why Max needed the spellbook now was a more pertinent matter.

While Della had ranted endlessly about their encounter with the ghosts last night, he'd wondered how she'd turned that snowball into flower petals. It could be a sign of alchemy, but that would cancel out all her other powers. Alchemists normally don't have dual abilities.

Why could she suddenly do something like this? Were her powers growing?

He'd gotten to thinking about various things the last couple of weeks. At first, he thought she could be a kinetic, a mutated string of witches with element-specific powers. That theory had quickly fizzled out. It wouldn't explain how she had used a spell to kill Eric Steiniger or today's events.

Sometimes, the only plausible explanation was that she was the last of an unrecorded species.

She didn't fit any typical mystical category, which worried him.

Max and every other witch worldwide had been taught that there are three archetypes of magic: physical, spiritual, and mental.

Physical magic consisted of practices such as alchemy, the act of transformation, or the art of potion-making. Being a familiar meant Max had physical magic in order to turn into a cat. Even sorcery fell into this camp. In most ways, physical magic was the 'science' of magic.

Spiritual magic was trusting that something would happen based on pure will or with the help of a higher power. The Universe, God, whatever you believe in. Some could argue and say prayer is a form of spiritual magic.

Mental magic contained telepathy, telekinesis, some kinds of divination—any magic that required pure brainpower.

Witchcraft was tricky since it could require all three at any given moment. With witchcraft, you would need to reach out to the Universe, call on your own strength, and sometimes use what was around you.

Max had always been confused by this, but he understood that everyone fit into a category. Those similar to werewolves, vampires—even Porter—were all in the physical magic community. People like witches, Seers, and voodoo practitioners were all spiritual. Diviners and mind readers were categorized as mental. Even—

Max's mind circled back to diviners. There were too many kinds of divination to count. He'd never gotten the hang of runes or tarot, and he was abysmal regarding tea leaves.

But he did know someone who'd had infinitely better luck. He also knew she may be good at another kind of divination.

Looks like he was going to have to add another burden to Della's plate after all.

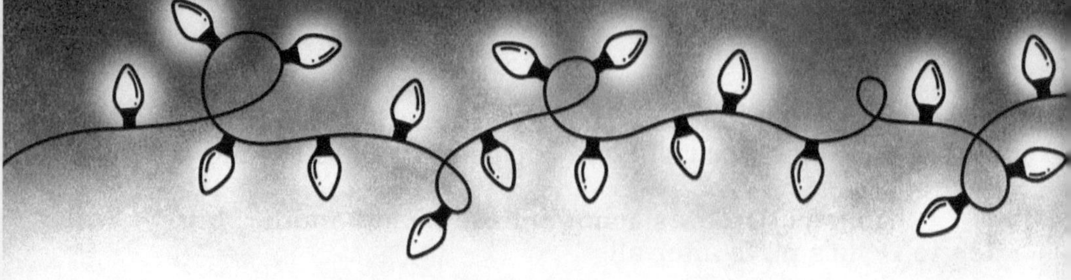

CHAPTER TWENTY-ONE

You Could Say She Puts the
'Sin' in Sincliar

Thoroughly shaken by everything that had happened the last couple of days—and fighting off a headache—Della drove the rusty old hearse into town with a vague idea of where she wanted to go.

They'd arrived late on Thursday, and now it was Saturday morning. Everything that had happened over the last two and a half days felt like it had unfolded over a month.

Her brain felt jumbled. Even if she tried to arrange her thoughts into something feasible, all she could see was Max looking like a ghost or his blood on her hands. So, instead, she turned the radio up so loud she couldn't hear herself think. Exactly how she liked it. The only time her thoughts slipped through was when the music stopped and made way for ads about Christmas tree farms and department store sales. Even those things set her on edge. Most people were counting down the days to Christmas like that special day would melt away all the problems the year had brought, but Della was looking at it like it was her funeral.

To top it all off, driving through Sycamore Heights alone made her realize how unfit she'd been to handle this Godforsaken town.

Or rather, how unfit it was to handle her.

Della had never liked the word ordinary. Ordinary implied that an object or being was just like the rest. Never changing. Never growing. Never differing. The town of Sycamore Heights was ordinary. Somehow, that made her skin crawl. It made her second-guess everything. Nothing was ever truly normal, right? Normalcy was a lie. This made her paranoid, more so than usual, which was hard to admit.

Driving up to what was now Sinclair Credit Union sent her spiraling. She couldn't help but wonder why the bank had been built like an homage to ancient Greece with its towering pillars and shining golden sign. That brought to mind Greek mythology—something she knew no one in this town approved of—and her favorite myth, the story of Medusa. The monster everyone blamed for unspeakable horrors. But it'd been Athena who had turned her into a gorgon when she really should have punished Poseidon. *Athena* had made her turn people to stone. She'd punished Medusa for something someone more powerful had done.

Della felt sorry for the gorgon. She'd always felt an affinity to her story. Especially now, staring at the bank, her mind plagued with all the horrors done unto her.

How could her father be so cruel? Why couldn't he be like Mavericks? Why did he have to say those things?

And why was Kimi defending him all of a sudden? What had changed in her short absence?

If she didn't force herself out of the hearse, she knew she'd sit there all day wallowing in sorrow. But that was a luxury for another time. Today, she had work to do. So, instead of scrutinizing herself, Della decided to scrutinize someone else.

At least the Universe had placed a lead in her lap.

Elvi Sinclair.

Sweeps into town. Her family buys the bank. Convinces the mayor to sell an integral part of the community to someone who doesn't know a thing about the town. Knew Ashton.

Elvi Sinclair: suspect.

Della dusted herself off as she dragged herself out of the hearse, wondering what mystery she may find inside the old bank. Its pillars towered above her, casting her in shadow. The sidewalk around it was cleared of snow, though the same could not be said about the other businesses nearby. If anyone needed proof that the residents here cared deeply about money, this would be it.

What once read Sycamore Heights Bank on a flashy sign above the door now read Sinclair Credit Union in a simple script. Della looked down at the business card Elvi had given her, then back at the sign. Sinclair Credit Union sounded like the name of a fictional bank in a poorly written novel where the author couldn't think of a witty title.

A sinking feeling erupted in her chest as her chunky teal boots marched down the sidewalk.

Poorly written novels always had the most obvious and lethal villains.

The looks she got as she entered the bank were some of the funniest Della had ever received. She'd forgotten how much she loathed seeing people wrinkle their noses and roll their eyes in her direction. In Moss Hollow, she blended in.

True, she was a freak, but freaks were welcomed there. By that logic, she could justify thinking the townsfolk of Sycamore Heights were freaks, and she was the normal one. Now, that was an idea she could get behind. Perhaps normalcy wasn't a lie. Maybe it was just relative.

She smirked at the thought, holding her head high. Della wasn't going to let anyone else bother her today. Not her parents, not her old classmates, and not Porter. This wasn't the first time she had bent this town to her will, and it wouldn't be the last. It was time to work her true magic.

"Good morning, ma'am," Della said kindly to the teller before her.

The woman looked up from the check she was looking over, took one look at her, and reached for the dial-up phone to her right.

Della's eyes flickered with frustration. She faked a smile, her eyes lifeless. "If I wanted to rob you, I would have at least brought a taser," she said, putting up her hands to show she wasn't armed.

The woman hesitated but ultimately moved her hand away from the phone. "Welcome to Syca—I mean Sinclair Credit Union. How may I help you?"

Della leaned on the counter, one hand in her pocket, the other flashing Elvi's business card. "I'm looking for Elvi Sinclair."

The woman nodded, pointing down a hallway. Della thanked her, then made her way down the hall. Nothing had changed except the names next to the doors and a new color palette. Everything was now gray and taupe, not gray and beige. Della couldn't help but roll her eyes as she sauntered down the corridor, finally finding the door that read 'Elvi Sinclair' in a flowery script. She knocked a few times, half expecting to be ignored.

Muffled voices ceased their conversation at the sound of her knock. There was a clicking of heels, then an exasperated sigh before the door opened. Della peered behind Elvi, watching a door to her left swing shut. From her angle, she couldn't make out any of the features of whoever had left, but the footsteps were heavy. Most likely a man. Cologne wafted into her nose, reminiscent of what her Grandpa Victor always wore. How strange.

"I wasn't aware you were on my itinerary," Elvi said, angrily adjusting her pearl-adorned powder blue cardigan.

Della shrugged. "I thought I'd pop in," she said in her sweetest tone.

Elvi smiled tightly. "What a pleasure. Make this quick; I have things to take care of."

Della stared at her, eyebrows together. Elvi returned

her scrutinizing gaze as she held the door open, sweeping her inside her expensively decorated office. It was odd how such a clean, open space felt so suffocating. In Mavericks' cluttered office, she felt at ease. Here, she felt like she'd been put on a pedestal for all to see.

Della followed Elvi inside, standing tall, her chin high to assert dominance. Though in actuality, Della knew she was much farther down the food chain than Elvi had ever been.

"I must admit, I wasn't expecting to hear from you so soon. Has something come up with Mayor Hawthorne?" Elvi asked.

"Actually, I was hoping to talk to you about something else," Della said flatly.

Elvi patted a chair before her desk as she walked over to her own. Her long fingers traced the back of it, her nails scraping the fabric, the sound echoing strangely. "Interesting. Why?" she asked, reaching for the pearls around her neck. This seemed to be her nervous tick. Della watched with curiosity as she spun a pearl between her fingers.

The pearl was a symbol of purity. Incorruptibility. Perfection. Spirituality, even. Yet, as Elvi fiddled with her jewelry, it was clear the opposite was true. Tainted was the word that came to mind. This woman lived and breathed lies. Della would have to remember that.

"I'm sure my mother has already informed you I work for a paper in Louisiana?" Della prompted, sitting tall in her chair, ankles crossed. Just a few months ago, she'd been sitting the same way in another part of town. An innocence she'd felt back then was absent now.

Elvi nodded. "The Moss Hollow Tribune, was it?"

Della loved how quickly a lie could travel when it was in her favor. Of course, she *didn't* work there. Who would ever work at such a boring place? But it was good that Elvi already had a name to go by.

"Correct. Contrary to what you have been told, I am not here for the holidays. I am here strictly for business matters," Elvi seemed mildly intrigued by this. Della took that as her cue to continue speaking. "Our paper reports on stories from across the country. We specialize in small-town mysteries. Readers love that sort of thing. I'm looking into the recent disappearance of Sycamore Heights resident Ashton John. If you don't mind, I have a few questions."

"You are a field reporter?" Elvi asked, almost to clarify, though Della wondered why she needed to do so. Maybe she was just being snide.

"Yes, ma'am," Della nodded. "I grew up here. That's

why I was sent back. I have connections my colleagues wouldn't. I'm just trying to do my civic duty," It pained her to acknowledge that as the truth. Della had always believed that if you had the resources to help, it was your job to do so. Even if you wished it weren't true.

"Well. . . I'm always willing to help a woman on a mission," Elvi smiled. She sat like a Queen on a golden throne, watching Della suspiciously, like she knew the peasant before her had plans to overthrow her kingdom. She gestured for Della to ask her questions.

"Did you know Ashton?" Della began, listening to Elvi intently and watching for tells and ticks, trying to figure her out. She didn't seem tense in the slightest. She seemed bored. Still, Della knew she'd catch Elvi in one of her lies sooner or later.

"On the many occasions I went to talk to your mother and Mayor Hawthorne, I spoke with him. He was just about as willing to give up the place as everyone else," Elvi said.

"Would you say you had problems with him?"

Elvi shook her head. "He was a nice enough guy, though I've heard the stories. I've heard *all* the stories." The way she articulated those words made Della uncomfortable.

"Would you mind elaborating?"

The Queen shifted upon her throne. "Why do I get the sense you're looking for a reason to blame me for his disappearance?"

"Because I know this town. I know these people. They're all bark, no bite. I start with the unknown. It's what I'm best at." That was about as truthful as Della would ever be.

Elvi scowled, staring her down. After a while, she leaned forward in her seat, tilting her head to the side. "I thought you were a hobbyist at best, but now I see you've got the skills of a true detective. A shame you're wasting those skills in such a Podunk town like Moss Hollow," she said, her voice even more condescending than it usually was.

Della scowled back. "It's a shame you've had to play dress up to fit in here," Della shot back. Elvi's eyes lit up in surprise. "Costume jewelry. Cheap heels. Thrift store cardigan. How regal."

"Miss Coleman, look at where I work, look at my job. I know when, where, and how to save my money."

"Or you don't have money to blow on such feeble things yet still need to keep up appearances," Della smiled.

Elvi rolled her eyes. "As if you didn't get that ugly pair of boots from a garage sale. Or better yet, a dumpster," she snapped, gasping dramatically.

"I don't like you," Della said coolly, sitting back in her chair, letting her professionalism slip away. She sat with her ankle resting on her knee, her fingers tented under her chin as she tried to deduce everything about Elvi. There was something off about her. Something she couldn't pin.

"Rest assured, the feeling is mutual," Elvi laughed.

Della glared at her, deciding it was time to throw caution to the wind. "Back to Ashton. Any weird behavior?"

"He was a recovering addict, Miss Coleman. The way he acted was far from normal." Elvi allowed herself to laugh again. "Can you elaborate on what sort of strange behavior I should have picked up on? Not everyone is a mind reader like you seem to be."

"Did he seem jumpy? Did he ever give you any reason to think he wasn't safe?" Della asked, yawning.

"Our conversations never went beyond the fact that I was interested in buying the historical society. Which he hated my guts for," Elvi assured her.

She was just as intent on watching Della as Della was her. Her eyes kept tracing her figure, lingering on the dyed ends of her hair poking out from her high ponytail. Sure, Della was an impeccable liar, but she wore her heart on her sleeves even if she was bending the truth. She wondered what Elvi saw. Did she see a formidable opponent? Or did she see a girl whose curiosity would get her killed?

"See, every time I think I want to believe you, I can't help but think you're lying to me," Della said haughtily. "Want to tell me why that is?"

Elvi was silent.

Della leaned forward, reaching for the brass plaque on her desk. She ran her fingers over the engraved metal, leaving behind oily smudges. "I think you know something."

"What exactly are you suggesting? That Ashton had something I wanted? That he ticked me off, so I did something to him? That maybe he knew something he shouldn't have? That I took matters into my own hands for whatever reason?"

"You tell me."

Elvi squinted at her as Della tossed the plaque back and forth between her fingers. This seemed to irritate her, which was precisely what Della wanted.

"I think we're done here, Miss Coleman," she finally said, quickly standing and straightening out her pastel pencil skirt.

"Why? Because I'm right?" Della asked.

"One press of a button, and I'll have you locked behind steel bars. I'll tell them you wouldn't stop harassing me. That you pulled a taser or a gun on me. Whose word do you think they will take? Yours or mine?" Elvi snapped.

Della tossed the brass plaque aside and kicked her feet onto Elvi's desk. "Oh wow, I'm so scared," she gasped, then shook her head disapprovingly. "I'll take my chances."

"That arrogance of yours is going to get you killed. You know that, don't you?" Elvi hissed, her face bright red. She looked like a ticking time bomb, but at this point, Della was having too much fun to care about what she'd do if she pushed Elvi too far.

"Is that a threat?" Della asked.

"Get. Out," Elvi spat, stomping her foot for effect.

The Queen's façade had fallen. She was easy to tick off. If Della pried hard enough, she knew she would find whatever Elvi was hiding.

"I'm not done asking questions," Della sighed.

"Oh, my dear, I think you are," Elvi snapped.

"The historical society," Della began, shifting gears. "I know a lot about that old house, but a lot can change in a short time. Have you noticed any cold spots? Odd smells? Strange noises? Any sign of a break-in at any point?" Della added the last part quickly, trying to cover the fact she was asking if Elvi had witnessed any ghost-like behavior. "Better yet, why were you there last night?"

"Your mother was right; you don't know when to quit," Elvi huffed, her eyes sweeping over Della again. Slowly, her anger softened to smugness. "And to answer your other question, I have keys and know you don't."

Della just shrugged. "I have familial immunity."

Elvi's eyes narrowed. "Can I ask you a question, Miss Coleman?" Della nodded. "What newspaper did you say you worked for? Moss Hollow Courier?"

Della smiled widely. "The Moss Hollow Tribune," she corrected sweetly.

Of all the words in the world, she chose 'courier.'

She knew something.

"I do my research too, Miss Coleman," she said softly. "What would your parents think if they knew? What do you think they would do? Would you still have that 'familial immunity' if they knew what you were doing last night?"

Della stood, her heart racing out of control. Alarms were going off in her head, telling her to run. "That's not your secret to tell."

Elvi lifted a daintily daring shoulder. "That's the thing with secrets. They're never really yours if you don't hide them well enough. You could have used a pen name. You didn't."

The Queen and the peasant stared daggers into each

other. They were caught in a dangerous game. Losing would be fatal for either.

Elvi sat back in her chair, smiling, an evil glint in her eyes. She was calculating all her options. The one thing Della had never expected this town to give her was someone with a brain that wasn't mush. Della had spent all her time trying to catch Elvi in a lie she'd forgotten her own tells. Her own lies. She'd underestimated the woman before her.

Elvi Sinclair.

A woman with corruption pumping through her blood. A woman who could see that same trait in others. Knew the smell of it like perfume, and Della practically bathed in it.

"I'll tell you what. If you ensure our conversations stay anonymous, maybe I'll have more information for you," Elvi winked. If she didn't know better, Della would have thought that statement was sincere. "But I can't guarantee the same for you. You are the anti-hero in this town, not me. Maybe you should try repairing some of the bridges you burned before accusing others. However, if you do the same, I'll try to keep your name out of my mouth. Understood?"

Della nodded, frigid with fright.

She felt small.

She hated feeling small.

"Good," Elvi whispered, looking bored again. "Well, I do hope whatever article you are writing does well. If you need anything else, don't hesitate to ask. For now, I'm going to have to cut this short." She batted her eyes sympathetically, holding out her hand for Della to shake.

Della wanted to protest, to ask more questions, to do *something*. But she was frozen. Unable to move, she stared at Elvi, her mind running wild with anxious thoughts.

"Miss Coleman?"

"Yes?" Della asked dully, snapping out of her thoughts.

"You can leave now," Elvi said coldly, removing her hand from hanging in midair.

Della scoffed at her, turning on her heels and exiting the office. As soon as the door closed behind her, she made for the exit, her mind racing again.

Elvi knew her secret.

She wasn't a reporter. She was a monster hunter. She didn't work with the law. She wasn't a detective. She was a vigilante at best.

And if Elvi didn't keep her word, Della's world would fall apart.

Who was she kidding? She'd made an enemy out of

Chapter Twenty-One

Elvi the minute they'd met. The first chance that woman got, she'd rat her out.

Della wanted to scream as she walked briskly back to the hearse, a gust of freezing wind ruffling her hair. Her eyes were set on the tops of her boots and the pavement beneath her feet. She was risking everything being here, and for what? Mavericks had to be wrong. She just needed to prove it. There had to be a plausible explanation for Ashton's disappearance. She had to find a reason to leave. Fast.

As she grabbed the handle to open the door, a butterfly landed on the back of her hand. It was a strange little thing—orange with brown spots and white outlines on its wingtips. The shape of its wings almost resembled a question mark.

She was momentarily fascinated with it, lifting her hand to the light and gently turning the butterfly from side to side.

"Where'd you come from, little one?" she asked quietly.

The butterfly fluttered its wings in response.

A burning sensation erupted above Della's ears.

Cold sweat broke across her forehead as another butterfly landed on her shoulder.

Then another.

And another.

All the same shape and gorgeous shade of orange.

"You're looking in all the wrong places," A misty voice whispered in her ear.

Della rounded, slipping forward in the slush beneath the hearse, startling the colony of butterflies that had landed upon her. The butterflies swarmed before her, more appearing from behind her. There had to be thousands of them. All were culminating into a singular shape—the shape of a person.

"Close," The figure of butterflies whispered. She could almost hear a smile in its wispy voice. "But not quite."

Suddenly, the butterflies broke apart in a cascade of iridescent light, the colony swarming around her in a flurry, kicking up snow and mud.

As quickly as it started, it stopped.

The butterflies hung suspended in midair, their wings flapping slowly. Then, one by one, they combusted into flames and dropped to the ground, leaving nothing but melting snow to show they'd been there.

Della shivered.

Not because she was frightened or even cold.

But because the butterflies hadn't been there at all.

Her legs shook as she slumped down to the sidewalk, panting heavily. Slowly, she leaned back against the door of the rusty old hearse, her eyes to the sky as snow began to dust her face in particles oddly reminiscent of ash. Her mind swam, and her body shook with anticipation.

"What do you mean I'm not looking in the right place?" she asked softly, shutting her eyes and putting her head in her hands.

She stayed there for a while, half expecting something to respond.

But apparently, her broken mind didn't have anything else to add.

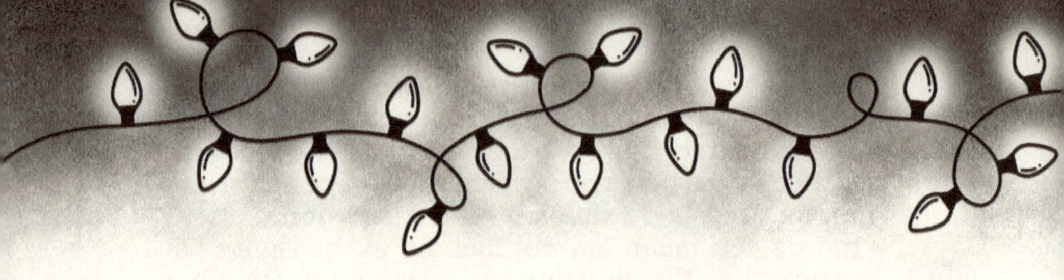

CHAPTER TWENTY-TWO

Malfunction

When Della finally collected herself, she shakily crawled back into the hearse. It was one thing to hallucinate butterflies. She could handle that. That would've been harmless. What was worse was driving, knowing she could pass out at the wheel or hallucinate something that could get her killed. Driving had never been her strong suit. She was anxious behind the wheel. Even more so since the last time she had driven the hearse was when Porter had been drunk. Right before the Grunches attacked them. Right before she killed Eric. Right before—

The kind of full-body tremor you get when thinking of things that deeply upset you coursed through her body. She hated it.

Della sighed heavily, eyes on the stoplight illuminating the falling snow. It refused to turn green. All she could do was sit there and stare, watching the light as it seemed to glow brighter and brighter red.

The light burst, scaring her so badly that her knee jerked up and hit the steering wheel. A loud beeping filled the air, resonating from the glove box. Someone honked for her to move. Someone else was yelling from the sidewalk about the broken light.

The beeping from the glove box ceased, but that didn't calm her nerves in the slightest. She leaned over and unlocked it, opening it to reveal a few of the EMF detectors Max had made. One of them had broken like the traffic light had.

Another honk, which Della promptly ignored.

She grabbed one of the other EMF detectors and switched it on, alarmed to see the device's dial shot straight into the red. As far as she knew, that always meant evil spirits. Because Max had made these EMF detectors with the help of magic, they usually told you exactly what was hidden just out of sight.

"Well, that's just great," Della whispered to herself. And probably to whatever spirit was causing the electronics to malfunction.

A knock on her window pulled her thoughts away from the supernatural. Her heart fluttered when she realized who was staring at her. A ranger hat with an ugly gold crest cast Kohen's face in shadow. His eyebrows were raised, his lips set in a frown. Shooting a disgusted look over his shoulder, he tapped the window for her to roll it down.

"I didn't break the stop light," Della said defensively.

"Never suggested you did, but now I'm not so sure," Kohen laughed. "You okay?" He eyed the EMF detector. "You seem jumpy."

"Yeah, I'm okay, big bear," she sighed.

"That's *Deputy Kohen* to you."

"Don't you mean officer?" Della smirked.

He laughed louder.

Kohen was so different than Kimi. You wouldn't even guess they were siblings if they were in the same room. And compared to Jasper, Kohen was practically a saint. He did have a holier-than-thou routine just like everyone else, though the stone-cold law accompanied his. Porter would like him when they got to know each other better.

"Where ya headed, little bear?" Kohen smiled. "Forget how to drive?"

Della shot him a bored look. "Haha."

He put his hands up in defense. "Hey, just looking out for you. You know how the civilians get this time of year. You holding up the line could cause some serious problems."

"Well, if you'd let me pass, I'd be on my way," Della said coldly.

Kohen only smiled, lifting the brim of his hat away from his eyes. "Only if you help me on a case."

Della's mouth hung open. "Are you serious?" she blurted out before she could stop herself.

Not once had he ever come to her for help. The last time she'd had a run-in with the law—snooping around the school after hours trying to catch a cheating husband and his mistress—he'd acted like he wasn't even related to her. She knew he only did it so Kimi wouldn't stop him from hanging around, but still, it hurt.

Kohen shrugged. "Word around town says my missing man contacted you last. I want to know what you know so that I can. . . know. . . what. . . you. . . know. . ?" He looked confused for a minute, which wasn't usual for him, then shook himself back to reality. "What do you say?"

"I say you are off your rocker," Della laughed darkly.

"You'd be right," Kohen gave her a cheeky smile. "Come on, Della. We both know you only came back because of good ol' Ash. Even if you won't admit it to your folks. I just need your brain matter. Come look things over and see if I missed anything. I'll do the same for you," Kohen said, a pleading look in his eyes. Someone honked. He rolled his eyes. He almost flipped off one of the impatient citizens he was supposed to protect but thought better of it at the last second.

"I don't miss things." Della tried to hold her head high but knew that was a lie.

"Everyone makes mistakes. You should know. Your dad's side practically invented mistakes," He laughed and winked.

Della knew he hadn't meant those words to sound like he thought she was a mistake, but for a second, that's how she interpreted it. Today seemed to prove everyone was out to get her.

He thought for a minute. "Tell you what. Meet me out at the construction site, and I won't tell your parents that I have you listed as a potential suspect in a missing persons case,"

Today was also proving that everyone had an ultimatum.

"I've been here for three days," Della scoffed.

Kohen narrowed his eyes at her, hands on his hips. While her family thought they had her pegged, Kohen really did. He might be the only person in the world other than Mavericks who knew what she was capable of. Otherwise, he wouldn't be asking for her help. Years of research had filled her brain with valuable information. How she used that information was what everyone seemed to worry about. She could solve countless crimes or cause them. Kohen may play favoritism, but she knew why he kept such a close eye on her. Della didn't know if he would defend her if worse came to worse.

"Well?" he asked.

"Fine," Della snapped, then drove off.

~ ~ ~

Several annoying Christmas songs later, Della crawled out of the hearse and into the cold. She stood in a clearing full of construction equipment and piles of dirt, shaking her head in disdain. This place used to be so beautiful. There had been a large pond in the center and rocks perfect for sitting and reading. A sanctuary from the stuffiness of Sycamore Heights, Della had escaped here countless times. But now her oasis looked like a dystopian wasteland. And felt like one, she realized as she squished and squashed through the mud caused by melted snow. Della didn't know what would be built here, but she had a feeling it was just another useless amenity.

Which made sense when she thought about it. Sycamore Heights was full of things like that.

Ever since she was little, Della had hated the idea of cutting down trees. How could humans do such a thing? Didn't they realize they were stealing land from the animals? Even now, she thought if her full-time job wasn't cryptozoology, she'd run away and become a tree-hugging hippie. Maybe she'd change her name to Solstice or something. If Elvi betrayed their vague little deal, she would end up as a traveling hippie, for she would have to run away and change her name. She'd have to pull a Quincy.

She didn't have much time to think about it all, however. Soon, Kohen's cop car pulled up next to her. He nodded towards a pile of dirt a few feet away, his hand on his holster. Della didn't follow him. Instead, she grabbed an EMF detector, ensuring it was on before stuffing it in her jacket pocket. It hadn't gone off on the drive over, but she suspected it would now.

"You expecting a bear to come barreling out of the woods?" she asked, watching Kohen's fingers clench around his gun so hard his knuckles turned white.

"Can't be too careful out here, you know that," he said darkly.

Della rolled her eyes, grabbed her book bag, and then slushed through muddy snow toward the pile of dirt. Inside her book bag were many useful investigating items: empty vials, gloves, a magnifying glass, a small footprint reference book, a trowel, and a polaroid camera Mavericks had gifted her. She slipped on a pair of gloves, then pulled out a vial and the trowel, bending to scoop some dirt into the tube. She dug a little further, looking for more bones. Max had updated her on Sebastian's findings before she left. Knowing this place had supposed human bones hidden in the dirt made her sick.

"What are you doing?" Kohen asked.

"My job?" Della laughed. "That's why you asked me to come here, right?" She glanced at him.

Her body tensed, waiting for him to say they hadn't talked earlier or for him to disappear in front of her. Thankfully, all he did was sigh heavily and nod. He must just not want her tampering with potential evidence. If that was the case, he should have swept this place clean the second he suspected foul play. Though from a mundane point of view, she had no idea why this place would be connected to Ashton's disappearance.

"What do you hope to find in that, exactly?" Kohen asked, kneeling beside her, watching her scoop dirt into a vial with morbid curiosity.

Della gave him a bored look. "I doubt you will like the answer."

"If you start drawling on about all that demon-hooey-bull-honkey, then yes, I won't like it."

"If you wish to dress like a barbarian, so be it, but you could at least try and talk like a civilized human being. Or at least something human-adjacent," Della sneered.

"Very funny," Kohen shot back. "I could make a quip about your neon green hair. How it makes you look like an alien."

Della raised her eyebrow at him, standing and shoving her vial of debris into her book bag, wondering what Max would find in this sample. Ghosts were tricky. Typically, they were confined to places or objects, sometimes even people. But on rare occasions, they could affect a larger area. If the ghost they spoke with last night had done something to Ashton outside of the historical society, this spirit could travel freely. Those were the kinds of spirits you had to be wary of. Hopefully, there was something in these samples that would tell them exactly what kind of 'demon-hooey-bull-honkey' was out here.

"What?" Kohen laughed, looking up at her with a confused expression. Her face must have betrayed her worry.

"Nothing," she decided to say. "Have you swept Ash's old trailer?"

Kohen stared blankly at her. "You do know what a cop does, right?"

"Why do I waste my time on you?" she sighed, then turned away from him, sweeping her hand through the air. "Why did you bring me up here? What exactly do you need my professional opinion on?"

Kohen ran a hand through his hair. He wore it long instead of braided today. Just like Mingan and Kimi, he seemed to have aged twelve years in a few months. Della was sure his hairline hadn't been so barren the last time she'd seen him. Nor had he had a single streak of gray hair before now.

"Don't you read the paper?"

"Not recently. Why?"

"Animals keep winding up dead around here. Poppy thinks there's a natural gas leak or something. That's why no one is up here working anymore. We sent everyone away so as not to end up with a casualty. Not to mention, the machines are acting up. Some of the guys couldn't get their chainsaws to work. It's weird," Kohen explained, kicking away a loose stone.

"So then, why are we here?" Della asked, backing away from the dirt and dusting off her hands on her corduroy pants. Gas leak? Why were they here if the place was supposed to be dangerous?

If he were Jasper's brother and not Kimi's, she would have thought her deranged family members had finally snapped and were trying to do away with the black sheep.

"I mean, someone has to figure things out," Kohen shrugged.

Della stared at him in awe at his recent stupidity. "What am I supposed to be looking for? I don't deal with gas leaks, I deal with—" She was going to say ghosts, magic, witches, and vampires but caught herself. "I deal with people. If I'm not here to find a hidden blood spatter amongst pine needles, why did you bring me here?" she asked breathlessly.

"I don't know, you tell me, D."

"Don't call me that."

"You love it when I call you that."

"I hatc it," Della corrected.

"No, you don't."

She scoffed. "Yes, I do."

"Agree to disagree," Kohen said, throwing his hands up in defense.

Della shook her head angrily. "If it's a gas leak, I can't help you. You need scientists or biologists. Or maybe even someone who cares. If you don't mind, I'll be on my way."

Nothing seemed out of the ordinary here. She had to admit there was an absence of birds, and the trees looked a little dead, but that wasn't a problem Della and her friends could fix. This was a human problem and a major waste of her time. Anger surged through her.

Screw it. Whatever scary thing was happening back in Moss Hollow didn't matter. She could handle it. All she had to do was get out of this damn town.

"Yeah, I guess you're right. But hey, at least I got a second opinion," Kohen said as she walked away. "And that opinion was yours!"

"Only took you eighteen years to listen to me," Della mumbled.

"What?"

"Nothing," Della snapped.

She made for the hearse but paused as Kohen walked past her.

"Hey, wait a minute. Elvi Sinclair. Opinion?" she asked.

He shrugged half-heartedly. "Annoying and gives me the creeps. Why?"

"Just wanted to feel validated in my judgment," Della sighed.

Kohen snickered to himself, waving as he slipped into his car and drove away.

Della returned his wave weakly, feeling defeated. She climbed back into the hearse, wrenching the EMF detector out of her pocket. Just as she made to toss it into the back, her eyes landed on the one that had broken at the stoplight. She sighed heavily, reaching for it. She wanted so badly to chalk it all up to coincidence. To try and tell herself that EMF detectors and stoplights must break all the time. Like faulty lightbulbs. Maybe the ghost they spoke with last night was just messing with them. That maybe nothing had gotten Ashton. But deep down, she knew something was off. Animals didn't like spirits, especially if they could sense the spirit had malicious intent. And ghosts were known to cause trouble with electronics.

"All right," she said to her reflection in the rearview mirror. She tossed the broken EMF detector away, instead pulling out the antenna of the working one.

Slowly, she walked the perimeter of the construction site. The device beeped several times, the rainbow spectrum on the screen lighting up. Every few paces, the screen flashed from green to white and back again. The lights on the detector kept changing as she passed by trees and heavy machinery. Red meant demons and evil spirits, blue meant the place was ghost-free, green meant a benevolent spirit lurking around, and white meant something entirely different. Usually, it settled on one color quickly. When it had flashed between all those colors at the historical society, that was the first time Della had seen it malfunction. Then again, she had only tested the EMF detectors in a few places. Nevertheless, she trusted Max's mystical programming skills.

Suddenly, the EMF detector shut off. She stopped, shaking and smacking it. The thing started buzzing and vibrating in her hand, the screen glitching. Della furrowed her eyebrows, messing with the tuning dials until it began sparking in her hands. She yelped, dropping it.

"Dammit," Della whispered, stepping back as the device continued to spark.

She reached for her phone to call Max, but it wouldn't turn on. Kohen was right; something was definitely messing with technology. But what? Just as she was about to turn and leave, something caught her eye from the forest. Slowly, she turned to see a pair of glowing white eyes. Deep in the woods, she could see the shadow of a tall figure. Rather than looking at her, it seemed to be staring at the EMF detector.

Della stepped backward, reaching for the Polaroid camera in her book bag, watching the creature. Whatever it was, it wasn't a bear. It was too tall, too thin. It came forward, sauntering toward a patch of light, a limp to its step. All Della could see was one gigantic, furry, bloodied, clawed hand.

"I've officially gone crazy," she murmured, snapping a picture. She wasn't sure what she wanted to see when the photo developed.

Because if a creature like this had been lurking in the forest all these years, she would have known about it. This had to be another hallucination. She looked around for something that would prove her right. Perhaps a hallucination of Theodore Heiser she could call a manifestation of her guilt. Or maybe a Grunch that came barreling out of the woods only to disappear into a swarm of butterflies once it reached her.

Backing away, she shook the Polaroid. Apparently, she hadn't gone crazy just yet. There it stood in the photograph.

The creature growled, startling Della, though the creature didn't seem to care about her one bit. All it was interested in was the EMF detector, which was now flashing every color on the spectrum simultaneously. Della couldn't remember what purple, yellow, pink, or orange meant, but she doubted those colors meant anything good.

The creature took another step forward, revealing part of its face: half of a wolf skull with moose antlers protruding from it—the tell-tale sign of a Wendigo.

"Oh shit," Della breathed. The construction had woken something up, just not the bears like everyone had thought.

At the sound of her swearing, the Wendigo finally looked up at her, tilting its face to the side like a confused cat. It grumbled something that sounded eerily like words before daring a step forward. The EMF detector began screeching loudly like a teapot ready to explode would. The Wendigo hissed and growled at it, charging forward.

Della stumbled backward, slipping in the mud and falling to the ground. The Wendigo glanced at her, then stepped on the EMF detector, lumbering over until its face was not three inches from hers. Its breath stunk of rotting flesh. The smell made her stomach lurch, yet at the same time, it was oddly comforting and familiar.

Della stared up at the creature in awe. She wasn't exactly scared of it. And it didn't seem like it wanted to hurt her in any way. All it wanted was for the EMF detector to be destroyed.

She swallowed hard, gathering her bravery. "Hello there," she whispered.

Was it her, or did it just smile? "Hell-o," it articulated, its voice like bones dragging against the walls of a dungeon.

Della's heart skipped a beat. The Wendigo leaned forward until Della was flat against the forest floor, blocking her from running—not that she wanted to. Maybe she should, but she was too curious.

A flicker of a memory danced in her brain. Something long forgotten, something she had a feeling her parents hadn't approved of. Suddenly, her head erupted in pain above her ears, where the brain stored memories. Her vision danced, the Wendigo swaying before her.

The Wendigo stared at her as if worried, then slowly backed away. Della scrambled to her feet, holding her head in her hands, the agony around her ears growing, making her whole head throb. Black spots danced in her vision. She stumbled to the side, trying to stay upright. Despite her best efforts, her legs gave out. She swayed to the side, collapsing in a shaking heap on the muddy ground. Every beat of her heart made her chest ache, each breath harder than the last. She lay on the ground, the world on fire with color and spinning like a kaleidoscope in her eyes.

Her shaking muscles relaxed as white-hot tears trickled down her cheeks. She could feel the vibrations of her heart beating faster and faster until—nothing.

Just emptiness.

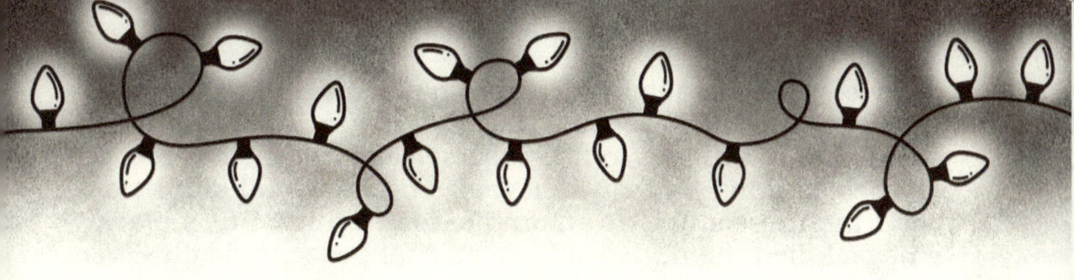

CHAPTER TWENTY-THREE

Dreamweaver

Max woke from a well-deserved nap with a sense of unease. His chest felt tight, his lungs like sandpaper. A throbbing in his head only intensified as he struggled to free himself from his sleeping bag. He had to brace himself on the door frame before leaving Leonel's room, tripping over his feet as he made for the stairs.

"What happened to you?" Sebastian asked as he staggered over to the couch.

Porter stood, putting a hand on his shoulder to keep him upright.

"Ei dunno, Ei just feel off," Max said, rubbing his chest, hoping that would dispel the tightness. "Ei've got a headache, too."

Waving Porter away, he sat heavily on the couch, closing his eyes. Porter knelt beside him, hand on his knee.

"Can you get him something, please, Seb?" he whispered. The floor creaked as Sebastian made toward the kitchen. "What's going on, buddy? Talk to me," Porter said, shaking his leg.

Max gave a half-hearted shrug. "My mind feels stuck in a fog," he said groggily.

"This is why I tell you to rest, Max," Porter said sternly.

That was the truth of it. A familiar's magic was turbulent. It controlled and leeched off them like a parasite. Their magic was bound to the witch they were devoted to to anchor their powers. If he had a witch, his powers would flourish. He'd be able to cast a spell without the possibility of dying. Mavericks and Nicoletta had tried many times to find him a witch. None had been a match. It wasn't something one could control. Some familiars trained for years with a witch only to find they weren't compatible. That's why so many familiars turned to black magic. It came so easily to them. They would spend a lifetime pumping their veins full of evil just to free themselves from their curse. If they couldn't find a witch, their powers would kill them, and they'd be stuck as an animal for eternity. But if black magic killed them, they'd have eternal peace in death. Even if they ended up in Hell in the process.

Porter knew this. That's why he worried so much.

"Hey," Porter said, shaking his leg again.

Max opened his eyes, taking the glass of water and ibuprofen Sebastian had offered him. He mumbled his thanks, the ice-cold water soothing the ache in his chest.

"Where's Della?" he asked, looking around the living room, hoping to see her.

"She's still out and about," Sebastian sighed.

Max's stomach dropped. The unease he felt when he woke up was back. "Have ya heard from her?"

"I'm sure she's fine. Let's worry about you, okay?" Porter said, giving him a reassuring smile.

Max handed his glass of water back to Sebastian, standing. Porter gave him a disapproving look as he made for the stairs.

"Ei'm gonna go back tuh bed," he lied.

"We'll check on you in a bit, all right?" Porter called after him.

Without looking at him, he gave a thumbs up.

At the top of the stairs, he leaned heavily against the wall, winded. He reached for his phone, dialing his dad. He let the line ring for a moment but eventually hung up. Instead, he dialed Della, hoping she'd pick up. He wasn't a Seer by any means, but he couldn't ignore this sinking feeling. The line rang, but there was no answer. He called several times to no avail. Pinching the bridge of his nose, he slid down to the floor. The ache in his lungs was back.

Why hadn't she picked up? She always answered when he called.

Up the stairs came Kimi carrying freshly folded towels. She paused at his feet, looking down at him in concern.

"Are you okay, Max?" she asked.

He nodded, struggling to his feet. Kimi had to catch him by the arm before he fell backward. "A little dizzy," he sighed.

"Are you hungry? I'll be starting dinner soon, but if you need anything, please feel free to raid the kitchen," she said, gripping his arm tightly.

Max pushed his palms into his eyes, shaking his head. "Ei'm fine, Mrs. Coleman. Ei think Ei just need tuh lay down again."

Kimi peeled his hands away from his face, placing her hand on his forehead. She frowned.

"Sebastian!" she called.

Like an excitable puppy, Sebastian came bounding up the stairs. Kimi handed off the towels to him, pointing at the hall closet. Without another word, she placed a hand on Max's back and gently pushed him forward. She led him to the door next to Cassie and Della's room.

"Don't tell Jasper I did this, okay?" she sighed, opening the door.

Kimi led him to the bed, removing the lightning-bolt print comforter to shake it out. She fluffed the pillows and clicked on the lamp, patting the bed with a kind smile.

"You may rest here. That way, no one will bother you," she said.

Max sat on the edge of the bed, looking around the room. The walls were plastered with band posters. An electric guitar hung near the door, its amp beneath, the cord sitting in a neat coil on top. A keyboard was pushed against the opposite wall, its keys gray from the dust. Stickers and spiders littered both instruments. Deductive reasoning aside, everything Della had said about Quincy told him this was his room.

Max felt close to Della here. He knew how much she ached for her brother to come home. They'd been inseparable growing up. He figured that was why making friends had been forbidden after he left. If her brother could leave, what was stopping everyone else?

"Thank ya, Mrs. Coleman," he said, shocked at how tired he sounded.

Kimi winked at him, perching herself on the edge of the bed as he lay down. Max let his eyes close as soon as his head hit the pillow. Kimi pulled the comforter up around him, tucking him in tight. Gently, she brushed away a ringlet away from his face. She stayed with him until he fell asleep.

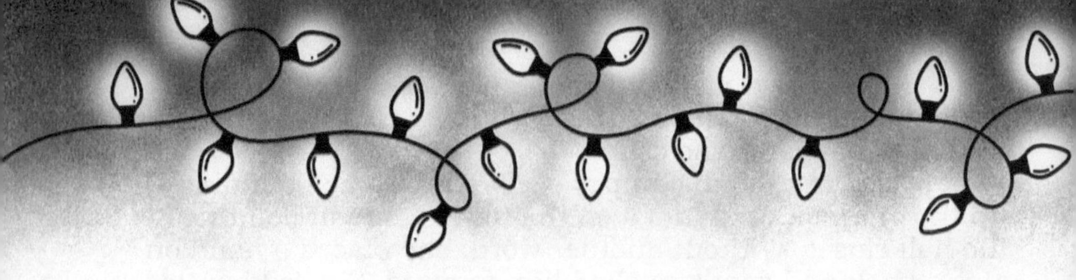

CHAPTER TWENTY-FOUR

Dreamcatcher

Della's eyes flickered open. Above her was a bright blue sky and fluffy clouds. Hot summer air filled her lungs. She sat up, dry grass scratching her hands. Her mind buzzed. This wasn't right. Hadn't it been cold? Hadn't there been snow on the ground?

She stood, brushing herself.

Someone laughed behind her. She turned to see her grandmother, Winifred, kneeling on the ground, planting flowers at the base of the giant totem pole at the center of the Mukwa reservation.

Della furrowed her eyebrows. She couldn't remember how she'd gotten here and where she'd been before. Her mind was foggy. In fact, she couldn't remember anything that had happened before this moment. No memories of her childhood. No memories of. . . two names were on the tip of her tongue, but she couldn't quite form them. This bothered her deeply. Those names were important.

Winifred looked over at her. "Well? Are you going to join me?" she asked, smiling happily.

Della just stared at her. She couldn't fathom why, but seeing her here didn't sit right. Wasn't there something wrong with her grandma? Wasn't she sick or something? Dread filled her as she backed away, ignoring the puzzled look on her grandmother's face.

When she turned, the sky began to glow with starlight, and the warm summer air turned cold.

"Grandma?" she called to the empty air around her. Her clothes were covered in snow, her skin and bones now feeling frozen. The reservation stretched out before her, but it was empty. The totem pole behind her was on its side, covered in snow and cobwebs. Worse still, the reservation looked like something out of a history book. Plank houses and teepees were everywhere she looked. There was no sign of modern civilization whatsoever.

"Hello?" Della called, walking along a dirt path.

"Grandma, where'd you go?" she shouted. She felt sick, like she had been running for a long time.

Footsteps.

Della turned, following the sound. Stretching before her was a set of footprints. *Bloodied* footprints. She tried to make out their shape, but her eyes refused to focus. They took a sharp turn to the right, leading into the forest. Della continued, squinting in the dark to see. Deep inside, she knew she wasn't meant to see this.

When she got to the forest's edge, she suddenly realized she had somewhere to be. The names she'd been trying to remember came back to her: Porter and Max. They were waiting for her somewhere, though she couldn't figure out where.

She looked over her shoulder. The sky was blue again. The reservation was as it should be. She could hear laughing in the distance. And there was her grandma, waving her over to where she was planting flowers.

Della looked back. The forest was dark, the trees covered in snow. A set of glowing eyes peered through the branches at her. Della knew she should be scared, but she wasn't. Those eyes weren't something to fear.

This Wendigo would never hurt her.

A new name was forming on her tongue. Just as she was about to walk toward it, a purple-black mist began to billow up around the Wendigo. The mist wrapped itself around its throat, choking it. The Wendigo cried, screamed, and tore at its throat, but nothing worked. Soon, it collapsed to the ground, bleeding from self-inflicted wounds.

The scene changed again. Now, she was at the historical society. The same purple-black mist was floating through the air like smoke. It wafted through the old house, anything it touched turning to dust. Della followed at a distance, peeking into open doors and down dark hallways. Nothing seemed out of the ordinary until she came to the room with all the Native American artifacts. It was closed with a rusty shackle and lock.

Della reached out to touch it, the lock disintegrating, turning to bright purple hydrangea petals as it fell to the ground. The door creaked open, the sound echoing in her ears painfully.

The sight she beheld made her wish she wasn't so curious.

Bodies.

Bodies piled high.

Women in bloodied gowns, men in tattered suits, children lying lifeless in their Sunday best. The only thing in common was that they were all dead. Della was about to shut the door when a hand sticking up from the bodies caught her eye.

"No," she whispered.

An ebony hand with splotches of tan. Max. And next to him was Porter. Mavericks. Nicoletta. Her parents. Kohen. Mingan. Leonel and Cassie.

Everyone.

Della took a stumbling step back, tripping over her feet and falling to the ground as footsteps scraped down the hallway.

"A shame, really. I didn't think I would have to go to such drastic measures this time. Thought you were smarter." That was a man's voice, though Della couldn't pin it.

She jumped to her feet, looking around wildly. The mist had disappeared, and she feared it had found what it was looking for.

"I mean, we have all heard the stories of the one with the dreams—the one who could bend reality. Honestly, I thought I'd be more impressed. Then again, you aren't very impressive." That same voice laughed. A figure emerged from the shadows, the purple-black mist engulfing him. Della couldn't make out any features, but she could feel the hatred and anger pouring off him.

"You killed them," Della spat, thrusting her hand forward as if that was supposed to protect her.

The figure laughed cruelly. "Not yet. But soon. This is just another one of your visions," the man sighed. "Take this as a warning, tell *mamankanois*, and leave."

Della furrowed her eyebrows. "Who—"

The mist shot at her like a torpedo, hitting her square in the chest and sending her flying backward. Her head collided with the floor, causing her entire mind to ring with pain. She could feel her consciousness slipping away. Her head was buzzing, feeling like it would implode. She shut her eyes tightly, trying to make it stop, trying to calm down.

As she lay there, she could feel something wet seeping into her clothes. Like she was lying in—

~ ~ ~

Her eyes shot open with panic.

Mud.

She was lying in the mud, staring at the looming trees and the dark sky speckled with stars. Slowly, she sat up, her head spinning. Though thoroughly shaken, she was glad she was still at the construction site. At least she wasn't sleepwalking. It was a pitiful silver lining, but at least it distracted her from the fact it had been the middle of the day before she lost consciousness.

Her vision sparkled with black as she stumbled to her feet. Her head was a lead weight sitting atop her shoulders as she staggered to the hearse. Something hot was trickling down her neck. Horror-struck, she reached up to feel something slimy and sticky. Blood. Blood seeping out of her ears. She caught her reflection in the window of the hearse. Her eyes were sunken. Blood was pooling on her lips, leaking from her nose. Her eyes were crying blood like a vampire's would.

A normal person may have thought this concerning. Not to say Della didn't. She was just more worried about how the windows and windshield of the hearse were frozen solid. The dark ice had even made its way inside the cabin. The door handle was frozen, too, giving a loud crunch as she pulled open the door. The entire steering wheel was frozen. Porter was going to absolutely annihilate her. She'd surely lose her hearse driving privileges after this.

Or maybe he'd be more worried about the blood pouring from her eyes, ears, and nose. She didn't know which scenario would be worse.

Freezing from the cold, terrified from what she had just witnessed in the depths of her mind, and wondering if the trees towering above her had eyes, she slipped into the hearse and drove away.

Her mind was reeling.

Mamankanois.

That word kept playing over and over in her mind. It meant butterfly. No one ever called her butterfly. Mingan, Kohen, Porter, and Max were the only ones who gave her sweet nicknames. Everyone else always referred to her as 'mole' or 'rat' or some other slight she hated. Not butterfly. Not mamankanois.

Where had she heard that before?

Unfortunately, driving down the darkened streets of Sycamore Heights hadn't jogged her memory. There was a curtain separating half her mind. One of the heavy velvet ones at old theaters. The kind you couldn't move on your own. Something was blocking her from remembering.

Butterflies.

Where else had she seen butterflies?

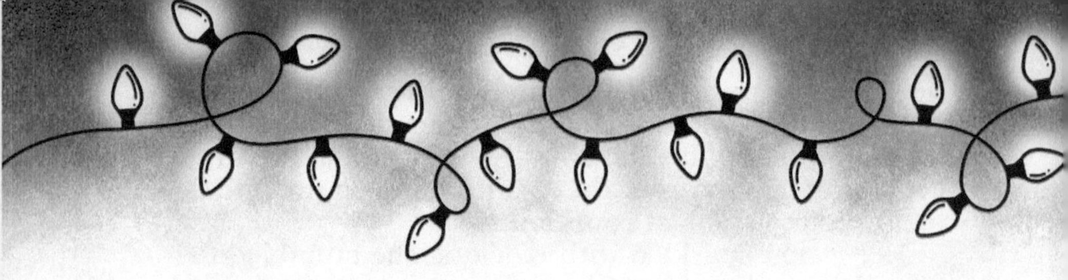

CHAPTER TWENTY-FIVE

Dreamwalker

Della was still trying to sift through her thoughts when she pushed open the front door to her parent's home and kicked off her shoes. The house was dark except for one tiny light in the living room. Max sat perched on the couch, nose stuck in a book, gripping the small lamp next to him for more light. As soon as the door opened, he whipped his head around to look at her.

"Hey! Ei've been waitin' all day for ya tuh come home," he said, shaking the book he'd been reading in the air. Della couldn't tell if he was worried or excited. "Ei wanna run a few things. . . past. . . ya. . ." He took a moment to take in the sight of her. His eyes widened, and he tossed the book to the side, standing. "What happened?"

Della studied him. She felt herself recoil from him as he edged toward her cautiously. She watched as his eyes slid over her frame. From the twigs and pine needles in her hair, the trails of blood on her face and neck, and finally down to the mud on her clothes. The look on his face turned from concern to fury. Della backed away, placing the couch between him and her. She furrowed her eyebrows, pulling at her long fingernails until her nailbeds screamed in pain.

"What happened?" Max asked again. This time, his tone was full of rage.

"I'm fine," Della shrugged. She felt her heart start racing. She didn't like the look in his eyes. It wasn't Max.

"Ei didn' ask if ya were fine, love, Ei asked what happened," Max corrected, slowly walking toward her.

Della wrung her hands, debating how to respond. She couldn't think of anything witty or comforting. She couldn't even think of a lie. So, instead, she succumbed to the thing she was trying to avoid.

"I went out to the construction site," she began, swallowing hard. Max paused, his foot hovering over the floor, watching her carefully. "Your EMF detectors were going off like crazy. There were eyes in the trees, and all of a sudden, a—a—a friggin Wendigo showed up, okay?" She was shaking with adrenaline. "I passed out. Woke up and drove here."

"Passed out as in 'mind-bending visions' or. . ?" Max asked, his tone harsh. He looked her over again, then took a step back, softening his pose. "Sorry. Ei'm not mad ya, Ei'm just worried," he said sternly. His eyes drifted away. Something passed over his face she couldn't describe.

"Mind-bending visions," Della said with a sharp breath. She stood anxiously before him, waiting for him to start yelling at her, lecturing her for her apparent wrongdoings, or for him to tell her how stupid she was.

"Are ya okay?" he asked. He shoved his hands in his pockets, looking at her through his eyebrows. Why did *he* look nervous?

She shrugged.

"Can ya tell me what ya saw?"

She swallowed hard, taking a step toward him. As she did, he reached for her, gently taking her hands into his own. He looked her dead in the eyes, and Della knew she couldn't lie to him even if she tried.

"I saw my grandma. We were on the reservation. It was sunny and bright and—and happy. And then it changed. It was dark and stormy and snowy, and it felt wrong, *really* wrong. I walked to the edge of the forest and saw the Wendigo again, but something attacked it." She let him mull that over for a second before continuing. "Then I was in the historical society and I. . ." Her words trailed off.

He shook his head out of confusion, giving her a questioning look.

"I saw you. I saw you dead," she finished. "I saw everyone dead."

She explained everything in as much detail as possible, skipping back and forth between what had happened with the Wendigo and the smoky figure. When she finally finished, she was out of breath, waiting for him to respond.

He pursed his lips and reached up to scrub at the blood on her cheeks. "C'mere," he whispered with a sigh, dragging her towards the kitchen.

He sat her down on the counter next to the sink, grabbed a wad of paper towels, wet them, then offered them to her.

He cleared his throat, reddening. "Want me, or. . ?"

"I can do it myself. Thanks," she smiled weakly,

graciously taking them, beginning to wash away the blood. She'd stopped bleeding sometime during her drive back, but somehow, she felt that didn't mean anything.

Max hopped up on the counter next to her, thinking as he stared at his hands. "Why wouldn' the Wendigo attack ya?" he whispered, more to himself than to her.

"Your guess is as good as mine," Della sighed, tossing her bloody paper towel in the sink. "What did that *thing* mean by 'tell mamankanois?'"

They sat silently for a long while, just staring at each other. Della finally felt herself calm down. She hated to admit it, but every time she had a vision, it shook her to the core. She'd spent her whole life wishing for magical powers, but now that she had them, it was scary as Hell.

Max's eyes lit up. He jumped off the counter, spinning around to look at her. "Maybe someone on the reservation goes by mamankanois or butterfly or somethin'."

"I can't think of anyone who does," Della said with a shrug.

Max stroked his chin in thought. "Maybe ya were pickin' up on someone else?" he offered.

"How so?"

He shrugged. "Like how ya did with Theodore. Entered someone's mind or whatever."

"I didn't enter anyone's mind, Max. I accidentally astral projected to him," Della sighed. At least, that's how Nicoletta had described it.

Max raised his eyebrow. "Della. Do ya have any idea how long it takes tuh learn how tuh astral project? Half a lifetime. Ya don' do that 'accidentally.' Plus, didn' ya say ya saw him in some forest clearin' with a bunch of crows? That sounds more like—" He froze, his eyes going glassy. "Ya've got tuh be freakin' kiddin' me," he breathed.

"What?" Della asked, following him to the kitchen table.

He snapped his fingers, and the spellbook she'd explicitly told him not to use appeared before him.

"Ei have a theory," he said excitedly.

Della squinted at him, crossing her arms defensively.

"Ya know what bibliomancy is, correct?"

"Obviously. Divination through books."

"Cool, so use it," he smiled, sweeping his hand over the spellbook.

Della laughed darkly, but then she realized he was dead serious. "Max," she scolded. "I don't know how to use bibliomancy. I can't even figure out the powers that I do have!"

"Della, Ei think deep down ya know more than what

ya'd like tuh admit. Now open the damn book so Ei can say Ei told ya so." He was acting like an impatient child, and it was honestly irritating her.

"I'm not touching that book, Max."

Max put a hand on his hip and tilted his head to the side. "Yer so incredibly stubborn, you know that?"

"Obviously," Della said with a roll of her eyes.

"Okay, if ya don' want tuh touch it, Ei'll make the pages move on their own. Just tell me when tuh stop, all right?"

Della thought for a second, staring down the old book as if it were a bomb she had no idea how to diffuse. Maybe Max was right; maybe it was just some ancient tome that everyone was freaking out over for no reason. It didn't exactly *look* evil. It was roughly the size of a decorative coffee table book and covered in weathered maroon leather. The front was embossed with magical symbols, ranging from pentacles, triskelia, and triquetras to runes, Viking compasses, and symbols Della couldn't name. Like Max, she guessed it was less of a spellbook and more a book of shadows, where a witch would record all their spells, rituals, potions, and other related subjects.

Slowly, she reached out to it. There was an energy surrounding it, dark and cloudy. But not necessarily evil.

"Conflict," Della muttered before she could stop herself.

Max gave her a questioning look.

She refused to hover her hands over it, instead placing both hands under her armpits as she slid off the counter. "Light and dark. The book itself is conflicted," she said. "Don't ask me how I know; I just do."

Max laughed to himself and snapped his fingers. The book opened to a table of contents so small and dense you'd need a powerful magnifying glass to read anything.

"Close yer eyes, hold out yer hand. Focus on the question you are tryin' tuh answer," he said. "Ask it what ya are."

Della tapped her foot anxiously but complied, holding her hand out over the book at a distance she deemed safe. She felt the pages move beneath her, a light breeze wafting up to her hand. The air was unnaturally cold, colder than ice, colder than the snow outside. She was starting to get antsy, feeling awkward just standing there with her hand hovering in midair.

"I don't feel anything," she said, dropping her hand to her side and opening one of her eyes.

"Yer not focusin'," Max sighed.

"It's kind of hard to do that right now, Max. My

head is pounding, I'm tired, I just met a Wendigo who act-ed like we were long-lost friends, and I feel stupid," Della screeched.

A mischievous look passed over his face.

"Do not quote *Star Wars* at me, Maximilian," Della huffed.

He smiled, coming to stand beside her, grabbing her hand, holding it back over the book. "It's just the two of us and an old musty book, okay? That's all ya need to focus on."

Della rolled her eyes as she shut them, breathing deeply.

The pages whirred to life again, that same ghostly breeze reaching her hand, chilling her entire body. Max held her hand tightly. She could feel his eyes on her, pene-trating every corner of her mind. Knowing he was genuinely trying to help and figure things out calmed her. Her mind quieted along with the rest of the world.

The cold wind turned scorching hot.

"Stop," she said, opening her eyes.

The pages fell into place with a dramatic flourish. It opened to a beautifully illustrated page on—

She gasped.

Max smiled widely. He walked back around to face her, holding the spellbook like a sword he was presenting to a knight.

"You're joking," she said, eyes widening.

"Nope."

"You think I'm a dreamwalker?" Della laughed.

She wanted to deny it. Dreamwalkers weren't mag-ical, at least not like Max and Porter or witches and were-wolves.

But what if they were?

What if *she* was?

"Ei don' *think* anythin', love. Bibliomancy never lies," Max said, an air of superiority to his tone. "There is nothin' that proves it wrong. All the cards point tuh this, and Ei have no clue how we didn' figure it out sooner. And come on, dreamwalkers can get into people's heads, right? What if ya did that tuh Theo and just did it again? But ya also saw the future, or at least a possible future?" He looked so proud of himself.

"But we don't know if that thing was actually talking to someone else, Max. This is just a—a—a—"

"A conspiracy theory?" he said with a devilish smile. "Since when were ya a nonbeliever?"

She couldn't argue with that.

"But Nicoletta said that I *was* astral projecting. You

really think she's wrong?" Della said defensively. "And what about me casting that spell? The one that blinded Eric? What about me killing him? I don't think dreamwalkers can do that."

"Nicoletta doesn' know shit, all right? She thought Ei was Faye Folk for an entire year before Mavericks finally told her Ei was a familiar," Max said with a roll of his eyes. He looked down, quickly reading through the passage she'd flipped to. "As for the spell and what happened with Eric, Ei don' know. But this book talks about how dreamwalkers are some of the most powerful beings this world has seen. It talks about yer kind bendin' reality—which Ei might add, ya did today—and if Ei had to guess, that's what ya did that day with Eric."

"Just sounds like witchcraft to me," Della sighed.

"Why are ya tryin' tuh fight this? Ei would have thought ya'd be happy," Max admitted, looking slightly hurt.

Della didn't meet his eyes. "I don't know. If I am a dreamwalker, that somehow means I've messed up. That I have failed my bloodline," she laughed darkly. "Maybe that's why my mind is so screwed up."

Max swatted her shoulder. "Don' talk like that."

She gave him a knowing look. "I love you for pretending you don't see it, but we both know I'm a screw-up. My mom said it herself. My dad thought I was screwed up the second I was born. Just about everyone knows it."

"More people who don' know shit," Max said, crossing his arms over his chest, still holding the spellbook, looking disappointed. "Ei wish ya could see what Ei see. Ei really do."

"Well, if you're right and I can get into people's minds, maybe one day I will be able to," Della sighed.

"Okay, listen tuh me. Seriously. Ya aren' a screw up. Ya don' mess up everythin' ya touch. Ya haven' failed anyone," he snapped at her, accentuating every word with a shove of his finger in her direction. "Those are lies told by people that want tuh see ya torn down, my love. Don' give any of those doubts any thought because it's *truly* not worth it."

The way he looked at her made her heart skip a beat. It was so powerful, so intense. Full of so much passion. He believed every word he had spoken. But it was more than that to her. That look made her want to believe him, too. Again, she knew she couldn't lie to him. At least not about this.

She took a shaking breath and said what had been on her heart for quite some time. "I feel like I'm being punished," she choked out, tears stinging her eyes.

Max nodded. If anyone understood, it would be him. "Ei felt like that for a while, too." He stared at her for a second. "Why do ya feel that way, though?"

"I need to tell you something," Della blurted out. She swallowed hard, wringing her hands again, anxiety coursing through her.

He nodded, sitting on the counter's edge, patting the space next to him. She jumped up next to him, sitting as close as she could. She could see his chest rising and falling quickly and saw the fear in his eyes that he was trying to hide.

"I feel like my mind is breaking." He gave her a bored look. That wasn't new news, but she wasn't joking. "Seers are supposed to see the future, and I haven't. Not really. I see parables. I see—I see riddles. That feels wrong to me. And my head hurts. Horribly. I feel like these visions or dreamwalks, or whatever they are, will kill me, and I feel that that's purposeful. I feel like I screwed up something, and now God or The Universe is trying to teach me the ultimate lesson," she explained breathlessly. "And it's not just that."

Max just waited for her to continue.

She knew she had to tell him. Knew he needed to know.

"I need you to promise me that what I say next, you won't tell him," she said, nodding her head upstairs, referring to Porter.

"My lips are sealed," Max whispered.

"I don't just see things when I'm out. It started that day at the hospital. I thought I was talking with Dr. Whitmore, but I wasn't. No one was there. But I swear to you, I thought there was. It's starting up again. I thought it was a one-time thing, but I could have sworn you were a zombie and were bleeding out from a gash on your neck this morning." She was talking so fast she didn't know if he had understood a word she'd said. "I'm scared of myself, and I hate it."

"That—That's a lot tuh take in," Max breathed, eyes wide. "Why didn' ya tell us sooner? Or me, at least?" He looked wounded. Like she had reached into his chest and ripped his heart out.

"Because I feel like I'm going crazy, and I don't want to end up in a psyche ward or worse," Della said, ashamed of the words leaving her lips.

Max didn't say anything.

"Are you mad at me?" she whispered.

He whipped his head around to look at her. "No! Of

course not! Why would Ei be mad at ya?"

"I figured you'd be yelling by now," she said sheepishly, not meeting his eyes.

A look of realization was spreading across his face. "Is that what happened every time ya tried tuh speak up? Someone would yell at ya?" He looked horrified.

Della sighed heavily. "My mom tried to be there, but with the twins and the historical society, she just got busier and busier. I couldn't talk to my dad about anything. Never felt comfortable enough to talk to Sebastian about a lot of things. My trips to the reservation were few and far between. I've had to keep so many things buried that I don't know how to tell anyone anything anymore. I observe. I focus on others. But when I have to sit down and tell anyone anything about myself, I feel trapped. I panic."

Max nodded to himself. "Ei get it, trust me, Ei do. But ya don' have tuh feel like that anymore. Not with me."

Della looked him dead in the eyes, her words getting caught in her throat. "But why?"

Max swallowed hard, looking away. "Can Ei tell ya somethin'?"

"Obviously."

Max was quiet for a long time. She could see the gears turning in his head. His face was reddening, his hands curling around the edge of the table. Part of her knew what he was going to say.

"Ei try my best tuh be honest. Ei spent my younger years lyin' tuh survive, so my goal now is tuh tell the truth whenever possible. So here it is," He paused to look at her. "Ei love ya so much, Della. Ya have no idea." He looked so guilty. His eyes were full of regret, but at the same time, he looked relieved. "Ei'm not sayin' that tuh put a wedge between Porter and ya. Believe me, Ei'm only—"

"There's already a wedge," Della cut in. A little too quick, a little too harsh.

Max inhaled sharply. "Ei've noticed. Wanna tell me why?"

"I love Porter. I do. But sometimes, I feel like the timing is wrong. Right person, wrong time. We're both struggling with so much, and I don't know if being together will make things better or worse. 'Cause right now, it feels worse," Della whispered. She almost couldn't stop herself from saying, 'And with you, it's always better.'

"Porter has always been difficult. But Ei've never seen him look at someone the way he looks at ya. Hell, he doesn' even look at his hearse that way," Max laughed.

Della smiled weakly. "I just don't want us to break each other's hearts."

"Ei thought yer only fear was giant man-eatin' crabs," Max said, nudging her playfully.

"Haha," Della snickered.

"Ei know ya don' wanna hear this, but maybe ya should talk tuh him about all this."

"I'm afraid of what he is going to say."

Max gave her a knowing look. "Ya shouldn' have one foot in, one foot out. That's not how relationships work. It's all or nothin', love." He swallowed hard, looking away. "Just know Ei'll be here tuh sift through the fallout."

Della chose not to respond to that. Instead, she stared at the tiles on the kitchen floor, quietly scrutinizing the dirt between the cracks and what looked to be a plastic fork hiding under the edge of the refrigerator. She tried focusing on anything and everything except Max.

But that was a difficult feat, she had to admit.

They were quiet for some time, and Della could tell Max was beating himself up for what he'd said, but she was glad he told her nonetheless.

"So, super sleuth, what are ya gonna do?" Max asked suddenly.

"About what?" she asked distractedly.

"Yer parents mentioned us all goin' tuh Church tomorrow. We can talk tuh that help group Cyrus mentioned." He was trying his best to cheer her up. Bless him.

"I think we should also talk with my aunt," Della said with a reluctant nod.

"Why?"

Della sighed. "Because she just so happens to be the mayor."

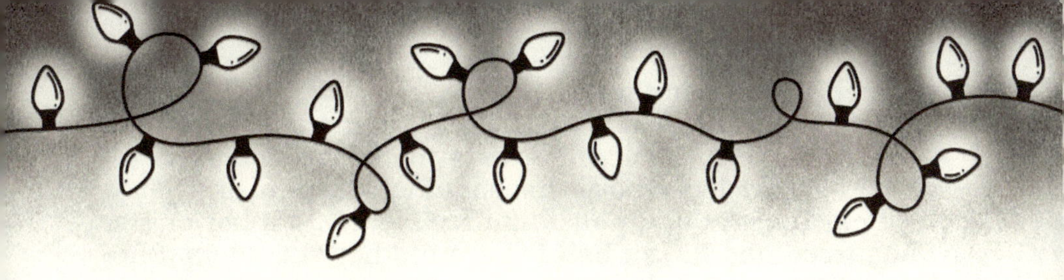

CHAPTER TWENTY-SIX

Sunday mornings were the Coleman family's most important day of the week. Like clockwork, they got up at seven o'clock sharp, ate breakfast, got dressed, piled into the family car, and headed out. It was the one day of the week that Jasper would yell at not only Quincy or Della but at Cassie and Leonel, too. It was like he could read minds. If the twins even thought about complaining, he would scream at the top of his lungs.

Della barely had time to wonder if anything had changed when Jasper had come barreling into her room, yelling at her and Cassie to get up and get dressed. Though she was irritated she had to get up so early, she took solace in knowing Jasper Coleman, the man with no shame, was still just as crotchety every Sunday as she'd remembered. She'd be terrified if he calmly asked them to hurry things along instead of shouting orders like a disgruntled skipper.

"This is gonna get old real fast," Max mumbled as Della helped him with his tie while they watched Porter fuss with his hair in the bathroom.

They'd decided to hide for as long as they could in there for multiple reasons, the biggest being Kimi wasn't speaking to or looking at Della.

"Oh, you have no idea. Christmas will be worse, trust me," Della sighed.

Porter made a disappointed face in the mirror. "I'm sure it won't be that bad."

"Then you don't know me or my family," Della laughed. Porter smiled, ruffling his hair a few more times. Della frowned. "You look fine."

"I just want to make a good impression."

"Trust us, no one will care," Max sniggered, then looked at Della, licked his thumb, and gently scrubbed at something on her cheek.

"What are you doing?" Della laughed

"Ya've got a bit of mascara there," he smiled.

Porter looked over his shoulder, scrutinizing her. He reached out and pulled the scrunchie from her hair so her green and brown hair fell around her shoulders. She usually tried to hide it when she went to Church, but today required her adventurous spirit. The boys stepped back to look at their handiwork, smiling sweetly. It was baffling how comfortable they were with each other. As an outsider looking in, she'd have thought the three of them had known each other their whole lives.

"Do a spin," Porter said giddily.

Della felt her cheeks flush. She spun, the skirt of her sparkly plum dress floating around her like she was spinning in a whirlpool.

"Beautiful," Porter said once she'd finished.

"Gorgeous," Max corrected.

Della imagined her whole face was burning red. "Suck ups."

Porter just laughed, leading them out of the bathroom. The rest of the Coleman family was piled into Jasper's car, so they decided to take the hearse. Just as Della had expected, Porter was livid. The mysterious ice from the night before had left water damage on his seats. Della tried to apologize, but he didn't want to hear it. He vowed that no one could ever drive his precious baby again. Della had to laugh at that.

It didn't take long for them to reach the Church. Every road led directly towards it in some way or another. With its towering steeples and manicured front garden—the snow had been pushed away into neat fence-like structures, ice sculptures dotting the grounds—it looked more like a palace than a Church. Porter was in absolute awe of the Sycamore Friends and Family Church. Max took it upon himself to point out that the ice sculptures were melting.

The Church was massive. Two stories, roughly half the size of a football field, full of extravagant statues of angels, stained-glass windows, and disgustingly uncomfortable pews. Despite all the ethereal aspects, the place still felt too human. Maybe it was the way the giant rugs stretching across the floor squished under your feet or the bathrooms that smelled of antiseptic.

Della used to love this place. Listening to Bible stories in Sunday school had been the highlight of her week. There was once a time when getting up for Church wasn't a chore—when Della read a passage from the Bible every morning. But people ruined it. The high standards and the pressure were too much for her to handle. Della couldn't remember the last time she picked up her Bible, but she did pray every night. That was the one thing she held onto. The one thing she still loved and believed in was God Himself—the love of Jesus. People couldn't ruin that part of her faith.

God kept the promises His creations couldn't.

Despite her loyalty to Him, she sighed bitterly as she led the boys inside. She spotted Sebastian and waved him over but wished she hadn't. Every head turned in her direction at the movement. She could already hear the whispers starting.

". . . is that the Coleman girl. . . oh my, it is. . ." One woman said.

"Who's that black kid? What's wrong with his skin? Bet him and the other one are trouble just like her." An older man said, eyeing Max like a vulture. Della searched around for his hand, gripping it tightly.

"I heard she was practicing witchcraft. I told her parents she was a bad seed, but did they listen?" a man said.

"I wouldn't doubt it. I still can't believe they let her dye her hair like that," his wife replied sourly.

Panic must've been written all over her face since Max squeezed her hand tightly, leaning close. "Ignore them. They don' matter," he said, giving the nearest gossiper a dirty look. As she squeezed his hand, she could feel his heart beating as fast as hers, their pulses in sync.

"She dropped out of high school in her last year. Pathetic," someone said.

Della held her head high, swallowing hard. She wasn't going to let them get to her. She squeezed Max's hand again, then let go. This was her world. She could be above them if she wanted; all she had to do was snap her fingers, and she could destroy this whole town. Another snap, and it'd rebuild to her liking.

Guilt flooded her at that thought.

Maybe she held onto her faith because the Universe had bestowed upon her a god complex.

Sebastian waded through the crowd, scowling at the assembly, shaking his head angrily.

"Screw them all," Sebastian whispered, taking a minute to do an odd little handshake with Porter before offering Della his arm.

Della gripped tightly to him, smiling. "Be cordial; I don't want to bring out the kraken," Della whispered back, her voice cracking. It hit then just how much she had relied on him all these years. Part of her wished he had come with her to Moss Hollow.

"So, we gonna find this support group now?" Max

asked, looking like he wanted to hide. He looked like a splash of color on a blank canvas here. Most would call it an accident, but Della would have called it art.

She shook her head, awkwardly unlinking Sebastian's arm. "Have to get through service first."

"Yeah, why do you think I brought my Bible? Get with the program," he said in a mocking tone.

Della smiled. They were all trying to make her feel better, which cracked her up.

They found a seat at the back, muddling through service as best they could. Well, Della and Sebastian muddled through. Porter had his Bible out, highlighting the passages the pastor was talking about, writing notes in a tiny journal he'd procured from the inside of his suit jacket, smiling happily. Max, on the other hand, was asleep, his chin resting against his chest as he snored. Sebastian found amusement in sticking pens in his hair, trying to see how many he could stick in before he woke up. Della couldn't help but laugh.

It hadn't been that bad of a service. She'd agreed with most of the pastor's points. Most. Not all. Very far from all. But per usual, worship was too long.

When service was finally over, and Porter had restrained Max from skewering Sebastian with a pen, Della stood, brushing herself off, switching to interrogation mode.

"You guys want to catch up with me later?" she asked, smoothing out the wrinkles in her dress. "I could use some extra ears around here. I won't be long."

"I'll trail ya, just in case," Porter said, a knowing look on his face.

Sebastian hesitated, searching her face, but nodded. He knew better than to ask questions. The last time he had gotten involved in one of her cases, he took her place in a holding cell. Della still felt terrible about that.

Max nodded, grabbing Sebastian by the wrist and pulling him toward God knows where.

Della inhaled sharply, swept her hair behind her shoulders, and then set off, Porter in tow. She didn't care to look at anyone; she just kept walking until she reached her destination. The Church had four quadrants: the main chapel, the children's chapel, the study hall and offices, and the meeting rooms. Ever since Della was little, the only place she allowed herself to venture alone was the meeting rooms. Every other sector made her stomach turn. Still, she didn't like it here. Even Porter looked uneasy. They exchanged a look, her skin crawling as she nodded to an open door.

When they entered, an overwhelming pickle juice

aroma filled Della's lungs. If they were alone, she would've gagged.

A woman was placing pieces of paper on chairs in the center of the room. "I'm just setting up. Can you wait out—" She looked up. "Delphee?" she asked.

For a girl who knew everyone in this town, it took Della a minute to figure out who this woman was. Again, those heavy velvet curtains in her mind were trying to keep the truth from her. However, this time, a name slipped through the cracks.

"Delphee Coleman," The woman smiled.

She had a kind face, slightly wrinkled, showing her age, her dark gray hair twisted in a bun on top of her head. Marion Warren. A grief counselor and someone whom Della had wished to forget.

"It has been quite some time since we last talk-ed. You can have a seat, and I'll introduce you both when the others come in," she smiled, offering two pens and nametags to her.

Della turned to Porter, who was lurking in the door-way, rubbing his neck nervously as he waited for Della to respond.

"Actually, Mrs. Warren, we are here to ask you a few questions," Della said, politely refusing the nametags, giving Porter a bored look, which he returned with a sympathetic smile.

When she turned back to face Marion, the woman's face lit up in recognition. "Of course! I'm always willing to answer questions!" she laughed. Della wanted to roll her eyes, but instead, she just smiled. "My goodness, look at you all grown up."

Della's eye twitched. "Yup," was all she managed. There was little she wanted to remember about grief coun-seling. She hadn't needed a shrink back then; she had needed her parents.

Marion smiled widely. "And you are?" she asked, ex-amining Porter.

"Porter Garroway, ma'am," he smiled.

"Pleasure," Marion bowed. "So, what are you two here for? We welcome anyone and everyone. No matter your addiction, we will help you get through it."

"I have a few questions about Ashton John," Della explained, taking a step forward.

"Oh," Marion said, obviously surprised. "What do you need to know?"

Della scanned Marion's face. She looked disappoint-ed that she and Porter weren't here to divulge all their secrets, but other than that, she just looked like a frail old woman with nothing to hide.

Della cleared her throat, putting on a sad smile like donning a mask. "First off, I'm very sorry for your loss, Mrs. Warren. It must have been a hard pill to swallow when you learned he'd gone missing." Pill. In a place like this, that was insensitive. Della silently cursed herself. Porter, on the other hand, had to stifle a laugh.

Marion nodded. "Ashton was a personal project of mine," she said, taking a seat in one of the chairs. "He was a very bright young man but plagued with trauma. I saw him outside this support group for grief counseling about his mother."

That triggered a thought. Ashton had lost his mother a few years back, which caused him to turn to drugs.

"You two must have been close then? In that time, did he ever confide in you that he was in danger?" Della asked, eyeing Porter out of the corner of her eye. He had discreetly grabbed a pamphlet that explained what happened in this little support group. He caught her watching him, and he gave her an innocent shrug.

"He had been acting odd for a week before he went missing. I had a feeling he was getting heavy into the drugs again," Marion said sadly. "I went over to his trailer one day to confront him. He drove off."

Della had to force her eyelids not to flicker in frustration. This sounded like an episode of a crappy soap opera a lonely housewife would watch. Not a clue to what had happened to Ashton. She tapped her foot on the floor, staring out the window behind Marion. This woman seemed to be using her caring nature as an excuse to know everyone's business. There was once a time when Della would have applauded such a deed. In a way, it reminded her of what Eric had done.

With a shiver, she shifted uncomfortably, turning her attention back to Marion's physical appearance. Her shoes were old and scuffed, her clothes rather plain. A loose sun dress over thick leggings, topped off with a cardigan. There were small holes in the cardigan and visible stitch marks on the dress from poor attempts at fixing it. Her clothes were either thrifted or very old hand-me-downs. Della guessed business hadn't been booming for Mrs. Warren.

"Was Ashton into. . . witches? Or magic?" Della asked carefully.

Marion looked like a little kid caught with her hand in the cookie jar. "I could have sworn you were asking me all this because of your job in Moss Hollow, Louisiana. Not because you were chasing some story for your blog," she said, her tone sweet and flowery. What a carefully crafted way of saying 'screw you.' "I still talk with your mom, you know."

Porter cleared his throat. "You—You saw Della? When she was younger?" he asked, eyeing Della cautiously. Della scowled at him, raising an eyebrow. Again, he gave her an apologetic smile.

Marion nodded. "I would talk to her for hours. She would sit and write in one of her notebooks, completely ignoring me."

Della finally let herself roll her eyes, taking a few steps forward. "Back to the subject at hand, it would be helpful if you answered my question, Mrs. Warren. I am just trying to help."

Mrs. Warren smiled widely. "Your definition of help seems to differ from the rest of us, doesn't it?"

Della smiled tightly. "It wouldn't hurt for you to answer the question, Marion."

"I think what my colleague is trying to say is that our questions differ because of our current leads," Porter smiled widely.

Marion's sharp eyes bore into Porter. She looked him up and down, seeming to make up her mind on something. "Ashton took a couple of odd jobs in town: the historical society, the dealership, a restaurant. I'm sure they have more information than I do. I didn't see him as much as I used to." She turned to look Della dead in the eyes.

"Thank you for your time, Mrs. Warren," Della sneered, turning to leave.

"Uh, just one minute," Porter said, catching Della by the elbow and spinning her back around.

"Something on your mind?" Marion asked.

Porter nodded, reddening. Not his usual magenta blush, but a deep, fiery red. "When you used to see Della, did she have seizures? Or talk about dreams?"

Della wanted to strangle him. No matter how guilty she would feel afterward, it wouldn't have compared to the satisfaction of seeing Porter cowering. How dare he ask that question. How dare he invade such private things. With Max, she knew he was genuinely trying to help her. With Porter, he was just fishing for information to use against her.

Marion's eyebrows furrowed. "Della had a very over-active imagination. Seems to me she never grew out of it. When I did get her to talk, she would spin some pretty tall tales. Her parents wanted that part of her. . . dealt with. Seems I didn't quite do my job."

Porter looked over his shoulder, discreetly nodding to prompt her to ask one of her carefully put-together questions. When Della didn't say anything, he took it upon himself.

"What kind of tales?"

"Well, after her grandmother died, she got it in her head that this whole town was doomed for destruction. That's why she takes those pills that keep her from dreaming. She'd have horrible nightmares, wake up screaming," Marion explained, looking innocent, but Della could hear the edge in her voice—the kind of mocking tone only high school cheerleaders were supposed to have.

"Yeah, well, Della is still here and has places to be," she smiled tightly, prying Porter's fingers from her elbow rather roughly. She hated being talked about like she wasn't standing there with them.

Porter winced against her fingernails digging into his skin, nodding. "See you around, Mrs. Warren."

"Heh. . . Yes, well, I surely hope not," she laughed sweetly.

Della stomped out of that room with the force of a hurricane. She was just glad no one else was in the hall to witness whatever she would allow herself to say or do to Porter. No word in the English dictionary, none of her flowery eloquence, no Latin phrase forgotten by time, nor new-fangled slang could describe her rage.

"Can we talk for a minute?" Porter asked, his fingers finding hers. He dug in his heels and tightened his grip as she tried to pull away. "Please? I have some things to say I don't want Max listening in on."

Della let her arm go limp, hoping that would make him let go. But it didn't. He only held tighter to her.

"I think you should talk to your mom about everything. You seem to be the only person who doesn't know why they did what they did. Maybe if you know, you won't—" Porter finally let go of her hand, timidly coming around to face her, a worried expression on his face.

"What?" Della asked, staring him dead in the eyes.

"You need to talk to them. I think they know more than they are letting on. And I can tell Kimi is worried about you," Porter explained. Worried wasn't the word she would've used. "I saw her looking at a file yesterday, and I know Max asked her about medical issues on her side of the family. I just think that—"

"Porter, do you think I'm dying or something?" Della asked blankly.

Porter rocked back and forth on his heels, shrugging several times. "No. Maybe? I hope not!" He ran his hands through his hair aggressively. "I don't know, Della. I just think that you should talk to them! I know you want to know what happened, no matter how much you try to deny it."

Della crossed her arms over her chest, biting her lower lip. So what? She was supposed to run home and ask about her visions? To try and understand? To wait for an apology? Too little, too late.

"I'll pass on the whole intervention thing," Della smiled tightly.

Before she could even make a move forward, he put a hand on her shoulder to stop her. "It doesn't have to be now. Just promise me you'll talk with them before we leave. Please. Because if you won't, I will. And I don't want you to hear everything from me."

"No," Della said, expressionless.

"Wh—What?" Porter blinked.

"No," Della smiled.

"Can I get a maybe?" Porter pleaded.

Della shrugged. "I'll leave that up to your imagination," she thought for a minute, then sighed. "If that's all you care about, if that's all you want to know, then fine. Ask them. Figure it out. Play detective. Team up with Max; he's already got some leads."

All he did was open and close his mouth a couple of times. Della smiled proudly, thoroughly through with this exchange. She turned to leave.

A hand around her wrist.

He spun her around, a playful look on his face. "I wasn't done," he said, still holding on to her, his lips only inches from her.

"Carry on then," Della dared him.

He leaned in closer, his eyes full of softness. Della inhaled sharply at the thought of him kissing her. But it wasn't anticipation. It was something else she could quite pin.

Porter closed the space between them with the softest of kisses. He kissed her with all his being, with passion and love. With yearning and wanting and promises of protection. But Della flinched. This didn't feel right. She turned her face away before he could kiss her anymore. Something was wrong between them. That's why she'd stopped him before.

"I told you, I don't want you to kiss me," she said before she could stop herself, pushing him away harder than she'd meant to.

Porter froze.

"You can't just kiss away whatever this is," she said, gesturing between them. "It doesn't work like that."

"Then tell me how I am supposed to fix it," Porter

pleaded. "I hate this."

"Me too, but I don't know how to fix it, Porter. I really don't."

He sighed heavily, backing away from her, looking at her hands like she held two loaded guns.

She slowly retracted her hands, clasping them together in front of her, sadness filling her. "I don't want this to be our cycle," she added, sighing heavily.

Porter gave her a funny look.

"We get mad at each other, and then you kiss me, thinking that fixes everything," she said, watching his face fill with understanding.

"Oh. . . I didn't realize that was a bad thing," he mumbled.

"Well, it's not."

"Okay?"

"But it is."

He silently repeated that to himself, looking confused. "What?"

"I don't know," Della breathed exasperatedly, removing her glasses and pinching the bridge of her nose.

Porter looked her up and down. "Okay, I won't kiss you anymore," he said, an edge to his voice. "Should have taken that hint the other night."

"It's not that I don't want you to kiss me, it's just—"

"It's that you don't want *me* to kiss you," he finished for her.

Della furrowed her eyebrows. "What do you mean?"

"I—" Porter ran his hands through his hair. "Nothing. It won't happen again, I promise. I won't jump you like that anymore."

"Okay."

"Okay." Porter nodded. He opened his mouth to say something else when Max and Sebastian came down the hall. "Can we talk more later?" he asked.

Della just nodded.

There was a fissure between them. Something was different now, and she didn't know what it was.

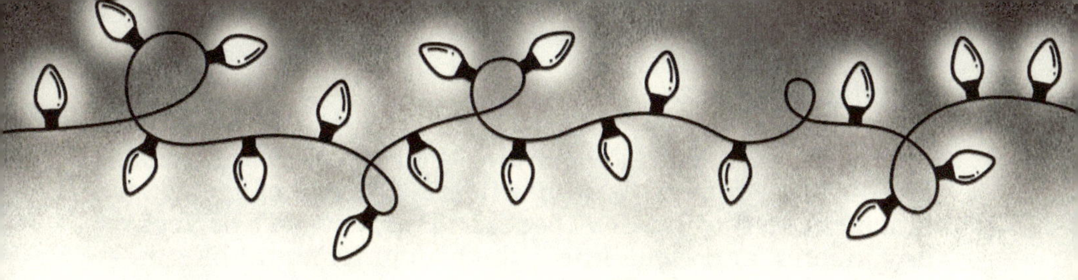

CHAPTER TWENTY-SEVEN

All Hail the Duchess

"Ei swear on my life if another person tries to ask me if they can pray for me, Ei'm gonna smite them," Max snapped as he and Sebastian made their way over to Della and Porter.

"It's not that bad. Some of them will," Sebastian laughed. "Did you guys get whatever info you needed?"

Della shrugged. "Not really. Hey, do you want to come with us to Poppy's?" She didn't really want Sebastian around, but the tension between her and Porter was suffocating.

Three's a crowd, as they say. But maybe four would be a balanced hunting party.

"Sure!" Sebastian said giddily.

Porter cleared his throat. "Who is Poppy again?"

"Della's rich aunt," Sebastian said matter-of-factly.

Max and Porter gave her a funny look.

"She's not rich—"

"Nope, she's loaded. And hot. Super-hot," Sebastian said dreamily. "Kinda weird, but hot."

"Okay, that's—No, please don't say that," Della stuttered, shriveling her nose in disgust.

Sebastian just shrugged, smiling excitedly. "Anyways, what do you wish to gain from Poppy?"

Della raised her eyebrow at him, shaking her head disapprovingly. "She's linked with the case I'm working on,"

"Oh, this'll be fun," Sebastian laughed.

~ ~ ~

Della didn't like to use the word hate, but that was the only word that came to mind when she thought of her father's side of the family: hate. Total loathing, even. She couldn't stand any of them.

Except Poppy Bennet-Hawthorne. Her aunt had as much hatred toward Jasper and the rest as Della. Della loved Aunt Poppy with all her heart. The two of them were black sheep that herded together. Poppy wasn't perfect by any means, and Della knew she was judgmental like the rest, but at least Poppy had the decency to pass that judgment onto someone deserving.

The thing about Della's family was that it was a big one. And the bigger the family, the more dysfunction and stupidity. Jasper had two full siblings, Rudolph and Felicity. Plus, his half-sister Poppy. Felicity was the oldest, Jasper and Rudolph fought for the middle, and Poppy was the youngest. Their mother, Claudia Bell-Coleman-Bennet, had been married to Christopher Coleman, who died *tragically* during a yacht accident. She remarried to a man named Victor Bennet and eventually had Poppy.

Poppy was happily divorced in her thirties, living in the biggest house in Sycamore Heights. She was a tall, curvy woman with mousy brownish-gray hair that stretched the length of her back. She was the spitting image of Victor but tended to act more like Claudia.

Her siblings despised her, for she was the baby of the family and got whatever she damn well pleased.

Which she sometimes used to help Della. How do you think she could afford an apartment in Moss Hollow? Jasper surely wouldn't have spared the money. Not that he had it to begin with.

Della knocked on Poppy's front door, eyeing her entourage cautiously. Porter looked like he was miles away, Max looked bored, and Sebastian was practically jumping out of his skin with excitement. Ever since they were little, Sebastian had tried to win Poppy's favor.

The door was wrenched open before Della could tease him about that.

Poppy—wearing a sheer maroon robe over frilly pajamas—flung herself onto Della, wrapping her in a big hug.

"Della!" Poppy screeched. She always said her nickname with such enthusiasm. After all, Poppy was the one who had given her that name to begin with.

"Hi, Aunt Poppy," Della said, embarrassed and breathless from her tight hug.

Poppy pushed her back, examining her. "Look at you! You look all sophisticated! I love it! I see you're still sticking with the green, trés chic."

Della nodded, her cheeks red. Compliments always made her feel awkward. Most of the time, she didn't feel she deserved them.

"The grandparents aren't here, are they?" she asked, peeking through the doorway.

"Nope, just me. Your cousins are out too, visiting their *father*," she said sourly as if that word was poison.

Poppy had married when she was eighteen and later had two teenagers: Christopher II and Chloe. Della was overjoyed to find they were gone. The little brats did everything they could to get under Della's skin. It hadn't been so bad when Quincy was around, but they practically tortured her once he left.

Poppy swept her inside, then finally noticed her niece had brought company. Her eyes lit up with a dangerous light as they slid over Porter, who cowered under her gaze. She looked to Della, her expression dreamy.

"You brought goodies," Poppy giggled.

"Hands off," Della warned. "They are half your age."

Poppy made a tsking noise, drawing an 'x' over her heart. "Fine, fine. Come on, darlings."

Poppy swept them inside, forcing them to remove their shoes and store them in the hall closet before she led them into her lounge. Della definitely hadn't learned to decorate from her aunt. The entire lounge sparkled under the light of a mini chandelier. Pale candles turned the air sweet, the smell reminiscent of citrus candies. Plush rugs and over-stuffed furniture matched the pink-and-cream-speckled walls. An elk skull with glittering lights around its antlers hung above the mantle.

Della counted two Christmas trees so far but knew there were more farther into the house. These were too small. One tiny tree on the coffee table, one around Max's height in the corner by the floor-to-ceiling windows. Both were flocked white and adorned with pink, gold, and brown ornaments. Both had presents beneath them. Every other tree that littered the house would have its own stack of presents. Each tree represented a different family member. Usually, the size of the tree represented Poppy's love for whoever's name was on the presents beneath it. A glance at the tiniest tree told Della the presents beneath it belonged to Rudolph. She smiled to herself. Rudolph, in some ways, was worse than Jasper.

"So, give me all the dirty details. What's the great Della Coleman trying to solve this time?" Poppy asked. She lay lazily across a couch, a glass of champagne in her hand.

Her guard Shih Tzu, Titus, ran down the hallway as if summoned. He went straight for Della, circling her feet, yapping excitedly.

"That's actually why we are here," Della began as Porter and Sebastian bee-lined for the tower of chocolates on the coffee table. "Ashton John. Spill."

Della sat on the loveseat in front of the window, Max hovering beside her. Titus jumped up on her lap and snuggled in, falling asleep instantly. Strange. Titus had never liked Della before.

Poppy smirked. "I figured that's all you came here for."

Della gave a half shrug. "Can't blame a woman on a mission. You taught me that."

Poppy saluted her with her flute of champagne before taking a dainty sip. "I'll give you the same long-winded explanation I gave Kohen. But. . . since you're my favorite, and you brought me playthings, I'll spice it up a little." Her eyes drifted to Porter.

Della rolled her eyes as Porter stared at her, eyes wide, caught eating a truffle mid-bite. Sebastian tried not to look hurt. Max gave a disgusted shake of his head.

"Poppy," Della sighed. Making men uncomfortable was Poppy's favorite game.

She pouted for a minute before finally collecting her thoughts. Poppy, being the mayor of this all-but-fine town, knew everyone's business. She was a bloodhound when it came to gossip. Nothing got past her.

"We hired Ashton at the historical society to give him a second chance. He was a hard worker. He helped fix up the leaky pipes and faulty wiring. I actually liked the kid. It seemed like he was trying to be a better person," Poppy said sadly. "He got along with your mother. Knew a lot about the house and the people who used to live there. For obvious reasons."

"What obvious reasons?" Max asked. He perched on the armrest of the loveseat, watching Poppy intently. Titus growled at him, causing him to recoil. Porter tried to hide his smug smile at that, but Della caught it.

"Ash's mom was Mukwa," Poppy said with a shrug.

Porter gave Della a look like he had been expecting this the whole time. Della glared at him.

Poppy gasped dramatically. "I know something the great Delphee Coleman doesn't?"

Della gave her an irritated look. "I had a feeling," she admitted.

Della thought for a long while, petting Titus, who didn't growl like she expected him to.

Ashton being Indigenous certainly changed a lot of things. Originally, she had thought whatever beast they were chasing was going after people who threatened the Mukwa tribe, but Ashton didn't fit that box.

"Did Ashton have any enemies? Newer ones? Did

anyone try to talk to him on lunch breaks or after his shift?" Porter asked before Della or Max could.

"Not that I recall. I've been preoccupied trying to juggle Chris and Chloe, the house, the construction near the reservation. . . pretty much everything," Poppy sighed. "Why? You think someone kidnapped him?" she scoffed. "For what reason? No one would pay ransom for him. No one even noticed he was missing for a week. He's probably downstream somewhere, having the trip of his life. Or he's dead in a ditch. Or maybe he took a page from your book and left this godforsaken town."

"People disappear for far less than ransom money, Poppy," Della said knowingly. Titus snorted as if he agreed.

Poppy couldn't argue with that. "Any other questions?"

Max gave Della a questioning look. She shrugged. Whatever he would ask couldn't be much worse than Porter asking her ex-therapist about her grief counseling days.

"Did Ashton ever call anyone mamankanois?" he asked carefully. "Or did ya ever hear anyone call him that?"

"Is that—Is that even English?" Poppy asked skeptically.

"It's Algonquin," Della sighed.

"Cool," Poppy smiled tightly. "But no. He didn't talk much to me or anyone else. Just your mom when he had to. Never saw anyone come pick him up or anything either."

"Dead end," Max whispered.

Della nodded.

"Okay, my turn to ask the questions," Poppy said excitedly, turning to Porter. "Staring with, who, pray tell, are you?"

"Oh, uh, me, I—Uh—I'm no one, ma'am." Porter swallowed hard, backing away, dropping the chocolates in his hands as if he thought they were poisoned. He positioned himself next to Della, staring at her with pleading eyes. He wanted out of here. Fast.

"I like nobodies," Poppy said with a daring smile. "They are always here for a good time and not a—"

"You make me sick," Della laughed, picking up Titus and placing him gently on the floor as she stood.

Poppy blew her a kiss in reply. "Will I see you at my party? All of you?"

"If I haven't solved my case, I'll be dragged here screaming. So yes, I guess," Della sighed. "Thanks for entertaining us." *In more ways than one*, Della thought.

"Of course! Always happy to have guests." She turned and winked at Sebastian, who practically fainted.

Max took it upon himself to grab the lovestruck idiot

by the collar of his jacket and pull him into the hall. Porter almost ran to follow them.

"They are just too cute!" Poppy said when they were out of earshot. "You know, when I was your age, I had to pick between Francisco Mon—"

"Not really in the mood for one of your stories, Auntie," Della laughed. "Usually, they end with me being scarred for life."

"Fair enough," she sighed contently. "My bet is on the handsome one."

"Which one is the handsome one?"

Poppy looked her up and down. "Darling, you already know. The fact you didn't say his name tells me everything."

"You're horrible, you know? You send me spiraling into an existential crisis every time I talk to you," Della pouted, knowing damn well she thought of Porter as pretty and Max as handsome.

"It does come with the last name, my dear," she said with a flourish of her hand. "Tell ya what. If you don't stay for Christmas, see me before you leave. I think you'll like this year's gifts."

Something told her whatever Poppy had wasted her credit limit on this year would be worth enduring Sycamore Heights until the end of the week.

"Deal."

"Alrighty. Now go, I have things to do, and you have a mystery to solve. Love you," Poppy said, waving her away.

"Love you too."

Della regrouped with the boys in the hearse. Even Sebastian had piled in. He had opted to leave his *Buick Electra* in the church parking lot on account of wanting to talk Max's ear off about one of their shared scientific inter-ests.

"Your family is weird," Porter announced when she slipped into the front seat beside him.

"Ha, you've got no clue," Della sighed.

"Now what?" Sebastian asked, poking his head in between them.

"Ei say we head tuh Ashton's last known place of residence," Max suggested.

Della nodded in agreement.

Porter cleared his throat. "Mind if I put in my two cents?"

Della shrugged. He shifted uncomfortably. "I mean, I'm invested in this as much as you guys are, but we haven't found any evidence suggesting this is one of *our* problems. Maybe we should leave this up to the cops and go ice skat-ing or something. Maybe Mavericks is wrong."

"True, but I have leads," Della said carefully, her voice high and squeaky. She glanced at Max, who looked out the window and pretended to ignore her.

Porter's face filled with darkness. "What?"

"I just think that we should follow the Ashton path wherever it leads us," Della said.

"*A missing persons case isn't exactly our kind of problem*," Porter said through tight lips.

"It was last time," Max said matter-of-factly.

Porter glared at them. "You suck. Both of you."

"You want me to give you directions? I know where Ashton spent his days rotting away," Della smiled.

"So do I," Sebastian said giddily. "Hit the gas, Garroway."

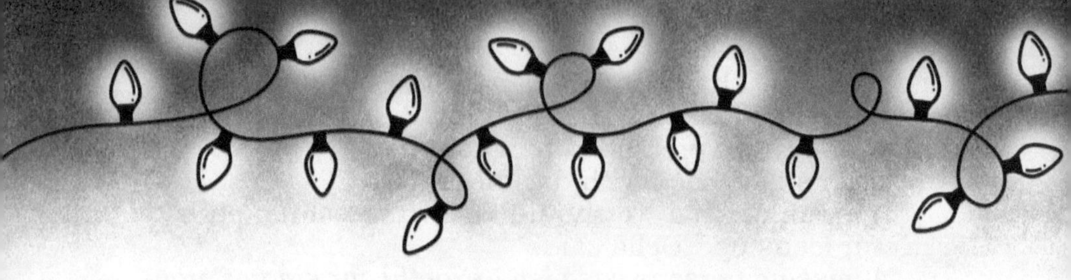

CHAPTER TWENTY-EIGHT

Dollar For Your Thoughts

Not long after, Porter parked the hearse in the driveway that led to Ashton's house. Well, 'house' was a generous word. The trailer before them looked worse than the car Sebastian drove. The trailer roof was caving in, the door was barely stuck to its hinges, and the steps were so rusted and broken that Della was surprised they were still attached to the rest of the desolate place. It was such a drastic change to the rest of the town. Part of Della liked it here. It reminded her of a more run-down Moss Hollow if that was even possible.

"You'd think a place like this wouldn't exist in Sycamore Heights," Sebastian said from the back seat, a glint in his eyes.

"You're drooling," she said. "Ashton lost his home shortly after I busted him," she told Porter and Max. The two events had been unrelated, but Della had felt guilty at the time.

"I kind of feel bad for the guy," Porter whispered, grimacing.

"Yeah, well, he made his choice," Max said sourly as Della stepped out of the hearse. He looked absolutely appalled by everything here.

The trailer park resembled a wrecking yard, and Della was sure most of the inhabitants thought of it as such. Old cars littered the small driveways between all the trailers in varying states of decay. Old tires peeked out of the muddy ground, and piles of moldy firewood lined the forest's edge like a fence. No wonder Sebastian liked it so much. He was a motorhead at heart, same as Porter.

"Disgustin'," Max breathed.

"All right, all right, I know it isn't the prettiest, but look how cozy it all is. In a place like this, everyone knows everyone," Sebastian winked.

"How is that any different from the rest of the town?" Porter asked.

Sebastian stood on the footboard of the hearse, leaning out, one hand grasping Porter's headrest so he looked like a pirate leaning off a ship's mast. "Down here is the hillbilly, redneck, 'shoot you in the foot if you make a wrong move,' part of town. It's where my soul belongs," he said, then saluted the sky. "God bless America!"

"Yeah, okay, step down off your soapbox there, Billy-Bob," Della said, lazily saluting back.

"So, what are we looking for, exactly?" Sebastian chuckled.

"Max and I are looking for clues. You two are staying in the car," Della explained, feeling once again like a tired parent.

"Then why am I even here?" Sebastian asked, looking hurt.

"Yeah, I don't like the sound of that either," Porter said, making to open his door.

"Yer our getaway driver," Max shrugged, then turned to Sebastian. "Ya said it yerself, if we step wrong, we get shot. Yer our eyes and ears."

"But—But what's in it for us?" Sebastian pouted.

"If we find money stuffed in the mattress or whatever, it's all yours," Della winked. "As for Porter. . . To be determined," Della said as politely as she could. Porter gave her a pointed look.

"Yes!" Sebastian smiled. "Thank you!"

Della rolled her eyes, pulling Max toward Ashton's trailer. His was one of the few that didn't have a beat-up truck attached to the front. Della made a mental note of that. You can tell a lot about a person by the state of their car and home. It seemed Ashton didn't care much about his belongings—like no one cared about him. Marion may have acted like she was heartbroken he was missing, but Della suspected otherwise. He was just a paycheck to her and nothing more. And Poppy? Poppy didn't care about anyone other than herself. Unless, of course, that person happened to have neon green hair and a rebellious spirit.

"We aren' actually gonna give him any money, are we?" Max asked, looking over his shoulder to wave at Sebastian as he scanned for onlookers. It seemed all the hillbillies were out for the day. That, or they didn't care too much about people poking around things they shouldn't.

"Ahh, Hell no," Della choked. "I am not going to be the creator of *that* mess."

Max smiled. Della had to do a double take. She was

used to Porter's melancholy smile, and until recently, she hadn't realized Max had shared his same sad grin. But this, this wide grin spreading across Max's face, this was true happiness. She loved it when her boys smiled.

"So, what are we lookin' for exactly? Weather-worn spellbooks? Demonic writin' on the walls? The smell of sulfur waftin' through the air? Oh! Ei know! Bags of bones hidden in the couch!" he laughed to himself.

"Are you making fun of me or yourself?" Della smirked.

"Little bit of both, if Ei'm tuh be honest," Max said with a shrug, stuffing his hands into the pockets of his faux-fur jacket. He nodded towards the door, a funny look on his face.

Della rattled the handle, surprised to watch it fall apart and disconnect from the door. She raised her eyebrow, bending down to look inside the empty socket. It was rusty all the way through. Carefully, Della reached into the hole and pulled the door open. The hinges squeaked and screamed at the movement. How old was this place? How long had it been like this?

"And that's a yes on the sulfur. This place smells like Nicoletta. Like magic," Max gagged.

Della raised an eyebrow. "You can smell magic?" He'd mentioned something like this before, but she hadn't cared to ask about it until now.

He nodded. "Sulfur and perfume. Ei can also smell yer anxiety."

Della blushed. "I'm not anxious."

Max scoffed. "Yer always anxious."

"You can't smell anxiety."

"Yeah, Ei can," Max said matter-of-factly. "Familiar, remember?" He flashed his cat eyes at her.

Della glared at him, sticking her tongue out. She wondered just how many abilities he had. That was a question for a different time.

For now, she turned her attention back to the trailer. Inside was a mess of its own. Piles of papers were strewn across the floor, some marked with muddy shoeprints. Spilled bottles of beer and pop cans littered the countertop across from her, making the trailer smell rancid. The pull-out couch had a few springs popping forth from it—it looked like someone had trashed it on purpose.

"Ei know that look," Max said as Della chewed her lower lip. "What are ya thinkin'?"

"I'm not sure yet. You check around here, and I'll see if there is anything in his bedroom," Della said absentmindedly, making her way to the back of the cabin where a door stood.

This door's hinges weren't rusty, the handle polished, free of dust. Della inhaled sharply as she pulled it open to reveal a small room. Where a bed should have filled the entire room, there was a wobbly desk with a single drawer. The walls were covered with newspaper clippings, printed articles, colored string, ripped pages from books, and crudely scribbled drawings. Della crossed to the desk, gingerly picking up a stack of papers. Scans of old documents were shuffled between photos of dark shapes looming behind even darker trees. Beneath that were more newspaper clippings. Some of which she realized were segments from past issues of *The Utopian Courier*.

"Hey, M—" Della looked over her shoulder, but something caught her eye next to the door she came from.

Each wall was so plastered with papers you couldn't see the wall itself. However, down by the baseboard, there was a metallic sheen. Della discarded the papers, bending to run her fingers along the metallic strip. Carefully, she began peeling papers from the wall, careful not to rip any of them. After a long minute of work, a small, rusty safe sat before her.

"What do we have here?" Della whispered, sitting cross-legged on the floor.

The only problem? Della couldn't crack a safe for the life of her. Cracking a safe had never come up in her detective career until now. She reached out to touch it but hesitated. She wanted to blame her imagination, but she swore she felt something move in the room. She looked around to see if Max had followed her into the bedroom, but he hadn't. No signs of ghosts. No flickering lights. Still, she felt something off.

Feelings. That word Mingan had always used came back to her. Whether it was panic, paranoia, or the paranormal, she didn't know, but she stood abruptly, deciding she didn't want to touch the safe or stay any longer than she had to in this dreary place.

"Hey Max, I need you," she called, looking over the papers she had taken from the wall.

Ashton was smarter than anyone had given him credit for, she had to admit. These papers were seemingly unrelated to a mysterious safe in the wall. More drawings of what looked like billowing smoke with eyes, another with a sketch of a clawed hand. Possibly that of the Wendigo.

"Max!" Della called again, another shiver shooting through her body like she had been plunged into ice water.

A sinking feeling erupted in Della's chest. She stood there frozen, clutching the drawings to her chest and peering through the doorway. No Max, but there was someone hunched over the rusty sink. There was something off about this figure. The way his silhouette was illuminated wasn't right.

"Hello?" Della called, taking a shaking step forward. "Sorry to intrude, but I—"

Della's words got caught in her throat as the person turned to her. Ashton John stood before her. But he wasn't looking at her. He was looking straight through her at the door to what should have been his bedroom. He looked different than how Della remembered him. His face was fuller, his once greasy brown hair was smooth and combed, and the dark circles under his eyes were gone.

"Dammit," he swore, looking over his shoulder. His voice sounded far away, muffled like she was hearing him through a vent.

This wasn't how things had sounded or looked when she'd visited Theodore. This wasn't a dreamwalk or a vision. This was something else entirely.

Della watched as he crossed to the window above the tiny dining table. In the distance, she could hear a running car and a pair of footsteps. He peered through the blinds, his face illuminated by headlights. Ashton swore heavily, glancing at his couch. Della realized now that the sofa—and the rest of the trailer—was in pristine condition. Either she was seeing something from a long time ago, or someone had indeed trashed the place.

A knock on the door.

"Just a second!" Ashton said, turning quickly toward Della. What frightened her most was that he walked right through her like she was a ghost. Not the fact that she was possibly seeing a memory.

Though baffled, she turned to follow him, seeing him unlock the door she had come through. An awful large padlock hung from the handle, a chain connected to the bathroom door to keep it shut. That hadn't been there before.

Another knock.

Ashton grumbled, doubling back to the front door. He ripped it open, faking a smile.

"Mr. Kitchi, Ms. Sinclair, how may I help you?" he asked.

Della peered over his shoulder to see Kohen and Elvi at his doorstep, both looking disgusted. Kohen was dressed in civilian clothes, but Elvi was a goddess in a pantsuit. Della couldn't help but scowl at her.

"We're just checking in on you," Kohen said, looking around Ashton's trailer with a keen eye. Della didn't know what he could be looking for.

"Aww, you are so kind," Ashton said. He blushed. The rotten little sneak could fake a blush.

Elvi smiled tightly. "Have you thought any more about our offer?" *Our* offer?

Ashton's smile faltered. "I'm not selling it, Elvi. It's rightfully mine."

"Then where is it? You say you care about that historical society. A peace pipe like that would fetch a pretty penny. A penny that could be used to keep the lights on," Elvi said coldly. There was desperation in her eyes.

All this over a peace pipe? Why?

"You people are always about the money, aren't you?" Ashton replied, his words just as harsh.

"I'm prepared to offer double for it," Elvi proposed, reaching into her purse and flashing her checkbook at him. Kohen gave him a reassuring nod.

"Even if I said yes, I don't have it on me. Why do you folks want it anyway?" Ashton asked. He glanced over his shoulder at his bedroom door. Della could see the regret on his face. He shouldn't have done that. This mysterious peace pipe was probably hidden in his safe.

Elvi followed his gaze, a smile pulling at her lips. "My family is a collector of these sorts of artifacts. Call it the family business."

"Artifacts people like you shouldn't have," Kohen said gruffly, his eyes narrowing. Della had never seen him like this. He was usually so happy-go-lucky. And why the Hell was he in cahoots with Elvi?

"Au contraire. That peace pipe is *my* family business, so I'm sure you understand why I must say no," Ashton smiled, then looked at Kohen. "In fact, it's *our* family business. You should be honoring that."

Kohen crossed his arms, squaring him up. "This isn't about us, kid."

Ashton yawned. "Alright, cool. Have it your way. If you don't mind, I'm actually trying to get the place cleaned. I have company coming over in a while."

Elvi frowned, replacing her checkbook in her purse. "You have no idea what you have gotten yourself into, Ash."

"Ms. Sinclair, I don't really care." With that, he slammed the door in her face. He stood there for a while, fists clenched, staring at the door like he expected them to break it down.

When he finally removed himself, his face was full of exhaustion. He turned towards the bedroom again, walking swiftly back. Della followed, finding she could pass through the door as he slammed it shut. Ashton ripped open the drawer, taking out a pen and paper. He began to write a letter, but it wasn't the one he'd sent her. This was different. His handwriting was smoother, and this one had been dated November fifth. He'd either decided not to send it and rewrite it later, or someone had done that for him. After he'd gone missing, which Della realized she didn't have an exact date for.

Della was watching his face go through a multitude of expressions. He didn't seem to know what he was writing, yet he did it with such passion Della knew it was important. She knew he believed he'd seen something. That something was wrong here. She moved closer, trying to read the rest of the letter, hoping to find new information, but her eyes refused to see what was on the page. She could read her name, date, and first line, but everything after that was all jumbled-up letters and numbers. It was like she was looking at some other language, like—

Someone was pounding on the door. Muffled voices wafted in through an open window.

Either Ashton was ignoring the ruckus, or the sound wasn't part of this memory.

Della turned back to him, trying to focus on that page. She had to figure out what it was. It was more than curiosity; it was an overwhelming feeling that she had to know.

Pressure was building in her forehead and around her ears as she hovered over him. She could make out *'Elvi Sinclair'* and *'help me,'* but that was it. The blurriness reminded her of trying to read without her glasses. She shut her eyes, rubbing her temples. Why did this keep happening?

When she opened them, Ashton was gone. She looked over her shoulder to see Max coming down the hall.

"Yeah, what do ya need?" he asked, scanning the room. "Geez. This is worse than the common office at The Courier."

Della just stood there, mouth hanging open. She felt like she had been. . . wherever. . . for ages, but to Max, it seemed like it had been seconds.

"Ya look like ya have seen a ghost—Wait, have ya seen a ghost?" he asked, paling.

"No ghost, but uh. . ." She paused. "It happened again."

"What?" Max asked, looking more frightened with each passing minute.

"I was here, but I wasn't here," Della said slowly, fully aware of how stupid that sounded.

Max furrowed his eyebrows. "Ei—Okay."

Della facepalmed. "Can you get into that safe over

there?" she asked, gesturing towards the wall. She could explain better later.

Max hesitated before turning to where she was pointing, cracking his knuckles. He bent down to the safe, staring at the keypad, one hand on the handle. Della watched curiously, ignoring how lightheaded she felt.

"This is easy. It's so old that Ei can see the wear around the numbers he used. Ei just don' know the order. Zero, one, three, eight. Any thoughts," Max asked.

Della shut her eyes and thought for a moment, trying to visualize Ashton in front of the safe. When she opened her eyes, she half expected to see the ghostly memory of him sitting where Max was. Sadly, her powers didn't seem to work when she wanted them to. Instead, she had to rely on cold hard logic. Those numbers seemed familiar. His birthday? No, that wouldn't make sense for his age. The day and year his mother died?

"Try zero, three, one, eight," Della shrugged.

Max punched the number into the keypad, a tiny beep resonating through the room soon after. Max tried the handle. It moved. "How'd ya guess?" Max asked.

"The third of June, two-thousand-eighteen. I think that's when his mom died," Della explained, bending down beside him as he opened the safe door.

Rusty, old nails and salt came pouring out of the safe. Max jumped back, kicking a nail away from him.

"That's sad," Max said quietly, peering over Della's shoulder. Carefully, she touched one of the nails. She expected it to burn her finger, but nothing happened. Dream-walkers aren't affected by iron like witches. Good to know.

Though she still wasn't convinced she was a dream-walker at all.

Della nodded. A thin bead of sweat was forming on her forehead. She went to wipe it away, her forehead hot against her hand.

"Why didn' the cops clear this place out?" Max asked, looking around with a quizzical look.

"The cops in this town are only cops so they can have an extra title or two," Della laughed, carefully digging through the salt and nails, only touching it since she knew Max couldn't. "It felt like I was the only one who cared about solving the crimes around here."

That was good enough for Max to believe, but he had a point. No matter how stupid she thought the local police were, they had protocols. Unless, of course, Kohen had *stopped* those protocols. But why? Why was he working with Elvi? Della was sure he'd hate the very ground she walked on. What did the two of them stand to gain by working together? They seemed to want different things. Della couldn't imagine Kohen wanting anything bad to happen to the historical society.

"Another question," Max began. "Why would Ashton have all that in a safe?" he asked, giving Della a knowing look.

Della held up a rusty nail to the light. Her head pounded as she craned her neck to look at him. "Because all of this protects against magic."

Max nodded. "And who is the only person in town that would know that?"

Della stiffened. "*Me.*"

"Doesn' it feel like all of this is startin' tuh revolve around *you*?" he asked.

Della nodded, returning to sifting through the salt and nails until she found something. As soon as her fingers touched it, electricity ran up her arm. Whatever it was, it was consumed with darkness. Pulling it out, she realized it was an intricately carved box. The box was as long as her forearm and a little thicker. Across the faces of the box were shapes—a dot inside a diamond, inside another diamond.

"This symbol means medicine man," Della explained, blowing the salt off it. Medicine men weren't evil, so why did the box feel this way?

The lid was almost flush with the rest of the box. If it weren't for a small chip at what Della assumed was the front, she wouldn't have known where to open it. Digging her fingernail under the chip, she felt the lip pop open. Inside was a peace pipe. Cautiously, Della lifted it. She had seen many peace pipes throughout the Mukwa reservation but never one like this. This one wasn't carved out of wood. It was made of bone, ending with a bear head carved from a black gemstone. Dusty beads and feathers hung from it. They seemed to move on their own.

"That thing looks like it should be in a horror film," Max shivered.

"See these feathers?" Della asked, holding the pipe up to him. Three feathers that were missing their middles hung from the mouthpiece. "Each of these represents that the owner of this had 'counted coup' five times."

"Okay, it's my turn tuh say what ya always say tuh me. English, please," Max laughed.

"'Counting coup' means that whoever owned this had gotten close enough to their enemy and returned safely. In this case, these feathers signify the warrior did that a total of fifteen times. And these red dots—" Della explained, pointing to the red dots that littered the shaft. "—most likely mean that the owner had successfully killed their enemy."

"So, whoever had this was not someone ya would want tuh mess with?" Max asked, scowling deeply.

Della nodded, carefully replacing the peace pipe in the box and shutting it. The sight of it made her skin crawl.

"Remind me, what were peace pipes used for?"

"Peace pipe is the Americanized term. They're better referred to as ceremonial pipes. Sometimes, they were used to seal a peace treaty, which is where that term originated," Della began. "Every tribe is different. A lot of people tend to generalize things without doing research. But honestly, the Mukwa people are pretty basic. Hate to admit it. They were influenced by many of the other tribes here in Washington. The Mukwas, as well as many other tribes, used the pipes during deep meditation periods. The pipe would supposedly bestow upon whoever used it great power or knowledge. Some believed they were talking to The Great Spirits. But like most religions, you would only get these gifts if you led an honorable life."

"Wow," Max breathed. "Is there any way of knowin' who that belonged tuh? Maybe our Wendigo used it? That's why it killed Ash? Maybe it was lookin' for it?" His eyes were full of giddy hopefulness.

"We can ask Mingan, but I'm not so sure the Wendigo is to blame for Ashton's disappearance," Della said, struggling to heave herself off the floor. Her legs jiggled like jelly.

"What makes ya say that?" Max asked, instinctively helping her, keeping her from falling over.

"It knew me, Max. It spoke to me," Della explained.

A pause.

"Last time a cryptid came barrelin' out of the woodwork, Porter got brainwashed, and ya almost died. Sorry if Ei'm not keen on trustin' this fellow," he laughed darkly.

Della looked away, half embarrassed, half hurt. She knew the dangers of the Wendigo, but they were missing something. In her heart of hearts, she knew that to be true.

Max raised an eyebrow. "Well, now that's over. . . Back tuh the whole 'Ei was here, but Ei was not here' thing." He gave her a stern look, taking her book bag and slinging it over his shoulder.

"It felt like a memory or something." She swayed a little as she disconnected from him. "I'm fine, just dizzy," she said before he could ask.

Max blinked at her dully. "Continue."

"I saw Ashton, Elvi, and my uncle Kohen. Elvi and Kohen wanted this." She shook the peace pipe box. "But Ashton said it wasn't theirs to take. It was his. Ours, actually, as in the Mukwas."

Della briefly explained everything. Neither of them could figure out why the peace pipe was so important. And what had Elvi meant about collecting artifacts? Is that the real reason she'd bought the historical society? To collect artifacts that didn't belong to her? How typical.

"So, we have a peace pipe, a missin' guy, a Wendigo, a ghost, and no way tuh tie them together," Max sighed, counting each problem on his fingers.

"Just the historical society," Della added.

"Maybe we should do another séance," Max said, wiggling his fingers in the air. "Unless yer too scared."

Della smiled weakly, lost in thought. "Wait, what if something was trapped inside the pipe?"

"It's entirely possible,"

The two of them were quiet for a minute before Della cleared her throat, making circles on the floor with the tip of her boot. "Can we leave now?" she asked quietly.

Max met her eyes, giving her a simple nod. He crossed to hold the door for her.

"Are we gonna tell Porter about yer vision?" he asked.

Della's heart somersaulted at the thought, but she knew she had to tell him. She was about to joke about how ostriches are better off with their heads in the sand, but the words caught in her throat and jumbled in her mind. She tried to form a sentence but couldn't even think properly. Red filled her vision as blood pooled from her eyes. Suddenly, Max was pushing her up as she staggered to the side.

"Hey! Ya with me?" he screeched, ripping the peace pipe's box from her hands as he tried to keep her from falling over.

That spot above Della's ears was burning, like someone had placed hot coals around her head like a crown. She ripped off her glasses, pinching the bridge of her nose, trying to collect her thoughts.

"Ya with me?" Max repeated, brushing her hair from her face and wiping away the blood from her cheeks.

All she could do was nod. A flicker of a memory was just out of reach. If only she could grasp onto it. If only she could remember. It was something about Kohen. Something he had said a long time ago. Something about—

"I think it's time to leave," Della choked out, shaking, feeling feverish.

"That's for damn sure," Max whispered darkly.

He took her hand, leading her outside. Her legs were wobbly as she crawled off the steps. Doubling over, she gasped for air, her lungs burning with the effort. This was different than the other times she had had visions or used her powers.

"Do ya need me tuh carry ya?" Max asked, only half joking as he placed a trembling hand on her back. She laughed weakly.

"Nope, I'm good," she said, stumbling back into him as she stood back up. Black specks danced in her vision. Her head was heavy yet felt floaty at the same time. She blinked and shook her head, the black dots turning to colorful lines that danced around like fireflies. She reached out for Max to stabilize her, but it didn't exactly help.

"Okay, well—" Max trailed off, swiveling around towards the woods. "Something is in the—"

"What happened?" Sebastian screeched, running up to them. Porter wasn't far behind.

"I'm fine," Della said groggily.

"You don't look fine!" Porter shrieked, showering her and Max with snow as he slid to a stop.

"I'm good now. I just needed some air," Della sighed.

"Ei really think we should—" Max began, alarm in his voice.

Della turned to him. He'd gone pale, his hands shaking as he chewed on the collar of his sweater. Della peered over his shoulder to try and see what he was so freaked out about, but there was nothing but shadows in the darkening forest. Still, she could feel eyes on her, just as she had when the EMF detector went off in the hearse.

"Max?" she breathed.

He whipped his head around to look at her, eyes wide. His nostrils flared as he grappled for words. Porter furrowed his eyebrows, looking between them out at the woods.

"What happened?" Sebastian repeated, taking Della's face in his hands. He looked terrified.

"I just got lightheaded," Della shrugged, blinking the blood from her eyes, still watching the trees.

"Okay, I'm Hella sure people don't bleed from their eyes after getting lightheaded," Sebastian said accusingly.

"Something moved," Porter breathed, an odd edge to his voice.

Della turned to him, watching his eyes go gold, his hand on his gun. "What kind of something—"

Her words trailed off as a bright orange butterfly landed on Porter's shoulder.

Porter ignored the confusion on her face. "Something big," he whispered, stepping in front of Max, taking his pistol from its holster and checking the chamber for bullets. "What do you sense?" he asked Max. The butterfly stayed with him, fluttering its wings expectantly.

Chapter Twenty-Eight

"Somethin' dark," Max shuddered.

"Della is bleeding out, and you guys are worried about something in the woods?" Sebastian snapped. "Hello! Life-threatening problem over here!"

Porter's shoulders sagged with irritation. The butterfly flew up and circled his head, then did the same to Sebastian and Max before finally zooming off toward the woods behind the trailers.

"If a bear comes barreling out of the woods, we'll all be bleeding out, Seb," he sneered, using his offhand to beckon them all back.

Della stepped around Max to watch the butterfly make figure-eights at the forest's edge.

"Not a bear," Della whispered, making to follow the butterfly.

Max grabbed her arm, startling her. She turned to him, stumbling away at the sight that met her eyes.

Max once again had that cut on his throat. His skin was gray, and those bruise-like dark circles had appeared under his eyes. But this time, the same malady appeared on Sebastian and Porter. She whimpered, yanking away from Max as he tried to grab her arm again. No, their wounds weren't entirely the same. They still looked empty and devoid of life, but Porter had cuts on his wrists and throat, and Sebastian had a gushing hole in his head.

What was wrong with her? Why was this happening? Was this how it would be for the rest of her life? Seeing her friends like this? Was she seeing them after their last moments? The moment she would lose them?

"Della, what's wrong?" Porter asked, his voice sounding almost demonic. She remembered this same tone from the vision she'd had after she'd killed Eric. And now that she was trying to rationalize everything, she'd seen Porter look like this in a vision when she'd had her seizure.

Was this a warning? That she had to stop this from happening like how she'd saved him and the kids from Eric?

Again, Max reached for her, but she didn't flinch away this time. When he touched her, her sight returned to normal. Worried expressions replaced pasty, dead-looking faces. Max was staring at her, eyes wild, reaching up to touch the side of her face. She realized now she was crying, tears mixing with the blood from her eyes.

"She's burnin' up," Max whispered over his shoulder. "What's happenin' tuh ya?" he asked, searching her eyes.

She wanted to say she was fine. That they didn't need to worry, that everything was peachy keen, but she couldn't. At the same time, once she said it out loud, she knew there'd be no going back. She knew something would be set in motion if they knew what was wrong with her.

"I just want to leave," she choked out. "Take me to Mingan's or my parents. I don't care. I just want to go."

Max looked to Porter, who shook his head and gave a halfhearted shrug.

"Then let's go," he said quietly.

Sebastian sighed heavily, mumbling just loud enough for Della to hear. "All this—bloody eyes and some weird-ass box—but no money in the mattress?"

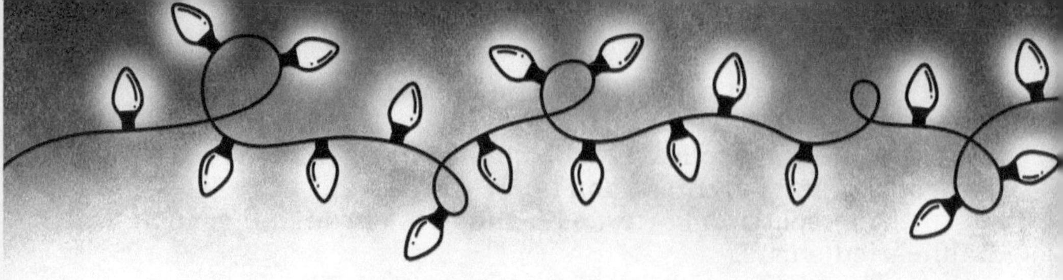

CHAPTER TWENTY-NINE

The Truth: REDACTED

Max and Porter had decided taking Della back to Jasper and Kimi's in her current state was a terrible idea. They'd brought her to the reservation, letting her lead the way to Mingan's cabin in silence.

Awkwardness hung in the air as the four of them sat huddled at Mingan's kitchen table, each with a coffee or hot cocoa in hand.

Della was hunched over a stack of books she'd found at the longhouse on the way over. Old photo albums, a book full of the names and deaths of tribe members—anything she thought would be helpful. There had to be some clue as to why the Wendigo was poking around and who the peace pipe belonged to. So far, she hadn't found anything of use. Not even a description of the peace pipe lying before her tucked inside its box.

Mingan didn't seem to mind a group of surly adolescents appearing on his doorstep. In fact, he was making them sandwiches. However, Della was too preoccupied with downing ibuprofen as she read to care about food.

"How much can you take of that before it gets dangerous?" Sebastian asked, slowly taking the bottle away from her.

"I took the max amount on the bottle. I'll be fine," she said with a shrug.

The boys exchanged a worried look, earning them an evil glare from Della. Her well-being could wait. Bigger fish to fry and all that.

"So, are we just going to ignore the bloody nose and freak out you had?" Sebastian asked. Having him around was getting irritating.

"Apparently," Max sighed, his eyes on Porter.

"I'm fine. I just have a headache," Della grumbled,

angrily flipping through a book.

After skimming through useless reading material, Della sat back in her seat, staring into space. The ibuprofen was helping, but her mind and body still ached.

Max cleared his throat, staring down Porter like he had lasers for eyes. Della looked between them, noticing how each of them seemed extremely nervous. Max was also nodding not-so-discretely in Della's direction. Porter gave Max a mildly questioning look. Max widened his eyes. Porter furrowed his eyebrows. Max shook his head angrily, turning to Della.

"Ei swear tuh—" he mumbled. "Running yourself intuh the ground over this isn' gonna help anything or anyone. Maybe ya should—"

"I'm not running myself into the ground, Max," Della said hotly, surprising even herself with her tone.

"All we're trying to say is—"

"I need to figure this out," Della hissed, standing. "You guys just don't understand."

"Maybe that's because you won't sit down and talk to us," Porter said, reaching for Della's hand. She yanked it away before his fingers could even graze her.

She turned her back to them, arms crossed, staring at the floor. They were worried for her and had every right to be, but she hated when they coddled her even more than feeling stuck. Still, she knew arguing would get her strapped to a kitchen chair or handcuffed to the bathroom sink so she wouldn't run off without them. But what other option was there?

"Talk to us," Porter said pleadingly. "Please, Della."

"Sebastian, can you do me a favor?" Della asked.

"Anything."

"Go wait in the hearse for a minute, okay?" She turned back to give him a knowing look. He knew that look and to bounce when she suggested to do so.

Without a word, he slipped out of the kitchen. The front door clicked shut not long after.

Della leaned against the table, removing her glasses, using the heel of her palm to rub her eyes.

"You guys know something I don't, so spill. We can't be a team if you don't tell me what's going on," Porter said softly.

Della sat, sweeping all the books out of her way. She dropped her voice to a whisper in case Sebastian had only pretended to leave.

She and Max told him everything in excruciating detail, from her hallucinations and visions to what happened with the Wendigo. Porter sat quietly, his face darkening with every word.

When they'd finally finished, all he said was, "You kept all that from me?" He sounded heartbroken.

"I'm sorry," Della whispered.

Porter mumbled something under his breath as he sat back in his chair. His leg bounced nervously beneath the table as he stared down Max.

"I know you guys are worried about me, but I need you two to accept that no matter what happens, I will not stop solving a case. Especially when lives are on the line. There is a missing person who could be dead for all we know," Della said, looking at them pointedly. "This is what I do. This is how I work. I don't care if I get a gunshot wound to the knee; I will crawl through this godforsaken town until I freaking figure this out. Because I know this is bigger than just Ashton."

"I get that, but Della, you can't solve a case if you're in a coma in a hospital bed," Porter hissed, looking away. "And dammit, you shouldn't have left me in the dark all this time."

"She was afraid how ya were gonna react. And don' even joke about things like that," Max snapped. Della stepped on his foot before he could say anything else.

She could tell he wanted to say more, but miraculously, he bit his tongue. For all his wit and sass, Max tended to bottle things up like the rest of them. And just like Della and Porter, everything he bottled up found its way out eventually. Della had thought this was when he'd finally blow a fuse, but apparently, Max was even stronger than she thought.

Which, if she was being honest, she envied.

More than that, she was thankful he'd kept whatever he thought to himself. Della had always hated loud noises, especially yelling. It brought back bad memories of all the times her parents had fought with her and Quincy. Back when she was still a little ignorant, she would try to de-escalate the situation, but it rarely ever helped. The older she got, she realized it was best to give up and let her parents fight.

But she wasn't ready to give up on *this* family just yet.

"I think we all just need to calm down, okay?" Della said softly. "Porter, I'm so sorry I didn't come straight to you with any of this. I really am. I hope you can forgive me."

His shoulders sagged as he turned away, shoving his hands in the pocket of his hoodie. "Whatever. Apology accepted."

Max took a steadying breath, his eyes twitching with

irritation. "Ei'm sorry too."

"Just don't let it happen again," Porter whispered halfheartedly.

Mingan cleared his throat, startling them all. His expression was something halfway between boredom and irritation.

Sorry, Grandpa. Della signed, reddening. Fighting with Porter and Max alone was one thing, but knowing they'd had a very judgmental audience this whole time was extremely embarrassing.

You three need to communicate better, he said with a roll of his eyes.

"What did he say?" Max asked.

"He's making fun of us," Della sighed.

Porter crossed his arms, pouting like a brooding teenager. "What do you want to do next?" he asked gruffly.

"We need to get into that desk," Della said, leaning back in her chair and staring at the ceiling. "We shouldn't have left without forcing it open."

"So we're prioritizing desk, now?" Porter said under his breath.

"Porter," Della scowled.

"Fine, Della, what do you want us to do? Because you're sure as Hell not going back there. Argue all you want, I forbid you," Porter snapped.

"Ya forbid her?" Max laughed darkly.

"Knock it off," Della groaned. "Please. Just for, like, two seconds?"

"Fine," the boys snapped, turning away from each other.

Della shook her hands like she was choking them behind their backs before taking a calming breath.

"So, it's decided then," she announced. "You two will go back to Ashton's, and Sebastian and I will continue looking into the peace pipe."

"We didn' decide on that," Max said with a loud *huff* at the end.

"I've decided for you," Della said tightly. "Go drive off into the sunset in the get-along-hearse, will you?"

"How exactly are we supposed tuh get intuh the desk? The place was cleared except for garbage."

Della shrugged. "Maybe the keys to it are in evidence at the police station. Call Jacobson and see if he can run his mouth for you guys. And talk to Kohen while you're at it, okay?"

They mumbled and grumbled but decided not to protest her grand ideas further.

One of these days, listening to them argue would end

in her death.

Sebastian appeared in the kitchen moments after she heard the hearse's motor whir to life. She couldn't tell if the look on his face meant he was concerned or intrigued.

"They seemed grumpy. What happened?" he asked.

"Don't even get me started," Della groaned.

"That bad?"

She nodded, turning to Mingan. He was scowling deeply, staring at the peace pipe's box.

Do you know something? Della asked.

His eyes flicked up to hers, his scowling turning sour. *I might,* he signed back. *Check back later.* With that, he left her and Sebastian alone in the kitchen.

Della sighed heavily. That was very unlike him. He usually jumped on any opportunity to tell her random factoids. He even texted her absurd facts about the world weekly.

Sebastian seemed to think the same thing. If he was keeping something to himself, it was cause for worry.

"You want to go stop by *Sun & Star Antiques*? You can drive Mingan's car," Della offered, hoping the owners had the information she desperately needed.

"You had me at drive."

CHAPTER THIRTY

Phone A Friend

This was a one-time favor, and Porter knew it. Jacobson had given Porter so much grace these last two months. Covering for him when he couldn't bring himself to come to work. Checking in on him at home once Porter confessed why he had been one of Eric's 'rescued children.' Waving all the minor offenses Della should've had on her record. He knew that, eventually, all that grace would run out.

Anxiously, he dialed the direct line to MHPD, sitting heavily on the hood of the hearse while Max sat messing with an EMF detector next to him.

"Hello, this is Moss Hollow Police Department. How may I help you? And if this is Cheryl, no one is coming to inspect your pipes. No one hid rats in them. If you are this concerned, hire an exterminator," Porter sucked in a breath. The voice that greeted him was none other than the new Deputy, Zane Newton. It went without saying that Porter and Zane hadn't gotten along.

"Zane, can you pass along to the Chief? I need to talk to him," Porter said, trying his best to sound formal.

The entirety of MHPD had been rigorously checked from every angle to ensure the remaining law enforcement was clean. Zane had come up a little *too* spotless for Porter's liking. Everyone had dirt on their hands, no matter how small the particles were. Either Zane was an angel—which no one in their right mind would seriously believe—or Mr. Newton was a tremendous liar on and off paper.

"Well, look who crawled out of the sewers? HEY, CHIEF YA GOT A SLACKER WHO WANTS TO SPEAK WITH YOU!" Zane screamed through the receiver, his voice burning Porter's ears. "Awe, bummer, Jacobson is out as of the moment—Hey!"

"Newton, get back to work. Go bother someone willing to put up with your shenanigans for once." That was the voice of Chief Skeeter Jacobson. "Porter! How are things in Washington?"

"Could be better, sir. I was wondering if you could do me a favor?" Porter asked, shivering against the biting cold. Or maybe from nerves.

Silence.

A deep, exasperated sigh.

"What do you need?" Jacobson asked.

Skeeter Jacobson was one of the only people in town Porter gave a damn about. Born to Hillbilly parents in a town where education wasn't exactly appreciated, he'd done well for himself. He was only a few years older than Porter—twenty-six if he remembered correctly—and he would be putting himself through law school if Eric hadn't died. Porter and he had a strained friendship, but there was mutual respect. Anyone who grew up in the bayou and made it out alive deserved respect no matter how they turned out. More so if they ended up with a heart of gold.

"I need you to contact the local police in Sycamore Heights," Porter said, smiling innocently, forgetting no one could see him.

Another draught of silence. "What am I supposed to say? Is this—" Jacobson lowered his voice. "—a magical problem? I know you said The Courier needed you."

"Uh, yeah, I just need to look at some evidence. Tell them Ashton John's anonymous relative from Louisiana wants us to collect his belongings."

"That is a pretty lofty lie."

"Skeeter, please. We need to—"

"We? Who all is down there again? Just in case things go south when I say that an anonymous relative wants a group of kids from the boot to come steal evidence," Jacobson snapped. "And don't call me by that damned name. You know I hate it."

When Jacobson had been appointed Chief, it had come as a surprise to everyone except Porter. The former Deputy was one of the quickest minds regarding their line of work. He could spot a liar just as fast as Della. He spent all his free time watching videos on the science of deduction and honing his perception skills.

In all honesty, he was a savant.

Even if he had blown up the communal microwave on several accounts. That man loved to leave the tin foil on his leftovers. Common sense was where he was lacking. It was all book smarts in that brain of his.

"Please. This is important!" Porter pleaded, removing himself from the hood of the hearse to stand in a foot of slushy snow.

"Will innocent people die? Are you dying? Will the Earth explode if I do not help you?" Jacobson asked.

"It's a possibility!"

"What the Hell is wrong with you people?" Jacobson snapped. It was more of a legitimate question than Porter would have liked to admit it. He was especially hung up on the 'you people' part. Who else had been contacting him? Mavericks surely wouldn't contact the police. He was too proud to do that.

Porter cleared his throat. "Some would say we are cursed. Personally, I would agree." That was the truth.

"You have no idea how much I would like to call bullshit on that and tell you that you can't talk back to me, that I am your commanding officer, but I can't. Why, you might ask? Because we live in Moss-friggin-Hollow, Louisiana!" Jacobson whisper-yelled. "Where my ex-boss practiced witchcraft, and werewolves run my favorite restaurant! What's next? Ambrose and his posse are vampires?" he laughed darkly.

"Well. . ." Porter didn't have the heart to finish his sentence. He had tried to keep Jacobson as out of the loop as possible but had quickly realized that wouldn't work.

"You have *got* to be kidding me," Jacobson breathed. "I knew they all sucked, I just thought they sucked metaphorically. Fine—Fine, I'll see what I can do. I'll holler when I get through." With that, he hung up.

Porter stared at the sky momentarily, one hand on his hip, the other resting on his forehead, still clutching his phone. "God give me strength," he whispered, knowing he'd need it today.

"And give me a warm blanket while yer at it? Ei'm freezin' over here. Ya know that, right?" Max shouted at the sky, messing with a bunch of buttons on the EMF detector until it started screaming at him.

"Aren't kitty-cats supposed to be warm? What with all that fur?" Porter sneered. "Got everything you need in that big bag of yours?"

They had stopped by the Coleman household, glad the rest of the family was still out for the day. They'd grabbed what they could carry, then left before anyone could show up. Porter swore he heard Max grumble a thank you for grabbing everything, but he wasn't sure.

"Haha. So funny." Max rolled his eyes, clutching his book bag to his chest. "Ei hope so. Ei shouldn't need too much. Just a few gloves, maybe some abrasives in case there's any blood. Grabbed some plastic bags, too." He thought for a moment. "Got a couple more EMF detectors just in case this one gets messed up. Also brought my ghost hunter's kit."

"You kept the ghost kit?" Porter laughed.

Not too long ago, Della had gifted them both a small metal lunchbox full of items that were supposed to ward off, trap, harm, or lure ghosts.

"Well, yeah. Ya didn'?" Max asked, trying to hide the horror in his eyes.

"I mean, I didn't pack it with me. I would have thought you wouldn't have either. Seeing as you have magic and all," Porter smiled.

"Yes, but Ei'd rather be over-prepared than un-der-prepared."

Porter watched Max expectantly as he received a text from Jacobson saying they were good to go. All he did was sit there and stare at the device in his hands while picking the dried skin off his lips. Porter squinted at him. Max was a scaredy cat, but he was rarely anxious like this.

"Hey. . . uh. . . sorry I yelled at you," he said awk-wardly, playfully punching him in the arm. Maybe it was best to put pride aside for the time being.

Max looked him up and down. "Ei'm—Thanks. Ei'm sorry too," he said dully.

"Max," Porter sighed.

He stared at him expressionlessly, though his eyes revealed how sad he was inside.

"You're like a brother to me. You know that, right?" Porter asked.

Max nodded, a thin smile pulling at his lips. "Of course, Ei do, ya little shit. Ya know Ei'm the older brother, though, right?"

Porter smirked. "Sure." He figured it best not to mention that just because he skipped a grade or two didn't make him older.

Max stared at him for a minute, and Porter knew he wanted to say something—something that he wouldn't like—but for the time being, he only hopped off the hood of the hearse.

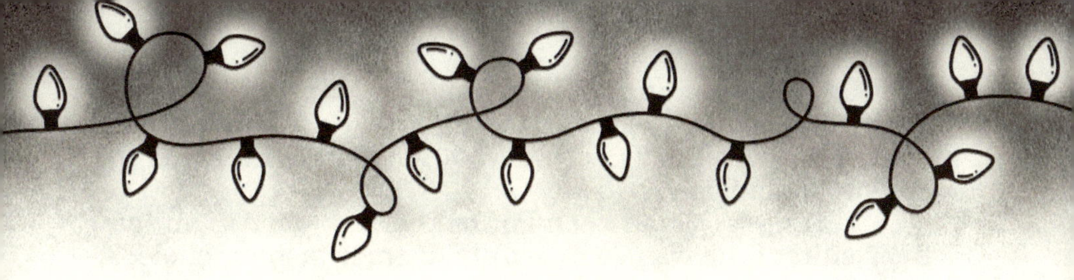

CHAPTER THIRTY-ONE

Cats Are a Mortician's
Best Friend

In a perfect world, Max wouldn't be galivanting around in Porter's shadow, freezing his skin off. He wouldn't be standing in a police station, experiencing the highest form of second-hand embarrassment, as he watched Porter fumble his way to the evidence room.

No, he'd be home watching cheesy Christmas movies with his father, waiting for Nicoletta to show up with sugar cookies and snide remarks.

Yet here he was, playing the diplomat per usual.

At least he could pick on Porter as consolation. Max sometimes wondered if that was his true calling: causing the mighty Porter Garroway as much strife as possible.

"Ya look like ya just stole the crown jewels or somethin'," he snickered, following the lumbering fool through the Sycamore Tribal Police Department building.

For tribal police, this place was surely lacking 'tribe.' Without the lifeless, snooty policemen and women around them, there wouldn't have been any sign of human life. The entire station was spotless. No paper out of place, not a speck of dust floating in the air, and almost all the furniture was a dull beige—it was like a hospital, only worse.

Porter swallowed hard, pulling the collar of his shirt away from his neck. "We look sorely out of place in our merry and brights," Porter paused to point at Max's sweater. "And I don't think anyone here wants to cooperate with any out-of-towners," he whispered, nodding awkwardly at a passing cop.

Max rolled his eyes, looking down at his sweater. It was one of his all-time favorites, striped bright orange, magenta, and purple. It was the softest thing he owned and the most expensive. Back in Moss Hollow, he would have received many compliments. But here, he got side-eyed like he was walking around naked. So, what if he liked color? This world was too bland for his liking. It could use more color. That was partly why he thought Della's hair was the epitome of fashion.

Besides, it had been Porter's idea to change out of their suits. If he was so upset about their fashion choices, he had only himself to blame.

"Jacobson called. We have nothin' tuh worry about," Max yawned, holding the door to the evidence room. "Let's just do our job so we can leave."

Porter rocked back and forth on his heels and fiddled with the strings on his navy blue sweatshirt. He looked as nervous as Max felt on the inside. Max sighed heavily, looking over his shoulder and into the evidence room. It was devoid of onlookers. Perfect. All they had to do was get what they needed and get out. It wasn't that big of a deal. The guy at the front desk had given them the keys and told them to hurry. It wasn't like they were breaking in. Why was he so antsy? Unless, of course, he wasn't nervous about this particular situation. . .

"Get what we need, then we can leave," Max reiterated with a smile. A tight, get-yer-shit-tuhgether-or-Ei-will-deck-ya kind of smile.

"Fine," Porter sighed, pushing open the door at last.

He crossed toward a tall shelf at the back of the room, ignoring his surroundings as he began to search for anything of Ashton's. The front desk guy had been helpful enough to describe where they were meant to find anything of interest.

Max leaned against the doorway, irritated. Part of him wished he had stayed with Della and Sebastian, but that would have been entirely too awkward. Maybe if Sebastian hadn't been there, he'd have asked to stay. In all honesty, he wished for once it could just be the two of them.

"Find what we needed yet?" Max yawned.

Porter nodded. Grabbing a small box off the shelf, he quickly exited the room, pulling Max along by the sleeve.

They were just about to make it back into the cold when a tall man with a crooked smile stepped in front of the door, his hands on his hips.

"You two honestly think I'm letting two 'representatives' from Moss Hollow Police Department walk out of here with that?" he asked.

"Kohen!" Porter said, feigning excitement. "Max, this is Della's uncle."

"Pleasure," Kohen smiled. "Getting a suspicious call from my delinquent niece's new hometown was cause for alarm. But seeing as Chief Jacobson and his number are legitimate, I see no reason to stop you from looking through all that."

"Thank you, sir—"

"However, I'm not letting you two bring all this back to the super sleuth."

The boys exchanged a dissatisfied look, reluctantly riding Kohen's heels when he gestured for them to follow. He led them to his office, depositing them inside with promises of donuts and coffee.

When they were alone, Porter set the ugly peach-colored box on Kohen's desk, rifling through it methodically. Inside were bags with the crest of Sycamore Tribal Police Department stamped on them. Max grabbed one, setting to work. Nothing interesting in the poor fellow's wallet, just his cards, I.D., some cash, and a punch card for *Ole Joe's*. Nothing in the pockets of a ripped-up jacket, nothing weird in the papers stapled together that read 'glove box.' The only thing of use seemed to be the keys.

Max turned to Porter to find he'd gotten distracted by the books littering Kohen's office.

"Anythin' interestin' over there?" he asked. He hadn't intended it to sound so sassy, but his voice betrayed him.

Porter glared but nodded. "A few books on Native American mythology. Do we really think Kohen and Elvi are working together to get the pipe? Why?"

Max shrugged. "If Della's parents knew about her powers and put her on faux meds tuh hide them, whose tuh say the whole family doesn' know? Kohen may be Sycamore Heights' version of us."

"What about Elvi?"

"Still workin' on figurin' that out."

"Bummer," Porter sighed, standing next to him, eyeing Ashton's keys. "Think you can cast a duplication spell on those? I don't think Kohen will let us borrow them.

Max rolled his eyes, taking the keys out of the bag. Five different keychains hung from them. One of a mountain range, another of a tribal-looking eagle, one of a cloud, another of a leaf, and finally, one that said 'Welcome To Washington.'

"No, but Ei can cast an illusion."

Porter looked over his shoulder to stare blankly at him. For someone who favored science over magic, Max seemed to be the only one who knew anything on the subject.

"Grab me a pen. Ei'll put a glamour on it to make it appear as a set of keys. Ei'm unable to duplicate it. Ei'm not an alchemist," Max explained loosely. "My powers don' allow me tuh just make things out of thin air."

Porter tossed him a pen, then returned to scrounging through the useless belongings left in the box. Max was just about to comment on how smooth all this was going when he noticed something.

Porter's tense shoulders gave away the thoughts clouding his mind.

Max sighed heavily, cursing himself.

"Spill it," he demanded. He put the pen in the evidence bag the keys had been in, then whispered a spell, "*Trylle.*"

The pen shimmered, dissolving into a set of keys identical to the ones in his hand. The only way you would know it was a glamour was by holding it up to the light. Glamours work by bending the rays of light around an object to trick the eye. It was one of the lowest and easiest forms of magic. A child could cast a glamour bigger than this. Yet, Max's veins burned from the energy it had used.

Porter twisted the cross charm hanging from the chain on his ear, discarding a crinkled bus ticket. Max was expecting him to avoid the subject, but instead, he launched into a long-winded rant.

"Is it just me, or does this whole thing seem directly related to Della? I mean, first, it's her hometown, then it's the Mukwa tribe and all her visions—"

"Calm down," Max said, though not unkindly.

Porter took in a shaking breath. "I'm worried, Max."

"Ei know," he replied, staring blankly at him. "We kind of live in a constant state of worry when it comes tuh her."

Porter glared at him. "I'm trying to have a serious conversation with you. You do realize that, right?"

Without warning, Kohen opened the door, startling them both.

"Can I ask a good faith question?" he asked, offering them a donut as he edged past them.

"Of course," Max said with a smile, taking a powdered donut with one hand and pocketing the keys with the other.

"Now, don't laugh, but by any chance, are Della and Sebastian messing with some of the low lives around here?" Kohen asked, looking embarrassed.

"No?" Porter laughed, genuinely confused.

"All right, I'll take your word for it," Kohen shrugged.

"Why do ya ask?" Max questioned, an eyebrow raised.

Kohen thought for a moment, looking between them. "There's been a few reports here and there since she left, but we've been getting more now that she's back. Little things, y'know? Stupid things. Pranks. Was wondering if she'd enlisted Breckenridge into doing her dirty work but has decided to take matters into her own hands," he laughed.

"What kind of stupid things?" A strange sense of déjà vu was bubbling up in Max's chest.

"Shadowy figures lurking around at night. Multiple reports of people getting locked out of their houses, places of work, or cars. Their keys were nowhere to be found, only to appear inside in plain sight. The O'Malley twins said someone drained their car of gas while they were at a party. Patricia Durnell keeps calling about flickering lights," Kohen smiled. "I was honestly hoping the troublemakers were back at it. Then again, this reads more Quincy than Della. She wasn't much of a prankster, but I figured she and Seb thought they could get away with it now that she'd moved. All these weird reports keep coming from people who made her life a living Hell here."

"I definitely think you've got the wrong people," Porter laughed.

Max agreed, but he did note the oddity of these reports. Especially the flickering lights. He really hoped none of this was related to Ashton and the peace pipe.

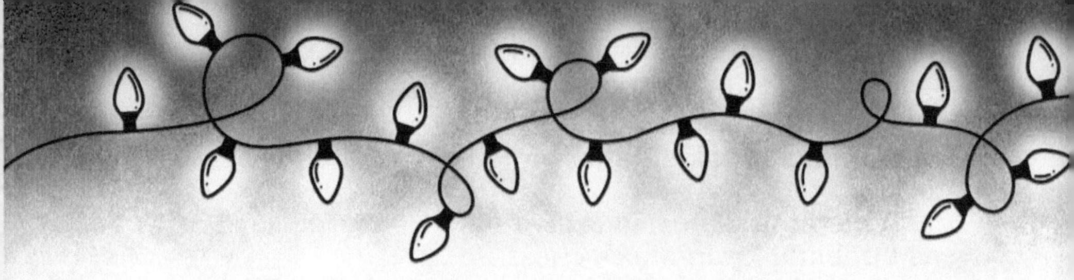

CHAPTER THIRTY-TWO

Collecting Dust

There were few in this town who tolerated Della and her never-ending quest for the unknown. Fewer still actively encouraged and entertained that lust for arcane knowledge. Of that small percentage were the two people who had allowed her to use their shop as the shipping address for her monthly Utopian Courier deliveries.

"Why exactly are we here? Late Christmas shopping or something?" Sebastian asked, looking giddy. Most of their belongings had come from this store.

"Yeah. Something," Della laughed.

Della swept open the door to *Sun & Star Antiques*, a small bell jingling behind her and Sebastian as they wove through musty-smelling furniture to the front counter. Sebastian tapped the service bell, giving Della a knowing look.

"Ouch!" A shrill yet flowery voice rang from behind the counter. A gaunt face soon met their eyes. "Sebastian! And, oh my! Miss Delphee Coleman! I didn't know you were back in town—HUGO DELPHEE COLEMAN IS BACK!" Enid Madigan, the sun of *Sun & Star Antiques,* screamed at the top of her lungs.

A door slammed open to Della's right, revealing a tall but gangly man with matted hair that reached his lower back.

Hugo Madigan. The star.

Where Enid was all sunshine and flower petals, Hugo was moonlight and bones protruding from piles of dirt. She wore a sundress despite the cold. He wore a scuffed-up leather apron and a pair of spectacles with extra lenses poking out the sides, making him look like a mad scientist.

Max would've gotten a kick out of them.

"Della!" Hugo exclaimed, throwing his hands up into the air. "Dear Lord, girl, it's been too long! You should have said goodbye before you left!" His voice was rough, and he smelled of grapefruits and bleach as he came to reel her in for a hug.

"Nice to see you both," Della choked out. Hugo was squeezing her awfully tight.

"You too, dear. What brings the two of you in today? We're having a sale on fine China!" Enid exclaimed, coming over to wrap her arms around Della and her husband.

"Enid, the girl has been here for two seconds, and you're already trying to sell things to her? Have some self-respect, woman!" Hugo scolded. "But really, all our fine China is up to seventy-five percent off until the twenty-fourth!" he winked.

Della wiggled out of their arms, smiling a little. "While I'm sure Sebastian is looking to add to his mother's collection, I have a few questions for you, if that's okay."

They nodded, linking arms with each other. Della had always wished her parents would be like Hugo and Enid. They loved each other so deeply. Not only that, but they were open-minded individuals, too. If it weren't for them, Della wouldn't know anything about ghosts, goblins, and ghouls.

She let her smile solidify as she thought back. The first day she visited *Sun & Star Antiques* was with Quincy. He used to want to work at this strange little shop. Hugo and Enid always filled their heads with stories of far-off places and mystical objects. Quincy had always asked how he would use said objects, and Della had always wondered how to find them. Quincy had never believed in those 'fairy-tales,' but Della had latched on to those stories as if they were the only thing keeping her alive.

"Sure! We're always willing to help a fellow Courier!" Hugo blurt out, then slapped a hand over his mouth so hard the sound rang out throughout the entire shop.

Della raised an eyebrow.

Enid rolled her eyes. "We know Percival," she said, giving Hugo a look out of the corner of her eye. "He's an old friend. When we heard Moss Hollow Tribune, we knew where you were going."

"Interesting," was all Della could say. It made sense. They had probably been stationed here to keep an eye on things.

She paled. If that was the case, then that's probably why Mavericks had insisted on her coming.

"What kind of case does Percy have you on?" Enid asked expectantly. The sparkle in her eye only furthered Della's suspicions.

"The usual," Della said, discreetly nodding toward

Sebastian.

"Ahh, I see," Hugo said. "Sebastian, my boy. We have a new selection of vintage comics; would you like me to show them to you?"

"Like you have to ask," Sebastian said, pulling him away and toward the book section.

When they were out of earshot, Della nodded towards a set of chairs in the corner that had been there since the shop had opened.

"I'm sure you already know. Ashton John sent me a letter. Said weird things were happening, and now he's missing. Thoughts?" Della asked.

"Hugo had felt a few disturbances as of late. We reached out to Percival not long ago to let him know."

Once again, Della's investigation skills were on point. But that wasn't what got her. Della stifled a laugh at the word 'Percival.' Very few referred to Mavericks as anything other than, well, Mavericks. Because that's what he was. Unorthodox, independent-minded, and eccentric.

"What kind of disturbances?" Della asked, settling herself into one of the chairs. She suddenly wondered just how close Enid, Hugo, and Mavericks were. Half of the things in this shop looked like they could have easily belonged in Mavericks' office. Or vice versa.

"The animals have been acting strange. Plus, there have been rumors of the supernatural in the woods. If you ask me, I'd say there was an unhappy ghost. Shouldn't be too much to handle, right? Especially for a girl like you," Enid said enthusiastically.

Della blushed from embarrassment. "I take it you read the October issue?"

She nodded. "I do believe you did Moss Hollow a mighty big favor."

Della shifted uncomfortably at that thought. "That's what everyone keeps saying."

"I've got him distracted for now," Hugo said, his leather apron squeaking as he walked over to them. He peered around a corner to ensure Sebastian was engrossed in the comics before settling on Enid's armrest.

Enid frowned at Hugo, who gave a questioning look in return. It seemed they wanted to say something, but neither dared to bring it up. Della found herself pulling at her fingernails in response to that. If they were anything like Mavericks, they knew far more than they wanted her to believe. Best to drop the subject for now.

"Have you had any interesting buyers stop in lately?" she asked, hoping to save the life-altering revelations for another time.

Hugo's eyes darkened. "Do you remember that old man who came in when you worked with us over the summer? The one that was obsessed with old records? He dared to try and return one he bought months ago on account of it breaking. He asked for a refund! Do you have any idea how idiotic that—"

Enid patted his shoulder to get him to calm down. "Why do you ask? Are you on the trail of something?"

The way they acted reminded her of Max and herself.

"Crappy customers are always fun to hear about, but I'm looking into one in particular. Has an Elvi Sinclair popped in at all?"

"The bratty banker?" Hugo asked.

"Yup, that's her."

Enid rolled her eyes. "Thankfully, she hasn't blessed us with her presence."

"What about my uncle? Kohen Kitchi."

They thought for a moment but inevitably shook their heads.

Why did it feel like every time she had a hunch, all she found was a dead end?

"Is there anything else you need, Delphee?" Enid asked. She looked dejected they hadn't been able to help thus far.

"I do actually need your eyes," Della smiled, pulling the peace pipe out of her book bag. "I'm going to go out on a limb here and say that you guys don't just sell old armoires and discount China."

"Knowing what you know, what do you need from us?" Hugo asked excitedly, standing. His words were tinged with magic.

Memories from the summer she worked here with Sebastian came back to her. He'd asked that same question to an elderly man before taking him into the one room they weren't allowed in.

She also remembered what that man had said.

"I'm looking to get something appraised," she said. She removed the peace pipe from her book bag, holding it out for them to see.

"Mind like a steel trap, this one," Enid said, taking the hand Hugo had offered her.

They led her into the back room, which was a glorified garage that had been redone in a somewhat tasteful manner. Tall shelves housed an array of glass bottles, vintage ashtrays, vases, and the infamous discounted fine China. The workbench in the corner was littered with Hugo's paints, stains, tools—anything and everything he could use to repair and repaint—and his preferred line of grapefruit-scented cleaning products. Old paintings whose eyes, unfortunately, didn't follow you stood in neat rows near the roll-up doors. Despite their mundaneness, Della had always refused to touch those old paintings. She recognized some of them even now. Apparently, Sycamore Heights wasn't big on oil paintings.

Della was hit with a wave of nostalgia along with the memory of when she and Sebastian had passed through the stained-glass door to her right, which led to Hugo's office. They'd practically begged him to let them work at *Sun & Star Antiques*. They'd been fourteen at the time. Those days seemed so far away.

Hugo took his place at the edge of an old rug in the center of the garage, standing tall and proud. "You have no idea how long we've wanted to show you this," he said, the somber smile on his face twitching with excitement. "Enid, my love, will you do the honors?"

Enid bowed deeply. "*Avdekket*," she whispered, taking Hugo's hand.

A puff of dust that smelled suspiciously like grapefruit wafted up from under the rug. Enid beckoned Della forward just as the carpet began lowering into the floor. Without hesitation, Della hopped on, feeling her stomach drop the same way it did when she rode elevators. This strange elevator went so fast that her hair flew up around her face. Enid laughed as she held down the hem of her sundress to keep it from blowing up.

"Enid is something of a stonemason," Hugo bragged, gesturing to the walls that grew taller every second. Della now knew how buckets descending into old wells felt.

Ornate sconces popped forth from the bricks, their eerie glow reminding Della of torches lining the walls of a dilapidated dungeon.

The rug suddenly stopped and spun, causing Della to come face to face with an old wooden door. Carvings of everything from kelpies to trolls adorned the door. At first, she thought the light was playing tricks on her, but the carvings were, in fact, moving. They swirled and morphed until the door was blank, save for a large keyhole in the center. Hugo removed his glasses, fanned out the many lenses, folded in the arms, and then stuck them into the keyhole. With a satisfying *click*, the door opened.

"Hugo, however, did the door. Wonderful, isn't it?" Enid said, pushing it open to reveal a large chamber that put even the exquisitely carved door to shame.

Crystalline floors seemed to pulse with what Della suspected was magic in its purest form. The ceiling was painted navy and gold, depicting constellations of ordinary and extraordinary varieties. Each of the walls had an inset bookshelf filled to overflowing with all manner of objects. The shelves closest to the floor held books, but the contents got weirder and weirder closer to the ceiling. Jars of glowing powders, bottles of bubbling liquids, glass cases with golden bones, and jewelry boxes that shook and rattled as Hugo walked by were just some of the surrounding oddities.

"What is this place?" Della breathed, completely in awe.

"This is where we keep all the magical artifacts," Enid said proudly. "Do you like it? We put quite a lot of work into it."

"Oh, it's wonderful," Della whispered. Immediately, she was drawn to a row of glistening weaponry hanging from the wall.

Hugo stopped her before she could touch the curved blade of a golden khopesh. "Poisoned," he said, grimacing. "We will be transporting it to a museum next week. Egyptian magic is some of the oldest. Wish it were talked about more."

"What form of magic is taught nowadays?" Della asked.

"Our modern-day witchcraft comes from Scandinavia. Strange, isn't it? The spells in most easily attainable spellbooks were written long ago in Old Norse. But magic has changed and adapted over the years. Very few speak and translate Old Norse. So now it has roots in Bokmål. Of course, some of the words have been jumbled around," Hugo explained.

"Modern-day magic isn't nearly as strong as it once was," Enid added. "There are a few who still practice in Old Norse. Their abilities are not to be trifled with."

"Oh yes! It's quite remarkable. And those who practice the Asiatic or African arts are a rarity here in the States. Their gifts are truly spectacular. You know, there are even nonverbal forms of magic created by the Deaf and hard-of-hearing community!" Hugo said, his eyes aglow with pride as he led her and Enid to the circular live-edge table in the center of the spherical room.

By the look of the table, it seemed Hugo was in the middle of one of his never-ending repairs. However, instead of wood filler and stain, he appeared to be filling the holes in a wooden chest with crystals.

"Let us see what you have here," he said, gingerly taking the peace pipe from her. His bushy eyebrows knitted together as soon as he touched it. "I can feel the negative energy resonating off of this," he muttered, quickly placing the box on the table and opening it carefully.

Enid was peering over his shoulder with the same concerned expression. She handed Hugo a pair of thick leather gloves and another set of multi-lensed glasses. Once the gloves were on, he took the pipe from the box, held it to the light, and peered through the hole. He frowned, gently tapping it.

"It appears as though it has been used recently," he said, more to Enid than Della.

That sadly made sense, knowing who'd been in possession of the pipe. Old habits die hard.

"Did you get this from your mother?" Enid asked, blowing on the feathers. She shivered, taking a few steps.

"It came from the historical society, yes, but Ashton had it hidden in his trailer," Della explained with a shrug.

"Ah, I see," Hugo laughed.

He nodded to Enid, who promptly turned on her heels, crossing to one of the tall shelves. Grabbing a small jar of swirling silver liquid as she went, she traced a symbol on the small space between the shelves. Out popped a rack with an array of tools, most of which Della had never seen. Much to her disappointment, all Enid grabbed was a dropper. Hugo smiled warmly at her when she returned, holding the pipe out over the table as Enid sucked up some of the silver liquid, dropping a few drops onto the pipe.

The liquid sizzled and sparked. It startled Hugo so severely that he dropped it.

Della panicked, reaching forward to grab the old peace pipe before it shattered on the table.

"Very, very dark magic," Enid whispered.

Hugo removed his gloves, tossing them aside. "Please put that thing back in its box, Delphee dear." He was shaking slightly as he leaned over to Enid. "It won't let me see it's past."

"What do you mean?" Della asked, quickly replacing the pipe inside its box. For now, she thought it best to stow the whole monstrous package back inside her book bag.

"Hugo practices a form of retrocognition through psychometry. He may see an object's past if it allows him," Enid smiled, looking ever so proud of her husband.

Hugo blushed. "It's by no means a rare ability, Enid dear."

"Oh, stop being so modest," Enid laughed, kissing him softly on the cheek. "His abilities are sought after in the *Dust Collectors* community. Percival himself has needed him a few times in the past. It's only fitting you've come to us as well."

"The *Dust Collectors*?" Della asked, following them over to a bookstand when prompted.

"He hasn't told you of us?" Hugo asked, visibly hurt by the notion. "While *The Utopian Courier* protects beings, we *Dust Collectors* protect things."

Della stopped listening when her eyes fell on the book in front of her. It was identical to Max's spellbook except for the color. Where his was maroon, this one was mossy green.

"Where did you get this?" Della asked, a shiver running up her spine.

"This Atlas was bestowed upon us many moons ago. One of the originals, I might add," Hugo said proudly.

"My—My friend has one identical to it."

"What color?" Enid asked, eyes widening.

"Maroon."

They shared a worried look. Enid tugged on a loose thread on her dress, staring at Hugo as though they could read each other's minds.

"Tell your friend to be careful," she said in response.

Hugo cleared his throat, opening the Atlas to the table of contents, which seemed more of an instruction manual upon further inspection. He placed his hand atop it, his eyes glossing over as he stared at the pages. The pages began to flip back and forth the second he lifted his hand. After a few tense moments, Enid sighed heavily.

Hugo shut the book, shaking his head in sadness. "The Atlas has no records of this peace pipe. My deepest apologies, Delphee. I wish we could be of more help."

"Don't worry about it. You confirmed more than a few of my suspicions, so it wasn't a total loss. It was lovely seeing you both," Della smiled, giving them a slight bow.

"Oh, you're too sweet," Enid laughed as they returned to the rug.

The mystical fibrous elevator whizzed back up into the garage, sealing their secret workshop from view. All this time, something incredible had been right under Della's feet.

Maybe Sycamore Heights wasn't as dull as she once thought.

"Please let us know what becomes of the pipe! We'd love to add it to our *Dust Collectors* record. Just in case anyone else comes across a similar object," Hugo said, patting Della lovingly on the shoulder. "And, of course, send Percy our regards. There is always a place for him at headquarters. We would love to have him if he ever wishes to return."

"I'll pass along the message, for sure," Della laughed.

While Hugo and Enid's mysterious double life was intriguing, Della could name a thousand reasons why Mavericks would have left such an organization. It all seemed too stuffy for him. Della had a feeling the *Dust Collectors* would have a million rules and regulations to follow. Such things were not the Mavericks way. Nor were they *her* way.

"Thank you again, I really appreciate this," she said, smiling to herself. "Have a—"

"Delphee," Enid said, wringing her hands. "Percy mentioned something I'd like to ask you about in his last letter."

"Oh, uh, of course."

"He said you'd been having visions. Has that continued?" The atmosphere and Enid's demeanor had changed drastically. Hugo put a comforting hand on her shoulder, giving her a sympathetic look.

"Yes, they have," Della said awkwardly.

Enid inhaled deeply, her shoulders sagging. "I see," she whispered, eyes dropping to the top of her shoes. There was a moment of tense silence before she made for Hugo's office. "If you'll excuse me, I just remembered I have to call a young lady about picking up a dresser."

Della waited until the office door had closed behind her before asking her question. "What was that about?"

"I'm sure you don't remember, but Winifred and Enid were close friends. We knew of her abilities. Enid had hoped they hadn't been passed on to you or your siblings. She took her death hard," Hugo sighed. "Please see yourself out, Della dear. If Sebastian has found a comic he likes, I trust you both to leave the money on the counter," he winked, and with that, he went off to presumably console his wife.

Della desperately tried to push down the bubbling questions this exchange had brought her. As always, *Sun & Star Antiques* had given her more than she'd bargained for.

With a heavy heart, she made her way through the shop to Sebastian.

"Find one you don't have?" she asked.

He shrugged. "I mean, yeah, but—"

"I'll buy."

"Cool, I have a whole stack," he said excitedly, looking up at her with his goofy grin.

"Gold-digger."

"Cheapskate."

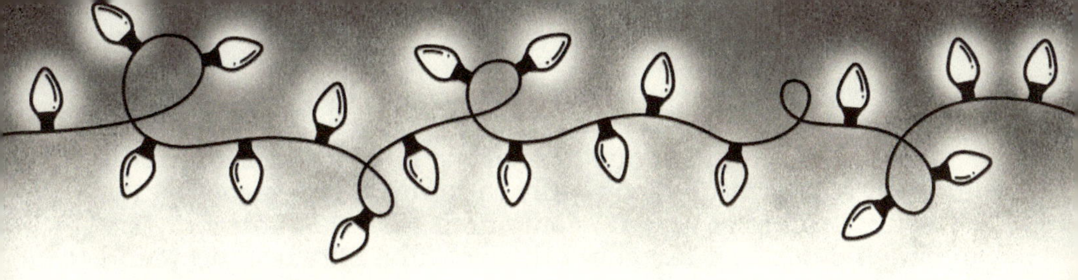

CHAPTER THIRTY-THREE

Listen!

The trip back to Ashton's trailer left Max and Porter with a drawer full of old tapes, an old tape recorder, half a keyring of melted keys, and burns on Max's hands. Ashton must've figured out how to do a protection spell on the desk. The second Max had touched it, his skin began to blister.

Despite how long those burns would take to heal, he was thankful this return trip hadn't ended in disaster.

Risking a healing spell was out of the question. What little magic reserve he had must be saved for moments of utmost importance. As far as he was concerned, blistering burns were far from important. Until they returned to Moss Hollow and Nicoletta, he'd have to settle for the human way of mending things.

Flexing his fingers, he winced against the pain. Hopefully, he could find something to wrap his hands in now that they were back at Mingan's.

Letting themselves in, Porter swung open the door to Mingan's cabin with a smug grin. Surely, he'd been expecting Della or Sebastian. Much to Max's bemusement, all they found was Mingan lounging on the couch. When he saw Porter's smile, he rolled his eyes.

Max decided at that moment Mingan Kitchi was his second-favorite grumpy old man. Mavericks being the first, of course.

Porter called through the house, but Sebastian and Della were nowhere to be found. A quick exchange of notes with Mingan let them know the pair had thankfully checked in not long ago. They'd promised not to get into trouble and bring back take-out.

A sense of ease slipped over Max. He hadn't realized how worried he'd been. Knowing they were safe—knowing *she* was safe—meant more to him than he'd ever care to admit.

Mingan took one look at his hands and trudged off with a disgruntled look, only to return a few seconds later with a roll of gauze and some anti-bacterial ointment. Trying his best not to agitate the wounds, Max began to tend to himself for once.

"Are we just going to sit here and wait for them to get back or. . ?" Porter asked, setting the drawer of tape recorders down on the coffee table. Yes, the whole drawer. Taking the whole thing had been easier than carrying each individual cassette tape.

"Or what?" Max asked as Porter flopped down on the couch next to him.

Porter gave him a daring look. "Want to play detective? I mean, we went through the trouble of getting this stuff. Why shouldn't we?"

"Ya just wanna rub it in her face that ya have knowledge she doesn', doncha?" Max laughed, wincing as he struggled to wrap his left hand in gauze.

Porter gave an innocent shrug.

Max nodded at the drawer, eager to find out what was so important that Ashton had spelled an entire desk to keep people out.

Porter leaned over and grabbed a tape from the drawer, holding it to the light. He marveled at it. Old tech must seem so obsolete to him. Max had grown up tinkering with all sorts of different devices. He could make almost anything with a hint of magic and a few spare wires. Meanwhile, Porter only knew how to restart his phone if it acted up. Max couldn't help but smile when Porter looked at him with questioning eyes, holding the tape and recorder out before him.

After a short how-to, Porter inserted a tape labeled 'October' into the recorder.

A whirring noise filled the air as the tape spun, promptly followed by static. Soon, they could hear a voice coming through the recorder.

"October fifteenth, twelve-oh-two. I have new information regarding a woman in town who has bought the bank," it said, the voice crackling and popping through the speaker.

Max hit the pause button, eyebrows knit together. "What is this? An audio diary?"

Porter nodded, pressing play.

"Her name is Elvi Sinclair. I did a little digging, and it's as though she doesn't exist. Complete clean slate. No social media. No public records. Not even another Sinclair

Credit Union," Ashton explained, his tone mirroring what a typical conspiracy theorist would sound like. Like Mavericks.

"I tried to confront Miss Sinclair about this earlier today, but she shut me down, which leads me to the real news. After I had approached her, I thought she had left. I went on break and saw her in the Native American exhibit, looking through the artifacts. She was on the phone with someone. I heard her say, 'It isn't here,' and tell whoever was on the other line that she'd 'keep working.' I—" A loud noise played over the recorder. "Ashton John, signing off," he added quickly. The tape spun, playing static once again.

"That's it?" Porter asked.

"Maybe try the other side?" Max shrugged.

Porter flipped the tape, visibly nervous to hear what Ashton had to say next.

"October twentieth, five-thirty. Elvi wants to buy the historical society. She claims she wants to help Poppy Hawthorne with her debt. I don't know what she's playing at, but she seemed pretty happy to hear that Poppy and Kimi Kitchi-Coleman were selling what they assumed were useless objects to anyone who would buy them. I have to cut this short. I have a date. Ashton John, signing off." The way Ashton talked so excitedly about his findings was cracking Max up.

Discarding his efforts to wrap his hands, he offered Porter another tape labeled 'October/November.'

This one opened with the sound of metal on metal. "October thirtieth, precisely midnight. I stole a peace pipe from the historical society. I could tell Elvi wanted it. I don't know why. But if she wanted it, I'm sure it's important. Other than that, things have been quiet around here. I did see something lurking in the woods this morning. I think it was a bear. Not sure. Probably nothing. But then again, I overheard Elvi on the phone talking about some monster in Louisiana. For some reason, I can't stop thinking about it. I think that girl who busted me for dealing drugs, Delphee Coleman, is in Louisiana. Could be a coincidence, but mystery tends to follow that kid." Ashton signed off, and the tape ran out.

Max's skin crawled. Della had mentioned Elvi seemed to know all sorts of things about them. That meant she knew about Eric and the Grunches. But this made it sound like she was getting reports about them. As Porter flipped the tape, his worry grew.

"November second, eight o'clock. I think there's a demon in my peace pipe. It's been rattling in its box since Halloween, and I could have sworn I heard a voice coming out of it this morning. I looked up how to ward off demons. Sounded like holy water was the way to go, but that didn't work. I think salt and nails are my best option. I hope that works. Elvi seems to know that I took the pipe. I'm afraid of what she'll do if I don't give it to her. I don't know what she's capable of." There was a loud bang and what sounded like sand—or salt perhaps—spilling. "HOLY SHIT! It broke out of the bucket!" The tape was empty after that.

"Is there another November one?" Max asked. Porter rustled through the box and procured another tape, his hands shaking as he pressed play.

"November third, eight-thirty-seven. Elvi Sinclair shows up at the front door with Deputy Kohen Kitchi. They're looking for the pipe. Willing to buy it from me, but I know in my soul giving it to them won't end well. Deputy Kitchi is that girl's uncle or something, but he rubs me the wrong way. I need to write her a letter before making any hasty decisions."

Porter paused it.

"That's what Della saw in her vision, right?" he asked. Porter nodded. They listened through the whole tape to make sure, then flipped it over.

"November seventh. I think I made a mistake. I decided to test a theory on the peace pipe and might've. . . lit it . . . Look! I'm not proud of it, but I figured if I shoved some sage in it and lit a match, my demon problem would be over. That's what the internet suggested, after all." A pause. "But a strange black smoke flew out of it and out my window. I think I released a demon on Sycamore Heights. I still haven't gotten a response from Delphee. She probably thinks I'm a fraud if she's received my letter by now. I mean, I would think I was a fraud," Ashton sighed heavily, and the tape shut off.

"Hey, there's another November one," Porter said, emulating Ashton's sigh.

This tape opened with a scream.

"November—shit—November ninth. Who cares about the time at this point? I've been looking into all sorts of Native American—gosh darn it! Excuse me, as I was saying, I've been looking into Native American spirits. I've been reading a bunch of books in the basement of the historical society, and I stumbled upon one full of weird Mukwa lore I've never heard of. I didn't unleash a demon; I unleashed a vengeful spirit. Not sure what is worse. Damn, this is like one of those cheesy ghost-hunting shows my mom used to watch. I have no—Ouch!" Heavy swearing over the sound of something dropping to the floor. "Oh, sorry. I'm also sitting here doing a ritual thing to protect my desk because now I'm afraid someone will come across all this and won't believe me, think I'm crazy, or Elvi and Kohen will find it all and get rid of everything. Dammit, how many times am I going to burn myself tonight?" A knock. The tape shut off.

"I think that was the day before he went missing," Porter said.

"How much ya wanna bet that Elvi was the one who knocked on his door?" Max asked.

"Seeing as that's so obviously the case, anyone who found these tapes would believe her to be the prime suspect in his disappearance. Her and Kohen," Porter said, sitting back, stroking his chin in thought.

Max leaned back, returning to his wounded hands, lost in thought.

What exactly was going on here? Sure, an old pipe containing a hell-bent spirit was cause for concern, but usually, *The Utopian Courier* handled those things. Elvi definitely wasn't one of theirs, so who was she working for? Narrowing down who would keep tabs on Moss Hollow would be like searching for a poltergeist in the fog.

And if Kohen knew about all this, what else did he know? Did he know what happened to Della as a child and why her parents pumped her full of harmful pseudo-medication? Did he know of Moss Hollow? He'd have to if he were working intimately with Elvi, as Ashton proposed.

Why hadn't he just come clean?

Was he trying to protect Della, or was something else going on?

"Just let me help," Porter sighed, breaking Max from his thoughts.

"It's fine. Ei've got it," Max grumbled, re-wrapping his right hand after giving up on the left for good.

He swore, wincing from the stinging pain. Unwilling to succumb to Porter's help, he struggled for a few moments more.

What he was trying to prove by this, he didn't know.

Eventually, he sighed, finally handing over the gauze.

Porter's smug grin had returned. Delicately, he wrapped Max's hands, meticulously ensuring every inch of burnt skin was covered and checking to see if the bandage was too loose or tight. He'd even gone the extra mile to find bandages to wrap around Max's fingertips. When he'd finished, he lifted Max's hands to the light, admiring his hard work.

"Now, was that so hard?" he asked. He was way too proud of himself.

"Thanks," was all Max said in return.

Porter winked at him, cleaning up their mess on the

coffee table. "I hope Della's come up with some clues by now."

"She said she was stayin' out of trouble, so Ei think we can count on it," Max laughed darkly. He flexed his fingers a few times, testing his motion range with his wounds dressed. "Said she was gonna ask around about the pipe. Don' know why we haven' just asked Mingan."

"I don't think she wants to drag anyone else into this. It's bad enough that Sebastian won't stop following us around."

"But Ei guarantee ya he knows somethin'," Max said.

"He does have a sort of Mavericks-type vibe, doesn't he?"

Max nodded.

The living room fell silent as Porter drifted off into his thoughts.

Max wasn't sure where Porter's mind would wander, but one little fact stuck out to him. Ashton had said the pipe had begun rattling on Halloween—the same day as Theodore and his brother's funeral.

The same day, the gravity of what had transpired sunk in.

The same day, he overheard something he shouldn't have.

Max's leg began to bounce up and down as he stared at his bandaged hands. Ever since he was a wee one, his ears had gotten him into trouble.

He'd known the silent war between Nicoletta and Mavericks had been raging for years, but what Della and the crew had done had changed things somehow. Lenora had been treating them differently. Less bubbly than usual. Richie was more talkative. The wolf pack at Bayou Gil's eyed them cautiously each time they dined.

Everyone knew something they didn't.

Mavericks had said he'd pulled all the strings to get Della to Moss Hollow, but why? He knew his father was a mastermind. Max loved him deeply. He knew to trust him. But Max hated being left out of plans. They talked about everything. There weren't supposed to be secrets between them.

Percival James Mavericks was a complicated man who'd existed for a very long time. His heart had always been in the right place, but stories had told him his father wasn't incapable of ruin and destruction. More often than not, those things followed him around like the plague.

Mavericks had sent them here for a reason, and though he'd tried to ease Porter's nerves, he knew it had to do with Della more than it did Wendigoes and spirits.

Mavericks and Nicoletta knew what her parents had done to her, which scared him. For all Mavericks talked about finding and sharing the truth with others, he'd kept so many secrets. For all Nicoletta talked about wanting Della to come into her abilities and be able to use them properly, she'd been holding her back during their lessons.

Max believed that whatever they knew, whatever they might've done, Della had a right to know. Keeping secrets from her like this would only end in heartache and feelings of betrayal.

"Are you just going to stew, or are you going to talk about whatever's on your—" Porter began, cut off by the lamp beside them flickering.

A freezing shiver shot up Max's spine as he jumped to his feet. "Somethin' feels off," he said, his face scrunched up in worry as the lights began to blink one by one.

"How off?" Porter asked. His hand was on his gun, though they were both well aware standard bullets would do nothing against a ghost.

"Like how I felt at the historical—"

Max's left side prickled with heat. He turned to see thick black smoke seeping out from the fireplace. Porter yelped in fright as the smoke began pooling in the center of the living room, collecting in two spots, building upon itself until a dark figure stood before them. The blob-like face of the spirit cut into a smile.

Max's heart was pounding along with the throbbing in his head. This spirit felt almost familiar. He reached behind him for Porter but found nothing.

The spirit stepped forward, mockingly tilting its head to the side. Fingertips glowing, eyes flashing back and forth from cat-like to human, Max backed away. The spirit screeched an ear-shattering scream before lunging at him. Tripping over the coffee table, Max found himself on the floor, the spirit hovering over him, its hands elongating into sharp claws. Its fingers grazed his skin, leaving a trail of stinging pain in its wake.

Max was frozen in fear, lying there staring at the entity.

Slowly, the spirit floated up away from him, its smile dropping.

Max scrambled to his feet, watching as the spirit paced back and forth before him like a wild animal stalking its prey. Its eyes narrowed as Porter appeared at Max's side with a handful of salt. Just as Porter aimed to throw the salt at the spirit, a fire poker emerged through the spirit's chest. It screamed, causing Max and Porter to cover their ears. It was almost as if Max could physically feel the entity's pain through its shrieks.

Mingan's face was barely visible through its smoky body. Anger flashed in his eyes as he dragged the fire poker through the spirit. It spun on him, slashing his chest with its long claws. Mingan screamed, falling to his knees, clutching his chest. The spirit reared up to cut him again, but Max was quick enough to stop him.

"*Skjoldet!*" he screamed, thrusting his hand forward. The spirit's hands slashed and thrashed at the invisible shield now protecting Mingan.

Porter tossed his salt on the ghost, but all it did was irritate the entity further.

It rounded on them. "TRAITORS!" the spirit screamed in a low and gravelly tone. No wonder Ashton had immediately jumped to the conclusion of a demon.

It kept screaming the same thing repeatedly, each time louder, less human, until all that was left was a high-pitched screech.

And then it was gone.

The ghost.

The smoke.

The horrible throbbing in Max's head.

Everything.

Porter slowly uncovered his ears, his eyes as wide as dinner plates. He stood gawking for a minute before his face darkened. Suddenly, he was supporting Max's full weight, struggling to keep him upright.

They heard a loud *POP!* and flames erupted from the fireplace. They curled around the mantle and leaped at the walls, leaving scorch marks behind that looked like hands.

The fire extinguished the exact second the front door opened.

"Hey, we brought dinner! Who wants—What the Hell happened?" Della's voice came as she and Sebastian rounded the corner.

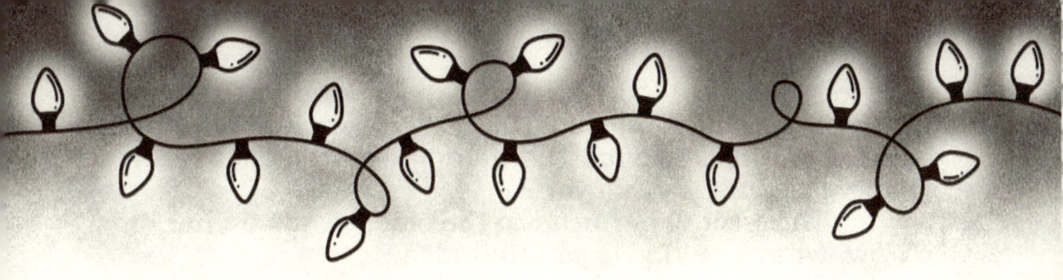

CHAPTER THIRTY-FOUR

History Lessons

Mingan's cabin was infinitely colder than the frigid air Della and Sebastian had come in from. Della's eyes fell on Mingan, who was grappling to his feet. He was bleeding, but it didn't seem too serious. Otherwise, she'd be in complete and total freak-out mode. Della shivered, handing their Chinese take-out to Sebastian and walking off toward Mingan in a daze. She couldn't tear her eyes away from the scorch marks around the fireplace.

Mingan took the hand she offered him.

That's when she saw just how bad the marks on his chest were.

What happened? she signed to him, panicked.

He waved her away, looking disgruntled. Maybe it was for her benefit, but there was no pain on his face.

What have you gotten yourself into, Della? Mingan signed back, placing a hand over his wounds afterward.

Della grimaced. *Seems like you found that out.*

He smirked, cupping her cheek in his hands. He then placed both hands on his shoulders, pulling them away into fists.

Brave.

Della's shoulders sagged, wrapping him in a giant hug. The tightness in her chest released.

"You all right?" Porter asked.

Della spun, seeing Max had collapsed to the couch. He'd gone so incredibly pale Della thought she was looking at a corpse. His amber eyes flashed back and forth between human and cat as he stared off into space.

"The animals," Della breathed.

He looked to Della, fear on his face. "What?" he asked groggily.

Before Della had a chance to respond, Sebastian

cleared his throat. "So, I'm going to go out on a limb here and ask an idiotic question," he began, shakily setting their dinner on the coffee table. "You don't work at some random paper in Louisiana, do you?"

Della tilted her head to the side, hands on her hips. "Now, what would give you that idea?"

Sebastian gave her a bored look.

Mingan tapped her shoulder. She turned to see him mirroring Sebastian's look. *Gather everyone in the kitchen. I have a story for you.* With that, he made off down the hall.

Della relayed the message, the tightness in her chest returning as Porter struggled to get Max off the couch. Together, they shuffled into the kitchen.

Sebastian began distributing Styrofoam containers of Chinese food. If anyone believed the truth of their hectic lives, it would be him.

Della stirred her chow mein, trying to find the right words. "I do work for a random newspaper in Louisiana. Just not the kind you're used to."

An ounce of recognition floated over Sebastian's face. "The Utopian Courier? That old conspiracy paper you used to have mailed to Hugo and Enid?"

"That's the one," she said, her cheeks burning red.

"The only time I remember you not having your nose in an issue of that thing was when Jasper confiscated your stash and threatened to burn them."

Della scoffed. "And now I've got an issue with my name on the front page."

"You're joking."

"She has it framed," Max yawned, resting his head on the table. "And highlighted."

"So does her boss," Porter chimed in, eyes glued to Max in concern.

"What exactly did we miss?" Sebastian asked, looking between Max and Porter in the same way a person watching a riveting game of tennis would.

"We got attacked by an angry spirit," Max groaned.

Porter sighed heavily, tugging on his earrings. "We brought home the contents of Ash's desk. Bunch of tapes talking about how the ghost was released and about Kohen and Elvi."

Della felt herself deflating. "Did you talk to him at the station?"

"He let us poke around. Maybe he's unaware he's an accomplice. Maybe he was just doing his job. Who knows. No jumping to conclusions, right?"

Sebastian patted Della's leg beneath the table, giving her a reassuring look.

Mingan returned in a shirt that wasn't full of mysterious claw marks. He helped himself to a heaping plate of food, taking a seat opposite Della, his eyebrows furrowed deeply over his eyes. Della knew that look only meant trouble.

You brought home a treasure earlier. May I see? he asked.

Della dug into her book bag for the peace pipe, sliding the box over to him as she wondered how this would go. If anyone knew the story behind this pipe, it would be him. Nothing happened on the reservation he didn't know about. He ran a tight ship. However, Della hadn't pried earlier for a multitude of reasons. Seeing as he was now harboring wounds from a ghost attack, she couldn't use the protection excuse anymore. The sweet taste of knowledge was on the tip of Della's tongue, but the longer she waited for his story, the less she wanted to hear it.

Mingan was the wisest person she'd ever known.

There was no doubt in her mind that he knew what she was.

Max had been right. Everything seemed to be revolving around her. It was only a matter of time before Mingan brought it up, and the rest of Della's world came crashing down around her.

Scowling deeply, Mingan popped open the box, taking the pipe into his weathered hands. Gingerly turning it toward the light, he scrutinized every part of it with a raised eyebrow.

Where did you get this? he asked after setting the peace pipe carefully back in its box.

Della reddened. *I don't think you want to know.*

Mingan smiled mischievously. There was about an eighty percent chance he already knew exactly where she'd found it.

"He knows about it?" Porter asked. His curiosity hadn't washed away the sadness in his voice.

Della nodded, gesturing for Mingan to begin.

This pipe would have belonged to one of our past Chief's children, he began. *This child was not a man you wanted to trifle with. While his father led our people with honor, this boy tried to lead with destruction. It was a dark time back then. The son took matters into his own hands under the guise of protection. Lots of blood was spilled because of him. He and the original Sycamores did not get along.*

Della relayed the story to the boys, watching the gears begin to turn in Max and Porter's minds. Sebastian looked like a little kid being read a bedtime story.

"I have never heard this story before," Della said,

signing the same thought to Mingan. Despite her best efforts, she didn't know everything about her Mukwa heritage. Some stories never made it on paper. Some never left a person's lips.

You wouldn't have. No one talks about the skeletons in their closet, do they? Mingan winked. *There were two sons: Ahiga and Huritt. Ahiga was older; he should have been next in line after his father, but he was reckless. His desire to protect his tribe turned him cold and bitter. He didn't trust anyone. Wouldn't speak to traders and travelers. The Chief, worrying for the future of the tribe, decided that when he died, Huritt would take his place instead.*

Something about the name Huritt stood out to Della, but she couldn't figure out why.

What happened to Ahiga? she asked, now fully invested in the story. So were the boys. They hung on every word each time she would translate what Mingan had said.

Jealousy. Ahiga was a great warrior, as you can see, Mingan said, pointing at the feathers and markings on the pipe. *But his ways were ruthless. Anyone with good intent or bad would feel his wrath the second they made a mistake. This pipe, he should not have had it. It is a sick talisman he used to fearmonger.* Mingan shivered.

But he didn't hurt the Sycamores? Della asked.

Mingan shook his head. *His father grew weary of him. He knew the Sycamores were trying to cultivate the land, which, in his eyes, would benefit our people. He knew Ahiga would disagree, so he sent him away. His wife was a powerful shaman. They sent him out into the world, telling him to return with things she could use in rituals.*

Della, being the great storyteller she was, could tell this story was about to go downhill real quick.

Ahiga spent many moons out in the wild, collecting ingredients as he was told to. When he returned, it was a welcome reunion until he saw his brother. Every member of the tribe loved Huritt. The Sycamores loved him, too. He was the Native they taught in exchange for help around their homestead. Huritt could speak English and was becoming a gentleman. Ahiga hated it. To him, Huritt was betraying both their tribe and his bloodline.

"From the look on your face, none of what he is saying is good," Porter whispered.

"I think I know what Ahiga's motivation is if that's whose spirit we are dealing with," Della said.

Mingan tapped the table to get her attention back on him. *Ahiga took it upon himself to cleanse the tribe of his brother. Every Mukwa knew the stories. Our tribe is rich in Algonquin and Cree traditions. Ahiga knew of the Wendigo.*

He knew what would happen if any of the tribe were to become one.

"They'd hunt them down and kill them," Della breathed.

"Who?" Max asked, looking terrified. Della shushed him.

"Huritt," Sebastian breathed.

You know the stories, too. If you are driven to cannibalism, you will be turned into a Wendigo as punishment. Huritt would never do such a thing, but Ahiga knew he could trick him. He would make a meal for his brother to show how much he missed him.

Mingan shook his head disapprovingly, wrinkling his nose. He had never understood Della's obsession with Wendigoes when she was little. She'd always thought he was simply disgusted by those stories. Somehow, this reason was worse. Knowing this wasn't just folklore but lived history made her sick.

The details are foggy on how Ahiga acquired such a gruesome ingredient, but he must have disguised the components well, he continued, his eyes full of sadness. *Huritt ate the tainted meal, and before nightfall, he had transformed into the Wendigo. Unable to control himself, he went after the Sycamores. His father and any able-bodied tribesman had to step in and get rid of him. Though they could not kill him, he was wounded. Huritt fled to the woods, never to be seen again. With Huritt gone, Ahiga took his place. The Chief was heartbroken over Huritt, which made him vulnerable. Ahiga convinced him to step down. Now Ahiga oversaw the entire grieving and angry tribe. He abused his power, turning the tribe against the Sycamores. He was the worst Chief we have ever had. And I sincerely hope no one repeats his mistakes.*

Mingan sighed, allowing Della to translate for a moment.

I do not know what transpired before this, but his mother grew suspicious and eventually found that Huritt becoming a Wendigo was not her beloved son's fault. The real evil being was Ahiga.

"Shit," Della whispered.

"What?" Max and Porter asked in unison.

"Stop interrupting!" Della and Sebastian hissed.

The Chief and his wife realized the only way to protect their tribe was to eliminate him. They used the pipe Ahiga had once made to boast his power to trap his spirit inside it. But now it looks empty, doesn't it?

Della's bones chilled instantly. "That's it? That's the end of the story?"

Chapter Thirty-Four

Mingan shrugged. *Until now.*

"What's he saying?" Porter exclaimed, looking frustrated.

Della quickly relayed everything Mingan had said. She was more convinced than ever that the Wendigo could help them. She had to find it—*him*—soon.

Porter's face darkened. "How would his spirit be able to escape?"

Depends. Mingan began, reading his lips. *If it was broken in any way, it could wiggle out.*

The boys looked at her expectantly. "Did Ash smoke out of the pipe?" she asked. Mavericks was going to love this. This was just the sort of wacky story The Courier needed.

Max shook his head, finally sitting up from the table. Some of the color had finally returned to his face. "He shoved some sage in and lit it."

"I can't tell if that's any better. Either way, he released a vengeful spirit, and now we're left dealing with the consequences."

Sebastian was quiet, lost in thought, as he finished off his bowl of fried rice. Now and then, he looked between Della and Mingan like they were nuts.

"Spirits are pretty straightforward, right? Sort of a trap and release situation, then we're good to go?" Porter said, suddenly looking hopefully.

Max nodded his agreement. "We still have tuh deal with the Wendigo, though."

"What do you mean, 'deal with?' He's not bothering anyone." Della hadn't meant to sound so defensive.

"Well, let's say he's the one scaring all the construction workers. That means he's bothering people. Even if he doesn't mean to scare or hurt anyone, that's what he's doing. And for all we know, the brothers could have made up and are working together," Porter said. "I'm sorry, Della, but we can't just let this guy run rampant."

"Are you suggesting we kill him?" Della scoffed.

"Yes," the boys said, straight-faced.

Della stood, shaking her head. "We're not killing anyone or anything else unless it's absolutely necessary. Huritt has given us no reason to take such drastic measures. It seems like he's trying to help."

"So, what do you suggest we do? Go talk to him?" Porter asked.

Della smiled brightly. "Exactly."

"And how do ya suppose we go about that?" Max asked.

"If you two are so concerned about the construction

site, let's start there. It seems to be a point of interest for Huritt," she said sassily.

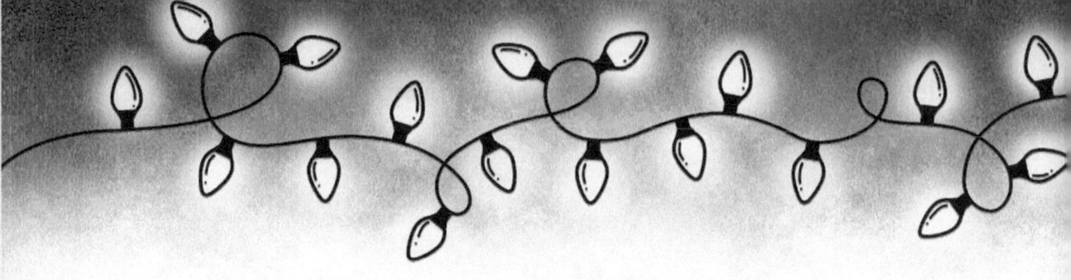

CHAPTER THIRTY-FIVE

Are We Really Surpised?

Sebastian had spent the first half of the hearse ride pestering them with questions they refused to answer. He spent the second half searching up Wendigoes on his phone. Della had to snicker. He was in way over his head. They'd tried to get him to stay behind, but he'd refused. It wasn't like he was new to all of this. Growing up with Della had given him a unique perspective on the world.

The construction site hadn't changed since Della's last visit. However, she hoped things would go a little differently this time.

"You guys aren't ditching me this time," he said as he scrambled out of the hearse to catch up with them as they took to the gravel path beyond where the hearse could fit.

"I'm warning you, Seb, you're going to want to stay in the car for this," Della sighed, weaving through the trees like a skillful hunter telling their protégé the hunt wasn't worth it anymore.

"As far as I'm concerned," Sebastian said loudly, running in front of them. He held his head high as he walked backward, pointing at them accusingly. "I'm the only sane one out here right now. The three of you are going on about Wendigoes and spirits like crazies. Do you want to end up in straitjackets?"

"Do you?" Porter yawned, lazily checking the barrel in his ancient-looking Colt Single Action Army pistol. "Anyone else having flashbacks? If something comes barreling out of those trees, you suckers are on your own. I'm not going to get bitten again."

"Wow. My prince charming," Della sneered.

Porter wolf-whistled at her.

Sebastian skidded to a stop. "That's it. I want to know what's going on. I want to know the truth—and not some—" He waved his hands through the air angrily. "—muddled up half-truth!"

"We are monster hunters," Max said simply. "While ya spend yer days wastin' away at a nine-tuh-five, the three of us are out there riskin' our lives to protect the world. We have killed the Grunch Road Monster, took an evil man tuh justice, and pretty much saved an entire town. More or less."

"I would say less," Porter argued.

Max pointed over his shoulder at him. "Yeah, well, guess what—" He inhaled sharply, deciding whatever he was going to say wasn't worth disturbing the feigned peace. "Anyways, ya don' belong out here. Go home."

"Oh so, I don't belong out here, but Della, who looks like she's going to fall apart if someone so much as touches her, does?" Sebastian snapped. "Don't you need a getaway driver?"

"You touch the steering wheel of the hearse, and the only way you'll be leaving this place is in the back," Porter warned.

"I'm staying! S-T-A-Y-I-N-G!" Sebastian screamed at the top of his lungs.

Della shook her head, stifling a laugh as she stepped past him. "Keep up, then," she called over her shoulder.

The four of them looked like quite a pair. Here they were, trudging through muddy snow like a colorful group of bards. Della was still in her plum Church dress, Sebastian in his suit. Porter was sporting a fandom hoodie, and Max looked like a model out of *Vogue*.

Della could barely believe it was still Sunday. That morning felt like months ago.

Like the last time she was at the construction site, the place was utterly devoid of life. Some of the heavy machinery had been moved, and a few loose candy wrappers littered the ground, blowing away like tumbleweeds, but other than that, things seemed normal. However, the broken EMF detector was missing. Hopefully, whoever found it couldn't trace it back to them.

"Are we sure we want to do this?" Porter asked, eyeing his surroundings cautiously.

Della nodded. "Trust me, okay?"

Excitement coursed through Della's veins. She was terrified of what would happen when she came face to face with Ahiga's spirit, but it was freeing knowing that even in her prejudiced, anti-magic town, something mystical had always been in the woods. There were people at The Courier who would kill for a chance to traipse through the woods looking for their all-time favorite cryptid.

Christmas had come early.

She winced at the thought of Christmas. It was the twentieth now. That fateful day was far too close. She had allowed herself to forget the upcoming holiday and Poppy's party on the twenty-third. Hopefully, they could exorcise Ahiga's spirit and hightail it back to Sycamore Heights before then.

Before they'd left the reservation, Della had bartered with Mingan for a thawed package of freezer-burnt fish. If Huritt was out here, maybe she could lure him to her with the smell of raw meat. Removing the bundle of fish from her book bag before handing it off to Max, she sat on a pile of cement bags.

In case their presence upset the Wendigo, Della instructed the boys to hang back.

The putrid stink of raw fish wafted into the air as she ripped the package open. The smell gagged her, but she guessed a hungry Wendigo would find it heavenly.

"Huritt! I got you some—" She looked down at the fillet in her hands. "—non-GMO, organic, fresh caught cod!" Though it disgusted her to do so, Della ripped off a piece of the fish and tossed it to the forest floor.

"Here, Wendigo! C'mere Wendigo! Come to momma!" Porter called, earning himself a glare from over Della's shoulder.

Max shushed him, and the construction site fell into silence.

Della waited a while before heading to the edge of the clearing, throwing the rest of the fish as far into the trees as she could. The trees seemed to go on for miles, eventually fading into an endless void. Such a sight used to fill Della with wonder. Yet now, standing here, watching the shadows play tricks on her eyes, gave her the creeps.

Della turned back to look at the boys. Max was shaking his head. It was like he could read her mind. Porter had a firm grip on his gun, staring past her. Sebastian just stood there with his mouth hanging open.

Each of them had a single orange butterfly on their shoulder.

Della's heart raced.

The butterflies had been trying to tell her something this whole time. But what? How did they fit into this?

The butterflies flew toward her, circling her before two landed on her outstretched hands. Their wings fluttered like they were spooked. The third hung in the air before her face, beckoning her into the woods.

"It wants me to follow it," Della whispered, making to follow the butterfly.

"What does?" the boys asked, appearing at her side.

"The butterfly," Della said dazedly, turning to give them a look she hoped conveyed how absolutely stupid she felt they were being, showing them her hands. The butterflies in her palm flew up, joining their friend.

"What butterfly?" Porter asked as Max grabbed Della's wrist.

"Are you guys blind? There are three giant orange butterflies in the middle of a black and gray forest," she laughed.

Porter opened his mouth to say something but was cut off by Sebastian swearing profusely. Della spun around to see two glowing white eyes peering out of the woods. There, in all his glory, was the Wendigo. One of the butterflies landed on the Wendigo's nose, fluttering its wings softly. Sebastian swore again, causing the Wendigo to recoil, slipping back into the shadows of the woods. Without thinking, Della wriggled free of Max's grip and ran towards it, ignoring the protests of her boys.

The Wendigo was large and lumbering but moved faster than any normal animal could, each step carrying it as if running full speed. Della followed as closely as she could, blocking out the three sets of footsteps behind her and Porter screaming at her to stop. The Wendigo ducked in and out of her sight, weaving between the trees masterfully. Freezing air burned her lungs as she ran after the creature she was sure held the answers she so desperately needed.

"Wait! Slow down!" she called to it, ducking under low-hanging branches, vaulting over roots that would trip her if she wasn't careful.

~ ~ ~

Porter skid to a stop. He'd lost sight of Della when Sebastian stumbled into a smaller tree and almost fell on him.

"How the Hell can she run so fast?" Max gasped, doubling over to try and catch his breath.

"All three of you need to get your priorities straight, or we can't be friends anymore!" Sebastian screamed. "A freaking monster just came strolling out of the words, and our lovely detective just bolted after it! Focus! Please!"

Porter inhaled deeply, taking him by the shoulder and giving him a tight smile. "We're accustomed to her running after danger. Nothing really phases us these days." He patted his shoulder and then turned to Max. "Can you hear her?"

"Vaguely," Max coughed, pinching the bridge of his nose. "Ei'm gonna kill her."

"She took off after a *monster!*" Sebastian yelled, jumping to exaggerate his point. "You aren't going to have a chance to kill her because it's going to get to her first!" he screamed.

"That's a good point. Max, lead the way," Porter said, feeling his stomach lurch.

Max sighed heavily, then took off to the left, running as fast as he could.

CHAPTER THIRTY-SIX

Crappy Decision-Making Skills

Della slowed, listening to the woods. They'd gone eerily silent like the construction site had been. Distantly, she could hear the snap of twigs. From the sounds of it, the Wendigo had slowed as well. She took off again, trying to corner it, hoping it would be willing to speak with her again.

If not, then she hoped Max and Porter showed up soon.

She'd spent many a day walking through the forests, twisting between the thick trees, waiting for adventure to find her. How had she never come across the Wendigo before? Or maybe she had, she just couldn't remember.

Her mind buzzed and burned as she tried to remember.

The Wendigo was only a few feet in front of her now. She stopped, gathering her courage, hoping she could outrun it if it attacked.

"Hey!" she called to it.

Her breath caught in her throat as it looked up, cocking its head to the side. Its eyes seemed to stare straight through her feeble body and directly into her soul. The Wendigo edged toward her, sniffing the ground. His gangly, matted arms shook, sending menacing waves of ripples through his fur.

"Lost?" he asked, his voice low and rumbling, like the sound the earth made before an earthquake split the ground apart. She could tell he wasn't happy she'd followed. He seemed offended.

Della just stared in awe at what she was seeing and hearing. It wasn't until he began to growl that she snapped back to reality.

"No," she said, adrenaline coursing through her. "I was looking for you."

The Wendigo straightened his head, squinting at her. He grumbled something unintelligible, turning away. He was two feet taller than Della, even on all fours. How terrifyingly beautiful.

"Wait!" Della called, running up to him, hands up in defense. "Please, Huritt, talk to me! I have so many questions."

The Wendigo ignored her and kept on walking. However, he was clearly trying to walk slowly so she could keep up. Della gave an angry little *humph* but continued following.

"It's okay if you don't have the answers, but I really think you do," she pressed.

Mavericks would freak out when she told him she'd been speaking with an actual Wendigo. In Washington, of all places!

"Huritt—"

"Do—not—call—me—Huritt," he growled.

The Wendigo made a sound that would rival the roars of dinosaurs as he turned to follow a rabbit trail, his long, bony tail nearly taking Della's head off.

"I'm sorry. Is there a different name you'd like me to call you?"

"Arlo," he said, looking over his shoulder at her. Della hadn't realized how sassy one choppy word could sound.

Della fell a few paces back, trying her best to act calm. "Well. . . *Arlo*. . . It's very nice to meet you! May I ask some of my questions now?" she persisted, unwavering as he stopped, turned back to her, and bent down to her level, sniffing the top of her head.

Huritt—or rather Arlo, as he preferred to be called—stepped over her. A sound akin to a laugh rumbled from his throat, telling Della he enjoyed getting on her nerves. Della pouted, continuing to follow him as he turned back down the path they'd just come from. This seemed to annoy him, which in Della's books meant they were even.

"Missed—you," he said after a while.

He stopped eventually, lowering himself to the forest floor, laying like a wolf, his front paws crossed rather regally.

"I, uh, don't remember you, though," Della said carefully, reaching out a hand to place atop his snout.

He nuzzled her hand like a horse, blowing his hot, steamy breath on her. Della couldn't stop her smile or the child-like laugh that escaped her chest.

A friendly cannibalistic monster.

Who would have thought?

"Why?" Arlo asked, studying her, his glowing eyes

sweeping over her.

She shrugged. "That's what I'm trying to figure out. Along with about a hundred other things."

"Ask—questions," he sighed, yawning, shaking his mane, showering her in dirt, twigs, bugs, and whatever else was currently in that matted mess.

"Have you seen an injured person in the woods lately?" Della asked carefully, scratching the top of his bonelike head, which he seemed to enjoy.

"No," he said, his tone a mix of sadness and anger. "Why?"

"A human went missing not too long ago. I have reason to believe that something like you killed him," she sighed.

"Not—my—doing," he huffed angrily.

"I know. I believe you." Which was the truth, though she didn't know why.

There was a strange, unspoken connection between them. An unbreakable bond that had spanned a lifetime, it seemed. Like two long-lost friends reuniting after losing touch for many years.

"Were we friends?" she asked softly.

He gave a simple nod and then looked out to the forest. "Long—ago."

"I'm so sorry I don't remember."

He grumbled to himself, his jaw chittering and clacking in a way that sent chills up Della's spine. She could tell his feelings were hurt, which baffled her.

"Is there anything else in these woods I should remember? Something that *would* want to hurt humans? Another Wendigo, maybe?" she asked, sinking to the ground, staring up at him in awe.

He shook his head, pine needles falling like rain on top of her. "No," he whispered gravely.

"Are you sure? Nothing new?"

He looked down at her, his eyes narrowing. Della didn't say anything for a while as they sat watching the sun go down, the trees turning into dark obelisks around them. Arlo seemed to be in a bad mood this evening, which made Della wonder if something had happened. She knew better than to believe he'd only come looking for her because he missed her. Especially if it meant coming this close to human civilization. Didn't he realize he'd be hunted endlessly if someone saw him?

Della shivered. "Is everything okay? You seem upset."

Arlo just nodded, lowering his head onto her lap. "Forest—angry," he whispered.

"What do you mean?" she asked, stroking his fur to

both get it out of her face and comfort him.

The forest was almost pitch-black, spare the light emanating from Arlo's milky eyes. Della realized with a pit in her stomach that she had no idea how far from the construction site she was.

"Bad—men," Arlo said, an ounce of fear in his voice.

~ ~ ~

Max's nose had never been wrong. Not once. He could sniff out anything he put his mind to. People were usually so easy to find. Yet, here he was, completely lost, unable to pick up Della's vanilla and cinnamon scent amongst the petrichor and pine. What good is a cat who can't smell his way to victory?

"Max," Porter said after a drought of silence so dense he didn't need his supersonic hearing to note the bugs crawling beneath his feet or the owls hooting in the distance.

"Shut it," he snapped.

"We should have found her by now," Porter sighed, pulling along a perplexed and almost deranged Sebastian, who kept mumbling, 'It's real. All of it. It's real,' which was driving the two of them insane.

"Ei realize that, Porter, but we haven' so shut up so Ei can focus," Max hissed over his shoulder.

"Yeah, well, if you weren't such a gentleman, she'd have her phone on her," Porter snapped back, pointing to Della's book bag hung over his shoulder.

Max gave him a dirty look but continued on.

"Can't you do—Oh, for the love of—Stop it!" Porter yelled, rounding on Sebastian. "Yes, monsters are real. So is magic. Witches. Vampires. Werewolves. Get over it!"

"Lay off it," Max sighed.

Porter swiveled around to him. "I can't! He's driving me nuts!"

Sebastian had gone silent, eyes glued to the forest floor. "Sorry. It's just a lot to take in," he squeaked. "I honestly thought you guys were just messing with me earlier."

Max nodded. "And we realize that, and we're sorry ya had to find out like this, but—"

"Are we?" Porter said, throwing his hands up into the air.

"Beg yer pardon?"

"Are we actually sorry, or are we just coddling him?"

Max thought for a second, looking Sebastian up and down. Eventually, he just shrugged and spun back around to keep trudging on.

~ ~ ~

Della furrowed her eyebrows. "What kind of 'bad men?'" she asked. "Was someone looking for you?"

He nodded. "Scary," he breathed. The fur on his back rippling though there was no breeze. She could have sworn he trembled.

A thought crossed Della's mind as Arlo shut his eyes, a sound like a broken lawnmower going over rocks resonating from him. Given her vision at Ashton's trailer and prior interaction with Elvi, she—maybe even Kohen—must know about him. What if they were the 'bad men?' What if that's why they wanted the peace pipe? Maybe they thought the peace pipe could somehow trap or destroy Arlo? Or maybe they thought it released him to begin with? She'd have to interrogate them after she found her way back to the others.

Arlo suddenly lifted his head, smacking Della's nose in the process. He stood, the fur around his skull-like face standing on end. A different kind of cold chilled the air. Something else was in the woods now. Arlo growled, stepping backward over Della so she was sitting beneath him. She guessed he thought he was protecting her.

"What's going on?" Della whispered, peering into the trees. As far as her human eyes could see, there was nothing there.

"*Darkness*," Arlo breathed, a growl rumbling in his throat.

Della's heart somersaulted as she scrambled to her feet. Just as she was about to ask Arlo if he could see anything, something whizzed past her, ruffling her hair with an unseen wind. Snow fell off swaying branches, disrupted by the invisible force. It had to be Ahiga's spirit.

Della cowered beneath Arlo as he pawed at the empty air. It didn't end well the last time she faced a monster alone. She wished she had better control over her powers or, better yet, knew exactly what she could do with them.

"Stay—under!" Arlo roared.

He didn't have to tell her twice. She edged closer to his back leg, afraid of being stomped by the front ones.

The spirit kept whizzing by them, kicking up freshly fallen snow, ripping branches off trees, tormenting them almost playfully, until finally, it stopped. Black mist appeared a few feet before Arlo, shaping itself into a body. It had the same white eyes as Arlo, though those eyes were lifeless compared to his.

It didn't speak, didn't move, just stared, its head

tilted to the side, looking right at Della. The mist where his mouth should have been broke into a cruel smile as it lifted a long, clawed finger and pointed at her. She didn't have time to react before it lunged at her. Della screeched, waiting for impact, but Arlo had put his front legs together to block the attack.

"RUN!" he screeched.

So, she did.

She turned on her heels and ran, ripping through the trees as fast as she could. Behind her, Arlo screeched in pain, which would have been horrifying enough without the loud thump that followed. She desperately wanted to turn back, but she had a sinking feeling the spirit wanted to hurt her more than anyone else. Which struck Della as odd. What would harming her accomplish? Did she unknowingly upset a centuries-old spirit? Knowing herself, it was entirely possible. Maybe it was the spirit she and Max spoke with the other night.

She didn't know how long she'd been running for, but suddenly, she was standing on what she thought was a path that led to a clearing dotted with rocks. Out of breath, she came to a stop, hoping there was a road on the other side or, at the very least, someone's backyard.

Trying to catch her breath, she walked into the clearing, a sense of dread filling her body. The forest was deadly silent—no hoots of owls, no wind, nothing except her footsteps crunching in the snow.

Then it happened.

Every inch of her skin burned like someone had poured boiling water over her. The burning traveled, seeping into her bones. She stumbled forward, gasping for air as shadowy tendrils erupted from her chest and flowed into the air before her, a misty form materializing. The spirit had flown straight through her. Whatever that was, it wasn't something Della ever wanted to experience again. It left her feeling empty and angry, its emotions lingering inside her.

Again, the entity's smokey face cut into a cruel grin. It reached out to her, shadows seeping out of the trees and wrapping around her ankles like rapidly growing vines as she stood. Shadows were meant to be cold, but these were scorching hot, burning her skin as they wrapped around her. She tried to move, but they cemented her in place. The spirit was laughing now. It took joy from seeing her in pain. This whole thing reminded Della of what had happened back in October.

But she wasn't going to let it end the same way.

Hands outstretched, trying to recall how she had felt that day, she called out to the Universe. She waited, eyes shut tightly, patiently expecting to feel some sort of power surge through her.

She opened her eyes to see the entity had its head tilted at her, looking bored.

"So, you're going to attack me and insult me? Low blow!" she snapped, thrusting her hands forward.

A tiny ripple of energy left her hands. The air rippled as if it were hot, but other than that, nothing happened.

The spirit laughed its eerie little laugh again, doubling over out of delight.

Della was fuming now. She hated bullies.

With clenched fists, she shut her eyes. She was a dreamwalker; she had to believe that. Max said she could bend reality, and she so desperately wanted that to be true.

But most importantly, she didn't want to feel as useless as she did now.

Because she wasn't useless. Maybe she was a screw-up like everyone said, but she wasn't useless.

In her mind's eye, her hands glowed with a dangerous purple light. She pictured the scenery around her, everything glowing with psychedelic colors that began swirling like a drug-induced mind-melting whirlpool. Slowly, the color melted toward her, turning to the same violent shade of lilac emanating off her fingertips. Acting on ancient impulsive instinct, Della thrust her hands forward again, a wave of psychic energy hitting the spirit square in the chest, sending ripples through its smoky form.

Della doubled over in pain, feeling like she'd been punched in the stomach. Whatever she'd been expecting, this was not it.

She looked up to see the spirit was unfazed. Della doubted she had done anything more than irritate it.

She braced for impact but should have focused on the shadows crawling up her legs. It was too late to act as something cracked beneath her. At first, she thought she had inadvertently broken her own bones from the amount of power she thought she'd used. But as her feet froze and the water soaked her legs, she realized how wrong she was.

This wasn't a clearing.

It was a lake.

The shadows pulled her down, causing her to fall back onto the snow-covered ice. She tried to move, but the tendrils pinned her to the cracking ice as they slithered over her body. All she could do was try to push herself up with her free arm.

Her hand went right through the fragile ice.

Soon followed the rest of her body.

Freezing water engulfed her, chilling her to the core.

The water was so cold it stole the breath from her burnt-out lungs. She gasped, the water like tiny daggers against her skin. The shadows writhed away, a wave of exhaustion taking their place. She couldn't move. Couldn't see through the dark water around her. Her eyelids flickered shut as she realized that this was her fate. She would drown in the middle of the forest, and no one would know.

Darkness clouded her mind as she felt herself sink, her lungs filling with water, her consciousness slipping away.

Her funeral had better be epic.

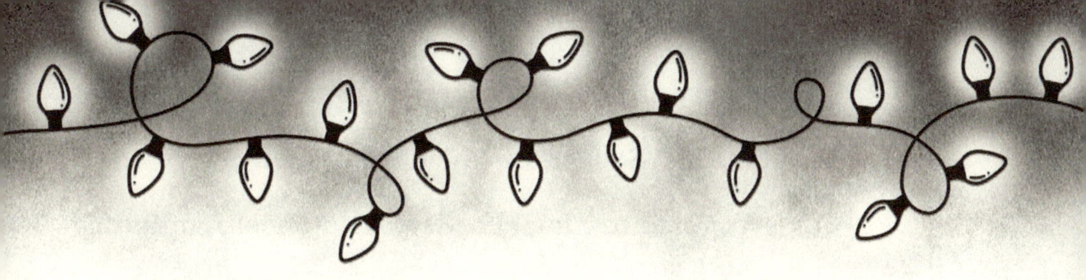

CHAPTER THIRTY-SEVEN

Losing

Max stumbled forward, suddenly feeling dizzy. Images flashed in his mind of bubbles, ice, and dark tentacles. His lungs fought to breathe. It was like he was drowning, what little life left in him trying to push the water from his lungs.

Porter gripped him by the elbow, steadying him. He said something followed by a very concerned expression, but all Max could hear was distant mumbling.

"Oh no," he breathed, shaking away Porter's hands, staggering backward into Sebastian.

As quickly as the debilitating dizziness came, it went, leaving Max reeling, his senses dull. He couldn't hear, couldn't smell. The world seemed gray. He hung his head low, pinching the bridge of his nose, a distant yet somehow familiar sadness replacing every thought and emotion.

"Wh—What do you mean 'oh no,' Max?" Porter whispered—or maybe that's just how Max heard it—as he took him by the shoulders, squeezing so tightly that Max thought he'd be left with broken bones.

"Ei don' know," Max said, shaking his head to clear his thoughts. "Ei don'—" He shrugged Porter off, confusion lifting, replaced by blood-chilling fear.

He did know.

He knew exactly what was wrong, and it scared him more than losing the rest of his nine lives. Scared him more than losing Mavericks or Nicoletta.

"Ei need my stuff," he quivered, shooing away Sebastian, caught in a daze as he backtracked through the forest.

"Hey! Slow down!" Porter shouted after him.

He hadn't realized he was running until Porter caught up to him.

"Talk to me!" he screeched.

"Ei need my stuff!" Max repeated, quickening his pace.

"What stuff?" Sebastian called from a few paces behind.

Max grumbled to himself. "Scrying stones! A map! My friggin stuff!"

"Scrying—Wait, that's for a locator spell! Max, you're a genius!" Porter said excitedly.

Max shook his head.

He wasn't a genius at all.

He was just a scared familiar who had lost his witch.

Or rather, his dreamwalker.

~ ~ ~

The boys had run back to the hearse at full speed without another word. Max was digging through the bags and boxes in the back for his scrying stones. Sebastian and Porter stood to the side, exchanging worried looks.

"Do—Do you want help?" Porter asked after a while.

Max crawled out of the back of the hearse as fast as he could, hightailing it to the front, all manner of magical objects tucked under his arms. He heard Sebastian whisper some infuriating question in Porter's ear, but he was too busy to care or take time to explain anything.

She had been in pain. Fading pain, pain replaced by numbness, numbness replaced by an empty chasm.

But why?

Why did *he* feel so empty?

Why couldn't he feel her pain anymore?

Why had this happened all of a sudden?

His heart somersaulted.

Focus, Max. He thought, his voice shaking inside his mind. He didn't know inner voices could sound anxious until now.

He emptied his arms onto the hood of the hearse, fumbling to arrange everything in neat little piles. Sebastian was on his left, peering over his shoulder, watching intently. Porter was on his right, his eyes boring into him, chiseling a hole in the side of his head. One of the scrying stones rolled off the hood with a splash as it landed in a puddle somewhere at their feet. Max ignored it. It was a smaller one, anyway. Too small to use correctly. Instead, he reached for the largest one he had.

"Max," Porter said sternly.

Emotional anchor. Ei need an emotional anchor, he thought.

Was this what a panic attack felt like? Simultaneously being hyper-aware of your surroundings yet completely disconnected from them? Or was he in shock? He'd never felt like this before. Not once. Why did his mind have to come up with so many horrible outcomes? He needed it to stop. He needed to focus. Do the spell right. Fix this. He needed control. Not panic.

"Max," Porter said again, this time louder.

Her notebooks. That'd be a great anchor. They are practically full of her soul.

He dug into her book bag, procuring the one notebook she carried with her despite it being filled to the brim with her ramblings. The margins were bleeding with ink; the front and back covers had been scribbled upon in moments when she wasn't at her best.

He held the scrying stone out before him—a crystal clear piece of quartz the size of his hand—and clutched her notebook to his chest, shutting his eyes tightly.

"*Finne, rof finne, Della,*" he whispered, his lips tingling with magic.

He waited a moment, afraid to open his eyes.

"Isn't there meant to be an image?" Porter asked, going stiff next to him. "What does it mean if there isn't an image?"

Max's eyes shot open. He peered into the scrying stone like a crystal ball, and only he could see its secrets. But there was nothing. It was completely and utterly empty.

"Th—that's fine. Some—Sometimes scrying stones don' work in places yer unfamiliar with," Max breathed, letting go of the stone, dropping it to the ground without a second thought. "Or maybe Ei'm still drained from the ghost attack."

Map! Use the map! his inner monologue screamed.

"Are you sure?" Sebastian asked.

He nodded.

"It's just a problem, and problems have solutions; ya just have tuh solve the equation," he whispered. More to himself than to them, unrolling a long stretch of weathered parchment on the hood of the hearse. "Sometimes there are multiple ways tuh solve problems."

"Do you need anything?" Porter asked, his voice tight. Max paused, hands shaking as he gripped her notebook so tight it bent between his hands. He nodded, looking to Porter, whose expression nearly broke him. His eyes were empty, his face pallid.

"Ei need yer knife," Max said, then turned back to the parchment.

He inhaled deeply, placing his hand upon the crinkly old paper. Navy blue lines shot across the page, twisting and curling into an ornate map of Sycamore Heights and the surrounding woods. This strange little map was among the many oddities Mavericks had picked up over the years. Came in handy during situations like this.

Focus.

Porter tapped his shoulder, handing over the old pocketknife he'd had since before they'd met.

Max's hands continued to shake as he grasped it, flipping it open, noting how the light reflected off the blade. It made it look less like a knife and more like the blade of a guillotine.

He wondered if Della had felt the way he did now when Porter had disappeared a little under two months ago. Had she felt as helpless? As empty? Even knowing that they'd be able to find him, had she felt this nagging sense of loss? Had her mind wandered to the places his did?

With every moment she wasn't there with him— *them*—his mind would march down deeper paths until there was barely a sliver of light. What if he found her dead? What if the Wendigo had hurt her? What if it had *eaten* her? What if they ended up more lost while trying to find her than she was? And then there was the question of what he would do if she were harmed. He had yelled at innocent EMTs on her behalf. He had threatened Porter. He was willing to drain himself of his magical life force to help her. What would happen if he had to admit he'd failed to protect her? That he'd failed Mavericks and Porter and Moss Hollow?

As he pricked his finger and watched his blood drip onto the magical map, he knew the answer.

He'd crawl through Heaven and Hell to get her back if she was dead. He'd fill his veins with black magic to resurrect her. He wouldn't be the hero that Porter always tried to be. Max loved her enough to be the villain if need be. He would burn the world down for her.

He clutched her notebook as if it held the secrets of the Universe. As if letting it go would destroy the world as he knew it. His other hand hovered above the map, glistening red droplets tainting the page.

"*Finne, rof finne, Della,*" he breathed. "*Finn det som er tapt.*" He squeezed his eyes so tight it hurt. "Please," he whispered, hoping that the God everyone spoke so highly of would hear him.

The silence that followed was deafening. He'd expected Sebastian or Porter to gasp in delight or fear or something. Anything other than dead silence.

"Max," Porter said quietly after a while.

"Sometimes it takes a second," Max whispered, refusing to open his eyes.

Minutes passed.

Nothing.

"Max!" Porter croaked.

"Just let it—Just give it a minute."

"M—"

"Shut up, Porter!" Max screamed, finally looking down at the map to see his blood seeping into the page and fading at the edges.

Porter swayed to the side before leaning heavily on the hearse for stability. "Not like this," he kept whispering over and over again.

Max couldn't move.

Locator spells always work.

They were the simplest kind of magic.

If you couldn't track someone, then that meant they were—

He couldn't form the word.

Porter slumped to the ground, looking like he'd been shot through the heart. Max couldn't imagine how he felt. They'd been at each other's throats lately, and for her to leave with unspoken words like this would ruin him. Porter rubbed his left wrist furiously, staring at the veins. His carefully formed armor was beginning to crack, and Max could do nothing.

Sebastian was quiet. You could see it on his face that he understood but didn't have the words or energy to say or do anything other than stare into the void.

This couldn't be how things ended. It didn't make sense. For her to go like this. Alone. Chasing a monster that was tormenting a town she hated. It was a meaningless death.

"It has tuh be wrong," Max snapped, rolling up the map and shoving it in her book bag with whatever else fit. All he left out was the notebook, an empty jar, and a few vials of herbs.

He'd expected Porter to snap at him, but all he did was nod.

"Seb, get him home," Max whispered, nudging Sebastian and nodding toward his dismal brother in arms.

Sebastian shrugged and mumbled to himself, offering Porter a hand up off the ground. He hesitated before taking it, refusing to meet Sebastian's eyes. Porter's movements were clumsy as he went to the passenger side door and tossed Sebastian his keys.

That's how you knew things were genuinely terrible.

When Porter Garroway let a stranger drive his hearse.

Max placed a few ginkgo leaves and a sprinkling of dried mugwort into the jar and shook it violently, only setting it down to rip a few pages from Della's notebook.

"What are you doing?" Sebastian asked lifelessly.

"This will take me tuh where she was last," Max mumbled.

Porter, who hadn't had a chance to open the door to the hearse just yet, whipped his head around so fast he winced in pain. "All you're going to find is a body," he said, his tone dangerously dark.

"Ei'm countin' on that," Max said curtly.

He crumpled up the notebook book pages and stuffed them in the jar. With a snap of his fingers, the odd concoction burst into flames, sparks dancing up into the air like escaping fairies.

"Max. That's dark magic," Porter snapped, eyes wide with fright.

"If ya have power tuh do somethin', why shouldn' ya use it?" Max said haughtily.

"You don't even know if you'll be able to resurrect her! It could kill you in the process, and I *will not* lose both of you. Not in one day," Porter cried. "I will put a bullet in your knee, Maximilian. Don't."

Max stared blankly at him. "Rather me than her."

Porter's eyes turned to two glowing orbs as bright as the sun. He lunged toward Max, but he was too slow.

"*Vimebes!*" Max screeched, and Porter dropped to the ground, landing in a patch of mud.

Sebastian took a step back, holding Porter's keys like a shiv. "Don't you dare do that to me."

Max glared at him. "Ei already have. Ya just don' remember it," he snapped. "Just get him home. Please."

Sebastian's hand fell to his side, a look of deep regret and remorse flooding his pockmarked face. He nodded, his eyes filling with a righteous sort of fire.

Max turned from him, capped the jar, shook the smoldering ashes as hard as he could until they began to glow, then threw the bottle at the ground, shielding his eyes as a bright blue light erupted from the shattered glass. He peered through his fingers and watched as the light began to turn into tiny glowing particles that floated about a foot over the ground.

"Lead the way," he whispered, nodding as they circled the rubble, thinking before forming an arrow and shooting off into the forest.

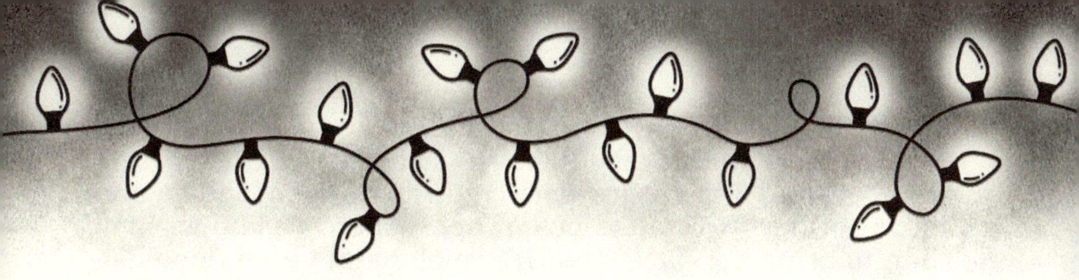

CHAPTER THIRTY-EIGHT

Searching

Max ran at full speed through the darkening trees, smacking branches out of his way, never losing sight of the magical GPS he'd conjured. There was no way to tell how far he was into the forest. Every tree looked the same, and time felt as though it had stopped.

His spell cut to the right before stopping, hovering in the middle of a shattered icy lake. Finding this place was like stumbling upon a thousand-mile drop. What was worse were the footprints that led right to the cracked center.

Max edged around the perimeter, unsure where the water ended and the ground began. The glowing blue particles a few feet away pointed down into the icy depths.

Something was floating in the water.

"*Mok,*" he whispered. The object flew into his shaking hands.

Della's glasses.

The world was it was collapsing in on itself. Max could barely hear anything over the pounding of his heart.

Before he realized what he was doing, he had ripped his socks and shoes from his feet, tossed Della's book bag to the ground, pulled off his thick sweater and jacket, and dove into the icy depths. The ice-cold sting of the water was like daggers against his skin. His raggedy old pants and a thin T-shirt were all that protected him from the cold. The lake was dark, the light from the surface sucked away by silt and frozen plants.

He swam to the bottom, looking around for anything remotely human-shaped in the dark. All he found was a decaying log and what felt like rusted handlebars. Every time he broke the surface for air, his panic and hopelessness grew.

There was no current.

No wind.

She would have sunk or floated.

There wasn't a body in this lake.

Max's worst fears were confirmed. The Wendigo must have got her. Without a locator spell, there was no way for him to bring her back. His GPS spell hadn't even done its job.

Max swam back to the surface, the weight of the day heavy as he lay down on the bank. Thick snow was beginning to fall as he lay there staring up at the sky, silent tears streaming down his face.

Maximilian McGregor-Mavericks was used to death in a way neither Porter nor Della could understand. He knew how death felt. Knew what it was like on the other side. He'd seen so many people die in his very short life, and although Porter had dressed bodies and buried long-lost loved ones, he hadn't lost what Max had. He knew that Della was not prepared for what lay before her.

Death was such a lonely thing. Even when you're doomed to wander the world as nothing but a restless spirit. You could try and protect those still living, but it would take years to learn how to use the strange new version of the world you thought you knew. In his experience, ghosts are few and far between. Even Moss Hollow, the paranormal capital of the world, was nearly empty on the other side. Most of the ghosts had found a way to move on by now.

But Della wouldn't be able to.

Her life was cut short before she had a chance to live it. There were thousands of things she hadn't done, things she didn't get to say, questions that no one ever answered.

What a horrible end.

Why did it have to happen to her?

Slowly, Max sat up, pulling his knees to his chest and burying his head in his hands.

Max had never been one for religion. It wasn't that he didn't believe. How could he not? He just didn't feel like God favored him. Or maybe all those nasty folks who had burned people like him at the stake were right. Maybe God did hate witches. Maybe he and all the others were damned for eternity. What was the point in thinking otherwise when no one proved him wrong?

But Della believed. Despite all the people that proved to her, organized religion lacked God in every possible way.

Della had never lost faith.

Neither had Porter.

Hell, even Mavericks collected Bibles. Max often wondered if the man had met God himself in his many years on Earth.

Maybe it was high time Max started sharing their faith. If there were any time to pray, it would be now. He hugged himself tightly, hoping his words met the right ears.

"Bring her back," he whispered angrily. "If not for me, then for Porter. If not for us, then just have pity. She's got so much good left tuh do. Don' let it end like this," He swallowed hard, looking to the sky. "Please, God. Please."

Emotion overflowed in his chest as he sat there, shivering, dripping wet.

Guilt for letting her down. For not being able to protect her.

Remorse for the things he never got to say and for some he had.

Anger because she was so headstrong, she went off alone.

Sadness because he'd never see the girl he loved again. Never laugh in the kitchen of The Courier with her. He would never feel the love she gave so freely when someone found a way into her heart. Most heartbreakingly, he'd realized they were connected by the threads of the universe a second too late.

"Just bring her back tuh us," he sobbed. "Bring her back tuh me."

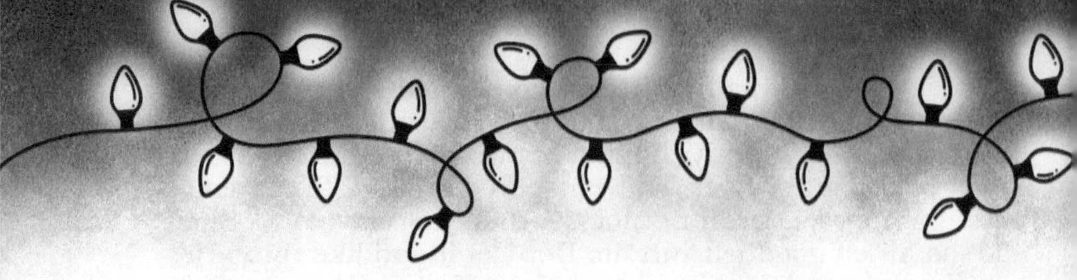

CHAPTER THIRTY-NINE

Perfect Timing

Porter jolted awake as his head banged against something cold. He shot up, pulling at what he thought was rope, looking around wildly. He was bound. Bound by rope. Back in Eric's grasp. His eyes wouldn't focus. He didn't know where he was. It was dark. Not even a sliver of light. All he could hear was his breathing. He reached out in the dark, his hands brushing some sort of sticky, leathery material. He recoiled, settling back into his seat, unnerved by how soft and plush it was.

His heart was beating so fast it hurt. How was he meant to escape a place he couldn't even see?

A sound to his left.

Wherever he was sitting moved ever so slightly.

He heard a heavy sigh as a light flared on.

He shielded his eyes, expecting pain to fill his body as his captor—

"Hey there, bud. You doing okay? You look a little pale." That was Sebastian's voice.

"What the Hell, Seb!" Porter screamed, finally realizing that he was buckled into the passenger seat of the hearse and that the sticky, leathery thing he'd touched was the dash.

Sebastian sat cross-legged in the driver's seat, eyebrow raised, a smug smile tugging at the corners of his lips. "The superhero is really just a man-baby, isn't he?"

"Shut up," Porter snapped, angrily unbuckling himself.

Everything came rushing back to him full force, knocking the wind from his lungs. He spun in his seat, searching the car for Max, who was nowhere to be found.

"Where—"

"No clue. He won't answer his phone. I was hoping

he'd come back after an hour or so, but it's been three, and his voicemail box is full, so I kind of gave up. Was wondering when you'd wake up," Sebastian yawned, looking him up and down. "You okay?"

"My best friend is traipsing around in the woods, and my girlfriend is—" Porter couldn't finish that sentence. Instead, he buried his face in his hands and tried not to break into a thousand pieces.

Sebastian only scoffed. "You really believe that? That she's dead?"

Porter ignored him.

He needed Max. Why had he left? Why did he always leave when he needed him?

Always.

They always left.

Why the Hell did everyone leave?

This wasn't fair. None of this was fair.

He had never hated his life more than he did now.

"This is all my fault," he breathed.

"Debatable, but no," Sebastian sighed.

Porter glared at him. "Could you cut the crap for five seconds and take this seriously. She is *dead*, Sebastian. She is *gone*. Max's stupid spell said so."

Sebastian's face went dark. "While you've been sleeping like the aforementioned man-baby that you are, I've had a lot of time to think, mmkay?" he began, arms crossed tightly over his chest. "Actually, I've *over*thought. But then I realized something. I don't know much about magic, and I can't say I believed in it before today, but I have *always* believed in Delphee Chrysanthemum Coleman," he snapped. "She's not dead. I refuse to believe it."

Porter just stared at him, mouth hanging open. He wanted to believe him. He wanted to have hope, but Porter was not the kind of person who could see light at the end of a tunnel. All he saw was darkness, and the shadows around him always tried to harm him.

"And it's not," Sebastian said sternly, turning away. "Your fault, I mean. Please don't—don't blame yourself for whatever tonight or tomorrow may bring."

"How are you so calm?" Porter asked, leaning against the window, squinting in the dark. He couldn't make out his surroundings but figured they were still at the trailer park.

"I'm not. I'm pissed off. Thought you could tell."

Porter rolled his eyes. "Just a little."

"What are we supposed to do? Are we meant to call Jasper and Kimi and say, 'Oh, hey, are we still on for Christmas Eve dinner? We are? Oh cool. Hey, by the way, your daughter is missing. Have a nice night.'"

Porter thought for a moment. "That may not be a bad idea."

Sebastian side-eyed him. "Are you crazy? Have you *met* Jasper and Kimi? They'll kill us. Screw the Wendigo, or whatever the frick it's called. I'd take it over the Coleman Disaster Duo any day. At least with a monster, I'd probably have a swift death."

"They'd call Kohen, wouldn't they?" Porter said, giving him a knowing look.

Sebastian's eyes widened. "And he'd freak out, too. He'd drop everything and start a search party."

Porter chewed his bottom lip, staring at his feet. "They'd search all night. They'd have to."

They exchanged a look. Neither of them wanted to be the one to call. How do you tell someone their kid is gone? How do you hide the fact you think she could be dead? At least as a mortician, Porter never had to be the one to deliver the bad news. He could find peace in digging graves and consoling broken-hearted loved ones.

He never wanted to be on the receiving side of it all. Not again.

Sebastian dug around his pocket for his phone, mumbling as he dialed Kimi's number. "If I'm right, and she's alive, I get the CD, all the money, and the keys to the hearse until you guys head back to Moss Hollow," he sighed as the phone rang.

"How did you—"

"You're missing the part where she's been my best friend since we were five," Sebastian laughed, then his face went blank. "Though I don't think she realized it until like three days ago. So smart, yet so incredibly stupid."

Porter couldn't help but nod at that.

Kimi finally picked up, and Sebastian put her on speakerphone.

"Hey, Mrs. Coleman! Kimi! Kimster!" Sebastian laughed.

"Breckenridge. What's wrong?" came Kimi's voice.

"Well, you know how Della and us guys had plans?"

". . . yeah?"

"Well, uh, you see, we—"

"Oh, for the love of—" Porter ripped Sebastian's phone from his hands. "Della's missing. So is Max," he breathed.

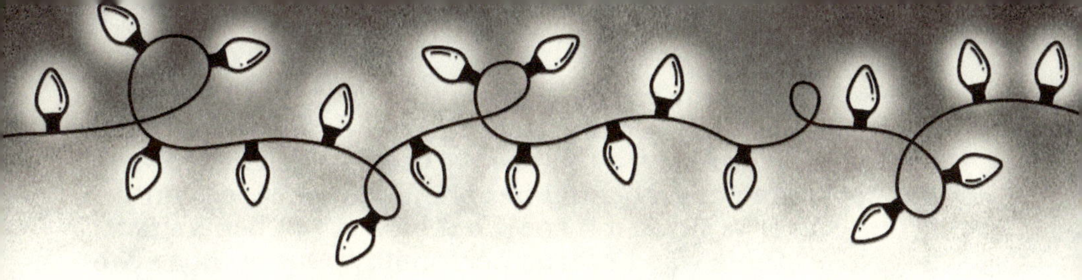

CHAPTER FORTY

"I'm suddenly regretting our decision," Sebastian whispered, fiddling with one of the buttons on his jacket.

"Oh really? You aren't having the *best* of times?" Porter whispered back, watching Kimi, Jasper, Kohen, and about five other cops argue over each other as he and Sebastian sat on the hood of the hearse outside the police station.

"Shut up," Sebastian snapped.

"No, you shut up."

"No, you."

"How about both of you shut up," Elvi Sinclair said sweetly as she and her twelve-inch heels click-clacked over to them. That woman had a strange habit of appearing out of nowhere.

"Why are you even here?" Porter asked. "Isn't this out of your wheelhouse?"

"A member of the community is missing. I must do my part to help find her," Elvi said matter-of-factly, adjusting the hem of her tiny sage green tweed skirt.

"Right, right, because you care so much about our damned little town," Sebastian mumbled.

Elvi straightened, smiling tightly. "Aren't you out past your bedtime, little boy?"

Porter tried and failed to contain his laughter, earning himself a glare from both of them. Remnants of hysteria were beginning to take hold again.

Elvi Sinclair was still a suspect in the disappearance of Ashton. Whatever platitudes and wit she used against them couldn't mask what they already knew.

She was bad news.

In more ways than one.

"If you must know, I had something to discuss with

Deputy Kitchi, but seeing as he is rather busy with the disappearance of his delinquent niece, I figured I would stay and offer my services if the need arose," Elvi sighed, sweeping her golden curls behind her shoulders oh so elegantly.

Porter wondered if she got a kick out of being insufferable or if this was her true personality. Out of those two options, he couldn't decide which was worse.

"How kind. Do you want me to give you a medal for your act of heroics?" Sebastian asked.

"Oh, honey. If you think I want anything your dirty little hands have touched, you have another thing coming," Elvi sneered.

Sebastian rolled his eyes and hopped off the hood of the hearse. "If you need me, I'll be drinking watered-down decaf, okay?" he snapped, then slipped inside the station.

Elvi sighed heavily, placing a dainty hand on her chin as she studied Porter. "How are you, Mister. . ."

"Garroway. And I'm about as good as someone in my position could be," he sighed, studying her with the same guarded expression.

Elvi smiled softly. "From what I've heard, Miss Coleman is stubborn and resilient. It's something I admire about her. I'm sure they'll find her in an exquisitely crafted lean-to without a scratch on her."

"I'll tell her you said that," Porter sighed.

Elvi laughed politely. "I would prefer you not. I admire a trait she has, yes. I admit, I could stand to learn a few things from your little super sleuth. However, I do not wish to get involved with your little band of misfits. I have a reputation to uphold and all." She looked him up and down in a similar way Poppy had.

Porter searched her dazzling blue eyes. "Something tells me you don't care much about that reputation."

She shrugged, taking a step forward. Since he was still slouching on the hood of the hearse, she was almost at his eye level. Those eyes of hers reminded him of the ocean. Beautiful, but dangerous. And the look on her face? It reminded him of a shark on the prowl.

"I could be swayed to forget it for a few moments. For the right price, of course," she smiled, taking another step. She was close now. Too close.

"Well, my dear Elvi. You're going to have to find another buyer," Porter smiled sweetly, leaning down to look her dead in the eyes. "Because I'm not interested."

Elvi curled her fingers under his chin. "We'll see about that," she whispered before disconnecting from him.

"I don't think we will." Porter shrugged, sliding off the hearse, towering over her now.

She snickered, pulling a thin business card out of her pocket. She shoved it against his chest, over his heart, lingering for a moment as he reached up and snatched it away.

It wasn't a business card at all.

It was a hotel keycard.

"You know where to find me, lover boy." she winked, curtsying. "If, of course, you want to talk."

He laughed darkly, offering the card back. "You just can't take a hint, can you?"

In response, Elvi leaned to the side, her eyes wide. "Ashton?"

Porter spun to see a man in a ripped-up t-shirt and jeans stumbling along the sidewalk, his eyes wide.

"You—You s—stay away from me," he said shakily, pointing at Elvi as if she were devil-spawn.

"Kohen!" Elvi screamed over her shoulder.

Kohen, still arguing with Jasper and Kimi, spun on his heels, an exasperated look on his face until he saw Ashton shaking and sputtering like a madman. His eyes grew wide.

Ashton wasn't dead, but Porter had a feeling they would all wish he was.

"Where the Hell have you been, bud?" Kohen said, fear on the edge of his voice. He practically ran over, placing himself between Porter, Elvi, and Ashton. The look he shot over his shoulder unnerved Porter, though he couldn't figure out why.

"Don't come any closer," Ashton said, hugging himself tightly.

Kohen put his hands up. "All right. I won't," he sighed heavily, tapping his foot impatiently. "Wanna tell me where you've been, buddy? We've been looking for you for weeks."

Ashton looked to Elvi, edging away. He shook his head. He mumbled something under his breath, putting his hands behind his back.

"Ash, I'm going to ask that you keep your hands where I can kindly—"

"I'm not talking to you," Ashton snapped.

Kohen dropped his hands to his side, his fingers brushing the gun strapped to his hip. "Is there someone you will talk to?"

"D—Della. Delphee Coleman."

Porter stiffened.

"That's just our luck, ain't it?" Kohen whispered. "Della is preoccupied, Ash. If there's something you can't say to me, then I will get you Marion or—"

"Only her!" he screamed, procuring a gun out of thin air and putting it against his temple. "I'm only talking to her."

"Kohen," Elvi breathed, protectively reaching forward.

Kohen shushed her, fingers curling around his gun. Porter knew what would happen next and wasn't prepared to let that happen. Without hesitation, he stepped in front of Kohen, reaching out to Ashton with open arms. Ashton stumbled back, fear in his eyes.

"Kid get—"

"I've got this," Porter hissed.

He dared a step toward Ashton, hands still raised. "That's a nice revolver you've got there, Ashton. It'd be a shame if you got blood on it. It would rust," he smiled. "It looks old. Family heirloom? I've got one of those under my jacket. Mind if I take it out?"

Ashton shook his head.

"All I want to do is drop it, okay? If I do that, and Kohen drops his, will you drop yours?"

He thought for a moment but nodded.

Porter smiled, never losing eye contact as he pulled out his gun and dropped it. Behind him, he heard a soft thud assuring him Kohen had followed through. Ashton hesitated but tossed his away, immediately rubbing his hands on his pants as if trying to clean them of an unseen substance.

"Della will be here shortly, okay? Until then, how about we go inside the station, get you some clean clothes, and make sure you don't hurt yourself?" Porter asked softly.

"I think I'd like that very much," Ashton said, more to himself than anyone else.

"Good, good. I'm going to hold on to this for a little while. Is that okay?" Porter asked, pointing at the gun he'd tossed.

Ashton nodded, promptly jutting his fists out before him. Kohen sighed heavily, reaching into his jacket for a pair of handcuffs. Porter stopped him as he made to cuff him, but Ashton only nodded.

"I'd feel better that way," he whispered, his voice shaking.

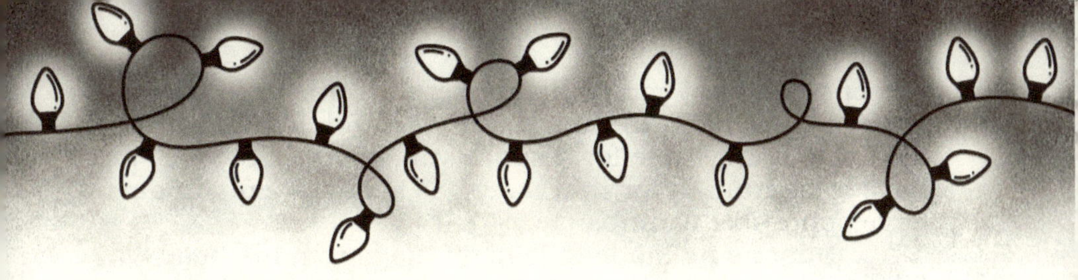

CHAPTER FORTY-ONE

Finding

Max had taken to roaming the woods, hoping he would catch her scent or find a miracle clue. But he was losing hope again.

It was easier to search as a cat, so he'd spent most of the evening with aching paws, fur matted with snow, and whiskers he was sure would freeze off. It didn't help that the snow was so thick in some places that he practically had to swim through it.

It was all so exhausting.

As he padded through the snow, he wondered how Sebastian and Porter were fairing. Hopefully, they weren't as lost as he was.

Who was he kidding?

They were probably wandering around looking for him, Sebastian utterly confused, and Porter thoroughly pissed off.

Max's frozen paws took him up a tree, where he sat on a branch that bent precariously under his weight. The forest was still eerily quiet. He'd thought by now he'd run into a deer or, at the very least, an owl. What exactly was out here scaring the wildlife? It was something mystical, for sure. He could feel it. Something watched his every move in the darkness, though it refused to show itself to him. The presence was familiar. Whatever it was, it was the same entity that had scared them at the historical society. The presence of it was dark and all-consuming, though not entirely evil. Hostile, for sure. But if it wanted to harm him, why hadn't it attacked?

Maybe it was confused by this form. Perhaps it couldn't tell who or rather what he was.

He debated transforming back. If it genuinely was hostile, maybe it had harmed Della. If not, perhaps the presence of the Wendigo had upset it. If this unknown being knew they were on the same side, it could help him. Maybe it was finally time for a summoning spell. However, he'd have to be human for that. Magic is tricky when you don't have opposable thumbs.

Just as he made to leap off his perch, his head was filled with such immense pressure that he thought it would explode. His paws slipped from the branch, causing him to tumble to the ground. He landed painfully on his side. Apparently, cats don't *always* land on their feet.

He sat up, his bones cracking back into place, his paws elongating into fingers.

That all-consuming pressure in his head was worse as a human. He wasn't dizzy this time. Everything was clear. Too clear. Too loud. Too bright. Too pungent. Even for him. What once was a shade of gray or beige began screaming with color.

Max stood, brushing himself off, peering into the dark.

Something inside him felt whole again. Warmth bloomed in his chest, the pressure in his mind dissipating, replaced by a sense of peace.

He snapped his fingers, and Della's book bag appeared over his shoulder. He clutched the strap of it tightly, taking a deep breath.

The familiar could feel his dreamwalker's presence once again.

God—at least that's what he wanted to believe—had answered his prayers.

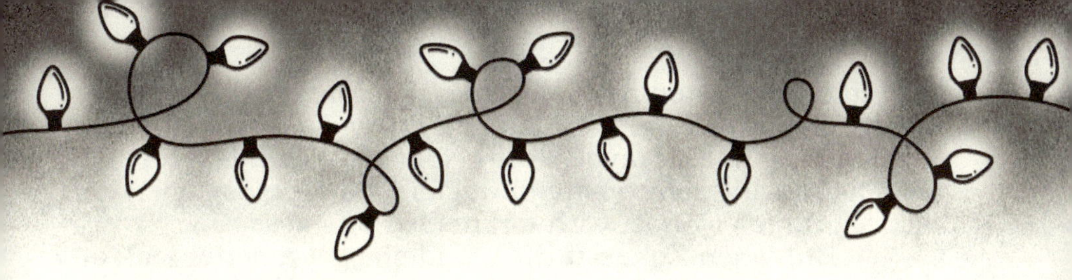

CHAPTER FORTY-TWO

*I'm No Expert, But Death
Shouldn't Feel Like This*

This time, Della knew she was dreaming. Knew this was only a flash of a memory, a vision, or whatever ephemeral word she would later find to describe it. She could tell by the pain around her ears. Immense pain radiated around her. Her very soul ached, but she welcomed the pain as if it were an old friend. It gave her hope that she was still alive.

Ghosts couldn't feel pain as far as she knew.

Yet, somewhere deep down inside her, there was a twinge of disappointment at the thought she was alive, and she couldn't figure out why it had come.

She could have stood there and pondered her emotions for eternity if her curiosity hadn't gotten the best of her. This vision was different. It wasn't like her usual ones. She wasn't a part of it. Looking down at her hands, her mind circled back to the ghosts-can't-feel-pain theory. She could see straight through her shaking hands. Yes, this was definitely different. It was more like she was watching a film made just for her eyes, like what she had seen in Ashton's trailer.

Jagged rocks lined the edge of the forest. Everything was silent as two figures ran through the trees. The rocks seemed important. Della tried to focus on them, expecting to find something morbid. No blood shimmered on the rocks. No broken bodies. She shivered, wondering why she had been waiting for that. She secretly hoped this would be a kinder vision. Maybe she would see a better glimpse of the future. One that would ease the fear in her heart.

But that didn't seem to be the case.

One of the figures—a man with a strange hat—called to the trees, receiving nothing but the rushing wind in his ears in return. He called her name. Della. Delphee. Over and over again, but no answer ever came. The man skidded to a stop, listening to the trees. He screamed her name again, choking down tears. Kohen. It was Kohen screaming through the trees. Maybe Della really was dead. Maybe this was happening somewhere in the forest as she assumed her astral form as a ghost with unfinished business.

But when Kohen turned, and she got a better look at his face, she realized this wasn't *her* Kohen. He was significantly younger than the Kohen she knew.

"Years do a lot to a person," she whispered, eyebrows raised.

The laughter of a small child suddenly echoed through the evergreens, though neither the figures nor Della herself could tell where it was coming from. Again, the child laughed, speaking to the darkening trees as if they were her friends.

"Della!" That was Jasper. He bolted through the trees, ducking under low-hanging branches, followed by Kimi, the two of them screaming her name. She'd never heard Jasper so scared.

Or maybe she had. Was this one of her repressed memories?

"Over here!" Della whispered at the same time a young girl's voice rang. Sweet and flowery. Innocent. It was her when she had been much, much younger.

"Della! Stay where you are!" Jasper called as a fourth set of footsteps echoed through the trees.

Young Della only laughed in response.

A growl.

Kohen ran at full speed in what he thought was the direction of the sound.

Jasper spun on his heels, reaching for Kimi's hand in the dark. She gripped his hand tight, tears welling up in her eyes.

"I'm going to kill him when we get back," Jasper whispered angrily, pulling Kimi toward the footsteps.

"This isn't his fault, Jasper. You know that," Kimi hissed, wiping the tears from her eyes.

"Do not try and defend him. Either of them. They knew exactly what they were doing, filling her head with that nonsense," Jasper snapped back, squeezing his wife's hand so hard she yelped in pain, pulling away from him. He rolled his eyes, cupping his hands around his lips, screaming at the top of his lungs. "DELLA!"

A shuffle of heavy footsteps.

A snap of twigs.

The sound of branches getting stuck on the back of an animal. A *large* animal.

"DELLA!" Jasper screamed again.

Hot air engulfed Della's—the present Della—body.

"Not now," she whispered. She wanted to see how this played out. This was her memory, after all, that was for sure. A memory she had forgotten all about.

Della followed Jasper's gaze. Out of the corner of his dark eyes, he caught a glimpse of a figure lumbering through the forest. Young Della giggled again, beckoning the figure towards her.

"Della, don't!" Jasper screamed, leaving Kimi in the shadows and rushing to his child's side.

A soft voice cut into her head. Her mind buzzed. Her heart raced. She didn't want to leave. Not now. She needed answers.

As Jasper ran through the trees, branches cutting into his skin, the creature disappeared. How was it so fast? It moved at lightning speed, just a knot or two slower than a vampire. Jasper screamed his daughter's name again, finally catching up to the creature, watching in horror as his daughter reached her tiny hand out to touch its hand.

"DON'T TOUCH IT!" Jasper screamed.

The figure rounded on its heels, revealing its true face. Its sharp claws scraped his daughter's hand, causing her to cry out in pain. Jasper would never know it had been an accident. All Jasper saw was a hideous, malicious being incapable of love or anything akin to such ideals.

Panicking, Jasper looked around for a stick suitable for use as a weapon. He grabbed a skinny log, rushing forward to swing at the beast. It growled at him, catching the branch, looking over his shoulder at the man's daughter. She was crying, asking her father to stop trying to hurt the creature.

"RUN!" Jasper screamed, whacking the beast alongside the head.

His daughter made no action to move.

No. No. This was wrong. This wasn't supposed to happen. That beast had been a friend. He—

Golden light erupted from somewhere behind her. All Della heard was a fluttering sound before the scene changed.

Suddenly, she was standing before a plank house on fire. Terror-struck voices filled her ears. At first, they spoke in a language foreign to her ears, but then it translated like she was watching a dubbed TV show.

A man stood before the burning plank house, his fists clenched around the peace pipe.

"Stop this now," the man said, turning towards Della, staring straight through her. She turned to see if someone was behind her, desperately hoping there was.

The face that greeted her was scarred and burned. His hair was braided, feathers and beads woven into the strands. Della guessed that he would have looked quite handsome without the fire casting a hellish glow on the young man or the evil smile on his face.

He almost looked like Quincy.

"I've done nothing wrong. You've brought this on yourself, Father," the young man said, his tone cold, snapping Della out of her thoughts. He swept his hands through the air with a slight flourish. "I am going to rebuild the tribe. No man will come to us and drive us out of our home! No one will be able to hurt us. If that means getting rid of those who stand in my way, so be it! If that means I am a monster, then Father, I shall become one."

The man, presumably the Chief from his regalia and assumed power, shook his head sadly. "Then you leave us no choice."

Della turned back to the young man just in time to see a spearhead erupt from his chest. The forest floor ran red with his blood as Della watched in horror. Behind him was a beautiful older woman with tears in her eyes. She knelt and hugged the young man in a way that only a mother could, placing a hand on his forehead as she did. She shut her eyes, her son screaming in pain. His skin was smoking, emitting the same shadowy black mist that Della had seen in her vision before and with Arlo in the woods.

The mist rose into the air, becoming a swirling black void that cast a horrid shadow over the scene. The son's body fell limp, held up only by his mother, who was sobbing uncontrollably now. Della looked to the Chief, watching as he put the peace pipe to his lips and inhaled. The pipe glowed a deep red as the spirit was sucked out of the sky and into the pipe.

When the last of his son's spirit was sucked into the pipe, the Chief collapsed to his knees, looking winded.

Thudding footsteps echoed through the forest. There were screams from people Della couldn't see as Arlo the Wendigo appeared, sitting at the forest edge like Della had seen in her other vision. He took one look at what had transpired and let loose an unimaginably loud roar. Della felt his grief course through her body as if it were her own. All the sadness and anger building up inside him was as powerful as a gale-force wind.

She hated having to see this. It was too much. Far too much. She didn't want to see this anymore. She didn't want to see any visions. Tears escaped her eyes as she turned away, refusing to look anymore. She wanted to run, to fight her way out of her mind, to rebuke this so-called 'gift' she had been given.

Suddenly, she was plunged back into the icy water that had brought her here.

She panicked, trying to fight her way to the surface. Her limbs dragged through the water like steel tubes, pushing her farther and farther down. Her legs ached as she tried to swim, burning from the cold.

Water filled her lungs again. She choked and sputtered but kept trying to fight through the darkness to find the surface.

Wait, where was the surface?

All around her was darkness as far as the eye could see. There was no light cascading down around from above. Nothing to show her where to swim. She was stuck down there on her own. She could barely even see her own hands as they fought to swim.

All she wanted to do was scream for help, but that would drown her further.

She was alone.

Again.

Back where she'd started.

Delphee Coleman had always been alone. And now she was going to die alone. For what? Because of her pride? Because she wanted to prove a point? Because she had a god complex? Because she needed to shove it down everyone's throat she was better than them? To show that she alone held all the answers?

How shallow.

How pathetic.

How so very human of her.

Where were her friends? She'd left them. She'd made the same mistakes she'd vowed never to make again. Where was Porter? She'd pushed him away. Her knight in shining armor couldn't save her now.

Maybe this was for the best. Death, that is.

Kimi was right. She screwed up everything she touched. Every time she tried to fix a problem, she only made it worse. Maybe the universe, God, the Angels—whatever she decided was real at that moment—were exacting revenge, righting her wrongs, and putting balance back into the world.

If that was the case, then that was fine by her.

She stopped fighting.

She stopped kicking.

She shut her eyes again, shutting off her mind. Her body went numb against the freezing darkness around her.

No, a voice in her head whispered. *Not yet.*

Della was vaguely aware she was floating up and up

and up. At first, she didn't realize her face had broken the surface—that she could breathe. That she was alive. Again, that disappointment returned to her, though this time, she understood why it had come.

Della thought she deserved death.

Oh, how wrong she was.

Her senses returned to her as her frozen body thawed. The numbness she had felt moments before was replaced with radiating heat. Her fingers were burning with frostbite. Her skin prickled with goosebumps. She shivered. This was somehow worse than the cold. All she wanted to do was give up, to sink back down, to take a deep breath and—

Wait.

That wasn't water filling her lungs; it was smoke.

Campfire smoke.

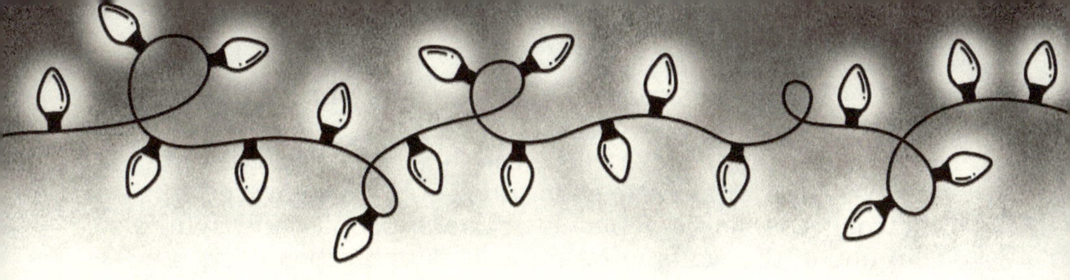

CHAPTER FORTY-THREE

Arlo

Della was aware she was lying on something soft and warm, but that didn't stop her mind from reeling. She could hear a crackling fire from somewhere nearby and smell the stench of cooking venison. She vaguely remembered that hands had wrapped around her waist before her vision. She remembered being pulled up. Someone had jumped into that lake and saved her: someone or some-*thing*. Fright coursed through her as she forced her heavy eyelids open.

Her glasses were gone, which made it difficult to see things clearly, but as her eyes adjusted to the dim light, she realized she was in a cave. Della blinked, reaching a shaking hand up to rub her eyes. Impossible. Why would she be in a cave? She must still be dreaming. . . But then, why did her head feel like it would explode? Why was her body cold and achy? Why could she feel every muscle move against each other like she was made of sandpaper? Slowly, she sat up, looking around for something that would prove she was back with the waking.

Or living.

Whatever. Both were damned in her presence.

Her hand brushed across something coarse and furry. She looked down to see it was an animal hide. She'd been lying on what looked to be a makeshift bed made from a deer pelt. Whistling wind floated through the cave, anger-ing the fire a few feet from her. The flickering light revealed that the cave was littered with old animal bones, more pelts, and garbage. Della made to stand, pain like pins and needles rushing up her leg. Instead, she returned to sitting on the warm hide, hugging herself to try and keep from shivering. Though the fire was blazing, she was still freez-ing.

The strange part? Della was sure she had been here before.

Another breeze made the flickering firelight dance across the walls of the cave. Each wall was covered in petroglyphs: some depicted animals, people, and symbols. On one of the walls, a name was carved repeatedly.

Arlo.

He must have saved her.

"Hello?" Della shakily called through the cave, listening to her voice echo. Her voice was weak, the syllables she spoke slurring together.

Something moved out of the corner of her eye. Slowly, the Wendigo moved into the light. His worn wolf skull face crowned with thick caribou antlers filled her vision. He moved closer, his mane of black hair and skeleton-like body looking quite evil in the flickering firelight. A long gash ran up his side, dripping thick blood onto the cave floor. Ahiga must have hurt him.

"Are you okay?" she choked out, overcome by a fit of coughing.

He tilted his head at her, his bony jaw chattering, his neck cracking. Della took this as irritation. As he sauntered over to her, he sniffed the air. His bright white eyes reflected the firelight like a mirror. Della couldn't help but think of her vision and the fire she'd seen moments before.

Della raised her hand, and Arlo shoved his snout into her palm. He breathed his hot, meaty breath on her, his eyes full of kindness.

"Della," he said roughly. The way he said it sounded like he was disappointed in her. He sat before her, tilting his head to the side again.

She nodded weakly, pulling her legs to her chest and resting her chin on her knees. The list of questions she could ask him would stretch for miles, but no words would form on her lips. Her brain was too stunned and weary.

"Safe—now," the Wendigo said as softly as he could manage.

Della tried to smile, removing her hand from the beast's snout. She opened her mouth to speak when his face and body began to shrink and melt. His fur began to disappear, replaced instead with ashy skin. His white eyes grew pupils, and his antlers transformed into greasy black hair that fell softly on his shoulders. Before her sat a smiling young man wearing the same clothes as Ahiga and the Chief had been in her vision. Only his were tattered and barely held together. Moth holes in his shirt hinted at scars across his chest.

Della stared open-mouthed in disbelief. Despite his

sunken features, he could have been another of Della's brothers.

"Arlo," she whispered in awe.

He nodded, smiling crookedly. He placed a hand on her chest. "Della," he said matter-of-factly. "You are bigger than I remember," His human voice was soft and kind, starkly contrasting the gravelly voice of his Wendigo form.

Della shrugged, looking down at herself. "I guess I am."

"What happened?" he asked, reaching out to touch her hair, looking concerned.

"I dyed it." At the word 'dye,' his eyes lit up with danger. "No, no, no, not die, like I colored—"

"Oh! Like how you dye fabric," he said, something clicking into place in his mind.

All Della could do was stare at him. This boy looked to be around seventeen or eighteen. Despite former knowledge, Della could feel the ancient aura resonating off him. It baffled her. This boy—this Wendigo could understand English. She would have thought his words would be choppy from what she imagined to be years of solitude. But he spoke with gentle compassion.

"You're freezing," Arlo said, sadness in his voice. "I—I was worried." He placed a hand on her forehead, staring at her with a stern expression.

"I think I'm okay," Della whispered, slowly prying his hand from her face. It was clear he didn't want to let go. "Where—Where am I, exactly?" she asked shakily.

"You call this my home," he grumbled, looking around the cave with a sour expression.

Della looked around again, her eyes tracing the pictographs on the walls. She knew it was a story—*his* story, to be exact. Some pictures matched what she'd just seen in the depths of her mind. Carefully standing, she stumbled over to touch the wall. Before her fingers grazed the beautiful inscriptions, Arlo jumped up and grabbed her wrist.

"No. Not for you," he said, glaring at the wall.

"What do they mean?" Della asked, her teeth chattering. It was warmer closer to the ground.

Arlo shook his head, his long hair rippling down his back, reminding her of Lenora. "A sad story," he muttered.

"About your brother?" Della asked, feeling faint.

Arlo stepped back, not meeting her eyes, though he nodded. Acknowledging that seemed to break his heart.

Della turned away, swaying a little, her feet and legs full of prickling numbness. Being frostbitten was not going to be fun. She looked down at her hands. Her fingers were purple. It hurt to move them.

She found she was gasping for air, her lungs burning with the effort it took to breathe.

"You're hurt. We have to get you back to your people," Arlo said, pulling her away from the wall and sitting her back down on the pelts. He grabbed a stray one, placing it lovingly around her shoulders.

"You have very good English. Have you been practicing?" Della asked, her teeth chattering from the cold. It was a stupid question, but she'd rather ask ridiculous questions than fall unconscious again.

"I listen. Campers talk, and I watch. English is easier in many ways than the Mukwa language," he explained excitedly. "When in Wendigo form, my brain gets. . . jumbled. The longer I'm not Arlo, the harder it is to break out of such a state. My words don't work right," he finished, rubbing her shoulders to try and warm her up.

His fingers were frostbitten too, but she guessed his had been like that for years. It looked like death had caught up to him, reminding her of how the Ambrose vampires looked.

Arlo sniffed her. "You smell like blood," he said, his voice full of worry. He pushed her hair aside, touching her ear lightly. When he pulled his hand away, his finger was soaked in red.

Della winced. "That's not good," she whispered, her eyelids heavy, her body violently shaking and shivering.

Arlo nodded, letting go of her shoulders and turning to the fire. He had constructed a makeshift spit on which he had set thin venison strips. He offered it to her, but she politely refused.

"Don't blame you. I hate the taste too," he thought for a minute, looking for the word. "Better now that I cook it." He pointed to the corner. "Campers think bear—bear—*bears*, get into their food. Not bear—*bears*, just me. I like the cans of beans." He looked frustrated with himself when he spoke.

"You like beans?" Della asked groggily, trying her best to stay awake. Her head was abuzz with dizzying pain. Images—forgotten memories—fought for her to see them, but none stuck.

"Ref-er-red beans," Arlo said with a smile.

"Refried?"

He thought for a second, then shrugged. "It's a possibility. I cannot read as well as I speak. Thinking in English is easier than reading it."

"Have you been out here all this time?"

Arlo smiled brightly. He jumped to his feet and ran to one of the walls, wiping away dust. Hundreds of lines were on the wall, like tally marks in a prison. "One for every year Arlo—er—I have been here," he began counting, got to thirteen, then came back to sit next to Della, clearly bored. "He—no—I know numbers but don't like them. I find them. . . weird."

"So, you just sit here, eating deer meat and refried beans?" Della asked, her eyes fluttering shut as another wave of freezing exhaustion flooded her.

He nodded, speaking with his mouth full. "Very good. But not just meat. Took chi-ips one day. Tastes nice."

"Chips," Della corrected, though not unkindly. She thought for a minute, shifting uncomfortably, wanting to ask the question at the front of her mind. "That's all you eat? Not. . . not humans?"

Arlo sighed heavily. "Don't like eating humans. Makes me feel wrong inside." He pointed to where his heart was. "You know this. I told you. You used to visit when you were smaller. Though you don't seem to remember him— me," he growled at himself. "Out of practice with words. Apologies," he mumbled.

He was right. Her only memory of him was the fragmented one she had just seen.

"So, have you eaten a human before?" Della asked, deciding she wouldn't want to hurt his feelings by admitting she couldn't remember him.

Arlo pointed behind him. "Once. That is why I am Wendigo. I didn't do it on purpose, it was—"

"An accident," Della finished.

Even on the brink of death, she had a job to do. At least Mingan's story matched up. Arlo didn't seem to be the lying type. In all honesty, he was probably honest to a fault. If Arlo had been out here all these years, and he hadn't eaten a single human being, then whatever had chased her through the woods must have gotten Ashton. However, Della didn't need convincing of that after almost drowning.

Della stared at the crackling fire, thinking.

"Questions?" Arlo asked.

Della nodded. "The animals, can you speak with them?"

"Yes. . . but they don't like me much. I eat them. Rabbit is Arlo's favorite," he smiled. "Uh, my favorite." He made a funny expression, growling as he bit his bottom lip in anger.

"Have the bears been acting weird?"

"All the forest is acting. . . weird. . . won't go near humans, hiding more. Bears started sleeping later than other days—years." He thought for a minute, counting on his fingers. "Yes, years."

Chapter Forty-Three

"Have you been to the construction site?"

"What is. . . construction site?"

"The place where people are building things out in the forest."

"Not before I saw you. . . heard chatter, though. The squirrels do not like the big monster."

"What monster?"

Arlo's eyes widened. "They say it's as big as my cave. Its hide—" He thought. "—s. . . *skin* made of colored metal."

"That's not a monster; it's a machine," Della smiled.

"I do not know that word," Arlo said, scratching his head and staring into the distance. "They also say there is another thing out there. Arlo thinks—I think—I *thought* it was something from the past, but now I am not so sure." Sadness tinged every word.

Della wanted to pester him with more questions, but the more she spoke, the harder it was for her to breathe. She closed her eyes, stretching her hands out toward the fire. Her muscles continued to burn as she moved, her arms shaking with the effort it took to keep them out before her.

"I need to get you to the other humans. You have been asleep for a long time, barely breathing," Arlo said darkly, standing and brushing himself off.

"How long?" Della asked, opening one of her eyes to watch him.

"I forgot the word for it, but it's a longer part of time. Not day, but shorter," he said matter-of-factly.

"Hours?" Della yawned. She'd been hoping for thirty minutes at most. But now that she cared to notice, she realized her clothes were completely dry. So was her hair. Maybe the drowning she'd thought she'd just experienced had all been in her head. That thought terrified her.

"Yes, that," Arlo said dismissively. He grabbed another pelt to place over her shoulders, pulling her up off the floor. He took her face in his hands, staring deep into her soul. "You are very hurt. Hurt like I was before I was Wendigo. I can get you to the town and to your funny-looking white men and the man that smells of cat," he whispered. His dark eyes were full of fear, though she could tell he was trying to hide it.

"I don't know if that's a good idea," Della breathed.

"It is! Della can't stay, so Arlo will leave. Not like I care about this place. It smells." He spoke with so much salt on his tongue, you'd think he was Gen Z, not. . . whatever generation he was.

Della looked him over, wincing. The funny-looking white men and the man that smelled of cat would have a heyday when they saw him, but Arlo was right. She would have no idea how to get back to town, and if she was right, she was suffering from hypothermia. If she traveled alone and lost consciousness, she would die.

"Lead the way, then," she said, nodding towards the cave entrance. "You think you can get me to the reservation?"

"The tribe?" he asked. Della nodded. "Of course! I can find anything. I found you, didn't I?"

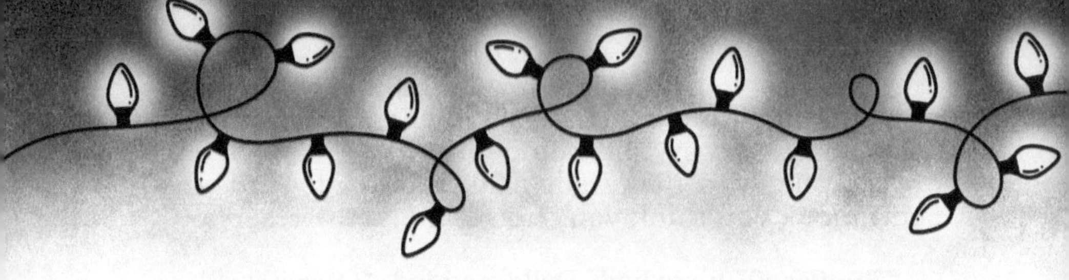

CHAPTER FORTY-FOUR

Sorta Safe, Not Very Sound

Arlo reminded Della of Leonel in most ways. He was fascinated by even the most mundane things, especially that she had left Washington and moved to Louisiana. He wanted to know everything. From how the airplane she had taken to get there worked to what this strange Louisiana place looked like. She was thankful for the onslaught of questions. The constant thinking about how she should explain kept her alert.

Plus, she could tell he envied her, which amused her. If anything, she was jealous of him. How Arlo traversed the forest made her wish things had been a little different, and she would have remembered him. She could've learned from him. He leaped over rocks and ducked under branches so effortlessly it was almost like a dance. He would stop occasionally to hoist her over bigger rocks, though she had tried to convince him he didn't need to. He was as stubborn as the other men in her life, if not more.

On top of that, she couldn't even imagine how sweet the years of solitude in the wilderness would be. He was living the dream while she had been stuck in a twenty-four-seven nightmare.

"Why 'Arlo?'" she asked, taking his hand as she stepped over a slippery rock.

He gave her a questioning look.

"'Arlo isn't Indigenous. Why do you go by it?"

"I picked it. I like the sound of it."

"Why?"

"Because 'Arlo' doesn't have a horrible past. 'Arlo' was the boy the Sycamores taught English. 'Arlo' was the boy Della played with in the forest. 'Huritt' was the dreamwalker who failed to protect his family. 'Huritt' has a horrible past. 'Huritt' is dead," he said sourly.

"But your given name is beautiful," Della said sadly. Many Indigenous people had their names changed because settlers couldn't pronounce them or worse. She wouldn't have given it up for anything if Della had been given a name like his. But instead, she was stuck with a street name.

"Maybe," Arlo chose to say. "But Arlo is, too."

Della cleared her throat. "How did you find me?" she said, deciding it best to change the subject.

"When?"

"Every single time," she shrugged.

"Could feel your presents. No. . . wrong word. . . presence! I know when you are in the woods and always follow you. Like how I knew where you were when you were—I don't know the word, but it is like swimming in water but not being able to swim," he whispered the last part, not wanting to upset her.

"Drowning," Della said.

"Yes, that! Of course, I jumped in to save you, but I had feared you were already lost. I am a good healer, though," Arlo said, puffing out his chest.

"Yes, and humble, too," she coughed.

He gave her a funny look. "I don't know that word. . . Is Della—Are you okay? You are turning the color of the day sky."

Della hugged the pelts tighter to her, nodding.

Arlo squinted at her. "Arlo—Arlo—*I* do not believe you."

Every time he messed up his words, he looked frustrated and angry. Della hated it. She wondered if he had been punished for using the wrong words long ago. What had he gone through?

Nevertheless, she gave a half laugh, walking closer to him to try and leech the warmth off him. The sky turned purple as the sun began to inch up the horizon, but the forest was still darker than she had ever remembered.

"Do not fear the forest. It won't hurt you if I am with you," he whispered, feeling around for her hand. He gave her an odd look when he finally gripped her hand as if he could physically feel the pain coursing through her body.

He didn't talk much after that, only stopping to tell her to stick close or not wander down this or that path. Della was beyond freezing. She could feel her body slowing with the cold. Snow fell in thick blankets around, bathing the world in white. Wind blew the particles into their faces, making it even harder to see without her glasses. The forest had always welcomed Della with open arms, but tonight, danger lurked around every corner. Sharp rocks jetted up from the forest floor, waiting to claim their next victim, steep drop-offs materialized when she least expected, and branches slapped her in the face, making her wonder if the trees were mad at her.

She and Arlo pressed on for what felt like days, Della hugging herself tightly, her heart skipping a beat every time she lost sight of her guide. However, Arlo always seemed to know where she was. If he wasn't gripping her hand, he appeared out of the snow, smiling like he had just found what he'd been looking for all his life.

Arlo halted, hesitating before continuing.

"What's wrong?"

"Something is following us." He spun, peering into the trees. "Stay," he said sternly, then disappeared.

~ ~ ~

Max was running again.

He could sense her. Everywhere. Like a beacon of light radiating from a lighthouse during a storm. Every step he took brought him closer.

He skidded to a stop.

That smell.

Vanilla.

Cinnamon.

Max spun on his heels, scanning the trees. They were still quiet, but the rest of the forest was suddenly abuzz with chatter. He could hear animals scurrying around in the distance, sensing the same thing he could.

He shut his eyes, trying to calm his rapidly beating heart and block out everything except this strange and overwhelming feeling that was mounting inside him. He turned slowly, following the beacon.

Vanilla and cinnamon.

The smell was stronger now, mixing with the pull he felt, leading him where he needed to go. He jumped over roots, batted branches out of his way, and nearly tripped on loose rocks.

Footsteps echoed through the trees, accompanied by faint, far-off voices.

Vanilla and cinnamon.

~ ~ ~

Arlo had been gone for too long. Something must be wrong.

"Arlo!" Della called through the snow, her teeth chattering.

Maybe he wasn't as agile as she thought. Maybe he had fallen somewhere. How would she know? How would she be able to help? Her legs wanted to buckle as panic coursed through her. If she allowed herself to give in to it, she wouldn't be able to press on.

"ARLO!" she screamed at the top of her lungs, her body finally refusing to work against the cold. She fell to her knees, her bones like ice. Her hands were blue and purple, her hair stiff with snow.

A sound like thunder met her ears. She tensed, shutting her eyes, bracing for impact, expecting pain.

But it never came.

And that wasn't thunder.

She looked up, heart racing at the sight.

~ ~ ~

He ran to her without hesitation, sliding to his knees, scooping her up in his arms, squeezing her so tightly he thought she might be unable to breathe. She hugged him back, running her freezing hands through his thick hair.

"Max," she whispered, melting into his arms, burying her head in the crook of his shoulder.

Vanilla and cinnamon.

The smell the girl he loved carried. The scent of her magic.

"Della," he breathed.

"I'm okay," she mumbled, wrapping her arms around him, almost to prove he was there.

"Are ya sure? Yer shakin'," he said, gripping onto her as if she would disappear the second he let go.

She nodded. "I'm cold."

Max couldn't help but laugh, pushing her ever so slightly away so he could see her face. Her skin was paper white. Dried trails of blood marred her throat. Her eyes were adorned with dark circles. He squeezed her shoulders, placing his forehead against hers.

"Don' ever do that tuh me again, ya hear?" he choked out, staring deep into those all-consuming brown eyes of hers.

Della only nodded. "I'm sorry," she said, her words barely a whisper. Tears stung the corner of her eyes as she shut them.

"Hey, hey, stay with me, okay?" Max screeched, panic seizing him.

"I'm exhausted."

"Ei know love, Ei know," Max breathed, hugging her icy body to him.

"She needs human doctors," came a voice from the trees.

Della shook her head. "No doctors."

Max turned to see a young man with gaunt features and long dark hair peering around a tree.

"Sorry," he said, edging toward them. "I took a wrong turn." His face was full of worry, eyes locked on Della.

"It's fine," Della mumbled groggily. "You can trust him. I trust him."

She sighed heavily, her limbs going weak, her head lulling to the side. Max shook her gently, but her eyes stayed shut. In his heart, he knew she'd be okay, but that would never stop him from worrying.

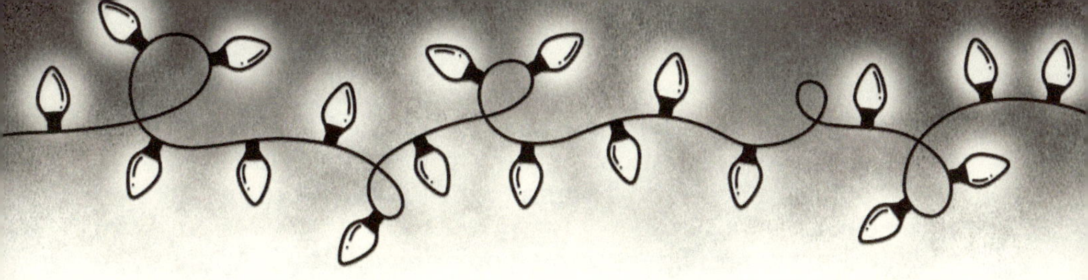

CHAPTER FORTY-FIVE

Eavesdropping

Kohen was pacing back and forth in his office, eyes locked on Porter. He'd been expecting a lecture about how you shouldn't step in front of a man with a gun affixed to his head, about how stupid he was, about how Kohen didn't trust him in any way, shape, or form. But Kohen was quiet. If he was anything like his niece, that was worse.

Ashton still refused to speak to any of them. Even when Porter explained who he was and his relationship with Della, he ignored him. Whatever he needed to say was for her ears only. That could mean a multitude of different things. The last time a guy in a cell had information for her, he'd ended up dead. The thing was, Porter was more afraid of everyone else's safety than Ashton's. Something about this whole ordeal didn't sit right with him.

Where had he been all this time?

Why did he look like he'd gone ten rounds with a chainsaw?

Why was he so antsy about Elvi and Kohen?

He needed Della, and he needed Max.

Porter cleared his throat, tired of watching Kohen dig a trench in the floor from pacing so much.

Kohen finally paused and looked at him. "Can I ask you something?"

Porter only shrugged.

"Why the Hell did you do that? He could have shot you. Or himself. That was stupid," Kohen sighed. "But it was also brave. To an extent."

Porter cast his eyes to the floor, wringing his hands. "I've been where he was. Afraid. Thinking the only way out is through the end of a barrel or the blade of a knife. Or maybe he thinks he could make a point with his death. Been there too. And while I don't know if I truly believe that's what is going on in Ash's head, I do know I had some-one to tell me how wrong I was. He needed that, too," Porter sighed. "Beats you shooting him in the kneecaps."

Kohen scoffed. "I wasn't gonna shoot him in the kneecaps."

Porter smiled. "I know your niece, okay? Apple doesn't roll too far from the tree."

"That is correct," Kohen laughed, placing a hand on Porter's shoulder. "Ever think of a career in—"

"I work at the morgue at MHPD. Got a badge to prove it," Porter said quickly.

"Not what I was going to say, but good for you," Kohen smirked. "I was going to say, have you ever thought about pursuing a career as a therapist? I think you'd be very good at it."

Porter's jaw dropped. "I—I—I never thought about that."

Kohen squinted at him. "Consider it. You'd help more people than you would in a morgue."

Kohen patted him on the shoulder and opened the door for him.

If only he knew how much those words impacted Porter.

"Thanks. I think I will," Porter whispered.

His head was spinning, the taste of possibility sweet on his tongue. Very few had seen potential in him.

Kohen winked at him, waving him away. "Go find Seb, will ya? I'm going to wrangle that search party."

"Yes, sir," Porter said with a bow, exiting Kohen's stuffy office a little happier than he had entered.

He'd barely made it a few doors down when hands yanked him down another hallway. Sebastian clamped a hand over Porter's mouth, narrowing his eyes as he put a finger to his lips. Slowly, he let go of him, beckoning him forward with a finger. Together, they peered around a cor-ner, listening intently to the conversation floating down the hall.

". . . Jasper, you don't understand—" Kimi began.

"I do understand," Jasper snapped back.

"You're not listening to me! She had a seizure! It's all starting up again, I know it," Kimi whisper-yelled, despera-tion in her voice.

"If you had just listened to me, to begin with, none of this would've happened. She belonged in a psyche ward, Kimi, and yet you turned to—"

Kimi scoffed. "Sometimes I understand why she hates you so much."

"She can hate me all she wants; you know I'm right.

I knew trusting that idiot to fix all this had been a mistake. This is all his fault, and you know it. We should—"

"We should be more worried about our daughter's well-being now rather than what happened years ago," Kimi whisper-yelled. "She could die, Jasper."

Porter glanced down at Sebastian, whose eyes were shut, his face scrunched up in worry. He wondered how long Sebastian had been listening and what he'd heard.

"We are not getting involved. She made her choice. She's an adult now. You promised the second she moved out, we'd wash our hands of all this for the twins' sake," Jasper hissed. Porter's blood went cold.

"And I promised myself that if she ever came home, I'd welcome her with open arms."

"You can't fix her, Kimi."

"Then what the Hell do you expect me to do? She is our daughter!"

"Like Quincy was our son?"

Kimi swore.

They heard her sneakers squeak across the floor, causing Sebastian to push Porter back until they were out of potential eyesight. His face was grim as he stared over his shoulder, still gripping Porter's arms tightly.

"What all did you hear?" Porter asked softly.

Sebastian's face darkened. "More than I should've. I think they know something—y'know, about the Wendigo and Elvi. Kimi also brought up her mom. Is Della okay? I know Winifred had some stuff wrong with her. Do Della's bleeding ears have to do with that?"

Porter pursed his lips, hands on hips, unsure what to say. Sebastian was in this for the long haul. He knew that for sure. But he didn't know the guy well enough to know how much worry and stress he could take.

"We'll figure it out when we find her, okay?" he decided to say. Better safe than sorry.

Sebastian shrugged, finally dropping his hands from Porter's arms. "Is Elvi a Courier? Or a monster hunter of some sort? I think maybe we should talk to her."

Porter's hand went to the pocket he'd stowed Elvi's room key in. An embarrassed flush spread across his face. Visiting her was going to be a mistake. She'd left in a hurry after Kohen had drug Ashton inside. Porter would've stopped her if he were anything like Max and Della.

"I think you're right, but—"

Kohen came skidding down the hall, nearly plowing them over. Terror lit up his face. "He found her," he breathed. "Max found her."

Porter's knees buckled. "Is she okay? Where are

they? What happened?" he stuttered, stumbling forward, grabbing Sebastian's shoulder to steady himself.

"All I know from Mingan is that they are on their way here," Kohen said, trying to catch his breath. Relief was spreading across his features, but the terror in his eyes hadn't budged.

"Thank God," Porter whispered, clutching his chest as the constant ache finally began to disperse.

CHAPTER FORTY-SIX

Beyond Repair

Della didn't know how she'd ended up sandwiched be-tween Arlo and Max, but here she was, half awake, watching the world go by from the cab of Mingan's truck.

She'd be indebted to Max forever for recovering her glasses. Seeing was such a luxury, one she often took for granted.

Max had such a tight grip on Della's numb fingers that she thought her bones would break again. They sat quietly, clinging to each other. She could hear Max's rapid heartbeat in her ear. Could feel it resonate through her like the beat of a drum. Angry and scared and something else. Something deeper. The scowl on his face worried her. The feeling in her chest worried her more. Whenever she looked at Max, she saw a faint, dull red light emanating from him.

Arlo was to her right, face plastered against the window, tugging at the collar of the shirt Max had forced him to wear. He'd complained how these modern clothes were itchy and uncomfortable, but as soon as Max said he couldn't come with them unless he dressed like a modern human, he'd gone quiet and complied.

"Max, are you okay?" Della whispered, her voice rough. She was still shivering. At this point, she wondered if she would ever warm up.

He nodded, squeezing her hand tighter. "Perfectly fine."

Della was getting tired of quiet, tense car rides.

Mingan—who hated driving more than she did—fi-nally pulled into a parking spot outside the police depart-ment. He sighed heavily and nodded toward the door.

Max led her inside to find her entire family, Porter and Sebastian, all talking over each other. Porter looked so lost, the dark circles under his eyes telling her how badly this had affected him.

Guilt flooded her.

As if he sensed her presence, Porter turned, eyes widening.

She expected him to rush to her, sweep her into his arms, burst into tears, and tell her how relieved he was.

Instead, he slowly stalked toward her, eyes on Max.

"What the Hell happened?" he said as level-headed as he could, his face red and his hands clutched in tight fists.

"We'll tell ya later, right now—"

"No, I want to know now!" he whisper-yelled, looking over his shoulder. "Things just got a Hell of a lot more complicated. Ashton showed up—"

"Porter," Max snapped. "Look at her. Really look at her."

Porter rolled his eyes over to Della, noting the state of her. The dried blood she'd quickly tried to wash off. The mats in her hair were tangled with pine needles and branches, and who knew what else. How her skin had turned a deathly shade of white.

His eyes softened.

There were loud footsteps before Sebastian collided with her, pulling her into a gigantic hug. Soon followed Kimi and Kohen—even Poppy.

Della was swarmed with suffocating hugs and prying questions she didn't know how to answer. The room was starting to swim. At some point, Porter and Max were pushed away from her. She couldn't see them in the sea of faces around her.

"I really need to sit down," she tried to say, her voice small.

No one heard her. Jasper was drilling into her about how reckless she was about what would have happened if she had ended up dead. Kimi was crying hysterically. Kohen was just as livid as Jasper, going on and on about how Ashton showed up with a gun and requested her presence. How he could have shot her on the spot at his trailer. Poppy was fussing with her hair. Others yelled at Jasper for letting Della galivant around like this. Even some of Kohen's co-workers were telling her their every thought.

"SHUT UP!" Max screamed from behind. His hand found Della's, and he pulled her away, shoving her behind him. She collided with Porter, who wouldn't meet her eyes.

"That is enough questions for tuhday, thank ya *very* much. If ya want tuh continue arguin', so be it. But for the love of God, would someone please get us a medic!" Max screeched, accentuating every word with a jab of his finger in someone's direction.

Jasper rolled his eyes but nodded in agreement, pulling Kimi along as he presumably went to find a first aid kit. Kohen sighed heavily, waving everyone away.

It was Della's turn to squeeze Max's hands until his fingers almost broke.

He turned to her when all who were left were Porter, Sebastian, and Arlo. "Are ya okay?"

"I'd like to sit down," she said with a shaky sigh, pulling him toward the chairs near the front of the precinct.

Porter, Sebastian, and Arlo followed. The five of them found their seats, Porter and Max on either side of Della, Sebastian, and Arlo at her feet, happy to sit on the floor.

"What happened?" Porter whispered, not even giving Della a moment to catch her breath.

"Porter," Max scolded.

"We need to know, Max. She can't just run off like that and not answer our questions. We thought she was dead!" Porter snapped.

"Ei think the only thing we should be worryin' about right now is whether or not she has hypothermia," Max countered.

"I hate to say it, but I'm with Porter on this one," Sebastian sighed. "Also, who's this guy?" he asked, pointing a thumb at Arlo, who smiled brightly.

"Arlo. Arlo the Wendigo," he said, tipping his head in a mock bow. "Warm regards."

"What?" Porter and Sebastian asked, looking at Della with horror-struck expressions.

"He changed his name," Della yawned, pulling her knees up to her chest and burying her face in her hands.

"You do realize we need more than that, right? I mean, come on, Della. You scared the crap out of us! What the Hell happened, and why the Hell did you run off like that?" Porter hissed, shaking her shoulder softly.

"Leave her alone," Max said. "Seriously, Garroway."

Della glanced at Porter. He was outlined in a dark brown light, just as he had been at the reservation.

Della briefly told them about what happened with Arlo and Ahiga—just enough information to satisfy Porter.

"We can talk about all that later, all right?" Max whispered. "Preferably not somewhere with pryin' eyes and listenin' ears. She needs rest. She'll tell us every little detail when she's good and ready. Right, Della?" He smiled sympathetically at her, which she appreciated.

Porter rolled his eyes, sitting back in his seat. "You already know everything, okay? The rest of us are in the dark like always."

"What's that supposed tuh mean?"

"Guys," Della said, putting a hand on their chests.

Max's dull red aura flared. The brown of Porter's darkened.

"Nothing," Porter said under his breath. Crossing his arms over his chest, he looked away with a shake of his head.

Max glared at him, tapping his foot on the ground angrily. He muttered something under his breath, looking anywhere but at Della.

Sebastian was staring at the floor, looking like he wanted to run far, far away.

Arlo was absentmindedly fiddling with one of Max's shoelaces. Worry filled his eyes.

Della's chest tightened. Her heart was racing with anxiety. These were her people, and they were at their wits end with each other. These were her boys. Her family. She didn't want them to fight.

"Go work things out," she snapped, finally dropping her hands from their chests. "Come back when you've made up. I'm sick of it."

"I have nothing to say to him right now. I'm not mad at him," Porter said quietly, a rough edge to his voice.

Della's heart was pounding away in her chest. Max looked at her sideways, concern on his face. She knew he could sense her fear and hear the anxious beating of her heart. She gave him a pointed look. He nodded halfheartedly, grabbing Arlo by the elbow and motioning for Sebastian to follow him. The three of them walked away, mumbling over each other.

Della turned to Porter, leaning against the wall, tracing his face with her tired eyes.

"Want to talk?" she asked.

"You have got to stop doing that. Running off, I mean. I can't take this sort of—" He shut his eyes tightly, leaning forward with a heavy sigh, wringing his hands. "Dammit, Della."

"I'm sorry," she said softly.

"No, you're not, and that's the problem," Porter laughed darkly, startling her with how loud he'd gotten.

Della didn't have anything to say to that. He wasn't wrong, but she really was sorry. She knew she shouldn't have run off like that, but sometimes her curiosity got the better of her. Maybe that was a shitty excuse—blaming her actions on her curiosity like it was some outside force that didn't belong to her—but it was the truth.

"Why does this always happen to us?" Porter blurted out, looking at her over his shoulder. "Why can't we be normal?"

Della turned her attention to her feet. "I dunno, Porter."

"I hate fighting with you. I hate feeling like I'm never ever getting through to you. That's not how boyfriends and girlfriends are supposed to be," he said. She could hear the lump in his throat. "You are my everything, Della. Am I yours?"

Della couldn't look at him. Suddenly, she couldn't breathe.

Porter scoffed, nodding to himself. "You shouldn't have to think about that. The answer should be yes. Without hesitation, the answer should be yes."

"You—You are my everything," Della forced herself to say.

"But not like he is," Porter grumbled. "Not like this." He gestured loosely in her direction, and she knew what he meant.

"Porter—"

He stood, shoving his hands in his pockets. "I'm not going to keep doing this, okay? I'm sick and tired of feeling like I'm second or even third best."

"You are not second best, Porter!" Della snapped, struggling to her feet. Her bones creaked and cracked as she stood.

"Then stop treating me like I am!" His eyes were wild, glinting gold in the harsh light.

"Stop treating me like I can't be allowed to make my own decisions!"

"Della, your decisions will get you dead!" Porter yelled, throwing his hands out wide. "You run headstrong into danger for the thrill of it because you think you have something to prove. And I'm so sick and tired of this horrible ache in my chest because one of these days, there isn't going to be a second chance. There won't be enough magic to protect you."

"Way to jinx me, jerk," Della barked.

"Oh, grow up, Delphee," Porter replied, rolling his eyes.

Nauseating grief pooled in the pit of Della's stomach.

"Where do you see yourself five years from now?" Porter asked, catching her off guard. The intensity in his eyes scared her. "Because I want a family. I don't want to do this for the rest of my life. I want picket fences and manicured lawns. I want a stable job. I want a wife. What do you want?"

"I—I want that too. But there has to be a balance. I'm not just going to give this up for you. This is bigger than us,

Chapter Forty-Six

Porter. This is important to me."

Porter's shoulders sagged. All traces of anger on his face disappeared, replaced by a numbed shock.

"There we go. There's the truth," he said, sounding dazed. "Nothing is more important to the great Delphee Coleman than her stories. Not even me. Damn, you really are just like Mavericks. No wonder Max—'

"That's not what I meant, and you know it," Della sobbed, tears streaming down her face.

Porter opened his mouth to say something, but Della had had enough. Before he could react, she sidestepped around him, making for the door.

"Don't walk away from me!" he screamed at her.

"Isn't that what you want?" Della screamed back, rounding on him. "You're not coming to me intending to fix things. If you want to break up, just say so."

"All I've ever done is try to fix things," Porter said, his voice dangerously low. "You're just pissed because you can't handle it when someone calls you out on your shit. You want someone who will never stand up to you? Someone who coddles you? Someone who doesn't care whether your choices have consequences? Find Max. See if I care. I'm tired of this never-ending bullshit cycle."

"This has nothing to do with Max. Stop bringing him into it."

Porter marched up to her with unabashed fury. "It has *everything* to do with Max!"

"I have only ever had eyes for you, Porter!"

"Then why the Hell do you look at him like that? Why do you tell him everything? We were never even close to what the two of you have!"

"Maybe that's because you never put in any effort!"

That stunned him.

"Me? The one who planned every date? The one who always calls and texts first? Hell, Delphee, I even paid for everything. Yet I didn't put in any effort?" he laughed. His gold eyes seemed to swirl like flames.

"I didn't want fancy dates; I wanted you to be there. I wanted you to be present," Della sobbed, stabbing her finger into the palm of her hand to accentuate her point. "I wanted to come to you and be able to talk about everything. But I couldn't," she spat, hugging herself tightly. The lights above were flickering, casting harsh shadows on Porter's face.

"So instead, you turned to my best friend? Great move."

"Who else was I supposed to go to? Every time I bring things up, you shut me down! The only thing we ever talk about is TV and the weather. I need more than that," Della cried, grabbing his hands and squeezing them tight. "Maybe I shouldn't have gone to Max, but dammit Porter, I don't have anyone else. At least I was trying to make sense of this all. You didn't. I talked with Eloise. I know about you missing your therapy appointments."

Porter ripped free from her grip, standing with his back to her, breathing heavily. "She shouldn't have told you that."

"She didn't have to. I know you, Porter."

He turned to her, tears rolling down his cheeks. "No, you don't. And I don't think I know you either. Because the girl standing before me is not the girl I fell in love with. You are a shell of a person trying to fill a void with artificial highs. You make bad choices with bad consequences for the fun of it. You never listen to any of the people who care about you."

"As if you're any different," she scoffed.

"I am. Because I've decided I'm done with this. When we get back to Moss Hollow, it's over for me. I'm done trying to care. I'm done fighting for someone who obviously isn't going to fight for me." His words were like knives to her heart. "*We're* done, Della."

Every light around them exploded, showering them with sparks.

"I hate you," Della whispered, then turned and ran out the door and into the cold.

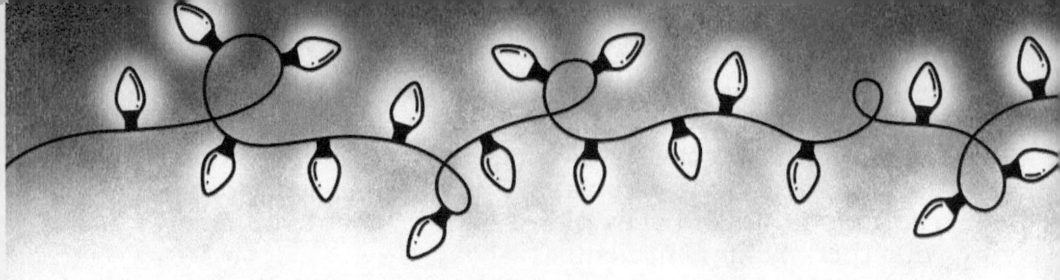

CHAPTER FORTY-SEVEN

*To Love Her Is To Hold The
Universe In Your Hands*

The cold stung Della's fingers and nose, but her tears burned down her cheeks like molten lava. No matter how hard she tried, she couldn't calm herself.

This was for the best, and Della knew it. She'd seen it coming from miles away. But that didn't stop it from hurting. Nor did it stop her from thinking she had made the biggest mistake of her life.

And the worst part? Everything Porter had said was a truth she already knew.

Delphee Coleman *was* a broken shell of a human being. She didn't know who she was outside of her conspiracy theories. She *had* been chasing artificial highs her whole life, and it had made her jaded, reckless, stubborn, and hard to love.

But if she was broken, then so was Porter. He'd asked her once if she thought he was broken. At the time, she'd thought he was just a little bent. Maybe then it had been the truth, but now? They were shattered beyond repair, and they only had themselves to blame.

They'd been convenient. At the time, they'd been the only option for each other. They'd settled, and maybe that isn't always bad, but it was for Della and Porter. What had happened between them wasn't healthy. If they couldn't find common ground now, how would they ever find it in the future?

Della knew that Sycamore Heights hadn't caused any of this. They'd been falling apart from the beginning. Still, she thought maybe if they'd just stayed home, they would've had a few more good weeks together.

No matter how she spun it, in the end, they'd always end up like this. Porter would always care too much, and Della would care too little.

She didn't want to end up like her parents.

Breaking up with him was a good thing.

So why did her heart ache like this?

"Della?" came Max's voice from behind. She turned to see him standing in the doorway, face full of worry. "What happened?"

She tried to speak, but there were no words for how she felt now. She sank to her knees on the icy pavement, crying inconsolably. Della hated crying like this, hated people seeing her as the fractured mess she was.

Max was at her side instantly, hugging her tightly and stroking her hair gently.

"Talk tuh me," he whispered.

"We broke up," she choked out, burying her head in the crook of his elbow.

Max rested his head atop hers, allowing her to cry as much as she needed to.

"Am I a bad person?" Della whispered after a while. The lump in her throat made the words come out like a squeak.

It took Max a moment to reply. For a second, Della thought he would say yes and agree that she was apparently public enemy number one.

"Della," he began, turning her face so she would be forced to look at him. "There is no one else on Earth like *you*. Ei have never met someone with such a sense of justice. Someone who cares so deeply for people she's never met. Someone whose sole purpose is tuh find and protect the good in this world. For all yer cynicism, yer the most optimistic person Ei know. Yer *not* a bad person."

This made Della sob harder. Max just held her, seemingly unbothered. They stayed like that until Della had no tears left to cry.

Soon, the two of them were just staring at each other, feeling as though the cosmos had stopped just for them.

Della thought back to the first day they'd met. Max had been so eager to help her. She thought back to them fighting late one night at Ambrose Apartments. They'd resolved their issues quickly, thanks to Mavericks. She thought of how he'd always been there for her. How he was always fighting her battles as if they were his own.

About how handsome he looked in the fading moonlight.

Max was more than her coworker.

He was her sidekick.

Her partner in crime.

Her best friend.

The question was, why did calling him that always

make her stomach turn?

The answer? Being friends with him was never going to be good enough.

For a girl well versed in truth, she'd been lying to herself—and Porter—for longer than she'd realized. It was high time she faced the music and spoke what everyone else already seemed to know.

"I love you, Max," she whispered, one last tear sliding down her cheek.

"Ei love ya too," he whispered back.

Della couldn't recall exactly how it had happened, but suddenly, his lips were on hers, and the ache in her heart had gone away. The falling snow around them suddenly glistened with a purple and turquoise glow. Tiny fireworks popped around them, illuminating their exhausted, tear-stricken faces.

Every kiss healed her mind, body, and soul. She could feel the frostbite fading from her fingers and the heartbreak subsiding.

"I don't want to screw this up," she said between hopeful, yearning kisses.

"Me either," Max said, pulling away for a moment.

He looked her over, and she knew he was the only person who had ever truly seen her.

And despite all odds, despite every morally gray, messed up, crazy thing she'd done, he loved her anyway.

All her life, Della had heard that you couldn't love someone until you loved yourself. But maybe having someone who loved you despite all your flaws and broken pieces would allow you room for that. If someone could see through your walls and still stick around despite what they saw, then maybe you could finally believe you were someone worth that kind of love.

Max made her feel like that.

He was her person.

Della just wished she would have realized that a lot sooner.

"I love you," she repeated, hoping he understood what that meant.

"Ei love ya too," he said, smiling brightly before kissing her again.

Max smiled brightly, using his thumb to brush snowflakes from Della's cheek. In his eyes, she saw her future. Her mind could play tricks on her, make her believe a false fate, but Della didn't believe in fate. She was the master of her reality, and that reality would include Max no matter what.

There they were, tumbling down onto the snowy

pavement, the falling flakes popping, showering them in colorful sparks soft as butterfly kisses.

Della decided that fireworks during a snowstorm—like Max's smile—was a memory she would never let herself forget.

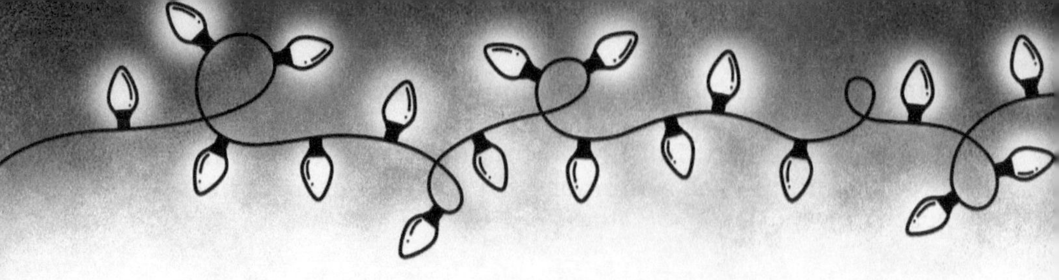

CHAPTER FORTY-EIGHT

A Bat in The Penthouse

Porter sat on the hood of the hearse, staring at the card Elvi had left him with. He'd looked up the address and found her hotel was about forty-five minutes away. In his book, that was far enough away from Sycamore Heights to allow him time to clear his head before he showed up on her doorstep.

He knew this wouldn't end well, but he was tired of sitting around. She had answers, and it was high time she gave them up.

Filled with rage-induced determination, Porter hopped into the hearse and tore off, the GPS on his phone screaming to slow down as he reached the freeway.

The more he thought about Della, the faster he drove.

That green-haired menace infuriated him.

He loved her so much, and this was how she repaid him? Emotionally cheating on him with someone he considered his brother?

How nice.

Merry freaking Christmas. Best present ever.

Ex-girlfriend of the year.

Part of him wanted to turn around and yell at her and Max some more, but that wouldn't solve anything. He'd just push them farther away. Yes, he was livid. Yes, he felt betrayed. But he didn't want them out of his life. He needed them. They were his family.

The hearse slowed as he realized blaming Della for all his problems wasn't fair.

Porter had always been a difficult person to be around. He couldn't blame Della for feeling alienated in their relationship.

They were two screwed-up individuals trying to fix

each other and make the other into someone they could feel safe around.

How had he not seen it before?

Porter had a lot of healing to do before he was ready to love someone the way he wanted to love Della. And if she couldn't wait for that to happen, then so be it. He believed in soulmates. Maybe his was still out there waiting for him. And perhaps that person would be everything he's ever needed.

But that person was never going to be Delphee Chrysanthemum Coleman.

With a heavy heart, Porter pulled the hearse into a parking spot, gazing up at the brightly lit hotel. Flipping the hotel key around, he found a room number had been scrawled onto the back in hot pink permanent marker.

Now or never, he thought to himself.

The bellhops and receptionist didn't pay him much attention as he wove through the overly decorated lobby, searching for the elevator. Mirrored walls inside the elevator forced him to gaze upon his reflection. His fluffy black hair stuck out in a thousand places. Deep dark circles adorned his eyes, reminiscent of the bruises he usually had. On top of it all, he was dressed like a grave robber.

He was suddenly extremely self-conscious.

The elevator opened on the sixth floor with a pleasant ding. Porter gawked at the fluffy carpet beneath his feet and the sparkling wallpaper around him. It was a strange feeling knowing he was way out of his league. He hurried to Elvi's room, knocking gently on an ornately detailed white and gold door.

The door opened to reveal Elvi looking as stunning as ever, her hair cascading in a golden waterfall of curls around her petite shoulders. Her pearl earrings glinted as she tilted her head at him.

"You're late," she said, a playful smile tugging at her lips.

Porter let his eyes sweep over her tweed suit. Elvi looked like she'd bought her whole ensemble from 'Mean-Girls-R-Us.' He smirked. She must have got her winning personality for free with such a large purchase.

"Did they find your girl—"

"She's not my girlfriend," Porter spat out. He reddened at his defensive tone, clearing his throat. "But yes, they did."

Elvi nodded to herself. "Well?" she asked, opening the door and beckoning him in.

"You said you wanted to talk?" Porter asked.

His jaw dropped as he stepped inside, taking in the

ultra-modern design of the room. If you could even call it a room. It appeared to be more of a penthouse. A crystalline chandelier hung from the ceiling, a glass table was set with rose-gold cutlery, and she even had an in-house bar—Porter had never seen such luxury. There were even candles in golden candelabras flickering away on a buffet by the door. It was Poppy's mansion on steroids. The only thing that didn't scream 'I'm better than you' was the cotton candy machine by the bar.

"I did say that, didn't I?" Elvi led him to the glass table.

On each side of an elaborate flower arrangement were pink and white plates and crystal glasses filled with— his nose wrinkled. He could smell the whiskey from here.

Elvi eyed him suspiciously. "Prefer something else?"

Porter knew he shouldn't. Last time he drank, things ended very badly. But he was tired and drained and had already made a handful of stupid decisions this evening, so why not throw a little alcohol into the mix? He was a happy drunk anyway.

"I could use a glass," he shrugged.

Elvi smiled to herself, pulling out a white velvet chair for him. Porter sat awkwardly, hyper-aware of the dirt his ripped-up jeans would leave behind. Everything was far too clean here. Everything had a place, and every place had a thing. Not a speck of dust, not a cobweb. Such a stark difference compared to where and how he'd grown up.

He kind of liked it.

In a way, he liked her, too.

Elvi took a swig of berry-red wine as she sat across from him. Most of her face was obscured by the giant floral arrangement between them: pale pink peonies, deep red carnations, baby's breath, and orchids. Every flower spoke to her femininity, elegance, and supposed wealth.

Porter picked up his glass, smelling it to try and pick up any sour undernotes, turning the cup towards the light to see if anything odd was floating in it. "Is it poisoned?"

Her laugh was as flowery as the bouquet. "Hardly."

Porter drank it dry in one swig, wincing as it burned his throat. Best whiskey he'd ever tasted. The flavor was smoky yet had a hint of silky honey and vanilla. Nothing like the crap back home he was used to.

"Not much of a whiskey girl, myself, but I've heard that one is good," Elvi said, peeking over the bouquet.

Porter shrugged. "It's fine, I guess."

"Coy doesn't look good on you, Mr. Garroway."

Elvi sat back lazily in her plush seat, swirling her wine like a member of the royal family. With her raised eyebrow and nonchalant posture, she looked rather bored.

"If I am to be honest, I wasn't expecting you to come by yourself," she said carefully. "I didn't take you for a lone wolf."

"Things change, I guess," Porter said tightly, watching the candles closest to him wave back and forth.

Elvi toasted to that. "So, they do."

With a snap of her fingers, a maid appeared from around the corner, a bottle of whiskey in hand. She refilled Porter's glass and then made for the kitchen, beginning to put together a tray of meats and cheeses.

"What can I do for you, Porter? I know you have questions."

Porter thought for a moment. Ashton was alive, so there was no reason to suspect any blood was on her hands. Yet he'd seemed absolutely terrified of her. Then, of course, there was still the matter of Kohen. What exactly had they said or done to him?

"I want to know about Ashton John," Porter said flatly.

Elvi's mouth twitched into a crooked smile. "Nothing to tell."

"Liar," Porter sighed, downing his second glass of whiskey.

The maid brought over the charcuterie board, offering to pour him another glass. He waved her away, figuring he'd better stop while he was ahead.

"Like I told Della, we didn't interact outside the historical society. I'm not quite sure why you and your band of misfits keep prying," Elvi laughed.

"Because we have eyewitness information that you and Kohen visited him at his residence at least once. Want to tell me why?" Porter asked.

He was enjoying playing this little game of hers. Especially since he knew he was winning.

Elvi's crooked smile dropped. "Who's your source?"

Porter took a piece of prosciutto and a slice of cheese off the charcuterie board. With a wicked smirk, he said, "That's classified."

She narrowed her eyes. "Mr. Garroway, trust goes both ways."

"Oh, I'd love to trust you, Ms. Sinclair. Want to help me do that? Start talking."

Elvi toyed with the string of pearls around her neck. Something about the way she did that unnerved Porter. She reminded him of the *Queen of Hearts*, and he guessed she was just as eager to cut off his head as the woman in the storybook.

Chapter Forty-Eight

"Let's try this again. What do you need from me?" she yawned.

This truly was a game. She wanted him to ask the right question. She was a genie. If he misspoke, he'd use up all his wishes.

"I need you," Porter began, leaning forward in his chair. "To tell me what you know about the supernatural."

Elvi set her wine glass down with a satisfied nod. "I think I can tell you more than that." She stood, sweeping her hair behind her back as she approached the cotton candy machine. "You have no idea how lucky you are I was assigned to this damn town."

This was all too weird.

Elvi glanced over her shoulder at him, looking mildly amused. "You don't have one of these at The Courier?" she laughed, beckoning him forward. "I would have thought Mavericks had found one of them by now."

At the sound of Mavericks' name, dread flooded Porter. Standing, he fiddled with the chain hanging from his ear. He should run. He should be in the hearse. He should be back at the precinct apologizing to Della for being such an idiot.

Maybe he'd spent too much time around her lately. Because, for once, he was too curious to be rational. This made him understand her a little more. But as with most things he did, it was too little too late.

Filled to the brim with anxiety, he came to stand beside Elvi.

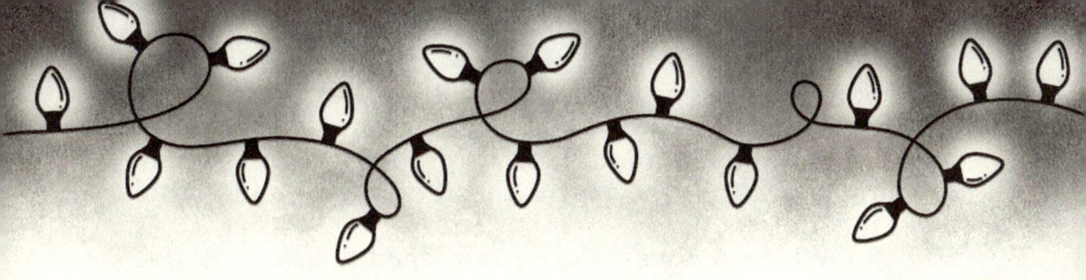

CHAPTER FORTY-NINE

P.O.I.

The cotton candy machine looked entirely ordinary. Nothing but a cart striped pink and white with an array of brightly colored sugars sitting on a small shelf near the wheels. Elvi grabbed one of the containers of blue sugar, poured some into the center pan, and then flicked the on switch.

Now, Porter had never gone to a fair or carnival and had never seen a cotton candy machine with his own two eyes, but he was pretty sure when you poured in the sugar, it wasn't supposed to glow.

"Hand," Elvi commanded.

Hesitantly, he took hold of her jewel-encrusted fingers. She thrust their hands forward with a rather aggressive tug so they hovered above the glowing, spinning sugar. Just as Porter was about to ask what she was doing, strands of warm sugar wrapped around their hands, traveling up their arms like the tentacles of an octopus. The cotton candy pulled them down into the spinning chamber, and suddenly, they were in a cyclone of electric blue that whipped at their faces.

Porter heard himself scream.

It only lasted a minute. Then, the freshly spun cotton candy began to part. Porter franticly batted away floating pieces of spun sugar, revealing what looked like the middle of a futuristic submarine. Stark-white walls were lined with huge windows that looked out into the ocean. When he looked up, he found windows in the ceiling, too. Colorful fish whizzed by, unbothered by the young man staring up at them in horror. In front of them stood a desk where a smiling man dressed in a gold suit sat. Elvi regarded him with a curt nod, shaking her hand free from Porter's tight grip. Behind him was another cotton candy machine, gold and white to match its surroundings. Standing on a pedestal, a spotlight illuminating it, the cotton candy machine reminded him of a shrine. Living in Moss Hollow had given him an open mind. But worshipping a cotton candy machine was weird, even by his standards. So incredibly weird.

"Where are we?" Porter managed to ask as Elvi led him to the desk and the smiling man.

She brushed the cotton candy from her clothes, then pointed at the emblem on the floor. The logo resembled a medieval coat of arms. A shield divided into four parts surrounded by intricate swirls was set in opal. A skull, a book with a pentacle on the cover, a scale, and a sword crossed over a rifle took up the quadrants of the shield. All of which were set in gold. The thin outlines of the crest seemed to be made of jade.

"The *P.O.I. Project* Headquarters. Location classified," Elvi said, holding out her hand to the smiling man in gold.

He nodded and then placed a lanyard in her hand. She, in turn, handed it to Porter. When Porter touched it, the card attached to the lanyard glitched like a computer screen, and suddenly, his face was staring back at him.

"Visitor pass. Stay close. Don't lose it," Elvi explained. Before saying anything else, she looked him up and down, pursing her lips. Porter glanced down to see he was also covered in wisps of cotton candy.

"Don't eat it," Elvi sighed, picking a piece from his hair.

Porter followed at a distance as she made for a hallway to the right, still taking in his surroundings as he brushed the cotton candy off.

The walls down this hallway had giant computer screens showing all sorts of digital maps, lists of people, and other odds and ends. Some of the names had places attached to them. Porter wondered if these were people working here or if they were people this *P.O.I. Project* monitored.

"What did I just get myself into?" he breathed as a hammerhead shark swam overhead.

Porter hoped he hadn't made a colossal mistake following her. The visitor pass eased his nerves a little, but this could all be a show.

"Hurry up," Elvi said coldly, stopping at a sliding door lined with blue light.

A flashing sign on the door read 'Containment Unit Four.' Elvi tapped the door, rolling her eyes as Porter gawked at the sliding mechanism.

"This stuff is straight out of a sci-fi movie," he muttered.

Elvi scoffed, though Porter caught her smile as she

whisked him inside a room whose only light came from the glowing blue lines on the floor, which resembled a motherboard.

"This is where we keep low-level threats," Elvi said, stopping before a dark glass case. She pressed a button, and the case lit up, revealing a rotting body with charcoal-colored skin.

Porter came to stand on Elvi's left, examining the body.

"Well, Mr. Garroway. What is your expert opinion?" she asked, procuring a pair of gloves and handing them to him.

"What, or rather *who* is this?" he asked, pulling on the gloves.

Elvi handed him a surgical mask. "The body of a revenant that's been terrorizing a small town in Indiana."

"The body shouldn't be in this state. It should be a pile of decaying bones," Porter said in confusion as Elvi opened the case.

"Magic has a funny way of preserving things like this, as you can see. Are you familiar with revenant lore? Decapitation is the only option in this sort of situation. We've subdued the entity for now, however." Elvi inhaled sharply. "Forensics wants to cut him open and see how he ticks."

Porter poked and prodded at the body, half expecting it to sit up and try to eat his face off. If that's what revenants did. He'd never heard of such a creature. Porter took his time examining the body, looking for any symbols carved into it. He had stumbled on a few bodies like this back in Moss Hollow. Some had been carved with ritualistic markings. The Courier had cleaned them up. Porter remembered one of Mavericks' lackeys mentioning vengeful witches with evil tendencies or something.

"Why are you showing me this?" Porter asked.

Elvi shrugged, shutting the case. "I figured you'd find a body like this interesting, undertaker."

She was right to a certain extent.

Porter followed her as she walked deeper into the room. All sorts of devices and artifacts were strewn across the worktables. Other dark cases were scattered at the room's edges, presumably holding other monsters.

"Want to see something cool?" Elvi asked. Hearing her use that word was strange.

Porter nodded. She led him to another sliding door with a keypad and scanner. Reaching into her jacket, she procured a card that matched his except for the color. Hers was a black so deep and dark it was as if she held a piece of the void. Elvi scanned the card, and the door opened, its hydraulics squeaking.

"We keep higher-level threats back here, but don't worry. They can't hurt anyone," she explained.

This room was lit a little brighter, though Porter wished it wasn't. Upon first glance, this room resembled the first, but the deeper they went, the more it changed. Tubes full of murky water held sickly-looking Merfolk suspended inside. Their gills pulsed like labored lungs, their long-clawed fingers twitching.

"These four were recently caught drowning sailors," Elvi spat, thoroughly disgusted.

They continued, weaving through the tubes. Beyond the Merfolk was a glass cage. In its center sat a mangled half-man-half-wolf. If memory served correctly, it was a Rougarou. Della would have loved to see this. More so, she would've loved to free all the monsters trapped here.

"We've had him since the eighties," Elvi said, knocking on the glass. The Rougarou turned and growled. "Learned pretty quickly we had to put blinders on him. Lost a few good agents to his parasite-like powers."

"Creepy," Porter admitted, glad Elvi didn't linger any longer. Even with the gaudy blinders and thick glass, Porter didn't feel safe.

Walking through this place reminded Porter of exploring a mad scientist's lab. All manner of beings were caged here. Porter didn't know how to feel. Being a descendant of Ahools, he somewhat sympathized with these beasts. But being someone who Grunches and an evil witch wannabe had brainwashed, he was glad all these monsters were locked up and away from the public.

The room started to dim again the further they went. Empty cages and tubes dotted the walls until they came to a slim tube in the darkest corner.

"This is what I wanted to show you," Elvi said, stopping a few feet before the tube. Swirling inside was some sort of glistening purple-black smoke.

"What is it?"

"Black magic in its purest form," Elvi said wistfully. "This tube is enchanted with a powerful barrier spell that requires the caster to be alive, present, and nearby at all times to function properly. That kind of spell wears a person down."

Porter eyed Elvi with a questioning look.

"The peace pipe, what do you know of it?" she asked, never glancing his way. The way she looked at the black magic writhing before them scared him. There was admiration, even love, in her eyes. But beneath that, he could sense resentment. She had a personal connection to it.

Porter shivered. "Not much. Why?"

Elvi finally turned to look at him. "It has the ability to contain immense amounts of power. We believe it is the only thing that can truly contain this kind of volatile magic. As well as the person who created such a monstrosity."

"Which is why you're here," Porter said slowly, trying to connect all the dots. "Where does Ashton fit in?"

Elvi's eyes twitched. "Kohen is well-versed in Indigenous lore. He and I had a fascinating conversation when I started poking around the historical society, which Ashton overheard. Ashton stole the pipe. We knew he had it, but he refused to give it up. We knew in his hands something terrible was bound to happen, but this whole thing has been blown out of proportion. In ways you couldn't even dream of," Elvi sighed.

"Okay. . . If you know who we are—which you obviously do—why didn't you just tell Della all this?" Porter asked. "If she understood, she would jump at the opportunity to help. That's kind of what she does."

Elvi sighed heavily, daring a step toward the black magic. "I'm not supposed to tell her."

"Who said?"

"Kohen."

Something bubbled up in Porter he couldn't quite explain. He had an awful feeling that the next words out of Elvi's mouth would change a lot of things.

"What exactly does Kohen know?"

"Way more than he should."

Why would Kohen want to keep all this from Della? They seemed so close. He trusted her enough to ask for her help and even trusted her companions enough to poke around the station. So, was he just trying to protect her, or was something else going on?

"The peace pipe held the spirit of a deranged shaman," Elvi said, spinning on her heels. The purple-black magic spun in a maelstrom-like vortex, outlining her in mystery. "But that wasn't the only thing trapped inside. And I'll tell you this: that shaman isn't the one wreaking havoc on the town."

"What's that supposed to mean?" Porter asked haughtily. "What does any of this mean?"

Elvi looked sympathetic, but she said nothing. Instead, she led him back to the cotton candy machine in silence. Again, she poured sugar into the machine, using pink instead of blue. Soon, they were back in her penthouse-adjacent hotel room.

Porter felt sick to his stomach. He wanted desperately to blame it on motion sickness but knew that wasn't the cause.

"I'd appreciate it if you relay what you've learned to Miss Coleman," Elvi said.

With a deep breath, she crossed to the mini bar, hovering behind it as if afraid. She stood there for so long that Porter wondered if she would ever follow through with whatever she had meant to do. Eventually, she pulled open a drawer, taking out a large gold envelope. She tapped it nervously a few times, then came back to stand before her puzzled guest.

"Please know this is above my pay grade," she said, handing the envelope over, leaving Porter even more confused.

Elvi returned to the glass table, crossing her ankles daintily as she sat.

"You and I are on the same side, Porter," she said quietly.

"I'm not following,"

"Just look at it," she pleaded, staring him down. "You wouldn't believe me otherwise."

Against his better judgment, he ripped into the file, finding a thick stack of papers inside. Each paper was embossed with the same crest and a swirling script that read *P.O.I. Project*. Besides that familiar mark, the contents of the documents were different. A handful of the front ones were forms filled out in neat handwriting.

On top was a form about Max. Every section was filled out detailing everything from his appearance to his powers and species, past transgressions, and beyond. Every magical being they knew had a dedicated page.

"What is this?" Porter snapped, shoving the papers back into the envelope.

"A peace offering," Elvi said, an air of sass to her tone.

"What the Hell is the *P.O.I. Project*?" Porter demanded.

"Ask our founder," Elvi said nonchalantly, picking up her wine glass.

"And how am I supposed to find whoever that is?"

Elvi smiled. "It should be pretty easy. You're smarter than you pretend to be. Wisdom comes from reading books, doesn't it?"

Porter made for the door, shaking his head in disdain and disbelief. Again, he felt way out of his league.

"And Porter?" Elvi called, stopping him before he could slam the door shut. "P.O.I.is prepared to use force to take that peace pipe. It is in your best interest this does not happen."

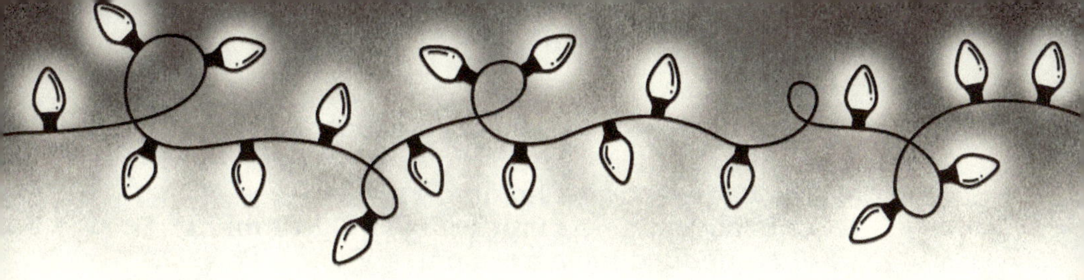

CHAPTER FIFTY

Infamy

Della and Max had dragged their shivering bodies back inside to find Sebastian, and Arlo had procured an array of snacks. Della figured they'd raided Kohen's mini fridge, which would only end in trouble. However, she was starving. Kohen could stand to share. The four of them were now sitting quietly on the floor, trading candy bars, oranges, yogurts, and bags of chips like school kids.

Everyone was exhausted. Too exhausted to listen to all the adults argue over each other about what to do about Della. Thank God she wasn't bleeding out. If that were the case—seeing how they handled problems—Della was sure she would've been dead by now.

"Still no word from Porter?" Sebastian asked. He was sitting on Della's right, peeling an orange for Arlo.

Max shook his head. "Tried his cell a few times. Ei'm sure he's just blowin' off steam."

Della grimaced. The last thing she wanted to discuss was Porter.

"You know what sounds really good?" Sebastian asked, handing over Arlo's orange. Arlo graciously accepted, trading him a half-eaten donut. "Those little chocolate-covered orange things Poppy always puts in your stocking."

"I can't believe you actually like those things, Seb," Della said with a wrinkled nose.

"It is baffling how many foods humans have covered in chocolate," Arlo laughed. "Though after tonight, I wish to try them all."

"You're my kind of guy, Arlo," Sebastian smiled.

Arlo gave him a funny look, most likely wondering what that meant and if it was a good thing.

"Hey, kids," came Kohen's voice. He sauntered up to them, kneeling, taking a *Twinkie* out of Della's hands.

"Hey!"

"Technically, these are stolen goods, so I'm just returning them to their owner," he said, sticking out his tongue. "How are you four holding up?"

The consensus was muttering and grumbling.

Kohen nodded his agreement. "Where's Porter?"

"We don't know where he disappeared to," Arlo offered.

Kohen turned to him, looking confused. "I'm so sorry. I don't think we've had a chance to meet. What's your name, young man?"

Arlo cleared his throat. "Arlo Cole—" Della shook her head wildly, mouthing 'McGregor.' Arlo gave her a questioning look.

Kohen turned to Della, who immediately smiled, feigning innocence. His eyebrows furrowed, but he turned back to Arlo expectantly. Della gave him a stern look behind Kohen's back, continuing to mouth 'McGregor.'

"M—Mick?" Arlo said slowly.

"You forget your name, kid?"

"He has major anxiety," Sebastian said through a mouthful of donut. "He's my cousin. Visiting from out of town."

"I see," Kohen said, seemingly satisfied. "Arlo Mick, you say?"

"Yes, sir."

"Nice to meet you, Mr. Mick."

Arlo nodded, dropping his eyes to the floor, focusing on his orange.

Max pinched the bridge of his nose, shaking his head in disbelief.

"Well, that was. . . enlightening?" Kohen asked, turning his attention back to Della. "Mind if I steal you?"

Della shrugged, taking Kohen's hand as he led her away from the safety of her friends. They ducked into an empty office, Kohen closing the door behind them.

He turned back to her with a soft smile, placing his hands on her shoulders. "Do you have any idea what kind of panic you caused?"

"The panicky kind?" Della asked.

Kohen leaned down to her eye level, giving her a parental sort of look. "Very funny," he sighed. "You okay?"

She shrugged. "Been better."

"I'm going to need you to be more specific."

Della sighed heavily, crossing her arms and tapping her foot nervously. "I've already had my once over by your lackeys. Hell, you even called an ambulance. I'm fine, big bear."

Kohen ruffled her hair, taking a step back. "You feeling up to talk to Ashton? He won't shut up about you. I think you have a fan," he chuckled.

"Are pigs flying? Because you've asked for my help way too many times lately."

"We can go check in the morning if you like."

With that, he led her to the small room where they were holding Ashton. Her visions, combined with what Max and Porter had heard in Ash's tapes, had planted doubt in Della's mind. Why did it have to be Kohen? Why couldn't it have been someone else? Literally anyone else.

Kohen opened the door to the small room where Ashton John was handcuffed to a table. His eyes were bloodshot, his face covered in bruises. Della wondered what had happened to him and if he'd ever tell them.

"Hey, Ash," she said softly, sitting in the chair across from him. Kohen stood behind her, arms crossed. Seeing as she'd been in a similar situation not long ago, she knew she had to handle this delicately.

"I'm not talking with *him* here," Ashton spat, turning away.

"This is our compromise, Ash. Take it or leave it. I'm not leaving her alone in here with you," Kohen said sternly, though not unkindly.

Ashton thought for a long while, anxiously tapping his fingers on the table. "I've changed my mind. I don't want to talk."

Kohen groaned behind Della.

"Why don't you want to talk in front of him, Ash?" she asked, genuinely concerned.

Ashton glanced at her, then at Kohen, and scoffed.

This was more than just Ashton being afraid of arrest. Hell, he was already in cuffs. This had to do with what she'd seen in his trailer.

"Kohen," she began, turning to him. "Why were you at Ashton's trailer before he disappeared?"

Kohen straightened. "I wasn't."

"Yes, you were!" Ashton snapped, banging his hands on the table. "You were there when it happened! It's all your fault!"

"When what happened, Ash?" Della asked.

"Don't listen to a damn word he says. He's obviously high as a kite and—"

"What happened with the peace pipe?" Della asked, dropping her voice.

Ashton trembled, shaking his head wildly. "It's not about the pipe anymore," he shivered. "You wouldn't believe me."

"Tell me," Della pleaded. "I can help, I promise."

He glanced at Kohen, then back at her, searching her eyes. He'd written to her for a reason. Some part of him knew she could help. All he had to do was get out of his own way.

"He's alive," Ashton said shakily. "That's why she wants it. Don't let her have it, she—she can't have it. Don't trust her. She's one of them."

"Who's alive? Who shouldn't I trust? One of who?" Della asked. She suspected the 'she' was Elvi, but other than that, she was utterly lost.

"Them!" Ashton hissed, pointing up to the sky. "They're everywhere."

Della furrowed her eyebrows, glancing over her shoulder to find Kohen glaring at the floor. "Care to add?"

He glared at her but said nothing.

Della inhaled deeply, swiveling back around to Ashton, who was muttering about government probes and listening devices. Was this what people saw when they heard her and Mavericks ramble on?

"Ashton. I need you to focus, okay? Can you tell me anything else? Anything at all?" Della asked, reaching forward to grab his hands. She squeezed them reassuringly, giving him her best apologetic smile.

Crazed tears were welling up in his eyes. "The Courier. I heard her talking to someone about The Courier. About you."

Della's smile dropped. "When?"

"Halloween," Ashton muttered the word like it was a curse.

"What did she say, Ash?"

"I think that—" Kohen began.

Ashton leaned in close, eyes full of crazed terror. He smelled of smoke and alcohol, but Della knew none of his craze came from any Godforsaken substance.

"They want you dead, Coleman," he whispered. "They know what you can do. *I* know what you can do."

Kohen cleared his throat. "Ashton—"

"Who, Ash? You have to give me more than that," Della said, searching his eyes for anything hidden beneath his fright.

"We're done here," Kohen snapped.

Ashton grabbed Della by the collar, spraying spit all over her face as he spoke. "He's alive, Coleman. It all ties back to the two of you. You don't understand. It's bigger than just stories. Theodore—"

"I said that's enough!" Kohen roared, yanking Della out of her seat and shoving her behind him. She collided with the wall painfully, her heart hammering alive.

"Theo's alive?" Della choked out.

"No! You're not listening—" Ashton screamed, standing, slamming his cuffed hands down on the table.

Kohen's hand was resting on his holster. "Calm yourself down, Ash."

He turned on his heels, grabbed Della by the collar, and dragged her into the hall. Neither of them could walk straight due to how bad they were shaking.

"If you know something, I need you to spill it. Now," Della whisper-yelled, shoving him away.

Kohen stuttered, gesturing wildly, unintelligible words flying out of his mouth.

"Kohen! This is serious!" Della hissed. "Theodore was—"

"You don't know shit about Theodore Heiser," Kohen spat, stabbing his finger into her chest.

Della stared at him with morbid awe, feeling like a caged animal. For the first time, she realized just how in over her head she was.

"You really think I was going to let you run off to Louisiana and not keep tabs on you?" Kohen shouted. "How the Hell do you end up in situations like this? You're eighteen years old. You're supposed to be a kid, not getting tangled up with government conspiracies."

"What the frick are you talking about?" Della snapped.

Kohen's hands dropped to his side as he stared at her. His eyes were full of fire, his lips set in a deep frown. He swore heavily, taking her by the elbow. They walked silently until they were outside the precinct, standing on the sidewalk.

The sun was beginning to rise, gentle rays of sunlight illuminating the freshly fallen snow. Sycamore Heights glistened like a diamond in the daylight. Della hated it.

"How much do you know?" Kohen asked, hands on his hips as he stared down at her.

"About what?"

Kohen gave her a bored look. "Astrophysics, genius."

"Wiseacre," Della snapped. "What do you know? What do you mean by 'government conspiracies?' How do you know about Theodore?"

"Theodore Heiser wasn't who he said he was. Neither was his brother, who, coincidently, wasn't even his brother. Their real names were Lazarus Everton and Enos Gunthrie, respectively. They were moles planted in Moss Hollow to live amongst beings like you," Kohen explained, looking her dead in the eyes as he spoke.

"Theo—L—Lazarus, I mean, said he grew up in Moss Hollow. Maybe you have the wrong guys?" Della asked breathlessly.

All this time, she'd known there were loose ends.

However, she didn't think those loose ends would be false identities.

"When Quincy left, I knew I needed to keep an eye on him," Kohen began.

"Kohen—"

"Just listen," he snapped. "Isn't that what you're good at?"

Della inhaled deeply, nodding.

"He was a roadie for a while, hooked up with a few bands. Ended up playing a show under the name Leland Kitchi at a restaurant called *Bayou Gil's Crab Emporium* in Moss Hollow. That name rang a bell, and I couldn't figure out why until you showed up to the reservation one day with one of those Utopian Courier newspapers," Kohen cleared his throat, shifting uncomfortably. "The two of you always had a penchant for weird things. I figured it wasn't a coincidence he ended up there.

I knew I could never get him to come home, but I could do all I could to protect him from here. I dug into the history of that town and found out all sorts of stuff. Hell, I even subscribed to *The Utopian Courier*. That whole town is a magnet for weird things, Della."

"Preaching to the choir, Kohen," she sighed.

"I, I know. I read your article. Good job, by the way. I'm proud of you," he smiled, glancing at her from the corner of his eye. She knew he meant it.

"Can we get back to the 'government conspiracies?'"

He laughed darkly, shrugging. "Quincy wound up writing for the Courier, too, under his stage name. He was featured in every issue. He traveled the world. London, Moscow, Zimbabwe—anywhere with a story. Everything he wrote seemed to have a tie-in. He was looking for something, a place he wouldn't name. All the monsters he wrote about, all the people he helped, they were all just happenstance. Every couple of issues, he mentioned an L.E. and how this mysterious person was helping him and his boss track down the biggest story of our decade.

Toward the end, his name was slowly pulled from the Courier. His last article was cryptic. I'm surprised it got published. There were hidden messages, but I couldn't make sense of them. A few months passed, and he hadn't written. I knew his address, so I sent him a letter. It was sent back, and inside was a printed note that read, 'Stop while you're ahead, Mr. Kitchi.'"

He let those words hang in the frigid air as Della stared at him. She wanted to be angry with him. How dare he keep this from her. How dare he know all this without telling their parents. Della could've had an address to send letters to all this time. She could've been in contact with Quincy until the day he disappeared. Della knew Kohen had only wanted to protect them both, but knowing this now felt like a bullet to the heart.

"I wrote to the Courier and asked why Leland Kitchi hadn't written anything as of late. A man named Percival James Mavericks responded, saying he'd left the Courier to pursue another line of work, but I wasn't convinced. So, I wrote to Ambrose Apartments, where he'd been staying, and they said he'd moved out. Quin vanished, Della. Without a trace," Kohen sighed heavily. "I've spent so many sleepless nights trying to figure out what happened to him and where he disappeared to. All I've found are stories that should've died with Lazarus and Enos."

"What kind of stories?" Della asked quietly, a dangerous edge to her voice.

Kohen's nostrils flared as he ran a hand through his hair. "I stumbled upon a forum created by a bunch of Courier fans. I figured asking them was the best bet. They didn't know what had happened to Quin, but one of them had unscrambled the hidden message in his letter. 'He betrayed us. I am left with such hopelessness. How can I protect her now? He won't let me.' That's what he'd written."

Della couldn't help but feel he'd been writing about her.

"I must've read through that whole forum hundreds of times. Mavericks wrote an old issue way back. He mentioned that same L.E. character. That article was vague but loosely aligned with what had happened with Theodore Heiser. I asked about that, but no one had an answer. I dug and dug and dug until there was nothing left to dig at. Years went by." He turned to look at her, smiling darkly. "Until a certain girl with neon-green hair published a story with the Courier."

"If you suspected Moss Hollow to be a dangerous place, why did you let me go?"

"Kid, you didn't say goodbye. You just left. And Kimi doesn't tell me shit. I thought you were still in Washington until I got the issue with your name on the front page."

"I'm sorry," Della said softly.

Kohen shook his head, hands on his hips. "Don't be. If you hadn't written that article, I wouldn't have logged back on to that forum to see I'd received a private message."

"From who?"

"Someone claiming to know who L.E. was," Kohen said. "They had irrefutable evidence that Lazarus Everton was Theodore Heiser and that he and Enos were planted in Moss Hollow to keep tabs on Mavericks."

"By the government?"

"By an offshoot."

"How do you know this person is telling the truth?"

"Because her grandpa put them on the case. Her family has been working for that same offshoot for generations." He gave her a knowing look, eyes full of hope.

"Elvi," Della breathed, her heart fluttering.

She shivered. That overwhelming urge to run as fast as she could and never look back returned. She was caught in the crosshairs of something she felt she'd never understand.

Kohen nodded. "Bingo."

"So, what? The two of you have been working on finding Quincy?"

"That's how it started. What all do you know about the—the ghost?" he stuttered, shivering.

"Enough."

Kohen thought for a moment, leaning back on his heels, arms crossed. His face had darkened tenfold. "I need to tell you something, and I need you not to freak out, okay?"

Della narrowed her eyes. "What did you do?"

"I didn't do anything, I swear!"

"Kohen."

He grumbled to himself, burying his face in his hands. "You kids make my life so difficult, you know that? God, why can't our family be normal?" He sighed, running his hands through his hair, looking at her through his eyebrows. "I've been trying to put the pieces together, but from what I've gathered, Jasper and Kimi did something that screwed you up as a child. I think that's why Quincy left in the first place."

"Wow. Really? Damn, what a revelation," Della said dryly.

"Delphee."

She rolled her eyes. "You're going to have to be way more specific, Kohen, because I can name about twenty things off the top of my head that majorly screwed me—and Quincy, for that matter—up."

"It's not like I can go up to them and ask, all right? I'm flying blind here," Kohen said earnestly. "Other than that, I know the peace pipe has bad mumbo jumbo trapped inside it. Or I guess it *had* something trapped in it," Kohen sighed.

"I know more than that, and I've been here for what, a week at the most?" Della said, wrinkling her nose.

"I know, I know. I was preoccupied with the whole Quincy thing. I'm a shitty deputy and an even shittier uncle. At least I'm not the one who smoked out of a peace pipe. Ash doing drugs literally brought on the end of the world."

"While I'd love to see that headline in the tabloids, he didn't smoke out of it," Della laughed.

Kohen smiled his goofy smile, turning so they stood shoulder to shoulder, staring at the sunrise.

"Damn, Della. I'm so sorry," he said, sounding wistful.

"What for?"

"For not believing you when you were little. For not telling you any of this," Kohen admitted. "All this time, the things you believed in so fervently were real, and even I thought you were crazy at times. And I had Mingan and Winifred as parents."

Della shrugged. "I don't blame you."

"Are you safe there?" he asked. "At the Courier, I mean. Even though they might've made Quincy disappear, nothing on the forum or in any issue makes me believe they're evil. I just—I just want you to be safe."

Della could never lie to Kohen. Since Quincy left, he'd been the closest thing she'd had to an older brother. Sometimes, he was the closest thing she'd had to a parent.

"I don't know, Kohen. But I like it there. I have friends now. I have a family," she said, looking at him sideways.

"I'm happy for you kid."

"Thank you," Della whispered. Again, she knew he meant it.

All of this was incredibly screwed up, but she trusted Mavericks and Moss Hollow. No, not trust; she had faith. Mavericks was a protector, just like her. They were cut from the same cloth. In her heart, she knew Mavericks loved everyone who worked for him like they were his children. He wouldn't have let anything happen to Quincy willingly. There was more to the story, and when she got home, she would weasel it all out of him.

But for now, she had Sycamore Heights to protect.

"Ash seems to know all this," she said, looking over her shoulder at the precinct.

Kohen nodded. "He overheard some stuff."

"We need to figure out what happened to him while he was—"

"DELLA!" That blood-curdling scream was Porter.

She turned to see him running at her full speed, looking terrified. He was running so fast that he barely had enough time to stop before plowing her over. He grabbed her by the sleeve, yanking her away from Kohen.

"Porter, what the Hell?" Della screeched, shaking free from his grip.

Porter was panting heavily. He had to take a moment to catch his breath before he could respond. "I—have—critical information," he coughed out, yet again grabbing Della by the sleeve and pulling her toward the precinct. "You too," he said over his shoulder, pointing at Kohen. "I know you know that we know."

"You people have got to stop saying things like that. All you do is confuse me," he said but followed them inside.

Porter beckoned Max and the others to follow, leading them all to Kohen's office, slamming the door shut so hard picture frames fell off the wall.

"Dude, what's the matter with you?" Sebastian asked, stopping him before he could shut the blinds on the windows looking out into the rest of the precinct.

Porter pried himself away from Sebastian, shutting the blinds and locking the door. "I just had an incredibly interesting conversation with Elvi," he said breathlessly.

"Why?" Max asked suspiciously, giving him an I-know-what-you-did look. "Ei thought we all agreed we don' trust her as far as we can throw her."

Porter ignored his scathing expression as he reached into his jacket, revealing a golden envelope. He handed it to Della, looking crazed like Ashton had.

"It's so much worse than that, Max."

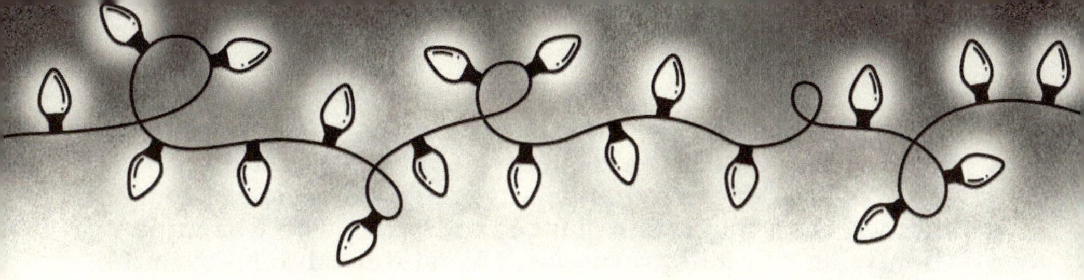

CHAPTER FIFTY-ONE

Super Sleuthin'

Della took the files out of their envelope with shaking hands, carefully reading through each before handing the pages off to someone else in the group. This was so incredibly messed up. No one should have this kind of information on anyone. Magical or not.

She remembered Porter saying there were other people like him in Moss Hollow who didn't fit the witch, werewolf, or vampire box—but she hadn't realized how many there were. According to these files, there was even a necromancer in good old Moss Hollow. Not that it surprised her. Of course, there had to be someone raising the dead when they weren't working their dead-beat job.

Utterly insane.

If someone had access to these files and the means, they definitely could find the perfect way to harm everyone listed.

The very last file in the envelope was about Mavericks. Della knew this was possibly the biggest invasion of privacy, but she couldn't help but scan the pages out of curiosity.

Immediately, she regretted that decision.

What she read under the column that said species made her heart somersault.

"The butterfly man," Della breathed, a flicker of a memory igniting in her mind. She stumbled, her mind buzzing, pain searing through the side of her head.

As quickly as the pain came, it was gone.

"What?" Max asked over her shoulder, steadying her.

Della shook her head violently, her vision swirling as she shoved the paper back inside its envelope, trying to calm herself.

Mamankanois.

Butterfly.

Now she knew why that word was so important.

Why was Mavericks entwined with everything?

"This doesn't change anything," she said, more to herself than them. She glanced at Porter, who was impatiently awaiting her response. "We still need to figure out what's going on with Ahiga—I mean the *spirit*. Sorry, Arlo," Arlo huffed and puffed but seemed to accept her apology. "We can deal with this at a later date."

"Is everything okay. . . ?" Kohen asked, handing over a file. "You. . . look like you've seen a ghost," he smirked.

Everyone seemed to hate that joke, seeing as they collectively groaned.

Arlo was side-eyeing her, but Della couldn't tell if he was worried for her or just intrigued by the sudden change in atmosphere.

"It does change things," Porter said. "This company is not just a small group of freedom fighters or something. They have an entire secret base somewhere in the middle of the ocean! Elvi says they want that peace pipe and are prepared to take it forcefully."

"She let you see the base?" Kohen asked, looking both hurt and concerned.

"Let them come. They aren't getting it," Sebastian shrugged.

"Della," Porter's eyes flashed gold. "They have an entire wing dedicated to traps, cages, tubes, and cells. Almost all of them have something inside. From mermaids to—"

"Do they have a unicorn?" Sebastian asked flatly.

"Yes!" Porter said, throwing his hands up in the air. "More than one."

"Ei really think yer gettin' too worked up over this right now, Porter," Max sighed.

Kohen opened his mouth to say something, but Della shook her head. She didn't think Porter could live through the shock if they knew what Kohen had just told her.

"It's not just Arlo's crappy brother, Max," Porter screeched. "That's why I'm worked up."

"I'm so lost right now. You have no idea," Sebastian said. Kohen nodded in agreement, looking back and forth between Della and Porter expectantly.

Arlo cleared his throat, curling in on himself. "It is my brother," he began, "but it's also you," he sighed, turning to Della.

Kohen's office fell eerily silent as every head turned to look at her.

"What—What do you mean?" Della asked.

Arlo placed a hand over her heart. "You. . . are not

whole," he said.

Della had known that for a long time. But hearing someone else say it, especially in this context, felt odd.

"Now, I might be new to all of this, but I'm not exactly an idiot, so I'm going to go out on a limb here and ask what we all are thinking: Are you saying that whatever has been happening around town has to do with Della?" Kohen asked. Though it was a valid question, Della knew he was rambling to save himself from spiraling.

Arlo only nodded.

"Makes sense," Kohen shrugged, his face darkening.

"In what way?"

Kohen almost laughed. "Everyone from the O'Malley twins to Patricia Durnell has been having problems. Aka, all the people who hate Della's guts."

Alarm lit up Porter's face as Max pinched the bridge of his nose. "I knew there was something we forgot to tell you."

"But Della has been gone for months," Sebastian pointed out. "How could any of this be her fault?"

Arlo rolled his eyes, pointing to Della's head. "She is not whole. She is broken." He turned to Max for help. "You feel it, too. You are her spirit animal, are you not?"

Della immediately spun to look at Max, whose eyes were the size of dinner plates. "You're my what?" she asked.

"That's a subject for a different time," Max said, his face reddening.

"I think that time is now, Maximilian," Della pressed.

"Listen, yer mind is broken, and apparently, that's causin' a bunch of issues. How about we focus on that, hmm?"

"How do we fix this, Arlo?" Kohen asked, donning his overprotective tone like a shield.

Arlo momentarily rocked back and forth on his heels, chewing his lip as he thought. "You would need to separate my brother's spirit from whatever part of Della is entwined with him. That's what I believe is happening, at least. Then we would need to reconnect Della with the part of herself that has been lost."

"And how do we do that?" Sebastian and Kohen asked.

"We need tuh hold a séance," Max groaned. "And then, of course, perform a controlled possession of sorts."

Della couldn't decide if her world was falling apart or if all the answers to her impending problems had been handed to her on a silver platter.

"What if we didn't have to? Hold a séance, I mean," Porter thought out loud. Everyone turned toward him, causing him to blush. "Kohen mentioned a bunch of people had been affected by this. If we follow the patterns, we can catch him—er—you? Them?" When no one corrected him, he continued. "We can catch them by surprise. They'd know what was happening if we tried to summon them or hold a séance."

Della thought for a moment, working out the details in her head. That might work.

"Pastor Clay on that list?" she asked, leaning toward Kohen.

"Yup."

Della inhaled sharply. "Who isn't?"

Kohen shifted uncomfortably. "Anyone with the last name Coleman, Bennet, Hawthorne, or Kitchi."

"Crap," Della mumbled.

"But," Kohen said excitedly. "They'll all be at Poppy's 'Pre-Christmas' Christmas Party' the day after tomorrow. Or—er—I guess just tomorrow. Anyway, it'll be like one big target."

"I was really hoping to avoid that."

"Kid, I'd be more afraid of skipping out on Poppy than a few ghosts."

~ ~ ~

Kohen had convinced Kimi and Jasper to go home not long after sunrise. He promised to take Della to the hospital and get her checked out, but instead, he and Porter drove everyone back to Mingan's.

The merry misfits crowded around Mingan's kitchen table, watching Della scribble away on the whiteboard next to his fridge. They had less than twenty-four hours to make a plan and figure out how to stick to it if something went wrong.

"We'll need somethin' tuh trap Ahiga's spirit in. Somethin' better than a peace pipe, no offense," Max said.

"Oh, trust me, there were so many flaws with trapping a spirit in a pipe, you have no idea. I'm surprised this hadn't happened sooner," Kohen laughed.

"Freaking Ashton," Della sighed.

"What do you need? We have an old antique store that probably has something that'd work. I can run down and pick something up," Sebastian offered.

"It would need tuh be somethin' imbued with magic," Max yawned.

"Trust me, Hugo and Enid will have us covered," Della smiled.

"We can try, but we'd need somethin' with a massive

amount of magical energy. We'd have better luck trans-formin' the peace pipe somehow rather than tryin' tuh make somethin' new."

"Oh! Della can do that!" Arlo said excitedly.

"How?"

"I can teach you," Arlo said, puffing out his chest in pride.

"Okay, so containment is my job, but let's try and get something from *Sun & Star* just in case," Della said, writing that down on the board. "Are you sure you don't want to try and reason with him?" she said, directing her question and a sympathetic look toward Arlo.

Arlo shook his head. "There is no reasoning with a. . ." He looked to Sebastian.

"Lunatic," he finished. Arlo nodded.

Their immediate friendship was strange yet beautiful.

"Right. No reasoning with a lunatic," Arlo muttered.

He looked beyond miserable. His brother's spirit was haunting an entire town, wreaking havoc on anyone who had wronged his oldest friend. On top of that, he'd just been thrown into a world Della was sure he had been trying to avoid for years. After all, why had he stayed in the forest for so long? If he hated that old cave so much, why hadn't he just left?

Della's mind buzzed with the memory of her father attacking him many moons ago. Her vision swirled, every-thing going dark, her head splitting with pain. She stum-bled backward, colliding with a chair. Her heart was pound-ing as she steadied herself against the table.

"Della?" came Sebastian's soft voice.

"I'm fine," she said quickly, pinching the bridge of her nose.

"You are bleeding again," Arlo said, appearing beside her, his hand hovering over her shoulder.

Della turned to him, slowly reaching up to wipe a trickle of blood away from her upper lip. "Normal at this point."

Arlo shook his head sadly, returning to his spot at the table.

Della removed her glasses and leaned against the kitchen counter.

"You sure you don't want to go to the ER?" Kohen asked.

"I don't have the money for medical bills nor the time to deal with the doctors," she sighed.

After a moment of tense silence, Kohen cleared his throat.

"What about the *P.O.I. Project* problem? What happens if they grab one of you thinking you have the pipe?" he asked. "Elvi made it sound like these guys are bad news." He gave Della a look that roughly translated into, 'I don't trust her, but I trust that.'

"We need to protect ourselves and the pipe, for sure. But keep in mind we have to do all this without exposing the general public to magic," Porter warned.

Max nodded his agreement. "We should put sensors up in Poppy's house. We can rig up the hearse with a few gizmos and have someone stationed out there monitorin' everythin'."

"I'll slip out after presents," Sebastian said. "Porter and I can go set up the sensors. Poppy seems to have a soft spot for us," he added with a cheeky laugh.

Porter begrudgingly agreed. "And after we regroup, I'm teaching you how to shoot a gun."

Sebastian's eyes sparkled with delight. "Really?"

"As much as I hate to say it, yes. I'm not leaving you without a way to protect yourself."

Della wrote their roles on the board, smiling. She loved how well thought out and cemented this plan was. Before her sat her dream team.

"I think we have quite the plan," Kohen said, gesturing loosely at the whiteboard. "But what if the spirit disappears after we confront it?"

"If worst comes to worst, Ei'm prepared tuh do a summonin' spell," Max sighed.

"Max is a wizard," Sebastian whispered.

"Witch," Max corrected.

Kohen seemed vaguely impressed. "I'm sure you guys are tired of my questions, but if Max is our spellcaster, Sebastian is preoccupied in the hearse, and Della is meant to just sit there and wait for half her soul, who will have the spirit channeled into them? Max said something about a controlled possession," Kohen said, a strange look on his face.

"I can't. I'm already a spirit. Technically," Arlo shrugged.

"I don't do possessions," Porter said quickly.

"So, I guess that just leaves me, huh?" Kohen laughed. Della wanted to protest him being possessed by Ahiga, but seeing as everyone else already had a role, this was his.

"We have a good start to the plan. For now, let's start gathering the things we need. If anyone thinks of something, please don't hesitate to speak up," Della announced, capping her dry-erase marker. "Go, team, go."

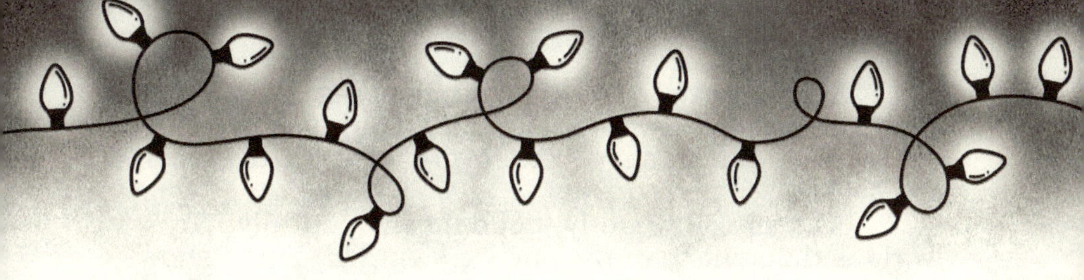

CHAPTER FIFTY-TWO

Learned Behaviors

Max led Porter and Sebastian out to the hearse, opening the back to reveal all the excess supernatural junk he'd brought. Kohen hovered nearby, watching from a respectful distance.

"How much stuff did you pack, Max?" Porter asked in horrified awe.

"Ya can never be too prepared," he said as he rifled through his bags, handing over a handful of sensors and miniature microphones. "Set these up wherever. When we head over tomorrow, Ei'll connect them tuh the server. Ei'll get ya each an EMF meter before that."

"Sounds good," Porter said. "Call us if anything happens."

"Will do."

"Seriously, Max," Kohen said. "Let's all keep in mind that Della is our number one priority."

That they knew for sure.

Max had almost lost her twice. He wasn't keen on going through that again.

"Side note," Kohen began, clearing his throat nervously. "What if we can't separate Arlo's brother's spirit and Della's magic or whatever?"

Max had been thinking about that, too.

"Let's just hope it doesn' come tuh that."

~ ~ ~

Della had been in the kitchen helping Mingan fix breakfast when Max returned after the others had left.

"That went surprisin'ly well," he said, taking the plate of French toast Della had offered him as they made for the living room.

Della snorted her approval, plopping down onto the couch next to Arlo, who was intently staring at the TV.

"Did Mingan show you how to work the television?" she asked.

Arlo smiled brightly, nodding energetically. "This world is different than the one I grew up in. These shows, as you call them, are intriguing. I am quite fond of the tele-vis-ion. Does everyone have one?"

Della shrugged. "After you teach me more about my dreamwalker powers, I'll show you more modern-day mar-vels. Deal?"

Della had been wandering in the dark for most of her life without a guiding light. Having Arlo here, having a teacher, was such a wonderful feeling. If anyone could an-swer her burning questions, it'd be him.

"Deal," he smiled, holding his hand out for her to shake. "What would you like to learn first?"

"Everything," Della admitted.

Arlo smiled to himself. He cleared his throat like a college professor would before beginning his lecture.

"When I was taught to use my powers, I had to make a lot of mistakes to find what worked for me. The first thing I did was figure out what emotion ruled my powers. For me, it was my fear. What is it for you?"

Della didn't need to think long to know that. "My an-ger."

Arlo nodded. "When you get angry, you lose control of the world around you. It's a turbulent emotion that, if left unchecked, is destructive. My fear was like that, too. I would end up hurting myself. I had to find a way to turn my fear into something else."

"Like happiness or something?" Della asked, sud-denly bored. He was beginning to sound like a self-help book written by someone who shouldn't be writing self-help books.

"I am trying to share my knowledge of being a dream-walker with you, and you are honestly hurting my fragile feelings," Arlo said with a humph. "No interrupting."

"Sorry," Della pouted, looking at Max, who had to stifle a laugh.

Arlo squinted at her accusingly for a moment before continuing. "Courage was what I was lacking. I didn't dare to face the world, let alone use my powers. What emotion do you think you're lacking?"

"You sound like a poet."

"Be serious, please." Arlo scowled. Della put her hands up in defense. "You need to take all that angry ener-gy and turn it into something beautiful. Transform it into a better emotion so you have the strength to believe in yourself and have control so you won't hurt anyone."

Della thought for a moment. She agreed. Anger was a dangerous emotion, and when paired with unchecked powers, it made a recipe for disaster.

"And how am I supposed to do that?" Della asked.

"Do you even know why you are mad half the time?" Arlo asked.

Della shrugged.

Arlo nodded. "Were you mad because I knew part of you was missing?"

"No, not really. But I am mad because I feel I have no say over anything happening around me. I feel like no matter what I do, everything just gets worse," Della said quietly.

She felt Max's eyes on her. It was as if he could see into her soul.

"The good thing is, with powers like yours, you *do* have complete control. The entire world bends to your will. You can turn the snow outside into starlight and back again. You can turn the trees into giant roses—anything. Della, you could create worlds. You just have to figure out how." Arlo smiled. "When you're overwhelmed, you see colors, right?"

Della nodded.

"Those colors are the essence of our world. Everything and everyone has their own color," Arlo said, searching for the right words.

"Like it's own frequency," Max added.

"I do not know that word, but okay," Arlo said with a shrug. "If you can isolate certain colors, you can start to change them, and with that, the world around you. I think Max will say, 'Change the frequency,'" Arlo said, looking around Mingan's living room. His eyes fell on a bowl where a tealight candle sat in decorative glass pebbles. He took one, scrutinized it, then handed it to her. "The colors are always around you. It's only when you start to lose control that they overwhelm you. Take a deep breath, focus on the rock, take in the colors it emits, then think of what you want it to be. It doesn't have to be much. You can just turn it into a different shape if necessary."

Della sighed heavily, holding the glass pebble out before her, taking in all the angles and sides of it, the color, the pockets of bubbles trapped inside it. She'd analyzed it enough that she figured she could describe it to a sketch artist in perfect detail if she had to. But no matter how hard she stared at it, she couldn't see any waves of psychedelic color.

"It's not working," Della said, letting her arm fall to

her lap.

"That's because yer lookin' with yer eyes, not yer mind," Max said exasperatedly. "Ya pay far too much attention tuh the world around ya, ya forget what's right in front of yer face."

Della gave him a dirty look but nodded, holding the rock tightly in her hands, shutting her eyes, and taking a big breath. Whenever Nicoletta had tried to teach her magic, she had told her to shut off her mind when casting a spell, but that hadn't worked. Maybe instead, she needed to let her mind run wild.

Instead of focusing on the world, she focused inwardly, going anywhere her mind led her.

She thought back on what happened with Eric and how she had let go and did whatever her instincts told her. She had done the same thing in the woods, too. That terrified her, but those were the only times she could control her powers.

Della's strength had always been her mind, no matter how broken it was.

She took a shaking breath, trying to absorb all the invisible color around her. When she finally breathed out, her skin began to prickle. Something ancient and electric was bubbling deep down inside.

Her eyes opened. This time, the rock was glowing an alluring silver. Della took that silver, focused on what it meant—true neutrality—and turned it into something brighter. The first color that came to mind was a deep, rich purple. Now it made sense why her eyes kept turning purple. Purple meant royalty, magic, and mystery—which was why she had always loved it. Slowly, the silver began to swirl and darken, turning a deep shade of plum as the rock grew beneath her fingers. Remembering she had to transform the pebble into something else, she focused on all her favorite purple things and picked one.

The rock grew to the size of her hand, the edges softening and rippling, splitting and morphing into the petals of a flower.

A perfect, shimmering hydrangea.

Della smiled to herself, holding it up for Arlo and Max to see.

"Holy shit," Max breathed.

When she looked up, Arlo wasn't looking at the beautiful flower in her hands, but her eyes. He was smiling widely, looking satisfied.

"Purple," he said with a nod.

"It's kind of my color."

Somehow, he smiled even wider. "Mine was orange.

When I wanted to bend the things around me, I had to change all the colors to orange. You'll do the same with purple."

When he put it like that, it didn't seem so daunting. "Do the different colors mean different things?" she asked.

He nodded. "I think you would call it an aura. Colors are like emotions; all of them are different. Some colors are harder to bend and manipulate. Was the rock silver?"

"Yeah, like neutral and easy to bend, right?"

"Yes. Most objects will be silver or white, but living things like plants, animals, and people have different ranges. If you focus on it, you won't just use the colors to bend things. It's like having a second set of eyes. You already use it with your intuition, but once you start seeing auras fully, you'll know for sure. Sometimes, even objects have colored auras. Traces of memories left behind by people. You can tap into that and see it's past."

She'd begun to pick up on that recently. Knowing that this was normal gave her a sense of peace.

And what is the opposite of anger?

Peace.

"Thank you," Della whispered.

"I am just doing what my family did for me. Something yours should've done long ago." Arlo smiled.

Della leaned forward and placed the hydrangea behind Arlo's ear. He smiled in such a childlike way. Sitting here with her and helping her seemed to be the only thing he had ever wanted to do. He looked at her like she was his little sister.

Della's heart ached at that.

"Can I ask you something?" Della asked. Arlo nodded, fingering the flower in his hair. "Do you miss your family? Or the Sycamores?"

"I miss everyone. It is lonely being immortal," Arlo sighed. "The way I try to see it is that people will leave us no matter what we do. I can spend my time thinking of that, or I can enjoy the time I have with all of you." He was very insightful for a being who had spent most of his life in a cave. "Why do you ask?"

"My older brother, Quincy, left us a couple of years ago. I did the same this fall, and sometimes I feel guilty for leaving like he did—even though I know I shouldn't. I worry about my family. Mingan, Kohen, and my siblings," Della sighed. "Max, Porter, Sebastian. *You*."

"Family is tricky. Yer stuck with people ya didn' choose, and they may get on yer nerves, but deep down, a part of ya will always love them. If ya truly are worried about them, maybe ya should tell them?" Max said, smiling sadly. "Better tuh say somethin' now than tuh wish ya would have when it's too late."

Della nodded, pulling her knees up to her chest. "Hey, I'm worried about you. There I said it."

He snickered to himself. "No need tuh be, love."

Arlo smiled at them both. "I think I like it here," he whispered.

"Me too," Max said, his face turning that lovely shade of maroon it did whenever he was trying to hide something.

Della hated to admit it, but this felt like fate. Like destiny. Sitting here with them, learning she was, in fact, in control—she knew everything had led her here for a reason. Every wrong decision, every shitty circumstance. All of it added up to his moment.

Della had always believed that everything happened for a reason. That's what the Bible, all those people on the internet with their tarot cards, Mavericks, Nicoletta—pretty much everyone—had told her.

Her own path wasn't any different. Sure, she seemed to have a little more say in the matter, but that was only by technicality. All she had to do was have a little faith and take it one step at a time.

But just like how she could turn a stone into a delicate flower, she would make the decisions for herself and not wait for someone to tell her which way to go. Nor wait for mysterious signs from the Universe.

"Arlo?" she asked, a dangerous smile on her lips.

"Yes?" he asked, looking confused.

"I think I'm ready to try transforming the peace pipe."

"Are ya sure?" Max asked. "That's like plungin' intuh the deep end after ya first learn tuh doggy paddle."

"I think she can handle it," Arlo said.

Della thought it was nice having people around who believed in her.

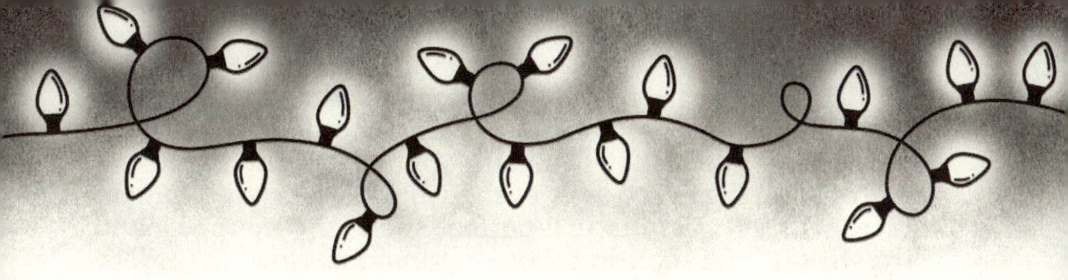

CHAPTER FIFTY-THREE

The Gift That Keeps On Giving

"**D**oes she creep you out?" Porter asked as he and Sebastian sat in the hearse, looking up at the mansion that was Poppy's home.

"In a good way," Sebastian said nonchalantly from the driver's seat. Porter had made good on their deal that if Della turned up alright, Sebastian could have the keys to the hearse until they left Sycamore Heights.

Porter raised an eyebrow. "That's weird. Even for you."

Sebastian didn't seem too bothered by that. "Is Moss Hollow's mayor living in a decked-out mansion?"

"Moss Hollow doesn't have a mayor," Porter frowned.

"Then Moss Hollow is doomed."

Porter choked out a laugh. "We do have a city council, but I'd have to agree with you. Mavericks, Max's dad, is one of the board members. If you didn't know him, you'd think he escaped the loony bin."

"Seriously?" Sebastian asked, wide-eyed.

Porter nodded. "And get this, he was voted in. And he hates it."

Sebastian just sat there in shock for a few minutes before shaking himself from his thoughts and nodding to the front door.

"Now, there are some things to remember about Poppy Hawthorne," he began. "If she mentions her ex-husband, tell her how much of a jerk he was. Don't stare at her slippers for too long. Don't touch anything that looks like it could be in a museum. If the dog doesn't like you, then you don't speak. You just don't."

"You act like she's a duchess or something," Porter said, wrinkling his nose at all the rules.

"Eh, maybe to some," Sebastian laughed.

He led Porter to the front door and knocked a few times, shivering as he looked over his shoulder. Porter followed his gaze. Snow was still falling from the night before, covering every inch of the world in a fresh blanket of ice. With all that picture-perfect snow, the house looked straight out of a painting. Porter grimaced. Now he understood why Della couldn't handle the picturesque Sycamore Heights. It was too perfect. He found himself waiting for something terrible to happen.

Just as he'd felt at Elvi's.

The door burst open, revealing Poppy wrapped in a silk dressing robe. She took one look at Sebastian, wrinkled her nose, and then swung the door open.

"What'd she get herself into this time, Breckenridge? Please tell me she didn't run off again," Poppy sighed.

"Not yet, thankfully. We're actually here to help with the party. Kohen mentioned something about the decorators not showing up?" Sebastian had turned into a gentleman. That just might have been the scariest thing Porter had ever seen.

"What do you mean w—" Poppy began but stopped when her eyes fell on Porter. Instantly, her attitude changed. She leaned on the doorframe, a devilish look in her eyes. "I remember you," she smiled, looking him up and down,

Nope. *That* was the scariest thing Porter Garroway had ever seen.

"He's almost half your age. Pull yourself together, woman," Sebastian snapped.

Poppy frowned, visibly sagging from disappointment. "Very well," she mumbled, then beckoned them inside. "I have so much to do. You have no idea how grateful I am that you boys showed up. I'll get the list I'd made for those low lives who didn't care to show their ugly faces."

When Poppy was out of earshot, Porter leaned down to whisper in Sebastian's ear. "I'm regretting letting you volunteer us."

"My thoughts exactly."

Poppy was practically jumping out of her skin with excitement when she returned. "I promise I'll make this all worthwhile. Hourly pay sound good?"

"Oh, you don't have to—"

"Of course, Poppy!" Sebastian said, sweeping her up in a big hug. "Did anyone tell you how beautiful you look today?"

"Oh, Breckenridge. You're too kind to me," Poppy laughed, ruffling his hair. She handed him the list and then pointed to the kitchen. "You boys help yourselves to whatever you please as long as it's not in a white container."

With that, she skipped upstairs, her robe fluttering behind her like the trail of a gown.

Sebastian's eyes nearly popped out of his head as he read through the list she'd given them. "Well, now I know where Della gets it from. That woman writes far too many notes."

Porter peeked over his shoulder to see an overly detailed four-page list. This was going to be a very long morning.

"I'll make coffee. You go get the sensors," Porter whispered.

The hours passed as they busied themselves decorating and hiding the sensors and mics, plugging them into any inconspicuous outlet they could find. At the end of it all, they were pleased with their handiwork. Every inch of the house was covered in glitter, tinsel, ornaments, lights, and faux gingerbread men. Poppy's house now looked like an elaborate department store display. She loved it.

"You two have to decorate for me from now on," she said, counting out a thick stash of cash for each of them.

"I'll come help with New Year's Eve if you want," Sebastian offered, dollar signs reflecting in his eyes.

"Heck yeah, you will!" Poppy laughed. "What about you, Porter?"

"Ahh, we'll probably be heading home soon. Seb can knock himself out, though. Give him my cut."

Poppy looked absolutely dejected. "You'll be coming to the party, though, right? It's the biggest event of the year. The Coleman family prides themselves on playing nicey-nicey in front of guests, y'know," Poppy winked.

"Except that one year when Cynthia and Rudolph got into it over his band," Sebastian laughed.

"Omigosh," Poppy gasped. "*Rebels In the Rose Garden*! Wasn't that the name?"

"Yup."

They laughed boisterously, leaving Porter as though he'd missed out on the world's greatest joke.

"Didn't you get a camcorder that year? Do you still have the fight on tape?"

"Okay, Poppy, no one says 'camcorder' or 'on tape' anymore, but yes, I can burn you a copy," Sebastian said, looking rather smug.

"No one says 'burn you a copy' either, Seb," Porter laughed.

Poppy giggled to herself, linking arms with them as she led them to the door.

"Thank you again for your help! Can't wait to see

you all at the pre-party! Make sure you have your gifts wrapped!" she said, humming a jolly little tune.

From the look on Sebastian's face, it was clear he hadn't had a chance to do any shopping. Porter suspected he'd have to take him shopping sometime later.

Yippee.

"Hey, Poppy?" Sebastian asked when they'd gotten to the front door. "Have you spoken with Ms. Sinclair about the historical society?"

"I did. Ms. Sinclair and I recently came to a mutually beneficial agreement," Poppy said, her voice high.

Sebastian and Porter shared a look. "You sold the historical society, didn't you?" they said in unison.

With a heavy sigh, she said, "I'm not proud of it. "I'm in over my head. I don't have the money. I can't save a dollar to save my life. Selling to Elvi is the best option we have."

"Damn," Sebastian breathed.

"What did Kimi say?" Porter asked.

"She agreed," Poppy sighed.

"Della's gonna be pissed,"

There was a sparkle in Poppy's eyes. "Maybe. I think she'll understand," she shrugged. "Make sure she's at my party, all right?"

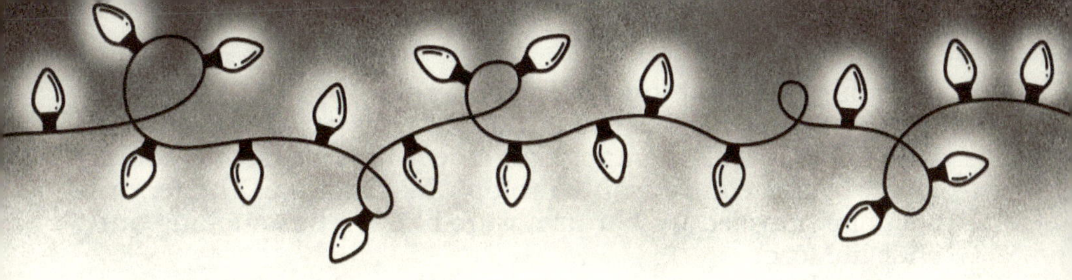

CHAPTER FIFTY-FOUR

Morph

Everyone—even Mingan and Kohen—was huddled around the table now. Della sat at the head of the table, holding the peace pipe in one hand, a half-eaten gingerbread cookie in the other.

Bless Mingan. He saw how nervous everyone had been and decided to bake cookies. Della was pretty sure she had the best grandfather in the whole wide world.

Everyone held their breath as Della finished her cookie, turning her attention to the peace pipe.

The aura surrounding the pipe burned like fire. The color closest to the pipe was a muddy brown, which faded to scarlet and finally to a mustard yellow. The anger and hatred resonating off the pipe made Della's head spin. Each time she tried plucking at the different colors, the peace pipe fought back. Waves of frustration traveled up her arms, ending with a pang in her heart.

"Don' be too hard on yerself," Max said reassuringly, taking the pipe from her hands and quickly setting it back on the table. "Just shut everythin' out. Let yer mind run wild with possibilities."

She nodded, sighing heavily, hovering her hands over the object, letting every noise and detail of the world around her melt away into the background.

As she let her senses numb, focusing only on her mind's eye, the flaming colors of the peace pipe grew brighter. The air had gone thick and humid. She could smell smoke. The pipe was fighting against her as best it could, the aura almost tangible to the physical world. Della spread her fingers, willing the aura to bleed into the air and wrap around her hands. The colors flashed and gnashed at each other. They were at war amongst themselves even more than they were at war with her. Della tried to calm them, sending out soothing waves of energy.

She could feel her mind and body straining against the effort it took to change an object that refused to comply.

All the aura wanted to do was consume. The tendrils of color traveled up her arm were like leeches sucking out her life force.

"It's not working," she said through gritted teeth.

Arlo took a deep breath, placing a shaking hand on her shoulder. "We believe in you. You are stronger than this. Deep down, you know it."

Della nodded to herself.

This inanimate object would not get the best of her.

No amount of fighting against it was going to work. Fighting her anger never worked either. Maybe she had to embrace it first, feel all those emotions in full before she could morph them into something else.

The mustard yellow edges of the aura began to sparkle as she focused on everything that had made her feel like she'd lost control.

Again, she thought of Eric Steiniger and the Grunches, how they'd ruined so many good things for her and Porter.

She thought of her fight with Porter and how her heart would always burn for him, even though she knew they would never work out in the end.

She thought of her parents and all they'd kept from her.

She thought of Quincy, how betrayed she'd felt when he'd left, and how worried she was knowing he'd been in Moss Hollow.

Hot, furious tears welled up in her eyes.

The muddy brown and yellow had disappeared. The entirety of the peace pipe's aura had turned a fiery red. It lashed at her, traveling over her arms like snakes.

It was time to let go of the anger.

It didn't serve her anymore.

It never had.

As her tears overflowed, she focused on the edges of the tendrils. Instead of forcing them into purple, she willed them to fade into shades of pink. From magenta to blush pink and finally to a silver-white like the rock had been.

With a twist of her wrist, she swirled the silver-white aura into a rich purple.

The aura wrapped itself around the pipe. All traces of anger and hatred were gone, replaced with a peace Della felt deep inside her heart.

Her mind was clear.

The pipe was finally ready to listen to her.

She thought of all the different things she could trap a spirit in. From the mechanical apparatuses often shown in movies to the witch bottles hanging from her apartment ceiling in Moss Hollow. A part of her wanted to turn the pipe into something unassuming. Just in case they couldn't destroy Ahiga. Something that you wouldn't think held such a powerful entity inside it.

But then, an idea came to mind.

Most of her trip to Sycamore Heights had been a nightmare.

And what best trapped nightmares?

A dreamcatcher.

She focused on that idea, imagining the pipe expanding into a malleable shape. The pipe followed her silent instructions, and the others watched in awe as it grew to the size of a salad plate. Before her, hovering above the table, was a pulsing bone-white blob. Della imagined what weaving patterns and adornments she'd want on the dreamcatcher. The blob separated into two circles, the second the size of a saucer. She willed the saucer-blob to become a medicine wheel dreamcatcher. A cross with the Four Sacred Directions morphed into shape inside a glowing hoop. The medicine wheel dreamcatcher connected itself to the larger hoop, which was weaving itself into a typical spiderweb pattern. The strings and outer hoops turned purple. Beads appeared on the strings, lilac, and turquoise in color. Two feathers appeared on each side of the medicine wheel.

In the center of the dreamcatcher, as if caught in the web, sat a bead in the shape of a butterfly.

When the dreamcatcher was finished, it floated down to the table, leaving Della winded. Her head felt a little dizzy, but other than that, the only adverse side effect she could feel was her lack of breath.

"Holy—" Sebastian breathed, taking the dreamcatcher into his hands, admiring it lovingly. It was perfect in every way. You know, other than the fact it was supposed to hold an evil spirit that just so happened to be one of her ancestors. "Money, Della. You could make us money."

"Dude," Porter scolded.

Della laughed, glancing at Max, who had a dark look on his face. He caught her eye and forced himself to smile.

"Nice touch," Kohen said, grabbing it from Sebastian. "All these little details represent protection and good health. Well, except for the butterfly. That represents transformation."

"Mamankanois," Della said with a smile.

Kohen's smile faltered. "What?"

Before she had a chance to reply, Porter butt in. "You

couldn't make something a little more inconspicuous?"

"Too inconspicuous, and I'd lose it," Della smirked. "Plus, it's just an insurance policy. Just in case we can't destroy the spirit, remember? If all goes well, I'll just have a cool souvenir."

Porter didn't seem to agree, but he shrugged it off anyway. His eyes lingered on her momentarily, then moved to Max, his face reddening. It only lasted a minute, but Della was sure Max glared at Porter. They stared each other down like they were communicating telepathically. Even the slightest change in expression and they would know exactly what the other was thinking.

Uh oh.

Della was about to ask what was wrong when Max stood abruptly, grabbing Porter by the collar.

"Ei need tuh talk tuh ya," he said.

With that, they disappeared into the living room.

Kohen, Sebastian, Arlo, and Mingan all busied themselves with looking at anything other than Della.

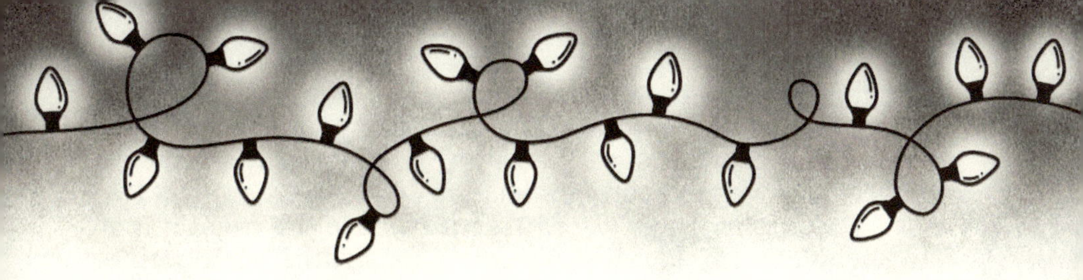

CHAPTER FIFTY-FIVE

Sharpshooter

Max and Porter sat awkwardly on the front porch shoulder to shoulder. Porter had a feeling he knew what was coming. His stomach was in his shoes as he waited for the lecture.

What surprised Porter were the words Max chose.

"Ei'm sorry," he said, his voice full of sadness. "Ei didn' mean tuh come between ya two. And Ei didn' mean for her tuh come between us."

"I know you didn't," Porter sighed, rubbing the back of his neck.

"Yer my brother, Porter. Ya always have been. Ei really don' want tuh lose ya over this. And Ei know she doesn' either."

Porter didn't want to lose them either. But how were things ever going to get back to normal? Their normal had been whatever this was since they'd met.

Maybe they all just needed to start over. Maybe they needed to find a new normal.

"You're my brother, too, Max," Porter said. Even though he meant it, it didn't sound very genuine.

They sat quietly, watching birds flit and flutter around in the gray sky. Nothing but the sound of Porter tapping his foot on the steps filled the silence.

"What are ya gonna do?"

"What?" Porter asked, whipping his head around to look at him, his eyes full of surprise.

"How are ya gonna fix things between ya two?" Max asked.

"I—I don't know," Porter admitted, the shock and surprise on his face fading to sadness and regret. "Part of me thinks I can't fix it."

Max shot him a pointed look. "Maybe ya *can't* fix

things, but ya should at least try."

Porter stared at him, his quizzical look fading to concern. "Why are you saying all this?" he asked, his voice full of worry. "I was expecting a lecture."

Max shrugged. "Because ya two are the most important people in my life. It's extremely frustratin' with both of ya at each other's throats all the time," he laughed, then looked away. "Especially when lives are on the line."

Porter knew him better than to believe that. He knew he was feeling guilty. Long ago, Max vowed never to steal anything again, but did that rule apply to hearts?

Max was wringing his hands nervously, studying Porter out of the corner of his eye.

"Ei love her, Porter," he said softly.

"I know you do."

That was the sucky part. He knew that was the truth and knew she loved him back.

Porter and Max had shared everything as kids. And when things came between them, when there was only enough for one, Max always stood back and let Porter have whatever it was.

But this was different. They'd liked the same girl many times before, but Della? Porter had never felt like this before. But he knew Max felt the same way. In fact, he knew Max's feelings were deeper than his own.

"Ei kissed her," Max blurted out, burying his head in his hands.

Porter inhaled deeply, eyes fluttering shut out of frustration. Why did he always get the shitty part of the deal? All he wanted was the kind of love you read about in fairytales. Was that too much to ask? And why did Max feel the need to tell him all this? That was a low blow.

Still, there was a teeny tiny part of him that was proud. The fact Max had actually kissed her was nothing short of a miracle.

"What do you want me to say, Max?" he eventually asked.

He shrugged. "Ei want tuh be with her. Ei—" His face reddened, a smile tugging at his lips. "Ei want tuh love her the way stars love the night. The way time loves eternity. Ei want tuh be able tuh promise her my tomorrows."

Porter blinked slowly. "Damn, you're down bad, aren't you?"

Max laughed to himself. "Ei guess so."

"The heart wants what it wants," Porter whispered.

Max nodded, his smile dropping as he ran a hand through his hair. "Ei feel guilty, though. Ei mean it, Porter, Ei don' want tuh lose ya."

"You—" Porter bit his lip hard, leg bouncing up and down rapidly. "You have my blessing if that's what you want." Not that he needed it, seeing as they'd already kissed.

"Ei really appreciate that."

Sometimes, all Porter wanted to do was be the bad guy. Playing hero, pretending to be the perfect stand-up person, was starting to get old.

"You really truly love her?" Porter asked. All Max could do was nod. Porter laughed darkly, standing. "Then don't break her heart, okay?"

"Believe me, Ei *won't*."

With a thumping heart like a lead ball inside his chest, Porter turned away.

Max's cold hand suddenly grabbed Porter's shoulder. Startled, he turned back to look at him. The look of Max's face made him redden.

"Ei smelled whiskey on yer breath earlier," he said sternly. "Ei thought we talked about that."

Porter just shrugged. "Old habits die hard, I guess."

"Porter."

"I'm fine, Max. I promise."

With that, Porter slipped back inside to find Sebastian.

~ ~ ~

"Hey. Why didn't you tell Della about the whole historical society thing?" Sebastian whispered, looking sideways at the back door to ensure no one was listening.

Porter had shoved a pistol into his hand and led him out behind Mingan's house, planting him a few feet in front of a tree.

"I'll tell her later. Doesn't seem like she needs anything else on her plate right now," Porter said, pointing to the tree. "Now shoot the tree."

Sebastian's hands shook as he pulled the trigger. Remarkably, the bullet hit the tree right where Porter had pointed. Porter stood staring, mouth hanging open.

"Oh, yeah, I probably should have mentioned I took a summer of archery. Granted, I've never tried to shoot a moving target," he said, his hands still shaking as he shot at the tree a few more times.

Porter rolled his eyes. "Bows are a lot different from guns, Sebastian."

Sebastian just shrugged. "Do you really think these *P.O.I.* folks will jump us?"

Porter nodded. "I don't trust them or Elvi one bit."

Chapter Fifty-Five

"If Elvi told you all this and gave you that file, why don't you trust her?"

"Something just feels off about this whole thing."

"Well, obviously," Sebastian said, emphasizing his words with a few well-aimed bullets at a branch blowing in the wind.

"You sure you've never had to shoot a moving target?"

"Nope," he smiled. "Y'know, we make a pretty good team. Max has his spells, Della has. . . whatever she has, we have our guns and your super strength, and Arlo is a Hell beast—"

"Wendigo."

"Whatever."

"You seem to be handling this all pretty well," Porter pointed out.

Sebastian shrugged. "I'd be more surprised if the lot of you *weren't* what you are," he laughed.

Porter showed him the ins and outs of the gun. How to put on the safety, how to load in another round, and even how to clean it in case Sebastian ever needed that sort of knowledge in the future.

"Can I ask you something?" Sebastian asked when they were finished. "Are you okay?"

"Yeah, I'm good."

Sebastian raised an eyebrow. "Dude, seriously."

"Really, Seb, I'm fine."

"So, you're not terrified of Della's new powers?" Sebastian asked, putting a hand on the back door before Porter could open it.

"I'm scared *for* her," Porter corrected.

"No. You're scared of what she can do. Same with Max," Sebastian sighed. "I don't blame you."

Porter scowled at him, looking him up and down. "Are *you* scared of them?"

"Not really. I know they would never do anything to hurt us on purpose. I'm scared something might happen to them, but I trust them. They are the smartest people we know," he said with a shrug. He thought for a minute, studying Porter's face. "If you have super strength, why don't you ever use it?"

Porter paled. "I haven't since—" He was about to say 'Since I killed a kid named Robbie,' but he thought better of it. "I haven't in a few years. There hasn't been a need," he lied.

"Can you, like, lift a car or something? A building? Or are you like punchy-strong?"

"You know, every time I start to like you, you say

something so incredibly stupid," Porter scowled.

"Same with you, gravedigger," Sebastian smirked, then shot at the tree without looking.

Again, he didn't miss.

"Hey, do you mind taking me Christmas shopping? In fact—" he began, causing Porter to roll his eyes, "—why don't we invite the whole gang along?"

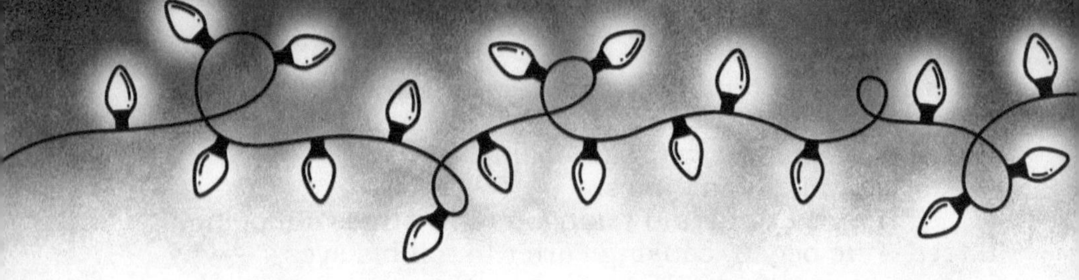

CHAPTER FIFTY-SIX

Normality

Not that she was trying to be dramatic but Della had a feeling what lay before them might be the most challenging mission they'd ever have.

Their grueling task was none other than Christmas shopping two days before Christmas Eve in a town whose prices did not reflect the average income of the residents.

Sparkling lights blinding them, holly-jolly tunes screeching in their ears, their limbs practically freezing off, the adventurers set off.

"Are we splitting up or. . . ?" Porter asked, already eyeing a bookshop. Della knew he'd walk out of there with more self-indulgent purchases than gifts.

"I mean, we have to at some point. I don't want Della guessing what I got her. Again," Kohen groaned.

Della gave him an innocent smile, prompting him to stick his tongue out.

"We also need tuh pick up a big thing of salt and go clothes shopping for Arlo," Max interjected. "He can only raid Mingan's closet for so long."

Max had found coffee within two minutes of arriving at the old yet well-kept strip mall. He currently stood behind Della, double-fisting what smelled like piping hot caramel macchiatos.

"What's wrong with Mingan's clothes?" Arlo asked, horrified, tightly clutching the thin button-up he wore.

"Well, for one, they aren't of this millennia," Kohen laughed.

Arlo squinted at him, crossing his arms angrily.

Della smirked. Was this what being a normal human being consisted of? Was this what friends did? It was almost too good to be true, like something from a movie.

"Tell you what, if you pick out some clothes, I'll show

you that art store I was telling you about," Sebastian said, causing Arlo's eyes to glimmer. That seemed to work.

The groups split off. Sebastian, Porter, and Arlo headed toward the bookstore while Kohen, Della, and Max began to wander around.

Della was distracted by the glittering displays around them. Memories from years ago—when she'd refused to believe things were as muddy as they were—flashed in her mind. It was all bittersweet. Christmas shopping as a family had been the one tradition she could tolerate as a kid. But it hadn't felt the same without Quincy. Without him, it all turned sour.

But today? Today, she was recreating those memories with her new family.

Maybe this wouldn't be such a grueling task after all.

Maybe, she thought, smiling at Max, *Maybe I can make this another memory I'll cherish forevermore.*

Max gave her a cheeky little grin and handed her one of his coffees, the cup burning her shaking hands in a pleasant sort of way. Caramel and whipped cream wafted up into her nose, mixing with the smells of a nearby candy shop.

"You drink off of this?" she asked playfully.

"Would ya care?"

"Not in the slightest."

Max sighed contently. "Weirdo."

As she took a sip, he slipped his fingers between hers. Her heart fluttered in that silly little way hearts do. Max's cheeks had gone maroon, his smile now a permanent feature on his face. Della noted how her heart soared, knowing she was the one to cause that grin.

At that moment, she realized she could admit how achingly handsome he was. Thick lashes over amber that always seemed to glow. Spirals of curly hair that sat like a crown on his head. Rich brown skin with splashes of ivory patches like clouds illuminated by the moon on a stormy night. A smile like a beacon of hope. Impeccable fashion sense—which she knew came from Mavericks, though he'd *never* admit it.

Della felt her cheeks burn in embarrassment.

It was also at that moment when Kohen cleared his throat and excused himself.

Together, she and Max walked the strip mall, window shopping before they decided where to spend their money.

They fell into easy conversation, the words flowing between them like they'd known each other their whole lives. They fit so well together. Like two halves of a whole.

Max swung their hands playfully, gesturing loosely

around them. "What do ya want for Christmas, Delphee?"

"I don't need anything, Max."

"Ah, see ya misunderstood. Ei didn' ask what ya *needed*, Ei asked what ya *wanted*. There's a difference."

"I see," Della said in a sing-song tone. "Well, if that's the case—" She dropped his hand, spinning him toward a chintzy little tchotchke shop. "I want you to go and find me the gaudiest piece of clutter you can find."

"Della," Max laughed. "C'mon. Be serious."

"I am," Della smiled brightly. "I love that sort of stuff. I guess I'm like Mavericks in that way. I mean, have you seen my apartment?"

"Noted."

"Now that we have that settled, I'm going to get *your* gift," Della's bright smile turned mischievous.

Max eyed her suspiciously. She half expected him to stop her. Instead, he gently kissed her cheek, then slipped away to find some random piece of trash she'd forever treasure.

~ ~ ~

Sebastian was a rare breed. He knew exactly what store, aisle, and item he was looking for. He was a no-nonsense shopper, making Porter's life very difficult. He was the sort of person who could spend hours in a single aisle and still not know what he wanted.

"Stop pressuring me," he groaned, holding two candles in his hand that smelled slightly different.

"I didn't say anything," Sebastian said defensively.

"It's the look," Porter sighed, handing one of the candles to him. "You have this impatient little look."

"That's just my resting face," Sebastian countered, giving a mild shrug as he smelled the over-powering candle.

Porter rolled his eyes. He decided on the candle he'd been carrying for the past fifteen minutes, putting it and a coordinating hand sanitizer into his basket. Hopefully, Mavericks didn't have something in this scent already.

Knowing him, he did.

It was the thought that counted, right? Maybe this would finally get him on Mavericks' good side.

"This one smells nice," Arlo said, appearing from the crowd around them with a bright blue candle titled 'Sea Breeze.' He rocked back and forth on his heels momentarily before clearing his throat. "May I get it?"

Sebastian grabbed it, sniffed it, wrinkled his nose, and set it in the basket. "We done now? This place is making me wonder if I'm asthmatic."

"Fine, fine," Porter sighed.

They paid, then continued to the next shop.

So far, they'd acquired Della, Mingan, and Della's parents' gifts and picked up a few things to take back to Moss Hollow. Porter knew exactly what he wanted to get Max, yet he'd had no luck finding the elusive object. Sebastian figured Kohen would be happy with a gift card to some outdoorsy place, so they ventured off to what he called the 'manly man's corner.'

Somehow, procuring a gift card turned into Sebastian dragging Arlo to the fitting rooms with a cart of clothing. Porter trailed behind, amused. Max would have a fit with all the flannels and cargo pants currently surrounding them.

"You get me a gift card?" Kohen asked, smirking as Arlo ripped a pair of pants away from Sebastian before slamming the fitting room door behind him.

"Is gift-guessing a family tradition?" Porter asked.

Kohen shrugged. "How goes the clothes shopping?"

"Like pulling teeth," Sebastian grumbled as he swept past, heading toward a rounder of beanies.

"Figured," Kohen laughed, shaking his head in disbelief. "How did we end up helping a Wendigo pick out clothes?" He had that look on his face most humans got when they started to believe in magic: that halfway crazy smile, those blank, glossy eyes.

Porter grimaced. He wasn't the only cop who'd had this discussion with him lately.

"Does this place have a website?" he asked, gesturing around. Kohen gave him a questioning look. "I think I'm going to need another gift card."

"Who for?"

"Skeeter Jacobson. He's the police chief back in Moss Hollow. I should get you two together. You can talk about how your minds are melting over Wendigoes and Grunches," Porter smiled.

"What's a Grunch? And more importantly, is his name *actually* Skeeter?"

"Yup."

"Seriously?"

Porter nodded. "You know that stereotype of the sort of swampy rednecks?"

"Yeah?"

"That's Skeeter."

Kohen laughed to himself. "I think you'd have better luck hooking him up with Sebastian."

"Right? What's up with him and the trailer park?"

"No clue. That kid's got a screw loose if you ask me."

They sat back on their heels, both with arms crossed over their chest, watching the chaos of clothes shopping continue.

Arlo slammed open the dressing room's door, face reddening. "I am uncomfortable."

"You look nice, though," Kohen offered.

Arlo's eyebrows furrowed deeply over his eyes. "It itches. It's too hot. And it's tight." He swept his long black hair in front of his face, trying to use it as a protective shield.

"Well, let's try something else, all right? Try to have an open mind, kid. We realize this is all new to you, but if you're going to fit in—"

"I didn't ask to fit in. All I wanted to do was make sure Della got to her friends safely," Arlo spat, brushing a strand of his hair behind his ear in frustration.

"You want to live in a cave your whole life?" Kohen asked. He could be stern in that older brother sort of way, which was baffling. He seemed so easygoing and laid back most of the time. Hearing such a tone startled Porter.

Arlo's shoulders sagged. He mumbled something that sounded suspiciously like 'no,' then dug through the mountain of clothes Sebastian had picked out. Kohen tried his best to help, offering to find something that wasn't itchy and asking if Arlo had a favorite color.

Without a shadow of a doubt, Porter knew Kohen was the type of man who would be a wonderful father.

An hour later, Arlo had finally found a few shirts, sweaters, and pants that weren't too scratchy or tight. He'd even picked out a beanie and a pair of shoes. Kohen had fronted the bill, much to Sebastian and Porter's relief.

Arlo wouldn't admit it, but they could tell he was pleased with the garments he'd chosen. The way he was parading himself around in a knitted hat with a chevron pattern was proof of that.

"I can't believe I'm saying this, but I've enjoyed this little outing," Kohen said, fist-bumping Sebastian as Arlo tugged his hat further over his ears. "Thanks for letting me tag along."

"We're happy to have you, Kohen," Porter smiled.

"No, but seriously. I couldn't take much more of Della and Max making those lovey-dovey eyes at each other." He shivered. "It's weird. I think of her as my little niece, y'know? But seeing those two all. . ."

Porter's brain shut off. He felt himself slouch into a protective posture, his eyes locked on the toe of his boots.

"Kohen," Sebastian chided.

"Sorry," Kohen grimaced. "When did they—Hey!"

Sebastian elbowed him in the ribs. "What's your prob—" His eyes fell on Porter's face. "Oh," Realization crossed his face. "Sorry."

Porter just shrugged. "Old news. We broke up."

A tense awkwardness filled the air.

Sebastian mumbled to himself, eyeing him cautiously. "I—Uh—I'm only saying this because I think you deserve to know. But they kissed," he blurted out.

The group fell quiet as Porter stopped dead in his tracks. He was suddenly hyper-aware of his heartbeat. How fast and loud it thudded as the group stared at him with guilty looks.

He cleared his throat, tugging on one of his piercings. "About damn time, right?" he choked out, promptly turning away.

This wasn't new news. So why did it feel like Sebastian's words were a knife to the heart?

CHAPTER FIFTY-SEVEN

Same Day Shipping

"**W**hat exactly did you guys buy?" Della asked in horror. Porter, Sebastian, Arlo, and Kohen each had arms full of bags from various stores.

"Most of these are for Arlo," Kohen laughed. Not his usual happy-go-lucky laugh. A weird I'm-in-trouble laugh sort of laugh. "Anyways, you guys ready to head home? Where's Max?"

"He said he had to put something in the car," Della shrugged.

Max appeared beside her as if on cue, with a sly smirk. "Find everythin'?" he asked, eyeing the knit hat on Arlo's head.

"I got a candle," Arlo said softly, proudly holding out the bright blue monstrosity.

Max looked like years of candle-related trauma had finally caught up to him. "Don' burn that near me,"

Della giggled, envisioning Mavericks' office and the perpetual scent of a thousand burning wicks trapped between those four walls.

The merry misfits crammed back into the hearse, setting off toward *Sun & Star Antiques*.

Upon arrival, they found the entire front window had shattered. Shards of glass littered the sidewalk, reflecting the yellow caution tape haphazardly placed across the broken window. Hugo stood in the center of the mess, a steaming cup of apple cider in one hand, his multi-lensed glasses in the other, which he was absentmindedly chewing on.

"What the Hell happened?" Kohen asked, eyes wide.

"There was a break-in," Hugo mumbled. He seemed dazed.

Della peered around Kohen's shoulder in shock. Upon closer inspection, Hugo's leather apron had a slash mark through it, and his hair was scorched on the ends. He caught her staring out of the corner of his eye, smiling as he smoothed a wrinkle from his apron.

"Are you guys okay?" Della asked.

Hugo shrugged, taking a sip of his cider. "It's a rather large wound, but she'll be fine. I sprayed it. She'll be okay. Should've bled out in my arms, but she's okay."

"Enid?" Sebastian asked, eyes wide as he pushed past Della to stand before him.

"Don't worry, it's like *Windex* and duct tape. It can fix everything," Hugo answered.

"I—What?" Sebastian asked, peering inside the antique shop. Della could see the fear on his face. "Do you need help cleaning up? Was anything stolen?"

"Does pride count?"

Sebastian shot him a disgusted look, sidestepping around him and disappearing inside through a space in the caution tape on the shattered window.

"Good kid, that one," Hugo said, directing his words to Della. "How may I help you, my dear?"

"Bad timing, I know, but do you have anything that could permanently trap an ancient, evil spirit?" Della asked, watching Sebastian set to work cleaning.

Hugo thought for a moment, beckoning them all inside. "Not currently, but I can order something from the archives. Of course, the object must be returned to the Dust Collectors. Please keep that in mind."

Max rolled his eyes. Della gave him a questioning look, but all he did was shake his head.

Hugo stopped at the door to the garage, looking around his shop with all-consuming despair.

Books were bent, fine China was shattered, and shelves were knocked to the floor. The entire place was in shambles. It would take ages for them to clean up.

Sebastian swore as he dropped a jewelry box. Porter rolled his eyes, disconnecting from the group to help him.

Hugo finally opened the door to the garage, leading Della, Max, Kohen, and Arlo to the mystical elevator rug. He tapped his foot on the edge. Faintly, Della heard Enid's voice from below. Though not as fast as the previous time, the rug began to lower.

The door to the chamber below was open, revealing Enid sitting at the worktable wrapped in a giant fluffy blanket. She smiled warmly at them, waving.

"You okay?" Della asked, sitting beside her on the edge of the table.

She nodded, patting Della's leg reassuringly. "Takes more than a few scratches to keep me down."

Della went pale. "Scratches?"

She nodded. "Hugo didn't tell you?"

"I think Hugo hasn't told us a lot of things," Kohen whispered, looking up in awe at the ceiling.

"We were attacked by a spirit early this morning. Friend of yours, I'm assuming?" Hugo asked. His face had gone dark with worry.

"More or less," Max sighed. His eyes had found the spellbook that matched his. Though he didn't go near it, Della knew he was curious. Still, he stayed by her side, standing protectively to her right.

"It called us traitors," Enid said, eyebrows furrowed. "Any idea why?"

Della pulled at her fingernails until her nailbeds screamed in pain. If part of her was mixed up with Ahiga, and they were causing chaos together, Della knew why they'd go after Hugo and Enid. Though she was enchanted by what she now knew, there'd always be a part of her that felt slighted they never told her anything before. In the broadest sense of the word, she did feel betrayed.

"I'm sorry," she whispered.

"Oh, child, don't fret too much. It's not your fault," Enid laughed.

"It kind of is," Della said.

Before she could stop herself, she'd told them everything. Hugo and Enid listened intently. She could see the gears turning in their heads and wondered what they were thinking. Enid would never blame her for what happened, but Hugo? She wasn't so sure. He was a lot like Max in that way. When harm befell those he loved, he was a force to be reckoned with.

"We will fix this," Enid said, squeezing her hand tightly. "Numerous objects in the archives can trap a spirit like this. Hugo will find one, and if your dreamcatcher doesn't work, we'll have a backup."

Hugo nodded, placing a hand on her shoulder. "You are not alone in this."

"You've got an army behind you, Della," Kohen added.

Della had never felt as loved as she did now. The seven of them would lay down their lives before anything happened to her. Would she ever let them do that? Hell no. But it was nice knowing there were people who'd pick up her broken pieces the same way she did for everyone else. They were willing to solve this to protect her simply because they did not want to live in a world without her.

Maybe she wasn't a cosmic mistake after all.

~ ~ ~

The group made their way home after saying goodbye to Hugo and Enid. Della joined in depositing their treasure troves in the living room, hoping the others wouldn't snoop. She'd been the only one with enough common sense to purchase wrapping paper and bags, so she'd had to divvy it between them all. Thankfully, Mingan had leftovers from a few years prior to make up for what they lacked.

Despite impending doom, Christmas truly felt like Christmas. The unease and awkwardness between the boys slowly faded away with every sip of cocoa and gingerbread cookie. Carols didn't sound like nails on a chalkboard, and Della even found herself singing along.

Was this what healing felt like?

Della sat back against the couch, taking in the sleepy faces before her.

Porter had a gingerbread cookie hanging out of his mouth as he used his foot to hold down wrapping paper while struggling with the tape dispenser. Sebastian was recording him discreetly with his phone. He'd use that as blackmail for years to come.

Arlo was sat in front of the TV, engrossed in a cheesy movie about an overworked CEO falling in love with an easy-going cowboy over the holidays. Mingan and Kohen sat gossiping during the commercial breaks.

Max had sat beside her for the longest time, absent-mindedly playing with an unraveled bow as he scribbled away on a card. At some point, he'd slipped outside, grabbing something from the hearse, which he wrapped away from prying eyes in the kitchen. He'd been the first and only one done wrapping all the presents he'd bought.

Della wished she could bottle this scene and keep it forever.

They deserved these moments of calm before the storm. Tomorrow could go any number of ways. Della knew they should go over the plan one last time and iron all the kinks out now so things would go as smoothly as possible, but she couldn't take this away from them. She knew the danger, but ruining this moment would forever haunt her.

If her last good memory of these people was this, she'd be content.

So, momentarily, she let herself pretend tomorrow was just another day.

Yawns and snores filled Mingan's living room as the exhaustion from early that morning took over. The sight was laughable. The boys were in a pile of limbs on the floor, save for Max, who was in the kitchen again. Mingan was sprawled out on the couch, a cookbook open on his chest. Kohen had fallen asleep to Della's left, snoring loudly.

Della grabbed a blanket off an old recliner as quietly as possible and gently placed it atop the boys. Sebastian grumbled something akin to a thank you and then drifted off to dreamland.

Max crept in from the kitchen as Della set up a makeshift bed in the corner.

He scoffed at the sight of Porter, Sebastian, and Arlo. "Like children," he whispered, catching the pillow Della had thrown his way.

"I'd take a room full of kindergarteners over these fools any day," Della snickered.

Max tiptoed around Porter's feet, settling on Della's blanket. He hugged his pillow to himself, smiling mischievously.

"Excuse me, sir, that wasn't for you," Della whispered, plopping down beside him.

"First come, first serve," Max shrugged.

Della rolled her eyes. Something about laying on the uneven carpet surrounded by the idiots she loved dearly made her so incredibly happy.

Max fluffed his pillow, lying next to her. "Hey there, Pluto," he said softly.

"Mars," she replied, nodding her head, pretending she was speaking to a rather dapper gentleman way back when.

"Ei had a great time tuhday. Wastin' time with ya, Ei mean."

"Thanks for the coffee."

"Extra sweet tuh combat your bitter little heart," Max laughed.

No, he giggled.

Like a schoolboy.

Della couldn't stop herself from laughing along, grabbing a stray pillow to hit him with.

So much had changed since the last time she'd hit him with a pillow.

Part of her figured she should feel guilty about how easy it was to love him. There should be a grace period, shouldn't there? To save Porter's feelings.

But she wasn't guilty.

Loving Max was like breathing. Simple, yet she couldn't live without it.

There was no denying that she had loved Porter, but maybe that love had to happen for her to realize what *real* love was.

She could let go of Porter so quickly.

But Max? Max was an anomaly—a once-in-a-lifetime kind of phenomenon. Like watching a lunar eclipse while the sky danced with the brightest aurora borealis you'd ever seen.

She couldn't live without him. Not at all.

It was like their souls had been intertwined since the beginning of time.

Max brushed a stray strand of hair from her face, his thumb lingering on her cheek. Della shut her eyes, wrapping her arms around him, burying her face in his chest.

Della had always thought that love was something you had to earn. You had to fight for it tooth and nail, or it wasn't worth pursuing. That's what she had done with Porter. She had fought for him—and with him, for that matter—but now she realized that love wasn't something you earned.

Love was a gift. When given with pure intentions, it could never be returned. When shared between the right people, love was like a garden. Sure, it required upkeep and maintenance, but in time, you even fell in love with maintaining it.

"Ya gonna tell me what's on yer mind?" Max asked, his voice full of sleepiness.

She smiled, looking up to press her forehead against his before shutting her eyes again. "I think you already know what's going on in my head."

"Can Ei guess?"

She nodded.

"Yer thinkin' that ya've finally found yer one and only *Robin Hood*," he whispered.

"You're sappy."

Max laughed to himself, planting a kiss on her forehead. "But Ei'm right, aren' Ei?"

"Tell you what," Della whispered. "I'll tell you tomorrow."

"Deal." Max nodded, burying his face in her hair.

Just as she was about to lose consciousness and drift off into some of the happiest dreams she would ever have, she whispered, "Max?"

He hesitated. "Yes, love?"

"I can't wait to see you in the morning."

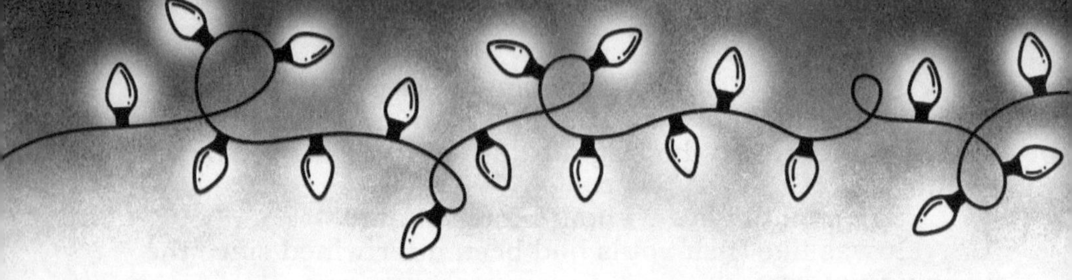

CHAPTER FIFTY-EIGHT

Premonitions

"**M**y God, they're adorable," Sebastian whispered, standing over Della and Max with his hands on his hips.

Porter did not share the same sentiment.

There they were, out cold, his arms wrapped around her, her legs draped over his. Both snoring so loud a passerby would have thought a motorcycle was hidden in the room.

"Someone get a picture. Preferably a polaroid," Kohen laughed, shaking his head in amusement.

Porter had to catch himself before his eyes rolled so fast they popped out of his skull. They'd broken up less than forty-eight hours ago. Talk about a fast rebound.

His face reddened.

That wasn't fair. Both of them—especially Della—deserved happiness. They deserved each other if he was being honest. Even if their happiness meant hurting their supposed best friend in the process.

Neither Porter nor Della were willing to make sacrifices for each other. So why should they stay together? Why shouldn't she be with Max?

Sebastian was watching him out of the corner of his eye.

Something unspoken passed between them.

"You know what," Sebastian began, pulling out his phone and tapping away giddily. "Let's wake 'em up."

Porter felt his lips pull up into an evil little grin. "Do it."

Before Kohen could protest, Sebastian played the loudest fog horn the internet offered.

Their noses collided as they woke with a start, eyes wide. Della kicked Max in the stomach with a literal knee-jerk response. Max's hand was caught in her hair. Their faces had gone so red it looked like someone had come in the night and sprayed them with a can of spray paint.

Glorious chaos.

Della stood, hands covering her face after Max had successfully freed his hands from her hair.

"You're an ass, Breckenridge," she mumbled, refusing to look at anyone as she made her way to the bathroom, slamming the door behind her.

"Well, good morning, Maximiliano. How did you sleep?" Sebastian asked. There was no use in him trying to hide the sly look on his face.

Max stood, brushed himself off, inhaled deeply, and then lunged at him, the two of them colliding with the couch as they went flying backward.

"Hey! Careful!" Kohen screeched, catching a lamp before it fell off the side table and crashed to the floor.

Porter allowed himself one last evil little grin before he removed himself from the living room, finding Mingan in the kitchen. A quick survey of the mess on the counter told him French toast was on today's menu. Together, the two set to work on breakfast, ignoring how the walls shook from the ruckus in the living room.

Arlo was sat on the kitchen table, scribbling away in the sketchbook they'd bought him yesterday.

"What did I miss?" he asked.

"Nothing unusual," Porter replied, peering over his shoulder to see he was sketching Della's likeness. "Wow, you're really good at drawing, Arlo."

"Thank—Thank you. When I was with the Sycamores, I expressed interest in the European style of art. They had a friend visiting who showed me how to paint," he explained, never once looking up from his drawing. "It was fascinating to learn about the differences in culture regarding art. Music, too."

Porter stood gawking at him for a minute. He spoke like a college professor.

Arlo looked up with a smile. "Would you like to hear about the differences I've noted? I've had quite a lot of time to think on the subject."

"Maybe another time," Porter said, giving him a light pat on the shoulder.

Kohen drug Sebastian and Max in by the ears, depositing them at the table like an angry mother dealing with her two rambunctious toddlers.

"He started it!" Max snapped.

"I don't care who started it, knock it the frick off! You're going to break something! Dear *Lord*!" Kohen snapped back, throwing his hands into the air. "How old are you, Max?"

Porter snickered to himself.

"Eighteen, ya a—"

"Wait, really?" Sebastian asked, eyes glittering. "I thought you and Porter were the same age."

Max grimaced. "Why do Ei feel like Ei shouldn' have said that?"

"Is our Max a super genius?" Sebastian asked Porter, hands clasped over his heart, making puppy-dog eyes.

"Skipped two grades," Porter smiled, wiping a fake tear. "I'm so proud of him."

"Ei hate ya both."

Kohen wrapped his arms around Max's shoulder. "So you're a real smart-ass, then?"

Max rolled his eyes, wriggling free from his grip. "And now Kohen's added tuh the list of those Ei despise."

"What'd he do this time?" Della asked from the hall as she pulled her hair into a ponytail. It'd grown out the last two months. Porter wondered why she hadn't cut it.

The neon green hair dye, however, was still holding on.

"They found out Ei skipped a few grades," Max sighed, sliding away from the fridge as Mingan gestured for him to move.

"Aww and boy genius is embarrassed?" she asked playfully.

The way she brushed past him on her way to the table made Porter's skin crawl.

"Viva la screw *you*," Max sighed, his cheeks reddening.

Porter knew that swath of maroon was not from embarrassment.

The crew ate breakfast relatively quietly. Arlo decided halfway through he did not care for French toast, so Kohen fried him up some bacon and sausages, which prompted Porter and Sebastian to ask for some as well. Mingan just rolled his eyes.

Della and Max talked in hushed voices at the corner of the table, smiling almost drunkenly at each other.

Porter couldn't help but think she'd never looked at him like that.

Beneath the jovial teasing and budding romance, tension was stirring again. Porter could see it in the far-off look Max had. In the way Sebastian kept side-eyeing Della. How Della's smiles never reached her eyes. How Arlo had picked the chair farthest away from the rest of the group. How Mingan and Kohen stole worried glances when they thought the kids weren't looking. How Porter's own heart was fluttering in his chest.

Somehow, this planned attack felt worse than running headfirst into unknown danger. Any errors from this point forward couldn't be blamed on ignorance.

Porter took a sharp breath. "If anyone wants to back out, now's the time to speak up."

Everyone paused whatever they'd been doing. That stirring tension was about to bubble over.

As gently as he could, Max set down his fork. "None of us can back out, Porter. This isn' just about a spirit anymore."

"I know," Porter sighed. "Which is why I want to make sure we're all on the same page."

Kohen nodded. "I know no one wants to say it, but if things go south, we lose more than a shot at trapping this ghost. Della's livelihood is on the line. I don't take that lightly, and I know none of you do either."

"But," Della said, looking each of them in the eye. "You can't let your worry for me hinder our plans. Trust me, I—" She bit her lip, rolling her eyes. "I—I'm terrified too. But if we don't do this, we're screwed. *I'm* screwed. Arlo says I'm broken, and I can feel it. I want this fixed. Whatever part of me is entwined with Ahi—the spirit—needs to be separated."

"Agreed," everyone responded.

Kohen stood, stretching and yawning. "Well, we have a few hours before we need to be at Poppy's. Is there anything else we need?"

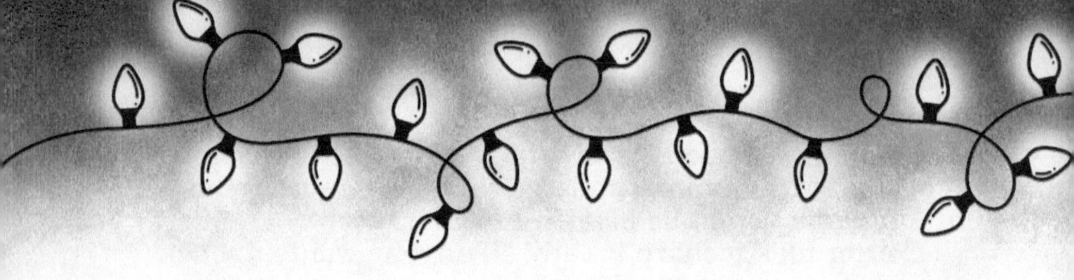

CHAPTER FIFTY-NINE

Caller ID

Arlo stopped scratching away at his sketchbook, a pencil in one hand, an eraser in his mouth, and a pen behind his ear. He looked up from his drawing, eyes on Della's hair.

"Kohen, can you ask Mingan a question for me?" he asked, tapping his pencil nervously. Kohen nodded for him to continue. "Can you ask him to cut my hair?"

Kohen's face went dark. "Why?"

Arlo stood, taking a deep breath as he straightened to his full towering height. "Our hair is sacred, I know that. Not once have I cut it before. But hair can carry memories. Della's carries memories of rebellion and adventure. Mine only carries heartache. I have lost almost everything that made me Hurrit. The only thing that remains is my hair."

"And by cutting it, you finally lay that all to rest?" Kohen asked, his face softening.

Arlo nodded. "I want to start over. Being with all of you has given me that opportunity. I want to regrow my hair as I regrow with all of you."

Kohen smiled, relaying the message to Mingan. "He says he'd be honored to help you begin anew."

Arlo was beaming. Della could see his aura glowing a bright neon orange. That color fit him, just as he said it did.

"Tell him I say thank you. He is the only one I'd trust to cut it."

It took an hour for Mingan to tame Arlo's matted mane of hair. By the end of it, it was cut to just above his shoulders. Arlo seemed lighter with the weight of his hair and the memories it carried gone.

He'd been spot-on with the rebellious aspect of her green hair. She'd only dyed it this color for so long to spite Jasper. Maybe when this was all over, she'd need to change her hair too. She was tired of feeling like everything she did was to spite Sycamore Heights.

Like Arlo, she knew today was a chance to start over.

But first, she had to ask a few questions about the past.

Slipping out of the kitchen, Della sat on Mingan's bed, back to the frosted window leaking sunlight into the darkened room. Specks of dust swirled around her, mirroring the dusting of snow blowing off the trees outside.

Her second chat with Hugo and Enid had left her with a sadness she couldn't seem to shove down now that the fun from last night was over.

There was so much she didn't know. She barely understood what the Dust Collectors were or what abilities Hugo and Enid had. And then, of course, there was the mess with Mavericks. The butterflies, his file in Elvi's *P.O.I.* envelope, and what Kohen had told her about Quincy all weighed on her.

The more she thought about it, the more she realized something must have happened long ago. Something she couldn't remember—something about *him.*

She'd been sitting there clutching her laptop so hard her knuckles had gone white. She sighed, opening it and typing in her password. Logastellus. Someone whose love for words is greater than their knowledge of words. A smirk tugged at her lips. No one would have guessed it in a million years.

Navigating to the *Facetime* app on her messy computer screen, she tapped his name. Mavericks had said to call if she needed anything. And right now, more than anything, she needed him. If she could snap her fingers and teleport him here, she would.

She just hoped he'd pick up.

The call rang a few times, and then suddenly, Mavericks was upside down on the computer screen. From the looks of it, he was at The Courier but was blocking too much of the camera for Della to see what exactly he was doing.

"Ah! Della! What a surprise!" Mavericks exclaimed excitedly, adjusting his glasses.

"You're upside down," she laughed.

"Oh! Yes, I do appear to be that way, don't I!" Mavericks laughed, then fell.

Headfirst.

His phone hadn't been upside down.

Mavericks had been.

"Are you okay?" Della asked as Mavericks picked himself up from the floor, fluffing his hair with one hand while trying to tap something on his phone with the other.

"Trying to get the ideas flowing, my dear! I've found hanging from the stairs in the common office tends to do the trick." He brought the phone so close to his face Della could see every pore and individual eyelash on him. "Where are Max and Porter?"

"Out and about," Della laughed. "We've picked up a few new Couriers, by the way. Sebastian Breck—"

"Ah, yes! Your blond friend with the bad acne!" Mavericks smiled, setting his phone somewhere so he could gesture while he spoke.

Della rolled her eyes. "Let's not lead with that if you meet him, okay?"

"Oh, of course!" Mavericks laughed, pushing up his half-moon glasses. "I'm assuming you called for a reason?"

"I have a few questions, but I just wanted to say Merry Christmas. My family celebrates today."

"On the twenty-third? How intriguing!"

"My aunt is really big on parties," Della smiled. "Anyways, we have a situation over here. You were right. There's a ghost running rampant in town. Want to guess what type it is and how we'll get rid of it?"

Mavericks' eyes sparkled with joy. "I mean, you can't put a reaper in a witch bottle now, can you?" he laughed, popping his collar. "What do you know of the ghost?"

"It's a black mist that was trapped in a peace pipe," Della said simply, watching the cogs in his head turn.

"Interesting. Sounds like a shadow person. And is the ghost violent?" Mavericks asked, procuring a book from somewhere behind the phone. A glimpse of the cover revealed it read *Epitaphs and Ectoplasm*.

"Yes. It's attacked me, Arlo, and the others," Della explained, phrasing it that way on purpose. Mavericks glanced at her questioningly as he flipped through the book. "Arlo is a Wendigo."

Mavericks raised his eyebrow. "Well, that is strange, isn't it? This Arlo, he is helping you?"

Della nodded.

Mavericks mumbled to himself something about not trusting anything that can grow back its skin, then clicked his tongue. "Well, the black mist is throwing me off. That could mean the spirit is having difficulty crossing into our world, or it isn't a ghost at all. Could be a demon. Hell, it could even be a rather strong poltergeist that has broken through the veil. But if I had to take a guess, it sounds like you are dealing with something akin to a wraith."

Della smirked. "You sure about that?"

"Honestly, you are killing me," he sighed, removing

his glasses and turning the book he was reading towards her. "Wraiths are usually either newer ghosts with unfinished business or harbingers of death. I suppose they can appear as a misty being, so yes, I'm sure. It's a wraith."

"Nope. Good guess, though," Della said with a wink. "It does have unfinished business, but it's centuries old. The Wendigo is its brother."

Mavericks' face dropped. "So it's just an angry spirit, then?"

"That's what we thought at first. But we changed our minds after Arlo the Wendigo saved me from drowning by its cold dead hands," she explained. "We've got a pretty cemented theory now."

"Wait, the Wendigo *saved* you?" Mavericks gawked at them. They nodded. "That is incredible! Not only does it speak, it does not seem to be driven by hunger! May I speak with it—uh, I mean, him. Apologies."

Della grimaced. "He's been weird about technology. I think talking to someone on a laptop would give him a heart attack."

"That's true. May I at least see him? Does he look like a skeletal humanoid figure or more animalistic? The horns and fur and all that?" Mavericks clapped excitedly.

"Well, as of the moment, he looks pretty human," Della said. She almost got up and stuck the laptop out the door to see if she could give him a glimpse of the terrifying creature that was scrawny little Arlo.

"Fascinating!" Mavericks exclaimed, disappearing off-screen to put his book away.

"Anyway," Della said, allowing her tone to become stern. "The ghost, or whatever you want to call it, is entwined with part of my soul. Would you happen to know anything about that? What about something called the *P.O.I. Project*? What about someone by the name of Leland Kitchi?"

When Mavericks appeared again, his face was ashy, like *he* was the one seeing ghosts.

"Mavericks?"

He shook himself, shakily reaching up to run a hand through his hair. He swallowed hard, then grabbed his phone, making odd noises as he began tapping the screen. "Uh, I have to go. You are—*kreeeee*—breaking up. I—*kree kree*—I need to go talk to a guy about a rat infestation," he said quickly, fumbling his phone around.

"Mavericks, that trick doesn't work on—" Della began as the screen went dark, showing nothing but 'call ended.' "—*Facetime*," she finished.

Well, that confirmed that.

Everyone seemed to have a different opinion on Mavericks. Some admired him, some feared him, others thought he had more than a few screws loose. Della knew him well enough to know most of his outward appearance was pure showmanship. He used his quirkiness to mask what was going on in his head, just like she did. Growing up reading his stories in rare issues of *The Utopian Courier*, Della knew how empathetic he was. He viewed the world through such an odd lens.

But just as the residents of Sycamore Heights could fake holiness for Church, Mavericks could have lied to her since the moment they met.

She wanted to trust him, so for the time being, that's what she would do. Hopefully, whatever he was hiding was about to be revealed. Maybe reconnecting with her missing pieces would unlock all those memories that made her brain melt.

But more than that, she hoped Mavericks was the man he tried so hard to be.

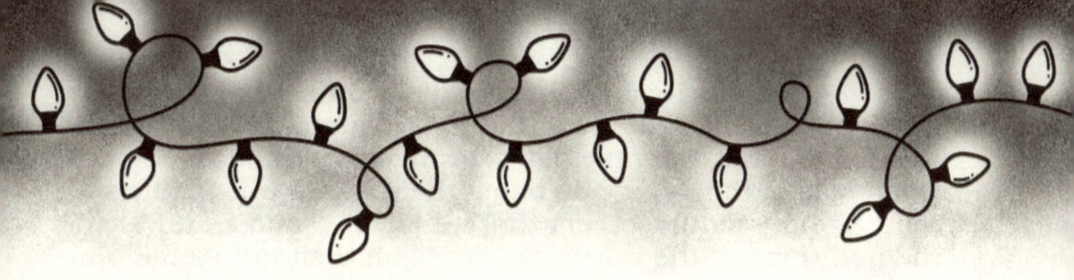

CHAPTER SIXTY

Burning Down the Christmas Tree

Della and the gang's arrival at Poppy's was met with hushed whispers. Anxiety surged through her as she looked around at the sea of faces in the foyer. Apparently, no one had expected them. Not even Leonel and Cassie, who immediately dragged Della over to their respective trees. Both were towering in the den, sparkling like diamonds. Della's was there too. Her's was the only tree that didn't fit the pink and white gilded age aesthetic. It was black with bat and pumpkin ornaments. With a guilty smile, Della noted it was taller than Cassie and Leo's.

When all else failed, at least she had Kohen and Poppy.

The clink of glasses signaled the drinking had begun as Della wove her way back to the group. Max and Della kept a quiet eye on Porter to ensure he wasn't indulging in the festivities.

"Everything's a go," Sebastian whispered in her ear. "The hearse is ready, too."

They'd wasted as much time as humanly possible getting ready to go. The entire Coleman-Kitchi clan was here, plus a handful of Poppy's respected—and despised—guests.

Pudgy Uncle Rudolph Lynch had found the piano—the remnants of his punk rock band's melodies weaving their way into *O Holy Night*. Aunt Cynthia was already fuming, the grip on her champagne glass so tight that Della figured it would break. Their son Finlay stood cowering behind his mother, the embarrassment almost killing him.

Grandma Claudia and Grandpa Victor had set their sights on a potential business partner: Elvi Sinclair. To her credit, Elvi was trying her best not to look bored as the Bennets talked her ear off.

Aunt Felicity and her car salesman husband, Marcus Leblanc, were parading around their daughters, Zoe and Madeline. They were the oldest grandchildren on the Coleman side of things. Poppy hated them. Della was indifferent. She didn't know them that well. But Claudia and Victor adored them in the way they adored all their grandchildren.

How they'd produced such prejudiced children was beyond Della.

Poppy was pouring herself a large glass of wine, taking a break from entertaining her beloved—and loathed—guests.

Jasper and Kimi sat alone on one of the plush couches, the only couple that didn't have a glass of liquid courage in their hands. Leo and Cassie had pointed out Della to them. Kimi had waved her over. Della pretended she hadn't noticed.

Porter checked the time on his phone. "This is going to be a long game of hurry up and wait."

"At least we'll get presents out of it all," Sebastian sighed. The group turned to give him a disapproving look. "I'm just trying to be optimistic."

Della rolled her eyes, adjusting the strap of her book bag. Inside sat the dreamcatcher. She could feel the power radiating off it like a beacon. She imbued it with the magic Nicoletta and the Weeping Crow coven would steer far away from. She couldn't wait to get back home and tell them all. They'd shun her for sure.

That is, of course, if I end up going home, her subconscious whispered. Her skin prickled with fear at that thought, wishing it never would've come.

"Yer gonna be fine," Max whispered, sensing her nerves.

"Promise?"

"Cross my heart and hope to—"

"Don't finish that sentence," Kohen snapped. He'd been making his rounds for the past half hour, doing a mental head count of everyone present and greeting anyone new at the door. Now, he sat on Porter's left, nervously tapping his fingers on the table.

Della stood leaning against the wall, keeping a watchful eye on Leo and Cassie. They'd roped Finlay into playing with them, though it was obvious he felt doing so was torture. It reminded her of Quincy and herself. They'd always try and drag the other kids into their schemes, though they'd had little success.

Her heart ached. She so desperately wanted Quincy to be here. Every year before, she'd kept her eyes on the door. She'd always thought he'd show up. He couldn't stay away forever, right?

But now she knew otherwise. Quincy wasn't coming home. He wasn't running around being a roadie for all his favorite bands while trying to make his own music.

Della rocked back and forth on her heels nervously, trying to push down the what-ifs regarding her brother. Whether he was alive or dead weighed on her.

Maybe Arlo could teach her how to enter his dreams.

If that's what Dreamwalkers could do, anyway. That was what the name implied, after all.

Out of the corner of her eye, she spotted Elvi lounging lazily against the staircase railing. When she realized Della had seen her, she beckoned her forward with a bejeweled finger.

"Uh oh," Sebastian whispered.

Della handed off her book bag to Max, rolling her eyes. "Better go see what Fancy Pants wants."

"You going to be okay?" Kohen asked, the color draining from his cheeks.

She shrugged. "If she wanted me dead, I'd be dead."

With that, she sauntered over to Elvi, making sure the expression on her face was less than friendly.

Elvi smirked, shaking her head to herself. With her silver dress and lacy cardigan, she looked like a killer mermaid ready to strike.

"What do you want, Elvi?" Della asked.

"Do I always have to want something, Miss Coleman? Can't two friends have a chat?" That smirk darkened as she disconnected from the wall, tilting her head at Della, taking her all in. "It's nice to see you up and about. I'm glad you're all right."

"Awe, don't tell me you worried about little old me," Della said dryly.

"Hardly," Elvi sighed. She looked over her shoulder, shifting uncomfortably. "Do you have it?"

"Have what?"

"Don't be cute, okay?"

Della squinted at her, crossing her arms over her chest. "Even if I did, do you really think I'd tell you?"

"So you do have it."

"You salty little—" Della cleared her throat as Cassie walked by. "Biscuit. You salty little biscuit, which I should just *smother* in gravy."

Elvi rolled her eyes.

"Nice catch," Cassie sighed. "Mom says it's time for presents." She shot Elvi a dirty look, then skipped off with Finlay in tow.

Elvi laughed to herself, leaning close to Della's ear as

she walked by. "I know you're not stupid, so don't do anything rash."

Della glared at her. "Vice versa."

As her stilettos clicked away, she said over her shoulder, "Oh, believe me. I've had plenty of time to think this over."

Della's skin prickled with fear. What exactly did she mean by that? Whose side was she on? Why was she looking for it if she didn't want P.O.I. to get the peace pipe? What game was she playing, and what were the rules?

"What did she want?" Max asked, startling her. His face was scrunched up in worry as he handed over her book bag.

"Nothing good," Della sighed, nodding to the living room where everyone was gathering.

Presents were piled high in the center of the living room, their glittering papers reflecting the shimmering lights of the Christmas trees. Poppy had escorted straggling guests into their cars, sending them off with a bottle of wine or leftover sweets. All who were left were the people she intended to spoil.

Or those who she took delight in disappointing.

There were only a few non-family guests left. Unfortunately, Elvi was one of those few.

As evening fell and the adults grew blotto, the tower of presents dwindled.

The older teens received the typical number of socks, clothes, and necessities. Here and there were trinkets and more frivolous things, but all in all, nothing special. Della hadn't expected anything more. Poppy's presents, of course, always had more thought put into them. Even then, Della could see the effects of her ever-growing debt.

Max and Porter had received a small basket of treats and sample-sized odds and ends. It seemed they'd been thought of last.

How charming.

Della had to hand it to them all; they roughed out the stories and the drunken stupor around them for longer than expected. When the children had run upstairs with their toys and the adults dissolved into their cliques, they thought it safe to slip back into the kitchen.

Porter and Sebastian retrieved their presents from the hearse, and together, they sat on the floor, enjoying their own gift exchange.

Porter somehow found a lava lamp for Max. Max had found him a cookbook based on a show he liked.

Della had assembled a new stationery set for Max, which he seemed to enjoy. However, nothing was going to top that lava lamp. On the other hand, he followed through with his promise to find the gaudiest piece of trash he could. A peacock whose tail feathers held pens with pom-poms on their ends. He said he'd bought something else but lost it on the way over. She couldn't help but feel that meant he wanted to give it to her in private. She, too, had something to give to him. And prying eyes weren't allowed to see.

Porter—much to his chagrin—ordered her a signed copy of a record she loved. She'd bought him a new *Vanish & Despair* hoodie weeks ago. Their exchange was awkward at best.

Sebastian passed around tiny bags filled with patches, stickers, and bookmarks he'd thought they'd like. Kohen had gotten them each a book. Mingan had crocheted them several items. Arlo had found rocks he said matched their auras.

Della sat hugging her loot. Her emotional cup was finally full.

As the din of the party behind them quieted, Poppy appeared before them. She held a half-empty wine bottle in one hand and an overflowing glass in the other.

"Della! I have a late gift for you!" she said excitedly, discarding her wine glass and grabbing her by the elbow.

"Uh. . ." Della looked to the boys, who nodded their permission for her to leave.

Della deposited her loot on the floor, then begrudgingly followed her tipsy aunt upstairs to the old bedroom she used to spend the night in. She'd begged and begged Poppy to paint the walls purple when she was little.

Memories of staying here were foggy in Della's mind.

Inside, Kimi and Elvi sat on the old twin bed, their conversation fizzling out as soon as the door opened. Jasper stood to the side, arms crossed, staring at the floor.

"Found her!" Poppy exclaimed.

"Miss Coleman," Elvi said with a pointed nod.

"Sinclair," Della said dryly. "Poppy, this is not shaping up to be a great gift."

"Oh hush, you," Poppy said with a roll of her eyes, squeezing herself between Kimi and the wench.

Della stood before them, an accusatory eyebrow raised. Kimi exchanged a look with Elvi, who procured a thin envelope from her purse. With a teasing flourish, she handed it to Della. It read 'Merry Christmas' on the front in glittery pink ink.

"What's this?" Della asked.

When no one responded, she opened it.

The contents inside made her knees buckle. It was

the deed to the historical society.

"Why—Why are you giving me this?" she asked, finding herself on the floor.

"Winifred and Mingan bought the historical society when they first got married. It's been in our family for a long, long time," Kimi began, wringing her hands nervously. "Winnie wanted that house to link the Sycamore and Mukwa legacies. If that house was passed to someone who didn't honor her wishes, she knew that'd never happen.

Winnie knew you'd want to honor both sides, too. Not long before she died, she put it in writing that on or before your twenty-first birthday, you'd become the sole proprietor of the historical society. Seeing as you were so young when she passed, someone else had to run it all until you were of age."

"That's where I came in," Poppy smiled, tipping her glass in Della's direction.

Kimi nodded. "Jasper and I didn't have the money nor the business sense to keep the place afloat, so we named Poppy as beneficiary."

"Some good that did," Elvi mumbled, rolling her eyes.

"Are you serious?" Della asked, her voice breaking. "Grandma left it to me?"

"She thought very highly of you," Jasper said softly as if he weren't talking to his problematic delinquent child.

"Why didn't you tell me sooner?" Della asked, shaking all over.

"You'd left for Louisiana," Jasper shrugged. "There was no sense calling you back just for this."

Elvi cleared her throat. "Anyways," she said, standing. "After several months of back and forth with lawyers, your parents, and Poppy, we've finally come to an agreement."

Poppy nodded. "Ms. Sinclair spoke with Vic and Claudia. They are willing to pay off the debt and make sizeable monthly checks in order to keep the lights on as long as you, Della dear, are calling all the shots."

"My parents had a rocky relationship with Winnie and Mingan, but the thing they had in common was their love for you kids. Plus, they'd hate to see that old house fall into the wrong hands," Jasper sighed.

"And now that I know how important the historical society is to you—" Elvi said, giving Della a knowing look. "—I've decided to retract my initial offer to buy it."

This whole thing had started because she'd wanted the peace pipe. Now that she knew Della and the others had it, what was the point in fighting for it?

"Y—Yes," Della said, trying to quell her excitement.

"Yes! What do I need to sign?"

"You realize you'd have dual responsibilities here and in Louisiana, right?" Jasper asked. Ahh, there it was. The condescending tone was back.

"If I own the historical society, then I can employ someone to act in my stead," Della said matter-of-factly. "I think I can figure it out, Jasper."

"Plus, you'd have a reason to come back and visit. You'd have to come check on things now and then," Kimi smiled.

Della's lips pulled into a content smile. This was the best Christmas gift anyone had ever offered her. "Thank you," she said, clutching the deed to her chest.

Elvi nodded. "You're welcome."

With that, she and Poppy left to return to the party below. The awkward chasm returned once the door had closed behind them.

Jasper shifted uncomfortably, crossing his arms tighter.

Kimi patted the empty space next to her. "Are you free to talk?"

Della nodded but held her ground on the floor, hyper-aware of the dreamcatcher in the book bag slung over her shoulder.

"What happened?" Kimi asked. Her entire countenance had changed. Fear crept up her spine, causing her to slouch in on herself. "Why were you out that night?"

"Following a lead," Della said, her voice small. "I told you, I have a job to do."

Jasper audibly rolled his eyes.

"While we realize that, you could've ended up dead. You can't just run off into the woods like that, Della. And you can't snoop around crime scenes, either," Kimi sighed.

"Contrary to popular belief, we do care about you," Jasper snapped, earning himself a warning look from Kimi. "You have to realize that playing detective will end in real-world consequences sooner or later."

"You don't think I know that?" Della laughed. "And I'm not playing detective; I am a *reporter*. I made the front page, by the way. Not that you'd care."

"Right, right. Front page of *The Utopian Courier*. I bet that was a difficult feat," Jasper laughed. "You were supposed to be interning at a respectable newspaper, Della. Not galivanting around for some—some nut job's psychotic conspiracy tabloid!"

"The Courier is respectable!" Della snapped. "We just have better things to do than report on the weather or who won the town bake-off!"

"Yeah, you report the lunacy of deranged townsfolk who believe in monsters!" Jasper shouted.

"Like you don't," Della snapped.

"Excuse me?"

Kimi stepped between them protectively, eyes on Jasper. "I thought we said we'd handle this delicately." She turned back to Della, feigning sympathy. "We are just worried, okay? You've obviously gotten yourself in over your head. You're breaking and entering, you've been parading around hunting things that *don't exist*—" The way she said that sent shivers down Della's spine. "—and now you're involved in Ashton's disappearance. Do you have any idea how worrying this is?"

"Why can't you just be happy for me? I have everything I have ever wanted, and you treat me like a social pariah!" Della barked.

The room chilled like someone had flung open a window to invite the snow in.

"Because you're *acting* like a social pariah!" Jasper yelled. "I had the displeasure of reading your little front-page article, and I am so incredibly disappointed in you, Delphee."

Della inhaled deeply. "I learned long ago that I didn't need your approval. Be disappointed all you want. I'm over it."

Jasper stood gawking at her. He almost looked hurt. He opened his mouth, rage filling his eyes, but Kimi stamped her foot down.

"Grandma didn't die from a heart attack!" she shouted.

Jasper went paper-white, taking several giant steps back. Della stood frozen, her heart thundering away in her chest.

"She had a seizure. A bad one," Kimi started, choking up. "She—"

"I know," Della finished, her voice gravelly from the tears welling up in her throat. "I know."

"What do you mean, you know?" Jasper asked, his eyes growing wider by the second.

"I played detective," Della said half-heartedly.

"Then you know about the—"

"Placebos? Yeah," Della laughed, turning away.

"Then why did you stop taking them? Do you have any idea what kind of danger you're in? You promised you'd always take them!" Kimi said sternly.

Della's blood ran cold. "Because I thought they were for migraines, mom. You lied to me!"

"To protect you!" Jasper screamed.

"No, Jasper, you did it to protect yourselves," Della snapped.

"It doesn't matter!" Kimi yelled. "You need to start taking your medication again. Before you start experiencing. . . *symptoms*."

"No," Della said simply.

"Della, you don't understand the severity of this," Kimi sobbed. "Winifred had a multitude of mental health issues. Some of which developed the older she got, including something akin to schizophrenia, split personality disorder, dementia—it was like she was living in a dream, or rather, a nightmare. She started taking those pills to stop it so she could live a normal life. That's all we want for you, Delphee."

Della looked back and forth between them, feeling somehow defeated. "My life has never been normal. I don't *want* to be normal," she scoffed. "And it's not your choice to make. If I'm old enough to be the sole proprietor of the historical society, then I can choose what happens with my health."

"Delphee," Kimi scolded.

"I am not normal. Our *family* isn't normal. Why do you try so hard to pretend like we are?"

"Because we love you, Della," Jasper began.

That mysterious cold had turned the air to ice.

Della glared at him. "This isn't love. This is you trying to control something you don't understand because you are a coward, Jasper. I know what I am. I know *who* I am."

The branches of a tree hit the window behind Kimi, startling her. The sky outside had gone smoke gray, a mighty wind kicking up snow, battering the mansion with it. Della's skin prickled and buzzed with anticipation. She could feel eyes burning holes into the back of her skull, but no one was there when she turned.

"Listen," Kimi said carefully, her eyes full of worry. "My mom had episodes. She'd be dreaming while she was awake, and those dreams—" She shook her head, a single tear rolling down her cheek. How dramatic. "—usually came true. Winifred called them visions, and these visions always caused seizures. It was horrible, Della."

Della straightened, her face a perfect picture of boredom. "Mom, I get that you—"

Kimi glared at her, which shut her up. "No one else in the family shared her gifts. Except you," she breathed, her voice barely audible. "You had the same symptoms, the same horrible nightmares that always came true. But my mom said that—" Kimi broke down again, crying uncontrollably.

A ringing sound erupted in Della's ears, her mind pulsing with pain. Images popped into her mind, gone before she could fully grasp what they were. Disconnected sadness bloomed in her chest.

"Winifred said that your powers were beyond her own, that your gift was different. We knew that whatever she experienced would be worse for you," Jasper finished, his voice bitterly mournful.

Della said as gently as she could, "I understand, believe me. You have no idea what these past few months have been like. But I'm *not* afraid of what I am. You poisoned and suppressed a part of me." She was trying the best she could to stop herself from shaking. "You tried to take away what made me, me, and I refuse to let you do that again."

"I didn't want to see you get hurt," Kimi whimpered. "I took my time; I did my research! There was never enough of anything in those pills that would harm you! They were only strong enough to keep—"

"Not immediately, but did you ever think of the long-term implications?" Della screeched. "*That* is what caused my seizure! Because my body couldn't handle—"

"Because your body wasn't used to your own power!" Jasper snapped.

"AND THAT IS YOUR FAULT!" Della roared, rage filling her bones. The world was swimming before her eyes, rippling, all the colors mixing. The anger she felt wasn't her own. It sent fire up her back like white-hot, razor-sharp claws had dug into her back.

"After Winifred died, you completely shut down. You were plagued with night terrors and horrible, horrible visions. How is a mother supposed to see their child like that, knowing what her future holds? What was I supposed to do, Della?" Kimi asked.

"You should've just been there to help me through it. I was just a child, mom! I could've figured it out as I grew older if you had helped!" Della screamed.

"I didn't know how!" Kimi screamed back.

Della swore, dropping to a crouch, holding her head in her hands. Her throat was tight with fiery tears.

They'd broken her into pieces in the name of love.

Had they never considered that Winifred's powers had killed her because she'd denied herself her magic? Had they never wondered whether they were doing more harm than good?

No matter how they tried to spin it, she knew the real reason they'd done all this was fear.

So, they wanted to be afraid of her? Wanted to treat

her like a monster? Fine. She'd bare her teeth and be monstrous. She'd be everything they hated so much. Because everything they hated, everything they feared, was what made her good, what made her the twisted hero she was. All those things they tried to bury were the same things Mavericks had chosen her for. The same things she valued most.

She wanted to give them something to be truly afraid of. To break something. To send furniture flying. To turn into a rage-filled monster and tear the room apart.

That burning sensation on her back intensified. A voice in her mind whispered, *Do it. Show them what you are.*

But she couldn't.

Because if she did that, if she gave into that feeling and hurt them, she *would* be a monster. But that wasn't who she was.

Pathetic, that voice growled.

Della stood, wiping away her tears. "I'm done. I don't want to talk about this any—"

The EMF meter in her bag screamed at her. Panicked, she rifled through her book bag to find it. The sensor was freaking out just as it had that day in traffic.

The lights above them flickered off.

A scream from downstairs cut through the silence.

The door behind her slammed open, revealing Kohen's alarmed face. "Uh, I hate to interrupt, but we have a problem."

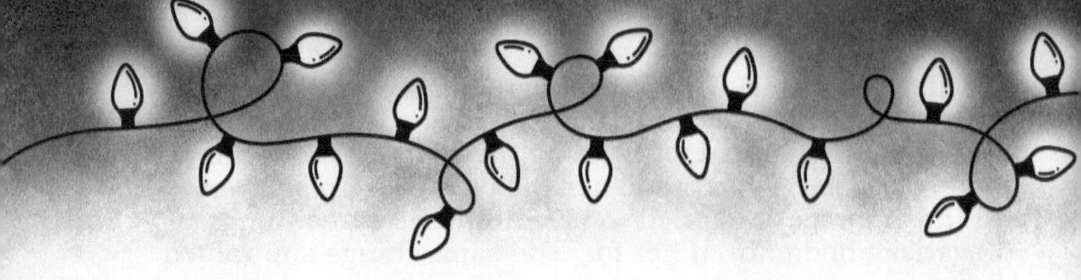

CHAPTER SIXTY-ONE

Crash and Burn

Della and Kohen took to the stairs two at a time, nearly plowing over Porter in the process.

"What happened?" Jasper said over their shoulders.

Porter looked between them, his eyes lingering on the half-dried tears on Della's cheeks.

"I swear to God I saw someone outside," came Poppy's shaking voice. She stood in the kitchen, peering out the window, wine bottle shaking in her hand. "Dressed in all black, just lumbering around out there."

"The lights have been acting up, too," Porter said pointedly, giving Della a knowing look. "I think someone should check on the electrical."

"I agree," Kohen said, nodding to where Max sat discretely checking his EMF meter.

This was it.

Ahiga was here.

Della knew he was toying with them, seeing how they'd react. Scaring Poppy like that was purposeful. He seemed to feed on chaos, and Della wouldn't let him have it.

"Poppy, I'm sure you just saw your own shadow. How much have you had to drink?" she asked, eyes on Max. His face was scrunched up in worry.

He whispered something to Sebastian, and with that, Sebastian ran outside to the hearse.

"I did *not* see my shadow, Della," Poppy spat.

"Poppy, just step away from the window, okay?" Kohen sighed.

The entire house chilled as the lights blinked off.

"Mom, what's going on?" Leo asked from the kitchen table.

"I'm sure the snow just took out a powerline. There's no need to worry," Kimi said, smiling reassuringly.

Jasper looked to Della, an accusatory look on his face. "What did you do?"

Just as Kohen was about to tell him off—Della really wished he would've lost it on Jasper—the window before Poppy shattered inward as if shot with a torpedo. She collapsed to the ground as black smoke began pooling into the kitchen.

Arlo jumped to stand protectively before Della, hands at his side, ready to protect her however he could.

"What the Hell?" someone screeched.

"M—Max!" Porter screamed, his voice shaking. Della didn't know when it'd happen, but his hand had found her forearm. He was gripping her so tightly that she almost screamed in pain.

Max stood frozen, looking dazed.

Porter swore, disconnecting from Della. He ran to where Max's bag sat on the table, procuring a container of salt. It was only when he shoved the salt into Max's hands that he snapped out of his trance.

Together, they set to work creating a sigil on the kitchen table, shooing Leo, Cassie, and Finlay toward the door.

"What are they doing?" Jasper demanded. He made for Della, but Kohen stopped him.

The smoke was building upon itself, creating Ahiga's form. It towered over Poppy, its face cut into a smile.

"Get away from her!" Della snapped, rushing forward. Arlo's hand stopped her before she ran headfirst into danger like usual.

Ahiga tilted his head at her. "Spared," he said, with a glance down. His claw-like hand pointed at Kimi, then Jasper. "Not so much."

Della stood before her mother and father protectively. No matter how angry she was with them, she wouldn't let harm befall them.

Ahiga lunged forward as Arlo slashed his arm through the air, his hand turning into a giant gangly Wendigo claw. An ear-piercing scream rang out as his claws collided with Ahiga's misty body. With Arlo preoccupying his brother, Kohen ran to help semi-conscious Poppy off the floor and to a safer spot near the walk-in pantry. Della pushed Kimi and Jasper toward the door. The rest of the family followed suit, screaming and crying as they ran for the safety of the outside world.

Beside her, Arlo's half-transformed body crashed into the wall. His face was scrunched up in pain as he slid down, his hand clutching his side, a red bloom spreading across his stomach.

The front door was wrenched open to reveal a fuming Elvi. As Della helped Arlo up off the ground, she watched in astonishment as Elvi bent down, removed her heels, and threw them at Ahiga. His body rippled, causing him to recoil in pain.

"Iron soles. Custom—" Elvi said proudly but was cut off by another loud screech.

Della turned to see glistening silver-white ropes around Ahiga's body, squeezing him tight. His slit-like eyes narrowed as he turned to Max.

"Kohen, we need ya," Max said, his outstretched hands glowing the same silver-white. "Now."

Kohen ran to him, hopping up onto the table, determination on his face. With a nod in Della's direction, he sat in the salt sigil, all trace of fear disappearing from his eyes.

Della knew in that moment there was nothing he wouldn't do for her.

Pulling Arlo and Elvi along with her, she stood beside Porter, covering her ears from the horrid sounds Ahiga was making.

The burning pain in her back had spread to the exact places those mystical ropes were squeezing.

Della glanced at Kohen, at the sigil on the table. It was a star inside a triangle. Each point of the star seemed to represent a different element.

Just like the mark on Jimmy's wrist back in October.

She vowed this wouldn't end the same way.

Max placed his hands on the table, shutting his eyes tightly. His spellbook had appeared before him, open to a page with the same symbol.

"*Fra død vikalle, ekablit igjen,*" Max whispered. "*Fra død vilkalle, ekablit igjen. Vikalle død.*"

Ahiga screamed, and the glass cupboards in the kitchen shattered. Kohen's muscles contracted against his will, his head lulling to the side.

"*Fra død vilkalle, ekablit igjen. Fra død vilkalle, ekablit igjen. Vilkalle død,*" Max repeated, his voice shaking.

There was electricity in the air. Della could feel it stinging her skin.

Ahiga's scream distorted as the silver ropes disappeared. His body arched, tendrils of smoke ripping away, traveling through the air toward Kohen. There was a sensation tearing in Della's chest, causing her to wince and stumble back into Elvi.

The edges of the salt sigil lit up red as Max spoke again. "*Vikalle Ahiga.*"

Squinting against the light, Della watched as Kohen's veins turned pitch black. He writhed and winced, the breath stolen from his lungs as his eyes rolled back into his head. Ahiga's screams faded with his misty form, his spirit engulfing Kohen.

The searing pain wrapped around Della's body disappeared, replaced with a dull ache as Kohen calmed.

For several agonizing moments, nothing happened. But then, Kohen's eyes shot open, revealing pits of swirling red hellfire.

The five of them watched Kohen carefully, squinting against the bright red light that had shot up from the sigil. Max was panting heavily. Della could tell the spell had drained him more than he'd expected. With a stumbling step backward, he swore, looking to Della.

"Ready?" he asked, worry flashing in his glowing amber eyes.

"For what?" Elvi asked. At some point, she'd retrieved her iron-sole heels. She stood clutching them to her chest, eyes wide.

Della nodded.

Porter motioned for Elvi to step back. Without a moment's hesitation, she did, joining him and Arlo in the archway that led to the foyer.

Max flipped through his spellbook, scanning a page for several infuriatingly long seconds. His hand now hovered before Kohen, whose lips were set in a cruel smile thanks to Ahiga.

Shakily, he reached up to hover his other hand before Della. "Ei will come for ya, always. Ei promise," he said. "If things go wrong—"

"I trust you," Della said, steeling herself with a shaking breath.

He nodded, inhaling deeply. "*Overføring av sjeler.*" whispered.

Ahiga's smile faltered as white-hot pain erupted in Della's skull. Her knees wanted to buckle, but she fought it, shutting her eyes tightly.

"*Overføring av sjeler,*" Max repeated, his voice hitching in pain. "*Fra Ahiga til Della.*"

Through her eyelids, Della could see neon purple light.

Her legs finally gave out, sending her crashing to her knees. Suffocating panic seized her chest, her eyes opening in fright. She gasped for air, staring at the reflection of her glowing purple eyes on the linoleum floor.

The floor dissolved before her, colors and patterns spreading from under her hands, the world glitching like a broken computer screen.

Boiling blood was pouring from her eyes, nose, and

ears. Scarlet drops hit the floor, bursting forth into strange glowing plants.

"NO!" Kohen screamed, his voice distorted.

Tendrils of shadow erupted from his chest, the edges bright purple. Kohen stood, gripping the tendrils like they were ropes. Della staggered to her feet, wiping the blood from her face as she beckoned the tendrils forward with a silent whisper. Kohen was pulling the tendrils back with all his might to no avail. They broke free from the barrier, shooting forward, connecting with Della's forehead.

Her vision blurred as someone screamed her name.

Her body arched back, her eyes burning as they rolled back into her skull.

As if she were drowning in the lake, icy darkness swept over her.

The last thing Della remembered was her head hitting the floor as soft purple light enveloped her.

~ ~ ~

Max stumbled to the side, feeling faint as he watched Della's head roll to the side. Before he knew what was happening, he'd found himself on his knees, holding his head in his hands. Voices swirled in his mind. The strangled cries of the dead fought over each other, clawing at his ears to be heard. Women and children screamed at the top of their lungs, calling out to him. The angered roar of fallen men drowned them out, deafening him.

It didn't stop until he felt a hand grab his shoulder.

"I'm fine," he choked, peering through his fingers at Della's unconscious form.

Struggling to his feet, he staggered over to her, collapsing to his knees again at her side. When he touched her, electric sparks of purple light traveled up his arm.

Dizziness took hold.

Black spots danced in his vision.

He blinked, and suddenly, he was lying beside her, his eyes fluttering shut.

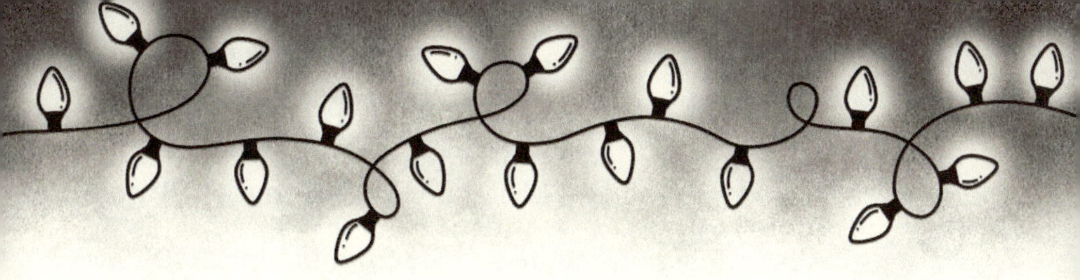

CHAPTER SIXTY-TWO

Porter rushed to them, skidding on the tile in the process. Max was burning, and Della was freezing. He shook them, but as expected, neither of them budged.

"Porter?" Arlo asked, his voice small.

"I—I don't know," Porter breathed.

There was nothing he could do.

He couldn't cast a spell and magic this better.

He looked to Elvi, thinking maybe, just maybe, she could do something. Anything.

Her giant blue eyes were on the table.

Porter looked up, feeling his stomach drop. Kohen's flaming eyes were fixed on Della.

Kohen just stood there, his skin so pale it looked translucent, his hair flying out behind him like he was floating underwater.

"Interesting," he said, though his voice wasn't his. It was low and scratchy, like something off an old record. "Foolish kids," he laughed. His eyes flicked to Arlo, a deep scowl appearing on his lips. "Brother."

Arlo growled at him, or rather Ahiga's spirit inside him. "Do not call me that," he snapped.

Kohen—no, Ahiga—squinted at him. "And what would you prefer? I have several choice words in my new-found dictionary. This body is—" He paused, studying his borrowed hands. "—a pleasant surprise. I'll be honest; I was hoping for the Dreamwalker. But he'll do."

Porter stood. "Can either of you exorcise him?" he asked, glaring at Ahiga as Arlo began to pace.

Arlo had stayed transformed, still stuck as a half-human-half-Wendigo.

"No," Arlo spat. "We'll have to wait for Max to wake up."

Porter's heart did somersaults in his chest. "I think we'll be waiting quite a while," he whispered.

Ahiga laughed. "What a shame."

"Where's the pipe?" Elvi asked. "With that spellbook, I can try to—"

"Absolutely not," came a voice from behind.

Porter turned to see a skinny older gentleman wearing a leather apron stained with what he hoped wasn't blood. He removed a pair of multi-lensed spectacles, stepping past Elvi with a pointed glare. Trailing behind him was Sebastian, alongside a tall woman in a bright yellow sundress.

Hugo and Enid.

Hugo whizzed past Porter, yanking Max's spellbook off the table. He shivered, immediately handing it off to Sebastian.

"What exactly are you playing at, spirit?" Enid asked, her voice full of disdain.

The swirling hellfire in Kohen's eyes flickered. "I am only trying to finish what I started. To protect my family, my tribe, from those who stand against us."

"Ahiga," Arlo snapped. "Nothing you have ever done protected us. Nothing you ever did—"

"You know nothing of what I've done!" Ahiga roared. "You know nothing of the burden I've carried!"

"You made me into a monster, Ahiga!" Arlo hissed.

Ahiga's eyes fluttered in frustration. "You were a sacrifice I was willing to make. You were too kind to those—those pollutants who founded this awful town."

"They were my friends!"

"They wanted us dead!" Ahiga screamed, stomping down hard on the table.

Hugo was instructing Sebastian how to use the spellbook, his eyes on Della and Max.

"How can you be so blind, even now?" Ahiga asked. "Do you have any idea what our people have gone through?"

Arlo inhaled deeply, straightening. "You cannot fight violence with violence, brother."

Ahiga scoffed. "Always the pacifist," he spat. "I should've just killed you. And I should've drowned her." He pointed at Della, the tip of his finger causing sparks to ripple across the magical barrier of the salt sigil. "She left. Left them to rot—"

"So did you!" Arlo snapped.

"Not by choice! Your idiotic father made me!" Ahiga screamed.

The table rumbled beneath him.

"*Our* father," Arlo said through gritted teeth. "He was

our father!"

The bright red light of the sigil was fading.

Ahiga rolled his eyes.

"I've had enough of this," Arlo growled, looking at Hugo and Sebastian. He nodded, turning away. "Do it. Trap him. Trap him now."

Porter grabbed Della's book bag, wrenching the dreamcatcher out of it, shaking off a pen that had wedged itself into the weaving. Hugo took it from him, holding it out before Sebastian, giving him a reassuring nod.

"You're not getting rid of me that easily," Ahiga said with a dangerous smile.

Kohen's foot stomped down on the table, the salt sigil blowing away. His palms thrust out before him, sending Hugo, Enid, and Sebastian flying backward.

"Do you have any idea how stupid it is to trap a ghost in a Shaman? How easy it is for me to take control of him?" Ahiga laughed.

Arlo's skin was melting away, his face elongating, antlers growing from his head. He lunged at Ahiga, his claws slashing through the air, hitting nothing as Ahiga leaned out of the way.

"Don't hurt him!" Sebastian screamed, scrambling to his feet.

Porter made a grab for Kohen's legs.

Every muscle in his body tensed.

"What the—" Porter exclaimed, frozen on the spot.

Kohen put his palm up in the air, levitating Porter. As he slowly clenched his fist, Porter gasped for air, his lungs tightening. With his other hand, Ahiga sent tendrils of smoky shadow towards Arlo. They wrapped around his limbs, causing him to roar in pain as they constricted like a snake around him. He reared, his horns scraping the ceiling.

"STOP IT!" Sebastian yelled at the top of his lungs. The spellbook pages were flipping back and forth, sending a breeze up to ruffle his hair.

Kohen's head tilted to the side.

"Now, why would I do that?" Ahiga snapped, thrusting his hands forward.

The pages settled, and Sebastian pointed two fingers at Arlo, fury filling him. "*LYS!*" he screamed, a stream of light flying from his fingers, shining around Arlo, the shadows disappearing.

Ahiga shrieked in agony. His power faltered, causing him to drop Porter to the floor with a painful thud. Elvi grabbed him by the collar of his jacket, pulling him up off the floor. Her iron-soled heels were back on her feet. In her hand was a glittering pink pistol.

Ahiga recovered quickly, thrusting his hand forward. A dark shadow stretched toward Sebastian. Hugo intercepted it, throwing orange powder on the ground, which erupted into flames. The shadow backed away, cowering like a scared animal.

While they'd been distracted, two shadows rose behind Sebastian. They lunged at him, wrapping him up in darkness. He cried in agony, the spellbook falling from his hands. Porter ran to him, unsure how to help but not keen on letting him die.

With a stamp of his foot, light scared off the shadows again. The look on Sebastian's face scared Porter shitless.

"Do it, my boy," Hugo said, reaching into his apron pocket to procure more orange powder.

"*Flyt,*" Sebastian spat.

The pages of the spellbook on the ground moved on their own, not stopping until they landed on a page full of dark magic. Sebastian scanned the page, took one last look at Hugo, and then spoke the spell at the top of the page.

"*KONTROLLERE SKYGGER!*" he screamed at the top of his lungs.

The shadows stopped, shaking like leaves in the wind. Sebastian stamped his foot down on the ground, and the shadows rushed at them, circling him, Hugo, and Porter like a pack of wolves. Sebastian thrust his hand forward, using his mind to pull the tendrils of darkness toward himself. He flexed his fingers into claw-like shapes, pulling the shadows off the ground and into two balls next to him. With all his might, he threw the balls of shadow at Kohen. They hit him square in the chest, sending him stumbling back a few paces.

Sebastian glanced at Porter, eyes wild. "Grab him!" he screamed.

Porter did as he was told, running to Kohen as Ahiga tried to regain his composure. The spirit didn't have time to react. Porter grabbed Kohen, tackling him to the floor, pinning his hands on either side of him as he screamed and cried out in pain.

"*ELLEF DØD, EKABLIT IGJEN!*" Sebastian screamed, Hugo and Enid instructing him, their hands out in front of them, pulling the spirit of Ahiga their way.

Kohen gasped for air as a spectral version of himself disconnected from his body and floated up into the air. His spectral form slowly turned into a person who looked like an older version of Arlo with scars all over his face.

"*ELLEF DØD EVIG DREAMCATCHER!*" Sebastian screamed.

Ahiga's spirit swirled in the air as a bright white light erupted from the discarded dreamcatcher.

The light sucked in Ahiga's spirit like a massive spectral vacuum.

With one final screech of horror, he disappeared.

They'd done it.

They'd trapped him.

Kohen stopped wriggling beneath Porter's grip, his eyes fading to their normal orange-brown. He stared up at him in shock, Porter still pinning him down.

"Never let me do that again," he whispered groggily. "Get off me."

"Gladly," Porter grumbled, standing, offering Kohen a hand up off the floor.

They turned back to Sebastian, who was looking at his shaking hands in awe and horror. "I can't believe I just did—"

Elvi appeared out of nowhere, sweeping the dreamcatcher off the ground. "Thank you kindly. I'll be taking this off your—" Before she could finish, a cookie sheet collided with the side of her head.

"What the Hell—" Poppy said as Elvi collapsed at her feet. "—happened to my kitchen?" she finished, brandishing her cookie sheet like a sword.

"We won," Sebastian said weakly, his voice shaking as bad as his body.

Porter took one look at him, and a lightbulb went off in his head. "Seb, are you okay?" he asked breathlessly, his eyes wide.

Hugo placed a hand on Sebastian's shoulder and nodded. "Breckenridge will be fine with some rest," he said, smiling proudly.

"That's just dandy," Poppy snapped. "But what about them?" she asked, pointing to Della and Max.

CHAPTER SIXTY-THREE

Slowly, Della sat up, blinking away the darkness. A breeze ruffled her hair as she stood, taking in her surroundings.

Black grass.

Purple pine trees.

A sky filled with the brightest aurora she'd ever seen.

"Hey—"

She yelped in fright, turning to see Max sitting a few feet behind her.

"What are you doing here? You scared the crap out of me!" she hissed.

He smiled, struggling to his feet. "Sorry," he shrugged, dusting himself off.

Della ran to him, wrapping him in a giant hug. "Where are we? Are we dead?"

Max squeezed her tightly. "Fortunately, Ei don' think that's the case," he laughed, gently pushing her away. "If Ei had tuh make an educated guess, Ei'd say we're here." He placed a finger on her forehead.

Della felt her heart drop. "Uh oh."

"Yeah," Max smiled, taking her hand.

"Any idea how we get out?"

"Well, it's *your* brain,"

Della turned to look at the forest of purple pine trees surrounding them. A path lined with tiny teal lights cut through the woods to her left.

One way forward.

She turned, her eyes scanning the forest behind Max. No path, no guiding light—just darkness.

No way back.

Taking a deep breath, Della made for the path. She pulled Max along, walking hand in hand with him through the trees.

They walked for ages, finding the forest littered with discarded toys covered in silvery spider webs. Della shivered. Something didn't feel right.

A bright light appeared up ahead.

The trees began to thin until the endless sky and creepy trees no longer surrounded them.

"Of course," Max sighed, gesturing to the sight before them.

Wooden filing cabinets stretched as far as the eye could see, standing as tall as a skyscraper. Each row was labeled in flowery silver writing. Some drawers had padlocks, some were already open, and some were hanging off their hinges.

"It's a mess in here!" Della said, aghast, crossing to the nearest drawer hanging free, carefully replacing it. When she put it back into place, papers appeared inside it.

"Are ya really surprised by that?" Max asked, a hint of laughter in his voice as he came to peer over her shoulder.

Della rolled her eyes, taking one of the papers. When she held it, it shimmered, a moving picture appearing across its lilac surface. It was one of her more recent memories—the day she arrived in Moss Hollow—something she thought about often. The edges of her vision sparkled, the drawing turning from sketch to photograph. Carefully, she tucked it away in the drawer, knowing she'd be sucked into the picture if she stared too long.

"Why do ya think we're here?" Max had his eye on a different drawer. One that said his name. "There are millions of drawers here. Are we supposed tuh find the memory of ya losing part of yerself tuh the peace pipe?"

"You act like I'm supposed to know."

"Again, yer brain."

Della sighed heavily, staring down the long hall of towering cabinets. "C'mon."

They walked in silence, taking in each and every drawer. Della didn't know if time worked differently in her mind than in the real world, but she was sure they had been walking for hours until they finally came to a crossroads. They hesitated, unsure of whether to split up or not.

Ultimately, they decided to keep heading straight and stick together.

They walked and walked, occasionally picking up fallen drawers or trying to open locked ones. Every time one of the drawers was replaced, a sense of peace washed over Della. And every time Max yanked on a padlock, her entire body filled with white-hot pain.

"Repressed memories," Max suspected, eyeing Della as she doubled over in pain for the seventh time, holding her head as if it were about to explode. "Best tuh leave them untouched for now."

"But what if what we are looking for is locked? I can't remember what happened, right? That sounds like a repressed memory to me," Della said, her voice tinged in pain, looking around with fear in her eyes.

"We'll cross that bridge when we get tuh it," Max said sternly.

Della was about to keep on walking when something caught her eye. One of the rows of drawers looked unusually flat and scuffed up. One of the handles was on its side, almost like a door handle.

Pulling it didn't work.

Pushing it did nothing.

Max cleared his throat, reaching around her. He slid the door to the right, opening it with ease.

"How—" Della began.

He shrugged.

Beyond the door was a pitch-black expanse. A foggy, all-consuming kind of darkness that made Della sick to her stomach. She desperately didn't want to go down that hall, but she knew the answers they needed were down there.

Together, they trudged on, their eyes eventually adjusting to the darkness. Max tried to flick a flame into existence, but apparently, his magic didn't work here.

Every drawer here was locked and covered in cobwebs that pulsed with faint lilac light. There was sadness here. Della could feel it all around her. She could feel the pain and sorrow and despair. The hopelessness. The fear.

"What was that?" Max asked, stopping dead in his tracks.

"Please tell me you're joking," Della groaned.

"Ei shit ya not, Ei saw somethin' in the distance. Somethin' ran by," Max whispered. Even in the dark, she could see his scowl. "Ya need therapy. Like hours and hours of therapy."

"Oh, shut up!" Della hissed, continuing forward.

"There could be a demon in yer mind. A sleep paralysis demon or somethin'!" Max snapped.

"It can't hurt you," Della said simply.

"But it can hurt *you*," he said quietly, searching in the dark for her hand. When he found it, he refused to let go.

Again, it felt like hours before they came to something of interest. It was Max who found it this time. One of the drawers was glowing purple, covered in rusty chains and far more padlocks than any other drawers. It was high above them, too high to reach.

"That's got tuh be it," Max said, craning his neck to see it. "How do we get up there?"

Della wished her mind had come equipped with one of those fancy rolling ladders libraries had.

As soon as she thought of it, she was atop a ladder, her face right next to the drawer. She heard Max swear from fright below. She couldn't see him, but the ladder shook, and she knew he'd grabbed hold of it to steady her.

"Ya okay?" he called up to her.

"Yup!" Della replied, unable to hide the smile in her voice.

She reached out to touch the drawer, the purple light glowing brighter as her shaking hand drew near. The chains, however, tightened, sending rust dust into the air. The padlocks shook, afraid of the contents they had locked away. They were trying to warn her that she didn't want to see what was locked in this drawer.

Of course, she didn't really want to see whatever memory was here. There would be no going back after this. This would change everything; she could feel it.

But she had to know. Curiosity had always been her weakness.

"It's okay," she whispered.

The padlocks stopped shaking.

"I'm not afraid."

The chains loosened.

The rusty locks faded to dust.

All except one. One last warning.

But Della had already made up her mind. She wished for a key, and one appeared in her hand. Shoving the key into the lock, she turned it, a click resonating through the air. The key, the lock, and the chain faded out of existence. Without hesitation, she pulled open the drawer and was suddenly back on the ground, holding it in her hands.

Max looked at her skeptically.

"Ready?" she asked.

He nodded as Della handed over the drawer, removing its contents.

One file.

One stack of crinkled papers the color of rotting plums.

She opened it timidly despite convincing herself she was brave enough to see what was inside.

A drawing appeared of the kitchen in her parents' home. Young Della was sitting at the table, scribbling away in a notebook. As the sketch turned into a photo and they were sucked inside, more of the scene appeared around them.

Her parents were at the door. She couldn't hear what they were saying, but she knew they were talking to someone. Quincy was sitting in the living room, listening intently. The look on his face told Della that he had been worried.

"Well, I'll see what I can do. Thank you for calling me first. Mustn't let this information fall into the wrong hands," said a voice all too familiar to them.

"Yer jokin'," Max breathed.

The man walked towards young Della and sat next to her. "Hello there. My name is Percival James Mavericks, and you are?"

"Why is my dad in yer memories?" Max asked shakily.

"If I knew why, we wouldn't be inside my brain, now would we?" Della said. It wasn't necessarily sarcastic.

Mavericks spoke again, a kind smile on his face. He looked younger, but not by much. "Oh! That's right! You're Delphee!" He tapped the notebook young Della had been writing in. "I like to write too, you know."

Young Della finally looked up at him. "Really?" There was a light in her eyes, the light of a child who desperately wanted to believe the world was a better place than people said.

Mavericks nodded. "I write truths. I write about people like you," he smiled.

Both versions of Della frowned, but only the younger one spoke. "I'm just a story?"

"No," Mavericks said with a sigh. "No, you're not just a story, my dear. You are something special."

Young Della looked over her shoulder at her parents, who were standing near the door, fear plastered across their faces. She glared at them, turning back to Mavericks.

"Most won't agree with that statement," Young Della said.

Tears stung Della's eyes. Mavericks was the reason her memories were gone? Mavericks had hidden her magic away? Why hadn't he ever said anything? She looked to Max, but he seemed just as upset and confused.

Mavericks winked at her younger self. "They are just jealous of you. A lot of people will be, Miss Coleman."

The scene suddenly changed. Young Della was now sitting at the top of the staircase, listening to her parents fighting. Quincy sat next to her, rage in his eyes.

"They're going to do something to me, Quin," Young Della whispered.

Quincy turned to her, his face darkening. "What did you see?"

"That's just it; I don't see anything. I didn't have any dreams last night. No visions. No nightmares. Nothing. I can't see anything beyond today," Della whispered, her tiny voice full of sadness.

"Mavericks won't let them hurt you. *I* won't let them hurt you," Quincy whispered fiercely.

Della eyed him. "Can you make me a promise?"

"Of course."

"Don't forget me. Whatever happens, don't forget," Della said, taking her brother's hand and squeezing it tightly. "Find a way to remember me."

Max reached for Della's hand and held it with the same passion and intensity.

"I don't remember any of this," Della quivered. She hadn't realized she'd been sobbing breathlessly this whole time.

Again, the scene changed. Mavericks and Della sat beside a small stream, watching a deer from afar. Mavericks was throwing stones into the water, watching them float away.

"I am truly sorry I couldn't help you, my dear," Mavericks said, a heaviness to his voice. She and Max were watching this scene unfold from behind them, but Della was sure he had tears streaming down his face.

"I'm not mad at you," Young Della whispered to him.

He looked at her. Not down at her, like most adults would with a seven-year-old, but *at* her. Almost as if he saw her as his equal.

"Why not?" he asked carefully.

"I don't think you have a say in the matter," Della sighed.

Mavericks was quiet for quite some time. "You are going to do great things one day, mamankanois. I know that for certain."

Both versions of Della gasped.

Mavericks turned to her and smiled. "Your grandmother used to call you that, right? Before she died? I knew her. She was my friend. She told me once that she had a vision about you. It was the only vision she'd ever had that didn't end in destruction. She saw you victorious." He flicked his fingers, and two golden butterflies appeared before them. They circled them slowly like a protective barrier.

"How will I be victorious if you are going to take my memories away?" Young Della asked. "If you're going to take away my magic, how can I protect myself?"

Max swore.

"What your parents don't know is that the spell won't last forever. I can't take away your powers completely, even I am not strong enough to do that. The medicine you'll take to subdue your remaining abilities will eventually stop working. One day, all your memories will come back," Mavericks explained.

"Why are they afraid of me?"

Mavericks' shoulders fell. "Because they do not understand. They were not born to see the world the way we do. You'd think by now they'd at least try and learn how."

"I'm angry with them," Della whispered.

Mavericks nodded. "I don't blame you. And when that day comes, and you remember, I think you will be even more angry than you are now." He thought for a moment. "If I could, I would take you far away from here. You belong somewhere else. Somewhere that you can be who you truly are."

"Why can't you?"

"There are people in this world that would stop at nothing to hurt you. There hasn't been a being like you on this Earth for centuries. Some want to use you and your powers. Others want you dead. And that is far too much for a young girl to handle," Mavericks sighed. "Even now, there are things that are drawn to you, like your Wendigo friend. He can sense your magic. It's like a pull to him. I doubt he'd hurt you, but you can never be too careful."

"I don't want to forget him," Della said sadly.

"In some sense, you will always have your memories. You just won't be able to access them. The older you get, the less you will try to remember."

"What if my memories don't come back?"

"Then I will find you and ensure they do," Mavericks said pridefully.

"Promise?"

"Promise."

The butterflies circling them closed in, dancing in front of their faces.

Mavericks turned to her, silvery tears making his wrinkles shimmer in the late afternoon light.

"I do so hope to meet you again one day. I'd like to offer you a job at my newspaper," he said, his voice cracking. "You can write the front-page stories."

Della smiled brightly. "I'd like that very much."

Mavericks nodded. "I'm not going to take that away from you, Della. I want you to keep writing. I want you to question everything. I want you to fight for yourself." He could barely talk now. He pointed at her heart. "I want you to always follow your heart, to trust your instincts. To be kind to those the world has deemed unworthy of love. I want you to be curious and courageous and adventurous."

"That does sound like yours truly, Della Coleman," Young Della smiled.

Mavericks laughed. "That has a nice ring to it. Sounds like a book title."

"Maybe I'll use it one day," she giggled.

Mavericks smiled lovingly at her. "I'll be looking forward to reading whatever story accompanies it."

He glanced at the butterflies. They were hovering inches from their faces, undecided on whether they should land.

"Maybe you could write about the things you believe in. Maybe start a blog?" he proposed.

The butterflies finally landed on their noses. They glowed brightly, fading respectively to purple and orange. They flew away, flitting over to the peace pipe that Mavericks had been holding. They landed on it, dissolving into the bone.

Della disconnected from Max, standing before her younger self and Mavericks.

The two of them were left with blank, lifeless expressions. Mavericks had not only taken away her memories but his own as well. He hadn't wanted to. Della knew that in her heart of hearts. She knew everything he'd said was the truth. That was something she admired about Mavericks. He always spoke the truth no matter how weird or strange it sounded.

The scene began to fade, and she and Max were suddenly back in the hall of memories.

"Are ya okay?" Max asked, his voice barely a whisper.

"No," Della cried.

"Ei'm—" Max began.

"I want you out," Della said gruffly. "Out now."

Suddenly, she was alone. She'd presumably sent him back to the real world.

The walls around her felt like they were closing in. Her entire life was a complete and utter lie. Everything. She collapsed to her knees, crying uncontrollably, hugging herself tightly.

How much of her life had been false memories?

This was why her mind was broken. All these memories shouldn't have been locked away. Without them, her mind had shattered. She didn't know how to use her powers, so they'd been trapped inside her, a fissure forming in her mind.

But she needed those memories now. All of them, no matter how painful they were.

Chapter Sixty-Three

She stood, shaking.

Her hands were already glowing bright purple, her bones illuminated in the dark. She conjured all her energy, her life force—everything—forcing it on the walls around her. Sparkling waves of lilac energy cascaded around her, and as they washed over the cabinets, the drawers flung open, breaking chains, padlocks, and shackles. Memory after memory flooded her mind, making her dizzy. But she didn't stop it, any of it.

She'd rather remember everything, even the horrible things, than have it all locked away.

Mavericks and her grandmother had called her a butterfly, but until now, she'd been a caterpillar trapped in a cocoon against her will.

Now was finally the time to break out of that chrysalis.

The waves of energy engulfed her. The bright purple magic looked less like energy and more like rifts in the universe.

That was it.

The Universe.

She'd always held a grudge against it, but really, it had given her a piece of itself. She shared in its power.

She wasn't a god. Wasn't trying to rival Him or His Angels.

But she could still create. That was her gift. Her imagination. Her mind.

She could create worlds if she wanted to.

If she could do that, she sure as Hell could solve any other problem this world would throw at her.

Because she was Delphee Chrysanthemum Coleman, the last dreamwalker of the Mukwa tribe and Kitchi name.

And she was tired of hiding it.

CHAPTER SIXTY-FOUR

The Rat and The Butterfly

"Took you long enough," came a voice from behind. "Too bad you won't make it out of here to share your newfound confidence with the world."

Della spun.

Before her stood a picture-perfect copy of herself. It was like looking in a mirror. You know, minus the fire-red tips of her hair, the stark black eyes, and the pulsing veins of evil magic.

"What are you supposed to be?" Della asked haughtily.

"I am your darkness, your Shadow Self. I am what you could become if only you gave in. I am all the parts you try so hard to hide. But news flash, I've been here the whole damn time, watching and waiting. Thank you for destroying that pipe. If you have your full power back, so do I," her Shadow Self spat. "Aren't you going to welcome me home?"

This was weird, even by Della's standards.

"Not quite. What do you want?"

"You abandoned us," her Shadow Self spat. "You let them take us away!"

Della rolled her eyes, crossing her arms over her chest. "And?"

Her Shadow Self smiled, revealing sharp teeth. "I think it's high time somebody else called the shots around here."

A gun appeared in her Shadow Self's hand. She aimed, wasting no time pulling the trigger. Della thrust her hand forward, imagining the bullet blooming into a rose. The bullet was eager to oblige, happy to become something less destructive. Della grabbed the rose out of thin air, snapping her fingers, watching as the gun in her Shadow Self's hand turned to silver sand.

"You really think I'm giving up without a fight?" she asked, making a *tsking* sound. "Come on, you know us better than that."

Her Shadow Self rolled her void-like eyes. "You talk too much," she snapped, lunging forward, her fingernails elongating into claws as her skin turned pitch black.

Della stumbled to the side, picturing the machete she had hidden in her apartment materializing in her hands. She smiled as it sparkled into existence. She swung it hard, slicing her Shadow Self's arm. She shrieked, clutching the wound in agony. Glittering plum-colored blood seeped out from under her fingers. She glared at Della, swiping her claws through the air, aiming for her throat.

As she dodged out of the way, Della imagined her chunky heels transforming into platform boots with spikes on the bottom. She kicked her Shadow Self as hard as she could, the spikes of her shoes covered in plum blood. Her Shadow Self clutched her chest, staggering back.

"Anger isn't as powerful as you think," Della said, standing tall.

"Peace won't get you anywhere. You need me for what's coming next. What do you think gave you the strength to kill that sorry excuse for a witch, Eric?" her Shadow Self snapped.

"I have *never* needed you," Della spat.

She swung her machete down, her Shadow Self thrusting up her hands. The air warped and glowed that deep rotten-plum color, her machete stopped in mid-air by an invisible force field between them.

"I have always been whispering in your ear, Della," her Shadow Self sneered, her toothy grin glistening.

She shoved her hands upward, sending Della flying backward. Della collided with the ground, her machete knocked from her hands.

"I am only as powerful as you allow me to be," her Shadow Self laughed. "You can feign peace and lie to your little friends all you want, but you're right, I do know you. You're far from a saint."

Della stood, brushing herself off. "Tell me something I don't know. Maybe then I'll start listening."

She reached for the machete, calling it forth. It flew into her hands, leaving behind a glittering trail of stardust. Della spun it with one hand, beckoning her Shadow Self forward with the other.

"If you're so big and scary, you should've been able to kill me by now," Della laughed. "But you're the one who's bleeding, not me."

Her Shadow Self screamed, rushing forward, her

monstrous hands grappling for their target. Della slashed her machete through the air and off came her Shadow Self's arm. She screeched, collapsing to her knees. Della lifted her chin with the tip of her blade.

Her Shadow Self laughed. "You can bury me deep inside these halls, Della, but you will never be rid of me. I will always be there, waiting for the day you fail, waiting for my time."

"Then you'll be waiting a long time," Della spat. "Have fun with that."

She inhaled sharply, beheading her Shadow Self without remorse. As the spectral body before her fizzled out of existence, Della collapsed to her knees.

She sat in the empty corridors of her mind, winded. Long had it been since she'd let herself sit alone with her thoughts. Usually, she didn't like where her mind wandered.

She and Porter were alike in that way.

Their minds were constantly out to get them.

But here, in the dark, the solitude was comforting. For the first time in a very, very long time, she didn't blame herself. She was not responsible for the things done unto her. Not anymore. And while there were still the screw-ups and mistakes she'd made alone, maybe it was finally time to start forgiving herself.

She even found it in her heart to forgive her Shadow Self for attacking her like that.

Footsteps echoed through the corridor—tiny, child-like footsteps.

Della stood, brushing herself off. Faint lilac light was traveling her way. Bracing herself for what was coming next, she walked toward the light.

Her younger self materialized before her.

Young Della, covered in cobwebs, dirt, and dust on her clothes, and pine needles sticking out from her hair, smiled brightly up at her.

"Hey, kid," Della laughed, kneeling.

"We grew up," her younger self replied. She seemed thankful to know that. To know despite the odds, they'd made it this far.

Della shrugged. "It happens."

"Thank you for coming back for me," her younger self said.

A light breeze blew the dust and pine needles away. Della licked her thumb, scrubbing dirt off her younger self's face.

"Sorry I made you wait," she sighed.

Little Della frowned. "It was scary in there. With Ahiga. He was very angry."

"Did he hurt you?" Della asked, brushing away cobwebs from her tiny bony shoulders.

"No," Young Della smiled. "We're tough as nails."

"And oh so humble, too," Della laughed.

The faint purple glow around her younger self grew brighter as the last of the grime vanished.

Hand in hand, they walked back through the corridors of memories, finding themselves on a black sand beach. The ocean here was made of galaxies. Della had never seen a more beautiful sight. They sat, kicking off their shoes, the gentle waves lapping over their feet.

In the distance, Della could see an island. No matter how hard she wished, no boat appeared to sail them toward it.

"We can't go there," her younger self sighed.

"Why not?"

"He's blocked us out," she whispered.

Della didn't have to ask who the mysterious 'he' was.

Young Della turned to her, not meeting her eyes as she fiddled with a slowly mending hole in her jeans. "Are we going to be okay?"

Della wiped a tear from her cheek. "I think so."

"I'm scared."

"Me too."

Young Della finally looked up. She studied her older self's face, a melancholy smile tugging at her lips.

"I'm really proud of the person we've become. Thank you," she whispered. "And good job fighting off that dork. She was mean."

Della smiled brightly, pulling her into a hug. At that moment, she didn't feel broken. She had become precisely who she was meant to be. Maybe she did believe in fate. Or perhaps, just maybe, she'd made her own destiny somewhere along the line.

"I'm going to protect you from here on out," she whispered, squeezing her younger self tightly. "And I'm going to live every day making sure I continue to make you proud."

"Then, can you promise me something?"

"Anything."

"Get rid of the green," her younger self frowned, twisting a stray strand of hair around her finger. "Purple suits us better."

Della laughed. "Deal."

Little Della giggled, wrapping her arms around Della as tight as she could. Her lilac aura consumed her as she faded into giant purple butterflies that soared into the twinkling night sky. They danced and played in the galactic sea breeze, each one a comet shooting off toward that lonely little island off the coast.

Warmth bloomed in Della's chest.

Her inner child was safe again. Free to roam her mind, reminding her of the wonder and magic they'd loved. She silently vowed to always listen to the tiny voice in her head whenever it told her to trust a little more and worry a little less. When that voice needed her, she'd be there whether it wanted her to love without fear or find joy in the littlest things. If that voice wanted to be heard, she'd voice whatever it had to say.

Della was ready to wake up now and wasn't scared in the slightest of what was to come.

After all, the Universe had been on her side since her birth.

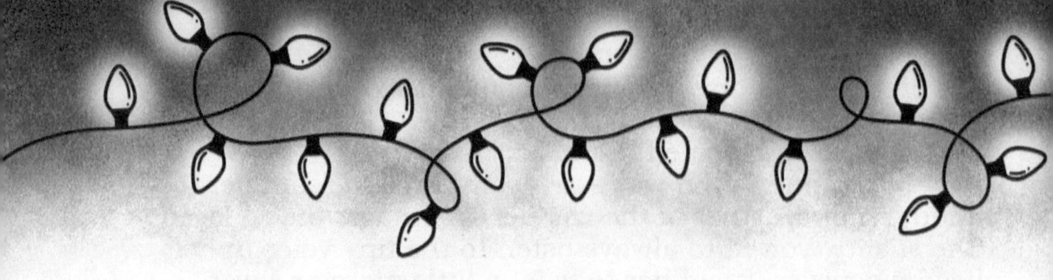

CHAPTER SIXTY-FIVE

Human Connection

Feeling was returning to Della's limbs in a cascade of pinpricks. She could hear a voice in the distance whisper a spell.

"Sebastian?" she asked groggily.

Someone, somewhere, breathed a sigh of relief.

Della forced her eyes open, a sea of faces swimming before her. She was still lying on the kitchen floor. Slowly, she sat up, blinking away the light.

Max was sitting beside her with his head in his hands. Without thinking, she hugged him, squeezing him so tight he complained he couldn't breathe.

"I'm sorry for kicking you out," she whispered, burying her head between his neck and shoulder.

"It's okay," he whispered back. "Ei'm glad yer okay."

He took her face in his hand, looking deep into her eyes. The glow of his eyes began to change to purple. Her own changed to teal. As they stared at each other in awe, their eyes faded back to their respective colors, then to all-consuming brown and flaming amber.

If they needed any proof that he was her familiar, this was it.

Max pulled her close, his lips finding hers. It was a quick little kiss, but it was enough. He pulled away, looking at her so longingly.

"It's a promise ring," he whispered.

"What?"

"The present Ei still have tuh—"

"I'm going to ask again: what the Hell happened to my kitchen?" Poppy screeched, cutting him off and startling Della.

You could always count on Poppy to ruin a good thing.

Porter offered Della a hand up off the ground, dusting her off as Max struggled to his feet. Poppy's entire kitchen was a wreck. Strange marks on the ceiling, weird plants growing out of the floor, scorch marks on the tile—Della grimaced. She'd make them pay to fix it if she didn't keel over from the massive truth bomb she was about to dump on her.

"Just lay off it, all right, Poppy?" Kohen snapped.

"Easy for you to say, your kitchen isn't a war zone!"

"It's hardly a war zone."

Poppy flipped him off.

Della couldn't help but laugh.

"Are you guys okay?" Porter asked, refusing to let go of Della's arm.

She turned to Max. He seemed drained, but somehow she knew he would be okay.

"Yeah, we're fine," Della smiled, pulling him into a hug.

Sebastian and Max joined in. Arlo too.

Kohen and Poppy.

Hugo and Enid. When had they showed up?

"What happened to Ahiga?" Della shrieked, looking up at Porter in fright.

"We handled it, don't worry," he smiled brightly, way too proud of himself. "You can thank Sebastian."

Della gave him a questioning look but eventually shut her eyes and enjoyed the giant group hug.

They stayed like that for a while.

They'd won this time. *Truly* won.

Mavericks would be so proud of her. That is, of course, after he answered all her burning questions.

"Uh, where's Elvi?" Sebastian asked, fear in his voice.

"Yeah, and the dreamcatcher," Kohen added, wriggling free from Poppy's grip.

Porter swore, breaking free from the hug to run outside and look for her.

Della knew she should be worried. Who knew what chaos this world would see if that dreamcatcher and Ahiga's spirit got into the wrong hands? But instead of fear, she just felt relief. They could deal with Elvi Sinclair and *P.O.I.* later.

For now, it was still Christmas.

For now, they could celebrate.

As the others went off to do damage control, Max pulled Della into the living room, reaching into his pocket to procure a tiny velvet box.

"Ei know it's kind of sudden, and we haven' even defined what we are, but Ei wanted ya tuh know that no matter what, Ei'm with ya 'til the end. People leave, and Ei'm so sorry they do, but Ei promise ya Ei won't," he said, opening the box, turning it round to show her a dainty ring with an amethyst shaped like a heart. "Ei'm with ya 'til the end. Of that, Ei'm sure."

He slipped the ring on her finger, sealing his promise with a kiss on her forehead.

"You want to know something super funny?" Della asked, making for the kitchen where her book bag lay discarded. She held up a hand to stop him from following, grinning like a crazy person.

She procured her own extra present, returning to him with outstretched arms.

In her hands sat an identical velvet box.

Max smiled brightly. "That is funny."

She opened it, revealing a silver ring with a band of turquoise around it.

"I'm with you to the end," she said, slipping the ring onto his finger. "Of that, I'm sure."

He laughed, pulling her toward him by the waist, kissing her as though he'd waited a millennium for this moment. She wove her fingers into his hair, collapsing backward onto the couch with him.

Della prayed to God no one would interrupt them.

Max stared deep into her eyes, cradling her cheek in his hand. There was admiration in his eyes, but she knew him well enough to know he was trying to bury his concern.

"What happened when ya kicked me out?" he asked.

"I had to fight an evil version of myself. I won, by the way," Della said, playfully flipping her hair behind her shoulder.

"My, oh my, what a brave dreamwalker ya are," Max laughed.

Della winked at him. "*Your* brave dreamwalker, you mean."

He buried his head in the crook of her shoulder, chuckling softly. "Dear God, Della, Ei'm glad yer okay."

There were tears in his voice.

Della rested her head atop his, twirling a piece of his hair around her finger. "Me too," she whispered.

She felt his tears soaking her shoulder as he sat there silently sobbing. Della hadn't realized just how worried he'd been. She squeezed him tight, reassuring him that she was, in fact, alive and well.

He lifted his head to look at her, a solemn smile on his lips. "Can we stay like this for a while?"

Della nodded, wiping a tear from his cheek. "Anything you want, love."

"That's my line."

She winked, snuggling onto the couch, savoring this moment for as long as possible. Someone was bound to come running in at any minute and ruin it. There were civilians with memories that needed wiping, a team that needed to be addressed, and a missing spy—her life was starting to sound like an action movie.

There would always be another danger to run off to.

But for now, she'd revel in these quiet moments with the boy who held her heart.

After all, who knew what their futures held?

"Thanks for navigating the darkness with me, Maximilian," she whispered.

"Anytime, Delphee, my love."

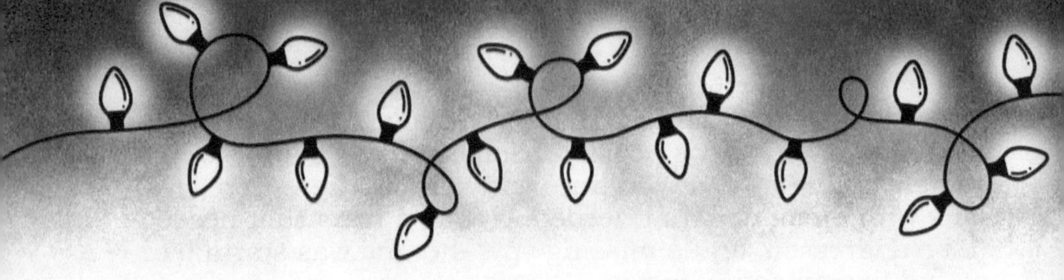

CHAPTER SIXTY-SIX

Christmas Day, Della pushed open the door to the historical society, Ashton and Kohen in tow.

"You have no idea how thankful I am for this opportunity, Della," Ashton said, depositing a suitcase by the front door.

Della shrugged. "You'll be safe here, and I know that everything under this roof will be safe with you watching over it."

Ashton smiled brightly, surveying his new home. Kimi had decided her days at the historical society were over. Her office was going to be remodeled into a bedroom. As long as Ashton took care of himself and the Sycamore House, he could stay as long as he liked.

"Mingan and I will be dropping by now and then to check on you, y'know, to make sure you haven't burned the place down," Kohen laughed.

"Much appreciated," Ashton said, making for the stairs.

He wrung his hands nervously, the wonderment disappearing from his eyes. It had taken hours to convince Ashton he'd be safe at the historical society. Whatever happened to him when he'd been missing still haunted him. He refused to elaborate further but promised he'd tell them eventually. He just needed time to collect his thoughts and get his life together. When Della mentioned Max could put up protective barrier spells and sigils, that seemed to ease his nerves.

Noticing her concern, he cleared his throat. "Hey, am I allowed to change things up around here?"

"In what way?"

"I just think it's a shame all our stuff is hidden away in a room upstairs," he shrugged.

"I'm sure we can make room down here," Kohen added, pointing down one of the many halls. "And I'm sure the Mukwas will be more than happy to donate a few new relics," he said with a wink.

Mingan was already spinning stories about his brave and ethereal granddaughter, the dreamwalker. In less than an hour, she went from being the butt of every joke to being respected as much as Mingan himself. When word spread of Della's plans to revamp the historical society, she was showered with praise.

"Hugo and Enid will help make sure things go where they belong," Della said, giving them both a knowing look.

"What? No more ancient Indigenous spirits wreaking havoc on the town? Bummer," Ashton yawned.

Kohen rolled his eyes.

Ashton laughed to himself, disappearing upstairs, whistling a Christmas carol as he went.

"So, uh, speaking of ancient spirits, what are you going to do about Arlo? Legally, I mean," Kohen asked.

"We have a guy," Della shrugged. Norman and everyone else at The Courier would have a ball forging all those documents.

Kohen blinked slowly. "I'm going to pretend I didn't hear that," he sighed. "But hey, mind using our last name?"

"How come?"

Kohen smirked, leaning back on his heels, admiring his niece, the great Mukwa dreamwalker. "He's a Kitchi through and through."

Della nodded.

"And so are you. Don't forget that," he said sternly, pulling her into a side hug before ruffling her hair. Della laughed, swatting him away. "You—all of you—are welcome here anytime. I hope you know that," he added, hands on his hips.

"I do," Della smiled.

Kohen rocked back and forth on his heels, glancing over his shoulder. Della gave him a questioning look, prompting him to sigh heavily.

"Porter mentioned something Ahiga said. He said I was a shaman or something. Mingan skirted the subject. Do you think Ash or, Hugo and Enid could help me figure it out? If I have some hidden power like you, I want to figure out how to use it," he said sheepishly, his face bright red.

"Worth asking," Della smiled. "As long as you're okay with being in a mystical classroom seven days a week with Sebastian."

Kohen snorted, rolling his eyes. "Maybe I should just figure it out on my own."

"Max and I will see what we can dig up," Della laughed, nudging him playfully.

"I appreciate that, little bear."

Ashton came bounding down the stairs, gesturing over his shoulder with his thumb. "Is there anything you wanted out of Kimi's office before I throw half her stuff in the dumpster?"

Della rolled her eyes, shrugging. "I'll do a once over. Try not to gouge each other's eyes out while I'm gone, okay?"

Kohen saluted her.

The energy in the historical society was different today. A fog had been lifted in a way. Della didn't know how she knew, but the spirits here felt calmer. As she walked past the small room that held all the Mukwa artifacts, joy passed over her. She wondered if Arlo and Ahiga's parents had been watching and what they thought. She wondered what happened to Ahiga. Was he burning in Hell, or was he stuck between worlds? Was he able to reconnect with his parents?

The door to Kimi's office was wide open. This space still felt a little dark, but Della knew that would dissipate as soon as Ashton moved in.

A few things were already boxed up—paperwork mostly—but the shelving units on either side of the room were still full. Della had a rough idea of what was in each box or tote. Most of the things stored here were broken beyond repair.

But Della had always had an affinity for broken things.

Scanning the room, a sliver of light caught her eye. She grabbed the stepladder leaning against Kimi's desk, propping it against the back wall. Della couldn't help but think of the file cabinets in her mind. Laughing to herself, she climbed the ladder, taking a small box off the top shelf. The box glowed with a bright white aura, beckoning her to open it. Once she was safely back on the ground, he set the container on her mother's desk and opened it.

Inside was a notebook bound in lilac leather, a dreamcatcher embossed in the center. As soon as Della touched it, the aura burst into swirls of purple. Inside was an inscription written in her grandmother's handwriting:

For Della,
May your wildest dreams come true, and the nightmares stay far, far away.

Love you forever,
Gramma Winnie

Della smiled, hugging the notebook to her chest. Della wasn't one to save pretty stationery for special occasions, but this notebook would forever be her most prized possession. Maybe she could use it to record all her visions. She had a feeling that was something Winifred did.

A soft breeze ruffled her hair. Della turned and, standing before her, was her grandmother. She was holding a sleeping baby, singing softly. She walked around Kimi's office, a look of mischief in her eyes.

"This will be yours one day, Delphee dear," she whispered, a smile tugging at her lips. "It will be your duty to protect our people and all those who seek us for protection."

There was a hand on Della's shoulder. The memory these walls held of her grandmother fizzled away as a spectral image of Winifred walked around to greet her. She was smiling ear to ear, that same mischievous look in her eyes.

"Good luck, my beautiful, beautiful mamankanois," she said, gently kissing Della's forehead before fading away, leaving behind ghostly dragonflies that peppered Della with teeny kisses.

Della wiped a tear from her cheek, tucking her notebook into her book bag before heading downstairs.

Kohen and Ashton were already arguing about how to redecorate and display all the treasures Della knew they'd be collecting. Kohen gave up, waving Ashton away, skipping over to Della, looking bored.

"Find anything?" he asked.

Della nodded. "Just an old notebook."

"Can always count on you to turn a bunch of junk into something beautiful," he laughed, putting his arm around her shoulders, leading her outside to where Max had been waiting for her. Porter had let them borrow the hearse for the afternoon.

"Ready to go?" Della asked as Max rolled down the passenger seat window.

"Ready if ya are," he smiled.

"I'll be back for dinner, kiddo," Kohen said, waving as she slipped into the driver's seat.

She told Max about what happened, for once excited to share what she'd seen. He listened intently, smiling brightly. She even let him flip through the notebook Winifred had left her. He had the same idea as her to use it as a place to record all her visions.

They stopped for lunch and coffee at *Ole Joe's*, marking this as their first official date as boyfriend and girlfriend—a concept which made Della's cheeks flush with childlike embarrassment in the best possible way. He'd promised her his tomorrows, and she couldn't wait to experience every day with him.

She also couldn't wait to see Nicoletta and Mavericks' reactions when they told them the nature of their relationship. She had a feeling Mavericks especially would be over the moon.

Before returning to Mingan's, Della parked the hearse in an alley.

"What's this?" Max asked, peering out at a wall that had been graffitied at least a thousand times.

Della smirked, laughing darkly. "All the seniors come and make their mark before going to college. Before I left for Moss Hollow, I spray painted, 'Delphee C. Coleman was here. Do not forget it.' over there," she explained, pointing to the middle of the wall. "I guess someone painted over it."

"Do ya want to redo it?" Max asked.

Della shook her head. "I don't feel like I have anything left to prove to Sycamore Heights. There are people here who love and accept me, and that's all that matters. The rest of them?"

"Viva la screw 'em," Max laughed.

"My thoughts exactly, Maxmilian."

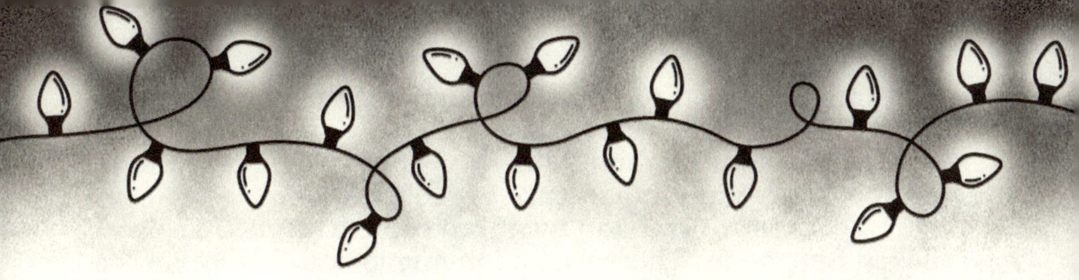

CHAPTER SIXTY-SEVEN

Until We Meet Again

Della stood breathless after helping Porter and Max pack all their luggage back into the hearse. It was early on the twenty-eighth, the sun just barely poking through the trees.

Snow was falling again.

This time, those glittery flakes brought hope with them.

She and the boys had spent their last few nights in Sycamore Heights back at Mingan's, allowing themselves a few days of much-needed rest. Max and Sebastian slept for most of it. Porter stress-baked. Arlo bonded with Mingan. Della began typing up her latest front-page story.

Per her family's request, she kept their names anonymous. The only people interested in the arcane were Poppy and Kohen. Everyone else lined up before Hugo when he said he could wipe away their memories of the strange ghost that had attacked them.

Della wondered what the difference between that spell and the one Mavericks had done was—just another question she'd have to find the answer to.

The only other people who hadn't wanted their memories wiped were Jasper and Kimi.

Della and her parents had come to an agreement. They wouldn't meddle in her life, and she wouldn't interfere in theirs. If she wanted to visit Leo and Cassie, she could. But she'd have to do so at Mingan's. They'd made it clear she wasn't welcome in their home anymore. There was no place for magic in the Coleman household.

They hadn't asked about the peace pipe or her memories. Della guessed that meant they didn't care.

Part of her had hoped they'd have a change of heart.

That maybe they'd roll up to bid her and the boys farewell.

But alas, they never showed.

Sebastian, Kohen, Mingan, Poppy, Hugo, and Enid, on the other hand, made sure to see them off.

"You sure you don't want to come with us?" Della asked Sebastian. There was a longing look in his eyes every time he glanced at the hearse.

"I'm sure," he smiled. "Hugo promised to teach me magic, anyway. I guess I'm his apprentice now."

"Be careful," Max scolded, flicking his head. "Don' get cocky. Humans aren' meant tuh do magic. The fact yer not ragin' evil is truly fascinatin'."

"I suspect young Sebastian has traces of magic in his blood. Trust we will keep you updated on how things progress," Hugo smiled, wrapping his arm around Sebastian.

Della was glad they'd found each other. Sebastian had always loved *Sun & Star Antiques*. She just hoped Hugo would keep him and Enid out of trouble.

"Oh! And Della, please give this to Mavericks for us!" Enid said, skipping up to the hearse with a basket of grapefruit-scented cleaning supplies.

"They do more than just clean," Hugo smiled, giving her a mystical little wink.

Porter took the basket and tried to find a space where it would fit in the back. Max had to help him.

"I'll keep an eye on them," Kohen smiled, ruffling Della's hair as he walked over with Poppy.

"Yes, I'm sure the five of us will have quite a few late-night conversations beneath the shop," Enid laughed.

"A good mayor knows everything going on in her town," Poppy said, a glint in her eyes Della couldn't explain.

"See ya around, kid," Kohen said, pulling her into a hug. "C'mon, Poppy. I owe you a coffee."

"You owe me more than that, Deputy," Poppy giggled.

Oh no.

Della knew that giggle.

"I think I'll be keeping an eye on them, huh?" Sebastian laughed.

"Please do," Della said with a disgusted shake of her head. "You heading out?"

"Yeah, my parents are pissed I missed Christmas morning. I'll have to tell them it's all your fault," he shrugged.

Della laughed, giving him a fist bump. They were never one to hug each other. Doing so now would feel like a goodbye, and Della desperately hoped they'd team up again. It was nice knowing how many people had her back.

Sebastian drug Hugo and Enid away, forcing them

into his old truck. Hugo looked displeased, but Enid was ready for an adventure as usual. Della knew that her husband taking Sebastian under his wing would be the greatest adventure of their lives.

"Almost ready?" Porter asked Arlo.

He nodded, staring at the hearse with a hesitant look. "I think so."

"If you want to stay, you can. Mingan is more than happy to have you," Della smiled, opening the door for him, already knowing his answer.

"No. I want to go with you. I want to see this Louisiana you keep talking about," Arlo smiled, tossing his sketchbook and pencil pouch onto the backseat. "I think I'll like it there."

He slipped into the backseat with Max, looking out at the world, a silent goodbye in his eyes. Della was overjoyed to be the one rescuing him from the place that had caused him so much heartache.

Moss Hollow would be good for him.

"Little bear," Mingan said, his raspy voice cutting into her thoughts.

She turned, seeing him smiling at her with tears in his eyes.

I am so proud of the woman you've become, he signed. *Your grandmother would be, too.*

Thank you, Della signed back. She hadn't told him what she'd seen at the historical society. Kohen had advised her otherwise.

Mingan waved away her thanks, placing a kiss on her forehead. *I love you. You are always welcome here.*

At least there was one spot in Sycamore Heights she could still call home.

"I hope I'm not too late to say goodbye," called an irritatingly sing-song voice. Della turned to see Elvi pulling up in a pale pink *Mini Cooper,* the window down, her hair flowing behind her. "Mind if we have a chat?"

"If that chat includes you returning my dreamcatcher, then yeah, we can chat," Della spat.

Elvi rolled her eyes, swinging her legs out of the car with the grace of a celebrity. "Can I get you without the snide remarks?"

"I don't know. Can I get you without the lies and half-truths?"

"Careful now, your little sister isn't here to stop our foul language," Elvi smiled. She took a large brown bag from the backseat and handed it over. "Here's your silly little dreamcatcher. Ghost-free, by the way. You're welcome."

Della took it cautiously, peering inside to make sure

it was the dreamcatcher she'd created. "Thanks."

"My pleasure, Miss Coleman." She sat lazily on the hood of her *Mini Cooper*, sizing her up.

Della glared at her. "What do you want?"

Porter and Max had appeared on either side of her. Arlo lingered in the hearse, craning his neck to see past Porter's legs.

Elvi shrugged. "Blame it on the Christmas spirit, but I'm feeling generous. I come bearing gifts." She looked to Porter. "For you, gravedigger, a warning. Someone in the police force isn't who they say they are." She turned to Max. "For you, witch, I unfortunately have nothing you don't already know. Although I'm sure that confirmed a few things." Finally, she turned to Della. "And for you, freak, I have four words. Ask Mavericks about Leland." She counted each word off, smiling darkly.

Della rolled her eyes, pushing down the dread bubbling in her stomach.

"Who's Leland?" Max asked, hands on his hips.

"She knows," Elvi said. "Believe me."

"I'm guessing you're not gonna tell me who the mole is?" Porter yawned.

She winked at him. "You'll figure it out. I believe in you."

Porter reddened, shifting uncomfortably under her gaze.

Flirting at a time like this. Did she always have to be so unbearable?

"What did you do to my brother's spirit?" Arlo asked, cowering behind Porter's shoulder.

"We exorcised him once and for all. He won't cause any more pain, I promise," Elvi said, drawing an 'x' over her heart.

Arlo didn't seem to believe her.

"Is that all? We have places to be," Della spat.

Porter held up a hand, earning himself a glare from Della and Max. He gave them each a pointed look, stepping forward.

"Are you one of us?" he asked, looking her up and down. "You didn't want *P.O.I.* to get their hands on the pipe, yet you told me they needed it to contain that black magic. What's your play?"

Elvi removed herself from the hood of her car, scowling deeply. "Unfortunately, I will never be 'one of you,'" she said, making a show of air quotes. "And my 'play' is protection."

"Yours or someone else's?" Porter asked, taking another step toward her.

"Let's just say we're allies, okay? That's all you need to know for now," she said, daring him to press further with that sparkle in her eye.

"We could protect you, you know," Porter said quietly. "If you truly are my ally, you're also my friend. And I am *very* protective of my friends."

Max nodded in agreement. Della gave him a funny look, but he only shrugged.

Elvi gave a half smile. "I'm glad to know I have earned that title in such a short time. But I'm going to decline. Double agents end up dead."

Porter leaned down, looking into her eyes. "Then I guess I'll meet you at my mortuary."

Max rolled his eyes, and Della about threw up in her mouth.

"Smooth," Elvi laughed.

Della knew Porter wasn't playing around. He meant what he'd said. No matter how untrustworthy she proved to be, Porter seemed to have a soft spot for her.

"I'll be in touch, undertaker," Elvi said, blowing him a kiss as she slipped back inside her *Mini Cooper*.

She shot Della a knowing look before driving off.

"Ei don' like her one bit," Max said, shivering.

Porter said nothing, returning to the driver's seat of the hearse red-faced.

Della stood staring at Elvi's bumper until it rounded the corner and disappeared behind snow-covered trees. Time would only tell what would become of Elvi Sinclair.

Porter honked at her to hurry up. Della imagined the boys were even more anxious to return to Moss Hollow now that she'd blessed them with her presence.

With a final wave to Mingan, Della slipped into the front seat of the hearse, casting a smile in her friend's—her family's—direction.

"Ready to go home?" she asked.

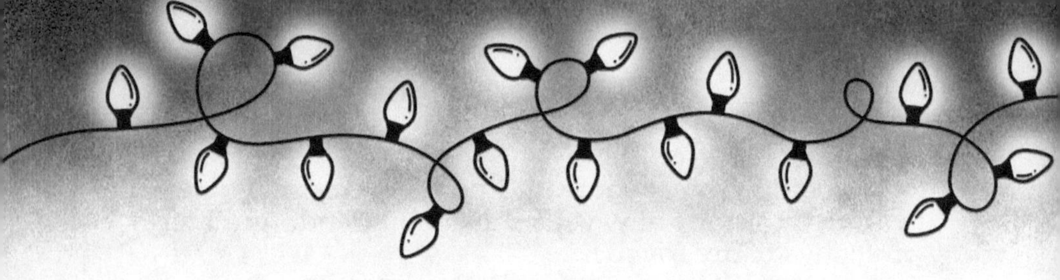

CHAPTER SIXTY-EIGHT

Parcels

"The prodigal daughter returns," Richie announced, opening the door to Ambrose Apartments for her with a gigantic smile.

Strike one. Richie rarely smiled and never had he opened the door for anyone, let alone her.

"Why are you so chipper?" Della asked, eyebrow raised in mock concern.

He shrugged, taking Arlo's bag from him as Porter honked a goodbye from the hearse. Della lazily waved over her shoulder, eyes locked on Richie.

"Just excited to have you home, I guess," he laughed.

"Did you get into rancid blood or something? You're scaring me."

Richie's smile faltered. "Again, just happy to have you home."

Della glared at him. "What happened, Richmond?"

A flicker of hatred passed over his face. "Do you need help carrying these up?" he asked, holding up Arlo's bags.

Della nodded, shoving her suitcase into his chest, leading him and Arlo toward the stairs.

"The elevator is fixed," Richie said, nodding his head the direction of the rickety old.

That was strike two. As far as Della knew, that elevator had been out of order since the nineties.

Richie smiled brightly, using the toe of his shoe to press the button. With a screech, the elevator doors opened. Arlo went in first, fascinated. Richie followed, making sure there was space between himself and Arlo for Della. She hesitated before joining them, not trusting him or the state of the elevator.

"So, how was your trip? Fight any monsters?" Richie

asked giddily.

Arlo opened his mouth to respond, but Della shushed him.

"You'll just have to read about it in the next issue of The Courier," she said carefully.

"Fun, fun," Richie replied, rocking back and forth on his heels.

He reached forward to press a button, and the elevator whirred to life. Della bore holes in the back of his skull with her accusatory eyes.

"Richie?"

"Yes, Miss Coleman?"

"What did you do?"

His shoulders tensed.

"Richmond Ambrose, what did you do?" Della spat.

He ignored her, smiling over his shoulder at Arlo.

The elevator doors opened, and Richie led them to her apartment door. Della unlocked it, allowing Richie to deposit their things inside. Arlo was in awe, disappearing inside his new home, unbothered by Della's worry.

There used to be three different two-o-threes—two on the right and one on the left, which was hers. Now, there was only one. The room numbers had been fixed.

Strike three.

Armageddon.

"Alright, drop it, bloodsucker," Della snapped. "What the Hell is going on?"

Richie's shoulders sagged. He looked Della dead in the eyes, the stark blue veins on his face pulsing. "We've been having a rat issue across Moss Hollow."

Della furrowed her eyebrows. "Seriously?"

Richie nodded. "Yeah."

"Is that code for something, or are you just being a freaking dork for the fun of it?"

"Yeah, something like that," Richie sighed.

Della rolled her eyes, finally crossing the threshold into her apartment. Arlo was already sifting through the snack cupboard.

"Oh, by the way," Riche said, clearing his throat and rubbing his nose with the heel of his palm. "I'm like, *really*, glad you're back. These rats have, uh, really put me through the ringer."

With that, he slammed the door.

Hadn't Mavericks mentioned rats? She swore Porter also said something about *Bayou Gil's* having a rat problem. What was going on?

Della stood staring at the door momentarily before turning to Arlo, whose hand was stuck in a jar of pickles.

He grinned sheepishly, yanking his hand free and putting the lid back on the jar.

"Sorry," he laughed. "I'm hungry."

"Help yourself to anything. This is *our* home now," Della said, sweeping her hands through the air.

Arlo nodded. "So I can have the pick-lees?"

"Yes, Arlo, you may have the pickles."

She laughed to herself, grabbing her suitcase, just about to hightail it to her bedroom when someone knocked on the door. Della sighed heavily, spinning back around and wrenching the door open.

"Richmond, I swear to—" Della said exasperatedly.

No Richie.

Just a package.

Della peered out the door, listening for footsteps down the hall. Ambrose Apartments was quiet, spar for Arlo loudly munching on his pickles.

Two voices fought in her mind. One told her to slam the door and leave the package for someone else to find. The other knew this was the start of a new adventure.

With one final look down the hall, Della grabbed the package and shut the door. The box was small—about the size of her hand—and wrapped in butcher paper. Arlo's eyes were full of curiosity as he followed her over to the couch. Plopping down on the sofa, Della tore open the package.

Inside was a single chess piece.

A broken king.

Della didn't need to gaze into the future to know this was a threat.

TO BE CONTINUED. . .

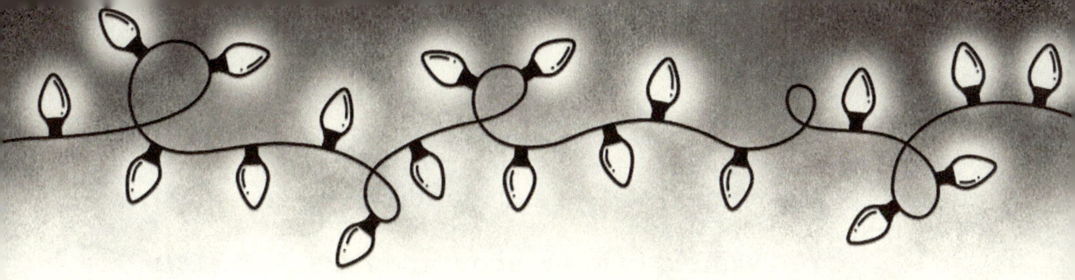

EPILOGUE

The door to his office slamming open that fateful January first came as no surprise. This was Delphee Coleman, after all. Her impatience was almost as admirable as her curiosity.

"You're early," he said, not looking up from his book.

"And you're about eleven years late—almost twelve. I've got a birthday coming up in a few months," Della snapped. "Put that down and start talking."

Mavericks flicked his eyes in her direction. He had to do a double take. "No more neon green?" he asked, finally setting down the almanac he'd been reading.

She flipped her freshly dyed hair over her shoulder as she sat next to him on the old couch near his office door. "Purple is more me, anyway."

"It surely suits you," Mavericks smiled.

"Cut the crap, old man," Della sighed. "When did you start remembering things?"

"Didn't I tell you not to call me that?" Mavericks asked, standing, clasping his hands behind his back as he paced before her.

"Humor me."

He rolled his eyes, studying her. He knew what was coming, and it would make her hate him. She'd never forgive him for the things buried beneath his feet. But keeping this from her any longer would end in consequences worse than her hatred.

"I started remembering several years back. Just fragments of things I couldn't put together. When I saw the title of your blog, something finally clicked. But up until recently, I still didn't have all the pieces," he admitted, watching her carefully.

She nodded to herself. "There's more to this than just

me, isn't there?"

He stopped dead in his tracks, locking eyes with her. "If you can believe it, this is bigger than even me."

"Mavericks," Della said, standing and crossing her arms.

"You wanted to know about the *P.O.I. Project*? It stands for *The People Of Improbability Project*. It was created to monitor and sometimes contain people like us," Mavericks said dryly, resuming his pacing.

"Were they the people who wanted to harm me way back when?"

"In a sense."

"You're being cryptic again," Della scolded.

"Originally, *P.O.I.* was started to be the magical community's voice within the government. Think of them like a mystical task force," Mavericks sighed. "I only know this, of course, because I founded it."

Della had gone eerily quiet. He could see the gears turning in her mind and knew he wouldn't like whatever conclusion she'd come to.

Mavericks sat heavily on the edge of his desk. "Things spiraled out of control, and now we're here."

"What exactly do you mean by that?" Della snapped. "Why can't you just say it like it is?"

Mavericks cast his eyes to his hands, noting the wrinkles and age spots. "Because Della, I'm trying to choose my words carefully."

"Mavericks. Elvi said—"

"Who?"

"A *P.O.I.* agent!" Della snapped. "She said that there is a mole in the police department here in Moss Hollow. She has an entire file on us. Do you realize how dangerous that is?"

"Yes, Della, I do," Mavericks snapped.

"Then act like it!"

"Do not take that tone with me!" Mavericks roared, standing. "While I am aware of your growing abilities, you do not know everything. So don't act like you do."

"That is the problem! I feel like I don't know anything!" Della cried, accentuating her words with a clap. "We are on the same side, Mavericks. Don't forget that."

"I know we are! But it was my job to protect you."

"Keeping things from me isn't protecting me. In fact, it does more harm—"

"You don't think I know that?" Mavericks asked, his voice dangerously low. "I have made more mistakes than I have lived years, Delphee. I don't intend on making any more."

Della took a shaking breath, removing her glasses and cleaning them with her shirt. "I know how much you love and care about us. But if Moss Hollow is in danger, I need to know. Multiple people have brought a weird rat infest—"

"It's not just Moss Hollow," Mavericks blurted out. "It's everything."

"How do we fix it, then?" Della asked, throwing her hands up in the air.

"I don't know! Why do you think you're here?" Mavericks snapped.

Della fell quiet again. She replaced her glasses slowly, studying him in the same way he had studied her.

"You told me you needed me for a reason, and I believe you. I *trust* you, Mavericks. I think you are one of the only people out there looking out for me. But I can't help you if you aren't truthful," Della said, steadying her voice as best she could. "So I ask this, knowing in my heart that you would never do anything to hurt me: What the Hell do you know about Leland?"

That took him by surprise, but he guessed it was coming eventually.

"That was my brother's stage name, what he wanted to publish music under. It's our grandfather's middle name," Della said, a pleading undertone to her voice. "My Uncle knows he worked for you. Elvi said to ask you about Leland, so this is me asking. What happened?"

Mavericks stiffened as he walked past her, flicking on the old jukebox behind her. That old song he loved so much whirred to life as the hidden door opened.

"I'm warning you, Della. You are not going to like what comes next," Mavericks said, gesturing for her to follow him as he took to the steps. "But you're right. I would never—*never*—do anything to hurt you. Or him. Or any of you."

Della nodded, hot on his heels. She followed him down that winding staircase until they reached the fatal secret beneath The Courier. Mavericks stepped aside, watching as her face lit up in recognition.

The young man in the cell turned to him, scrambling to his feet. "Della?" he asked, his black eyes full of surprise.

Della stood frozen on the last step, her mouth hanging open. "Q—Quincy?" she choked out.

He backed away, looking at Mavericks with hatred in his eyes. "How dare you," he spat. "Get her out of here. Now."

"Oh my God, Quin," Della breathed, staggering toward him, taking in the horrendous sight that was her beloved brother. Black magic left scars, and he was covered in them. "What happened to you?"

"Black magic," Mavericks said, following her closely. The barrier had held him this long, but he feared seeing her would ignite his powers in a way Mavericks couldn't control.

"Why—Why is she down here, Percy? What did you do?" Quincy hissed, pinning himself to the far wall, panting heavily.

"She remembers," Mavericks said simply.

Quincy's eyes narrowed. Mavericks grabbed Della back as her brother rushed at them. He collided with the barrier, barely even wincing at the electric pain Mavericks knew the invisible wall had caused him.

"Get away from her," he growled. "Get your hand off of her, now!" Purple-black tendrils whipped at the wall.

Della looked to Mavericks, her eyes full of horror. Mavericks gave her a reassuring nod, squeezing her shoulder tightly. The look on her face reminded him of the day he took away her memories and locked away her magic.

"With him behind the barrier, we are safe," Mavericks said, watching Quincy huff and puff, his magic swirling around him in a dangerous vortex. "He is not at full power."

"What happened to him?" Della asked, unable to look away from him.

"Don't listen to a word he says," Quincy spat.

"Quincy found a way to block the memory spell. When he was old enough, he came to me to reverse it. But every time he brought it up, I couldn't remember our conversation," Mavericks began. "Eventually, he gave up and decided to find out how to reverse it on his own. One thing led to another, and right under my nose, my star pupil became addicted to dark magic."

"How could you do that?" Della asked, surprising both Mavericks and Quincy. "Black magic? That was your grand plan?"

"I didn't choose this, he's lying. He made me this way," Quincy spat.

Della laughed darkly. "No one can make you do black magic, Quin. It doesn't work like that."

"You don't know him the way I do."

"Apparently, I don't know you either," Della snapped.

Quincy's eyes locked onto Mavericks. "Della, you need to get away from him. Now. He's tainted you."

Della rolled her eyes, scoffing.

This was not going the way Mavericks had expected.

"Sometimes I think Mavericks is the only sane one left on this stupid planet," Della sighed, turning to him.

"How long has he been down here?

"Five years," Mavericks sighed. "He was a Courier for three before that. It all went wrong after I sent him out to monitor *P.O.I.*, they corrupted him."

"LIAR!" Quincy roared, rounding on him. "You made me into this!" he screamed. He pounded on the barrier over and over again, beating his knuckles raw. "LIAR!"

"He tried to kill me," Mavericks laughed.

"Don't listen to him, Della. It's me, it's Quincy. I would never do anything to hurt anyone, you know that," Quincy said, the pleading look in his eyes sickening Mavericks.

"In a sense, he is no longer your brother," Mavericks added.

"Liar!" Quincy screamed again. "Della, don't listen to a word he says!"

"Oh, grow up, Quin, you're twenty-four years old. Act like it."

"You're seriously taking his side?" he asked, eyes wild with hysteria.

"Well, he's not the one dripping in black magic!"

"You were never stupid, Della, can't you see—"

"You're right, I'm not. But I'm also not your kid sister anymore," Della spat. "I can make my own decisions. And I choose Mavericks over the monster before me."

"How dare you—"

"I gave up on you long ago, Quin," Della sighed. "I needed you, and you left. Eight years I've waited for you to show up. I've gotten on fine without you. I think I can continue just the same."

With that, she turned and made for the stairs. Mavericks didn't stop her, but Quincy began screaming and crying—anything he could do to make her turn around. None of it worked.

"I HATE YOU!" he screamed at Mavericks. "I HATE YOU BOTH!"

Mavericks bowed to him, following Della back up to his office.

She stood in the center of his curated mess, her shoulders sagging. This was it. This was when she'd turn on him. He could very well lose them both in that moment. Max, too—he'd follow her to the ends of the earth, no doubt.

"Della, I know this is a lot to—"

She turned sharply on her heels, wrapping her arms around him, and cried.

Mavericks—disgusted that someone had touched him against his will—tried to push her away. Those attempts just made her cling to him harder.

He let her hug him, let her cry.

She needed him.

They needed each other.

"I'm so sorry, Delphee, dear," he whispered, stroking her hair softly.

"I am, too," she cried, looking up at him with her magnificent brown eyes.

"For what?" he asked, not knowing what she could possibly have to be sorry for.

"That I wasn't here," she sobbed, then buried her face in his chest.

His silk suit was going to need dry cleaning. Hopefully, her mascara and tears would wash out.

"Hush now, that's not your fault," he sighed, finally mustering the courage to push her away. "I screwed up a long, long time ago. You and your brother are taking the brunt of the consequences."

Della wiped her tears with the sleeve of her sw—no, that was Max's sweater. Why was she wearing Max's sweater?

"What do you mean?" she asked, her voice hoarse.

Mavericks shook himself from his thoughts, sighing heavily.

There truly was no going back now.

"In order to best understand the present, you must look to the past," Mavericks began, leading her back to the couch, "lest, of course, history repeats."

Tell me, Della dear, have you heard the extraordinary tale of the man in the paisley suit?

EXTRAS

HELLO, MY LOVELY COURIERS!

While I can't offer you a signed CD like Della, here
are some songs I think these characters would love!
I always have music playing while writing, and these
songs helped me get into my character's heads.
I highly suggest giving these songs a listen!
You might learn something new about our band of
mystical misfits. . .
(You can find full character playlists on
Spotify under Amelia_Rikstad)

DELLA:

I'm Not Angry Anymore—Paramore
Monsters In The Dark—MyKey
Paradise—Coldplay
Regarding Your Departure—Noah Floersch
Graceland Too—Phoebe Bridgers

MAX:

The Scientist—Coldplay
Flaws—Bastille
Ain't It Fun—Paramore
Welcome Home, Son—Radical Face
War of Hearts—Ruelle

PORTER:

Organ Donor—Jeremey Messersmith
I Lied—Lord Huron (Ft. Allison Ponthier)
Boyfriend—COIN
The Hearse—Matt Maeson
Twenty Long Years—Lord Huron

MAVERICKS:

Long Cool Woman (In A Black Dress)—The Hollies
Deleter-GROUPLOVE
Creature— half•alive
Time in a Bottle—Jim Croce
Light—Sleeping At Last

ARLO:

The Yawning Grave—Lord Huron
Frozen Pines—Lord Huron
The Moon Will Sing—The Crane Wives
The Cave—Mumford & Sons
Name—The Goo Goo Dolls

SEBASTIAN:

Out of Tune—The Backseat Lovers
Bounce Man—Twenty One Pilots
New Kid Blues—The Stardazed Trail
The Pantaloon—Twenty One Pilots
Viciously Lonely—The Backseat Lovers

ELVI:

Pretty In Pink—The Psychedelic Furs
LDQ (Little Drama Queen)—PUBLIC
Oh No!—MARINA
Time Machine—COIN
Look What You Made Me Do—Taylor Swift

QUINCY:

Eat You Alive—The Oh Hellos
Bones—Imagine Dragons
One Hit Wonder—Everclear
The Family Jewels—MARINA
All These Things That I've Done—The Killers

Hey kiddo,
Took this picture of you and the gang before you left. Figured you'd want a copy. Have fun monster hunting!
Miss you already,
Kohen

UTOPIAN COURIER PRESS 2023

TO KEEP UP WITH DELLA AND THE GANG, FOLLOW THE AUTHOR AT:

Instagram: utopian_courier_press
Facebook: Utopian Courier Press

AMELIA'S WEBSITE:

utopiancourierpress.com